The Second Year: A Midterm Conspiracy

(A novel)

Andy Furillo

A pale blue sky hung over the park in the center of town that burst with the fresh green bloom of early spring. A jam band's rhythm streamed through the trees and bounced off the surrounding city buildings and office towers, and a hundred freak dancers twirled in the middle of the public square.

The occasion was the unveiling of the first piece of public art to ever emerge from the scalpel of Lincoln Adams, a local wood sculptor who had been in the news recently. Hundreds of Link's friends and fans filled the park, to drink local beer, to sip regional wine, to pick at platters of food prepared and arranged by the all-star lineup of the town's celebrity chefs, to celebrate his work, and to dance to an uninterrupted groove of countrified jazz-rock with a touch of the psychedelic blues.

Link mingled the best he could among the masses – it didn't come naturally to someone who loved to read the news but had an aversion to being in it. A slim and healthy 6-foot-4, he was easy to spot as he strolled through the park under his white straw cowboy hat and his black T-shirt, the center of attention that he knew on this day he must endure. He chatted with his friends and fans who over the years had filled their homes with the forms that he released from their redwood and fir entrapment. He felt comfortable enough to stop and engage the stranger, the lunatic, the poseur, the philanthropist, or anybody who looked at him sideways, to accept their congratulations, uncomfortable as it was for a man who'd rather talk about the closest and best hiking trails, natural bodies of water where you could immerse yourself in summer, issues of sports and politics and the casual matter of being alive, than his own work.

With a go-cup that sloshed Sierra Nevada Pale Ale over its brim and onto Link's right hand, the artist submitted his left to the grasp of his public relations consultant. Her name was Manuela Fonseca, and she guided him in and out of interviews she had arranged with the local and worldwide press that had gathered for Sacramento's artistic event of the year. Until this day, Link had only spoken with Manuela over the phone. He had never actually laid eyes on her, hadn't seen the way she spilled out of a flowered mini-sundress strapped over her otherwise exposed shoulders, her bronze skin firm and glistening in the last rays of sunshine on the first warm day of spring. These first visions of Manuela laid Link to waste.

As the two of them lurked on the outer fringe of the dancers, Link took notice of another subject, a fellow not nearly as impressive or exciting in his appearance as Manuela, but still a starter in the lineup of Link's first-team drinking buddies. This was a young man who hung out in the homeless camps along the banks of the American River and the sidewalks of Ahern Street north of downtown, a derelict who made a name for himself riding the rails of hobo America: The Scrounger, a moniker for somebody who oftentimes appeared in public with his face full of blood or his eyes blackened after having lost another street fight that he had most likely instigated. At least that's how Link frequently encountered the Scrounger, although it had been months since he'd seen him, with or without the facial rearrangement.

And it was not until this day, in this park, to this music, that this artist learned something new about his derelict friend:

The Scrounger could dance his ass off.

In front of the bandstand on the north end of Cesar Chavez Plaza, behind the statue of the park's iconic labor-leader namesake, the Scrounger punched the air and kicked his feet to every beat from the drum kit. He snaked and slithered. He rocked and he rolled. He shimmied and he shook, with a twist and a shout. He convulsed himself into a protoplasmic heap and collapsed in a blob-splat to the pavement, in apparent exhaustion – a move stolen from James Brown – only to rise up in revitalized conquest, to spin from his bottom up to his back to his shoulders until he stood on his head. Faster and faster the Scrounger twirled, in upside-down 360s, the soles of his black-canvas Converse to the sky, until the Scrounger slowed, and slowed, and slowed – a little bit slower now, a little bit slower still, slowing to a full stop, until…

Boom!

4

Link wouldn't have believed it if everyone else hadn't seen it too. It appeared that somehow, the Scrounger did a back flip, pushed into flight with his arms and shoulders and further accelerated by an unaccounted force that he solicited from his hips and thighs. He swung up and over and a full 180 degrees backwards, sticking the landing. Still in a crouch and still looking straight into the band, the Scrounger shot the musicians a glance. He flashed them a signal, like a catcher calling for a fastball. He nodded his head – a one and a two, and he folded his arms at shoulder height. His head bounced as if it were Lawrence Welk's baton. His eyes locked into the drummer, and now, a transition, into a very passable *prisyadka* – the famous squat dance from ancient Russia, with fully-extended, synchronized kicks, straight out of the imaginary chair in which he sat. Right leg, left. Right leg, left. Right leg, left leg, right leg, left. Faster. Breathtakingly fast. His legs were a blur. They made you dizzy. His eyes stayed glued to the drummer. The drummer stayed right with him. The drummer kicked the bass. The thump of the bass synchronized perfectly with the time structure set forth by the Scrounger's bobbing head. Right leg, left. Right leg, left. Right leg, left leg, right leg left – repeatedly. The musicians looked at each other. Not knowing what came next, the musicians funked up the time. They laid down a little oom-pah. They knew nothing of oom-pah, but they did the best they could. They segued into a Cajun waltz. The Scrounger adjusted, slowing his style. The Scrounger stayed with the *prisyadka*. The polka-*prisyadka* combo worked. The whole thing worked. The crowd went nuts.

The Scrounger stayed low, to the slower time. He stayed in his squat. He kicked out of the crouch, left. He kicked out of the crouch, right. He held his back perfectly straight, his arms folded and unmoved at his chest. Then, in concession to the oom-pah, a wrinkle: he dropped to the pavement and alternately slapped his palms to the pavement across his body. He kicked and he slapped while the rest of the dancers stopped dancing and clapped in time. He scooted forward, through the gathering, the dancers parting like a Red Sea on command from Moses, while the Scrounger kicked and slapped and ambled around the plaza, up and down, a one and a two, to the oom-pah, past Manuela, and past Link, who noticed something else about the Scrounger's performance:

As the oom-pah snaked around the plaza, the Scrounger was picking up cigarette butts here and there and putting them into his shirt pocket.

*****

A blue canvas covered Link's project, and the only thing you knew right away about the thing is that it was big, about 15 feet tall, nearly three times the height of the Cesar Chavez statue that looked ready to lead a march across the street on City Hall.

There'd been a lot of that going on lately.

A few weeks earlier, the police shot and killed a young black man in his grandmother's back yard, about six miles from the plaza. The kid had been breaking car windows in the neighborhood when the cops got the call and sped down and spotted him hopping a fence under the searching spotlight of an overflying sheriff's helicopter. The cops unloaded on the kid when he pulled a cell phone on them and they thought it was a gun.

Every night since, hundreds of demonstrators marched through the downtown streets at rush hour to demand justice for the slain Devante Davidson. A couple times, they surrounded City Hall and took over the meetings. They'd already finished this evening's parade by the time of the unveiling, and a couple of stragglers hung around afterwards to help celebrate Link and grab themselves a couple of free beers. They ran through the spread of roast pork and local fruits and cheeses and grilled asparagus shoots and a salad table deep enough to stuff every vegan from the Tower Bridge to the Capay Valley. They stuck around to listen to the band that called itself Mind X and to watch this crazy dude bouncing around the park doing his Russian squat dance.

Link hadn't done much of anything the previous year, before he tore into the remains of a felled young redwood and pounded it with the chisel until his palms bled. He'd kind of been in an artistic slump, bugged at first by customers who thought they could buy his inspiration with outrageous six-figure offers, and later depressed by the outcome of the 2016 presidential election, and, later still, to be kidnapped by Russian mobsters who held him hostage in a ridiculous attempt to extort a piece out of him for their own oligarchic vanity. It didn't work, and the good news was that Link burst into the new year with a renewed inspiration. And here, in the receding light of the mid-April dusk, the mayor of Sacramento had been recruited to pull the cord on the mammoth piece of wood sculpture that would stand in perpetuity as a civic landmark not far from the memorial to Cesar Chavez.

For years, Link stood at arm's length from his own greatness. He never embraced it, and he certainly didn't embrace the public's embrace of his celebrity. In recent months, however, he worked on trying to understand that attention was no big deal. He needed to come to terms with his ability and his celebrity, to realize that his aversion to fame was the biggest ego trip of all. People recognize you on the street – so what? You put your soul in public view and you damn well better know that people will take notice. And you damn well better be ready to defend it. If he had the gall to go public with what he hath wrought, he knew he had to listen to everybody's brilliant and unsolicited opinions – in his face, on the street, on social media, in the public square. And Link thought it good, to subject his artistic exploration to debate, hatred, ridicule, adoration, love, scorn, sarcasm, wonderment, repulsion, adulation, execution, worship, to psycho-analysis. He became all right with criticism.

Mainly, he could no longer duck the reality of his prominence. As much as he recoiled from the thought of it, Link had become a gigantic story, from his ordeal the previous year that generated headlines around the world – "Artist Freed by Homeless Army," "Russians Thwarted in Kidnap-for-Art Ploy," "Investigators Say Artist Kidnap Linked to Russian Organized Crime Ring," "Was Link-nap Linked to Trump-Russia Probe?" He turned heads just walking around the corner from his house on D Street to his favorite coffee joint around the corner on E Street.

As he moved halfway into his seventh decade, he thought it made him better at what he did. He thought it sharpened his mind and opened his heart. He thought criticism made him more receptive to ideas that rushed out of places where the mystics insisted that your own personal energy connected with the pulse of life.

Of course the press was there, and Link was on friendly terms with most of it, especially the locals, including what was left of *The Sacramento Beacon*, the town daily that no longer covered the arts, or art openings, or the festival of Link's own return from the artistic dead. They calendared the opening in their events listing, but could not spare a body to finesse the event. A newsroom once 300 strong had dwindled to maybe 50. His last friend on the paper – and he used to know them all, at the newspaper bar where they all hung out – showed up for the unveiling only in his unofficial, personal capacity, and he soon became drunk.

The New York Times sent one of their guys up from L.A., and *The San Francisco Chronicle* had their Sacramento reporter on hand. The alternative weekly gave him a reefer the day before on the cover and a half-page walkup, memorializing the events from the previous year. *People* Magazine sent out a photo team with a reporter, and Link went out of his way to be especially nice to them. They'd been pilloried the past several months, when word got out that it was their puff piece where they called him "the Michelangelo of the Redwood" that created all sorts of artistic and political problems for him, such as his being kidnapped by the Russians.

Local TV newscasters set up on the edge of the plaza to go live at 11 on the unveiling. The host of the popular "Insight" program on the local NPR station was there with a crew to get cut-in sound – she'd had Link live in the studio a few days earlier to talk about his latest work.

Nearly half the people on hand for the unveiling of Link's new piece were currently experiencing homelessness. They mixed respectfully with the political and media elites, and the media and political elites had come to respect them, too, at least when they were around Link. He liked the homeless, and he liked their stories, and he kicked them down money and he bought them beers all night long and into the morning to hear their tales of hoboing across America. He found that once they had been befriended, there was no class of human more loyal. Street people – led by none other than the Scrounger – got him out of the fix when they got word of his predicament with the Russians and marched down to his studio and in effect held the hostage takers hostage until the cops arrived and the bad guys split.

Link did his best to make everybody feel comfortable with his discomfort of being on public display. One on one, he'd talk with any of them until the break of day. Assembled en masse, they made him nervous. With effort, and with Manuela at his side, he was able to stop and exchange sweet nothings with these people who had been buying his stuff for more than 20 years, long before fame caught up and overwhelmed him. They bought little donkeys and tiny totems, figurines of gyrating Indians and the indigenous plant life of Northern California – mini-Persian Oaks and golden poppies painted to full bloom. Over the past decade, his customers grew younger while his long, straight black braided hair turned grayer. He'd recently cut it.

He gave them all a moment, trying to call up a past recollection, some minor intimacy, perhaps, from a Bela Fleck concert back in '94 at the Crest, or Barry Zito's first home start for the River Cats at Raley Field in '00, or the afternoon they got totally plastered at Old Ironsides during the storms of '96 and they walked down to the levee and reached down and were able to touch the Sacramento River that had climbed to within a foot from the top, or the night they crashed one of Schwarzenegger's inauguration parties in '03 and got drunk on The Terminator's tab.

He talked to a couple of chefs and the former brew master at the Rubicon. The former metro editor of the *Beacon* broke in to say hello. A legislative staffer. Three auto body shop workers he knew from when he lived in an apartment on Q Street across from his old studio. A former reporter at the *Beacon* whom he once hustled into a weekend getaway at the coast and hadn't seen since.

About 15 minutes before the unveiling, the mayor walked over to extend his congratulations and to go over his remarks to be delivered to the crowd. Link congratulated the mayor for holding the city together in the wake of the Devante Davidson tragedy. Not knowing the mayor at all, the conversation fell into kind of a stiff chit-chat that really made Link jittery. A dabble of sweat popped out of Link's forehead while the mayor blabbed on about fixing the city. Link wanted to listen. Only his head was about to explode.

Manuela threw him a lifeline.

"Excuse me, Mr. Adams, I need you for a minute," she said, looking into the distance.

Link looked up from the mayor. The mayor saw the perspiration flowing down from Link's hairline. The mayor was not oblivious. The mayor also had to work the crowd. The mayor took the PR lady's cue and went to mingle elsewhere.

Manuela Fonseca whispered to Link:

"We've got a camera crew here that might be a problem," she said.

"Just one?" Link replied.

"Some are worse than others," Manuela said. "I have no idea where these guys are from. They're not from Sacramento, that's for sure."

Manuela let go of Link's hand.

"Wait here," she said, as she circled the crowd that had given way to the bouncing, scooting Scrounger and approached the two-man camera crew that had caught her attention.

*****

The one with the camera was a tall, fairly husky white guy wearing a tight-fitting and faded off-red T-shirt with short brown hair, brown checkerboard streaks and tan khakis. He looked to be in his late-20s. His partner stood shorter, blonder, thinner, and he carried a boomed microphone. He scurried in front of the bandstand in an attempt to interview dancers while the bigger dude filmed. He couldn't have been more than 22 or 23.

About the same time that Manuela walked up on them, they noticed her, and they swung their equipment in her direction.

"Hi, fellas," Manuela greeted them. "Hey, I'm helping Mr. Adams here tonight with the media. I don't believe I've met you guys."

The taller and older of the two took a drag on the cigarette that had dangled from his lips. He blew the smoke in Manuela's general direction.

"You're right about that – we haven't met," he said, voiced tinged with an accent from somewhere in the South.

"I'm Manuela Fonseca, and like I said, I'm helping out with the media," Manuela said firmly.

"Helping out with the media?" he asked. "What the fuck does that mean?"

The immediate hostility took Manuela by surprise.

"I guess that depends," she said, "on who you're with."

"Like, if we were with MSNBC or some lefty fake news organization, we'd get anything we want?" the younger, smaller guy said, with a confrontational lilt similar to that of his bigger, older partner.

This clumsy reveal of the men's worldview centered Manuela.

"This is a public park, I can't kick you out of anywhere," Manuela said, toughening up her voice. "If you're *accredited* journalists with a *real* news agency, I'll see what I can do to help you. Link's been doing interviews with reporters all day, and he already did one with the FOX crew that's here. Look."

She pointed across the street to the TV truck with the markings of the local FOX40 affiliate.

"You can say that we're independent," the bigger guy said, sobering a little.

"OK," Manuela responded. "I'll leave it at that. You can also say that you won't be doing any interviews with Mr. Adams, and that we'll be watching you very closely, and that if you come within 20 feet of Link, you'll be arrested."

"All right!" the smaller guy laughed. "Now we're getting somewhere!"

His partner dropped his cigarette on the concrete and crushed it out with his foot, and neither of them noticed when the homeless guy doing the crazy squat dance motored past them to pick up the discarded smoke.

2/*Up the Esquire*

Link had never before set foot in the Esquire Tower, the 22-story building at 13th and K streets in the city's epicenter. Never really had a reason. He'd been in the street-level restaurant many times, and it smelled as good as any in town, but he went there in his younger years mostly for the drink. He learned from the perspective of the skirt-chaser that it was a great place to get smashed. Also, it became a top lunch place for political dealmakers. From the first day it opened, it gained a reputation as an old-money place. Link's riches were more recently acquired. In a bar that catered to insiders, Link lurked at the fringe. The Esquire was a suit place, and Link didn't have one.

He rode the elevator to the top floor where all 10,000 feet of office space had been consumed by the massive MJ Public Affairs operation – about a dozen public relations associates and 14 lobbyists representing 72 clients with crucial business pending under the dome at the State Capitol building two blocks away. Water agencies. Oil. Booze. New car dealers. Drug companies. Manufacturers' associations. Professional associations. Foreign governments. Even a couple of social justice groups and anti-poverty concerns, if only to qualify the firm for *pro bono* write-offs.

Into the curvaceous white-carpeted lobby with the baby-blue walls and pictures of the eight founding partners lined up four to a side on both sides of the elevator, Link checked in with a young man at the reception desk who enthusiastically took the artist's information. Two minutes later, Manuela Fonseca welcomed Link into the inner sanctum of the town's most prominent chamber of political and entrepreneurial promotion and advocacy.

She led him by the arm into her wood-paneled corner office with a 270-degree view of the epicenter of California politics, it being the Capitol itself. Her view also took in the Senator Hotel, where the fabled fixer, Artie Samish, once maintained a suite. Artie had called himself "the guy who gets things done," which in the previous century meant making sure that liquor distributors and race tracks got what they wanted. To her right, she could see The Diplomat, the new bar on 11th Street where lawmakers raised money and hashed out policy over hash and eggs and Bloody Marys. Below and to the right of the Senator, she could see the corner of Chicory, a coffee place where the baristas couldn't be nicer and where some of the deals worked out during morning meetings of the political elite couldn't be greasier.

"Starting to get some reviews," Manuela told Link, who plopped himself into the black-leather couch across from her sparkling clean glass-top desk.

Manuela stood behind her laptop, the only thing on her desk besides a landline. Behind her, a cabinet decorated with five Emmy awards from her past life as an outstanding TV reporter for the NBC affiliate in Sacramento. Above that, a wall with several proclamations and designations that acknowledged her excellent work in the community. There was one framed glossy picture of a young man who appeared to be in his mid-20s. Link figured him for her son. There were no pictures of other children, or of a dad.

Art news and publicity were a whole new world for Manuela. She had been a hard-news woman for 15 years, chasing murders and covering local politics and trudging up to the mountains to stand in the cold rain and snow on the first nights of winter, when TV news crews filmed people putting chains on their tires, as if that was a story.

She had once hoped to catch on with the network, and she had her chances to move up to the San Francisco and L.A. stations. She had the look – dark, athletic, gorgeous. But she wasn't ambitious enough. Not enough, anyway, to dump her future husband when she got her offers from California's bigger markets. Then, about a decade ago, the worst thing in the world that can happen to a female TV journalist happened to her – she turned 40. She anchored a little bit on weekends, but she didn't like it. She thought about a career change, and MJ Public Affairs gave that notion a boost when they heard that Manuela might be available. With a kid in high school and a divorce in the books, she went for the money. At first, they ran her out of their suite in the new basketball arena where she schmoozed up corporate presidents and other prospective clients with her semi-celebrity, her good looks, her smarts, her easy manner. In time, she proved to be a terrific rainmaker, bringing in clients the company never knew existed, like the town's growing number of celebrity chefs and equally prominent brewmasters, bicycle racers, cage fighters and world-famous tattoo artists.

She brought in the Lincoln Adams account, too, and she found out the previous day that she liked hanging out with this cool, handsome, polite and talented Native American guy who was totally clueless about anything that had anything to do with promotion, of himself or anything else.

As for the reviews of the unveiling of his totem pole the previous day, Link seemed genuinely unconcerned.

"They are all entitled to their opinion," Link told Manuela.

The public relations expert scanned a story on her computer screen and printed it out. Still standing, she clicked back to the searchable stories on Link's re-opening the day before in Cesar Chavez Plaza. She found another and printed that one out, too.

"Some of them," she responded to Link's assertion, "are more considered than others. I'm telling you, I wish I went to the school that believed that all publicity is good, and the only thing that matters is that they spell your name right. My problem is I've been in this business long enough to know that is not the case."

14

"It worked for Donald Trump," Link said. "Wasn't most of his publicity bad?"

"His publicity had been mostly good for a long time before he announced he was running for office," Manuela responded. "The last ten years, the main thing people knew about him was 'You're fired.'"

"I believe that proves my point."

"People like the strong, executive image, Mr. Adams," said Manuela. "Even if it's not the truth."

"Please, call me Link."

In the clear light of Manuela's big office, away from the chaos and pressure of the unveiling, Link was able to really notice her. Long, thick, black hair. Skin the color of lightly-creamed coffee. Strong, big-boned shoulders. Thick through the torso but no extra ounces to be seen. All business in a light, tight blue dress suit and black high heels. Big brown eyes. Smooth skin spread over cheekbones on the high side. And, Link noticed, an ass that made you notice. He took her for 50, give or take a year, and somebody who spent a lot of time in the gym.

Manuela retrieved the printouts and took a seat in the nicely-cushioned chair behind her desk.

"Check this one out," Manuela said, as she pushed toward him the printed pages of a local arts and politics blog that called itself the RFC Post. The initials stood for River Fucking City, but you had to know somebody to know that.

"For nearly a year, the spirit had absconded from Lincoln Adams, the beloved wood sculptor and Sacramento institution who is as eccentric as he has become historic," the review read. *"For years he has thrilled his patrons and customers with works of originality that have blended mystical nativism with an eye for the absurd and a hint of terror. An inherent transcendence to his work has captured the legions of fans who say they 'get' Mr. Adams, but it was the high-priced competition for his work among actors, singers, politicians and other celebrities – and the free-market implications thereof – that nearly destroyed his artistic impulse. Criminal, foreign elements sought to coerce his creation. Their failure was his salvation, and last night at Cesar*

15

Chavez Plaza, Mr. Adams returned to action following his harrowing kidnap last fall with the unveiling of a piece that startled the city in a way it hasn't since they removed the cover from Jeff Koons's 'Piglet' outside the Golden 1 Center two years ago. The agony and the ecstasy have since died down over Koons's multi-colored reflective pig. Now, it's just part of the Sacramento backdrop. Only time will tell whether Mr. Adams's effort will be similarly accepted or ignored."

"Not bad," Link said, looking up to where Manuela was still scanning reviews and sipping coffee.

"There's more," Manuela said, without looking up.

"If Koons unnerved Sacramento with a young pig, it will take more time to see how critics and pundits and art aficionados and regular people on the street take to the sculpture by Mr. Adams. One thing you can say about it for sure: it is not at all swinish. In fact, there are many things you can say it is not. The difficulty people might have with this work is to describe exactly what it is.

"Indisputably, it is very tall, as most totems are, a full 15 feet in height, in glazed redwood, and it will stand as the most prominent statue in the plaza. In the context of one of the city's most prominent spaces, it serves as third base to the home plate that is the Cesar Chavez statue on the north side of the park. Across the plaza from Chavez, playing 'second base', is the traditional memorialization of somebody with whom few living residents of Sacramento are at all familiar: A.J. Stevens. Mr. Stevens, whose initials stand for 'Andrew Jackson,' supervised locomotive repair and manufacture for the robber barons of the Central Pacific Railroad. Employees of the enterprise thought so highly of his work some 12,000 strong attended the dedication of the statue on Nov. 28, 1889. The sign at its base reads, 'Erected to a friend of labor by his co-workers.'

"Approximately 11,750 fewer personalities appeared as witnesses to Thursday night's unveiling of Mr. Adams' most recent work. Earlier in the day, workmen transported by truck the piece from Mr. Adams' studio 11 blocks away and bolted it into the pedestal, a massive block of granite off to the plaza's east side, looking toward the William Coleman Memorial

16

Fountain, the distinguishing feature of the plaza since 1927.

"Now, for Mr. Adams' statue: its height, of course, is its most distinguishing characteristic, and after this abject fact is reported, it becomes difficult for an ordinary interpreter to understand what the author intended to accomplish. The sculpture stands on a dowel carved within a circular granite base, two feet high and exactly 10 feet in diameter. Compass point outward over the simple, shouted admonition: TRUTH. Reading upwards, as all totems are meant to be read, another 12-inch indentation is embedded in marble north and south, with smaller letters that demand KNOWLEDGE. East and west come with the added suggestion of KINDNESS.

"The one-word statements give way to a being with the torso of man and the lower body of a furry water mammal, an otter, judging by the looks of its webbed and furry feet. Their totemic arrangement comes together in an orange-and-red pastel blaze, suggesting fire, yet man and water mammal stand resolute in the swarm of the flame. The torso is wearing what appears to be Army fatigues, but the piece is interrupted in mid-girth by brilliant flames that surround what appears to be the light of a freight train bearing down on observers. The head of the human figure bears great resemblance to the mid-20th Century South American revolutionary, Che Guevara, whose likeness is now widely depicted in popular culture, on flags and T-shirts.

"Sacramento's mayor pulled the cord that removed the covering of the Lincoln Adams creation that will stand in the Plaza along with Chavez, Stevens, and the Coleman fountain. The mayor thanked Mr. Adams for his years of work, which has brought some acclaim to the city. It remains to be seen whether this effort – the sculptor's first attempt at public art – represents an elevation or desecration of our sense of place.

"Mr. Adams, in a very brief statement, thanked the mayor for his presence. He also mentioned a financial contribution from actors and other celebrities 'who made this piece possible,' and he gave another nod of recognition to a woman in San Francisco, a Leia Kahananui, 'for her inspiration.' A small inscription on the back of the totem also acknowledges Ms.

Kahananui. Another plaque mysteriously acknowledges 'The Scrounger'.

"The ceremony concluded with Mr. Adams saying to the gathering, 'I hope you like it.' He declined to answer any questions from the journalists who were on hand, although he did mingle for another half-hour.

"Mr. Adams, of course, is a talented fellow who stokes curiosity about his intentions. His popularity is unquestioned, and the significance of his latest contribution to civic culture is to be determined with the passage of time and the assessments of the future."

When Link looked up blearily from this lengthy write-up, Manuela unceremoniously began reading snippets of other reviews she stacked one behind the other on her screen: "…head-turning brilliance." "Ostentatious, self-absorbed, overwrought." "You call this art?" "An ambition achieved." "Lincoln Adams makes his mark on history." "Not worthy of public display." "Magnificent in its inaccessibility." "Memo to mayor: tear this thing down." "Sacramento's greatest piece of public art." "This makes 'Piglet' look like a Rodin." "Genius on display, in three acts." "Indecipherable." "Indescribable." "I want my money back – and I didn't spend any." "Priceless." "Another reason to stay out of downtown." And, "This will really put Sacramento on the map."

Link stretched back on the couch, fingers locked behind his head and his full 6 feet and 4 inches of length thrust forward, his left cowboy boot flopped comfortably over his right ankle. He had removed his white straw cowboy hat and placed it over his belt buckle. He nodded.

"I do not have a problem with any of it," he said. "People need to have their say. I welcome these discussions."

"I take it, then," Manuela said, "that you will be available for interviews?"

"I didn't say that."

Link never liked talking to reporters that he did not know and had not become drunk with. This worked well with the locals. Out of towners – he and them were hit and miss.

18

Manuela laughed at his reticence, just as a young man poked his head into the open doorway.

He looked to be in his late 20s to early 30s, dark-haired, soft-spoken, polite, respectful – and very anxious to meet Link, if the gigantic smile on his face was any indication. It was the way Link would have looked if as a kid he ever got a chance to meet Wilt Chamberlain.

"Hi, Manuela," the young man said, smiling, out of his white shirt and skinny jeans, with a haircut shaped into something resembling an arrowhead.

"Good morning, Jordan," Manuela greeted him. "Link, I would like to introduce you to Jordan Diaz. Jordan is an independent political consultant who does some contract work for some of our other associates. He's been dying to meet you."

Link stood up to shake hands with the young man.

"Independent political consulting," Link repeated. "Tell me what you're finding out."

The visitor, who upended his morning to meet the great Lincoln Adams, wasn't ready to talk about himself. He'd come to tell the artist how he'd been overcome by the unveiling of the totem, how it's exactly what Sacramento needed, how it gave the city identification, how it was every bit as significant as Cloud Gate, the gigantic stainless steel kidney bean in Millennium Park in Chicago sculpted by Sir Anish Kapoor that reflected the entire lakeside skyline, if you looked at it right.

Jordan tried to organize his thoughts but instead blurted out what had been on his mind from the second he got the text message from Manuela a few moments earlier.

"I just can't begin to tell you," he said. "My mom and dad used to buy your stuff when you were over on Q Street – we must have had twenty of your pieces in our backyard. My mom made stories up around every one of them while we sat outside on the hot summer nights. You've been a part of my life as long as I've been alive."

Now it was Link who was doing the smiling.

"I am deeply honored," he said.

Manuela watched the two men awkwardly beaming at each

other for a minute or two, before shaking her head and jumping in to help.

"Jordan," she told Link, "is one of the most brilliant young political minds in California. He's been hired by the national Democratic party to work on a couple of congressional campaigns in the Central Valley and a few more down in Orange County. Right Jordan?"

"And the high desert, north of L.A.," the consultant replied.

Link listened with the intent of an American who had always been interested in politics, but one who had never been consumed by them. Mainly, he had viewed politics as a spectator sport, and he rooted for the Democrats. They were not perfect, but neither were the Oakland A's, the baseball team he favored from nine stops away on the Capitol Corridor train route. The Dems mystified him with their inability to maintain a winning coalition the same way he could not understand why the A's traded away instead of paying their homegrown stars. Still, it had always been fun to watch, until this orange goon took over the White House and the country woke up every morning trying to get out of the way of a fastball aimed at its head.

All of a sudden, he gave a serious shit.

"What about it," Link asked. "Can the Dems flip the House?"

The question that had been consuming the country ran even more intensely with Jordan Diaz, who had embarked upon the most important gig in the biggest break of his young career. Out of UCLA, he moved home to Sacramento and got a fellowship that paid the rent for a year while he worked as a public information staffer for the Democratic caucus in the Assembly. Before his time was up on the fellowship, he met one of the city's most prominent political consultants who offered him a job doing communications on city council campaigns around the state. He got pretty good at it. He won a few races. He hooked up with three other young guys just like himself. The big-shot consultant rented them space in his red-brick I Street office in midtown and threw some work at them, legislative stuff, mainly, to maintain the Dems' two-thirds majorities in the Assembly and the state Senate. The consultant threw more work at them –

20

statewide office stuff, Treasurer, Controller, Lieutenant Governor. They won some more races. The four of them split off from the big-name consultant. They opened their own office, in the same part of town. They got calls from all over the country, more statewide races, U.S. Senate races, in places like New Mexico, Missouri, Montana and Indiana. They even got roped in to do some work for Hillary Clinton. They picked up congressional and legislative races all over the country, and when calls went out for organizing ahead of the 2018 midterms, each of the four got jobs in the seven congressional districts in California that the Dems thought they could snatch from the GOP.

Jordan took a seat on the other end of Manuela's couch and replied to Link, "I don't know what will happen, Mr. Adams, but…"

"Please. Just call me Link."

"…OK. Sorry. But this is going to be a much heavier lift than people might realize."

"How so?"

"Each district is its own mixture. They are all historically conservative, although the demographics are changing – especially the racial demographics – and the registration is shifting a little bit, too. There are now more registered independents and decline-to-states than there are Republicans. But these people are still fairly conservative, and even if they are repulsed by Trump, they aren't necessarily repulsed by their Republican congressmen and women. A good number of them are a little concerned that Republicans they otherwise might like aren't keeping the President from going completely off the rails. At the same time, they can't stand the people who are jumping up and down about Trump and wanting to see him impeached. So, it's a tough read. Take this district around Modesto, for instance."

Link nodded intently. He dug these face-to-faces with insiders who could tell what was going on behind the news he read religiously every morning.

"It's as tough a read as any of them," Jordan went on. "It goes

21

down to Turlock and up to Manteca and west to Tracy. They've got a kind of moderate Republican representing them down there now. He's married to a Mexican woman and he speaks Spanish, and he's playing up his Mexican connections by opposing Trump on building the wall and keeping the Dreamers here – he's okay with it. His problem is the right wingers don't like that kind of stuff. So now, you've got an ultra-conservative, anti-immigrant Republican who just took out papers to oppose the incumbent."

"Who's that?"

"Some doctor our of Manteca named Jacob Harland."

"Who's the incumbent?"

"John Bonham," Diaz answered. "Retired military. Navy man. Back bencher. Moderate. Vulnerable – he voted against Obamacare and for the Trump tax break for the rich. Polls terribly down there on those issues. We're pounding hard on both. Meanwhile, we think the right-winger is going to go all-out for the deplorable vote. Lots of historical ties down there to Oklahoma and north Texas, even Alabama and Mississippi. The Mexican population is growing, but the right winger could pull enough racists to knock us out. We don't think he has a chance to defeat Bonham, but he's got a good shot to finish second. We are officially worried."

The problem, Jordan explained – really on a roll now – was California's top-two primary system. The state's voters approved a new method of primary voting a few years back that lumped everybody in the electorate together, regardless of party, with the top two finishers moving on to the finals. The idea was that, somehow, it would moderate the state's politics, which it did not. In fact, it didn't do much of anything, except give Republicans a chance to preserve a couple of their seats in congressional districts where so many Democrats filed to run that they could put on a rodeo. They could get 60 percent as a group in any congressional district, but if Republicans finished one-two in any of the primaries, they'd keep the seat.

In the 10th Congressional District of California, four credible candidates put in for the office on the Democratic side and threatened to split the party's vote so badly that the Republicans would capture the top two primary slots. Right now, Jordan Diaz told Link and Manuela, the DCCC's most recent poll showed the Dems drawing a generic 55 percent. Bonham was attracting 30 percent, leaving 15 percent unaccounted for, and the under-the-table racist wild-card vote lurking as always as an under-the-table disrupter.

Link stroked his greying goatee.

"Democracy," he said, "can be a funny thing."

"It shouldn't be this funny," Manuela said.

Jordan rattled on about Orange County and how the Dems were in the same predicament in a couple of the districts down there that they were in Modesto. Jordan cited facts and figures. He cited statistics. He discussed changing demographics. He talked about campaign contributions. He had all the info on the most recent polls.

Link listened while Jordan talked. For him, like with most Americans, the political season came around only once every four years, like the Olympics. Everything else was pre-season – he only needed to watch it out of the corner of his eye while he went about his little life of watching basketball and baseball, going to see live music, hanging out with his pals over beers, and every once in a while knocking out a piece of wood sculpture. He let the insiders worry about politics and only allowed for them to alert him in case of emergency, like when Cheney invaded Iraq or when Newt Gingrich tried to run Bill Clinton out of the White House.

Like most Americans, he lived his life simply, hopefully, fitfully, and fretfully. He worked on his craft. He went his own way – until November 2016, when circumstances jolted Lincoln Adams out of his political casualness.

Some of where Link was coming from was personal. Like, for instance, what President Trump called "this Russia thing." The descendants of Sovietism, of course, had provenly hijacked the election through its manipulation of American social media and the theft of the emails it handed over to WikiLeaks, which played them up as if they were some kind of story, Link deduced. Yet the Russians didn't stop there. The theft of the presidency wasn't enough for them. They also had to kidnap him and try and force him into accepting their $1 million in exchange for sculpting them a likeness of a mob mistress who had seduced him.

Six months later, sitting in Manuela Fonseca's office, listening to Jordan Diaz lay out the most recent manipulations of the American system, something snapped inside Link's head. He realized that his Casablanca moment had arrived, that destiny had taken a hand.

"You know what," he said casually, interrupting Jordan's prodigious flow of political nerdiness.

Jordan and Manuela looked at him, the latter raising a stenciled eyebrow.

"It's time for me to get off my ass."

Jordan and Manuela looked at each other, not knowing exactly what to make of the pronouncement.

"Seriously," Link went on, slowly. "Like, I've been fretting in front of the television for nearly a year and a half. It has not made me a better person, and it has done nothing for the betterment of the country, or my own spiritual actualization. I think it's important that I take some action, of some sort. If nothing else, it could be a psychotherapeutic experiment."

Jordan laughed.

"I don't know anything about mass psychology," he said, "but I can tell you, you're not alone in the way you're feeling, and I can also tell you that thousands of people like you are signing up like crazy to go precinct walking in a lot of different places all over California."

"Precinct walking," Link said.

"Yes," Jordan replied, to what really wasn't a question. "To flip the House."

"Even in Modesto?" Link asked.

"Especially on Modesto. I'm telling you, Mr. Adams . . ."

"Please," Link interrupted. "One more 'Mr. Adams' and I'm moving to Modesto and never coming back."

"I'm sorry, Link. But there must be at least a thousand volunteers down there, working for the four candidates and two or three IEs that are opposing Bonham."

"IEs?"

"Independent expenditure committees. Labor unions, enviro groups, and the like."

"Where do I sign up?"

"Seriously?" Jordan asked, a little stunned.

"Like I said," Link went on. "I'm tired of sitting around getting angry. The more I think about it, it's no joke – doing this kind of thing would be the best thing in the world for me."

"Way better than a couch," Manuela broke in. "Or at least my couch. Now, if the two of you would please get out of here, I've got work to do."

Jordan and Link stood up and shook hands, before Manuela escorted them to the lobby of MJ Public Affairs.

Before they got on the elevator, the two men shook hands with Manuela, and Link felt her touch to be warm and soft. He smiled at her, natural like, and before the elevator door shut him in, he saw that she, was smiling at him, too.

3/*Mom*

Out the revolving glass door of the Esquire Tower, Link and Jordan stepped onto the K Street pedestrian mall into a perfect spring mid-afternoon under a fresh canopy of sycamore that shaded a meandering collection of Capitol suits and street people. The two of them signed off with Jordan and exchanged phone numbers and email addresses and agreed to get together soon to plot out Link's future as a political activist/volunteer.

Link proceeded down 13th Street, across sparkling green and

fresh Capitol Park where the emerging leaves on the giant red oaks on the N Street side fanned state employees and bums and mid-day lollygagging co-workers who spread out on the grass for a snooze. Nobody recognized him, which was good. On his way to R Street, it looked like everybody in town was checking their phones. He contemplated the possibility of them all reading the RFC Post review, and concentrated on his breathing. It always brought him back to the core of life, to his sense of "balanced detachment," a Buddhistic concept where the practitioner preserved a steadfast state of non-emotion within a heightened sense of awareness to sight and sound, to the feel of the beat of his heart.

He thought about heading over to his studio, where absolutely nothing was happening, which was OK, too, for now. He didn't have any logs to work, other than a few rejects that never fired, like racehorses on a bad day. He planned one of these weekends soon to drive up to Mendocino County to see the Witch Doctor, his main man and mentor who provided him with redwood trunks culled from what the old man in the mountains called his "sacred forest." They always met in the remote outpost of Covelo, at a red bench in front of an abandoned beekeeper's storefront, where the two had rendezvoused for nearly 30 years – Link driving up from Sacramento in a rented van, and the Witch Doctor emerging from wherever he was hiding out to lead him to the wood. Another visit was way overdue.

One block short of R Street, an impulse redirected Link eastward. Six blocks in that direction and Link knew it was his day. The bells clanged and the crossing rails dropped and a three-engine Union Pacific freighter rendered midtown immobile. Nothing pleased him more than to be stuck for 10 minutes while the train roared past. He used the time to take stock of his world and everything in it, including himself and his art and how he and it were getting along.

First, the oil cars, fresh from the fracklands of North Dakota. Southbound, they'd drop off at some miserable Kern County town for refinement into low-grade asphalt. Their tubular blackness preceded hopper cars carrying the nation's bounty.

The 2018 fleet of Toyota Rav-4s sped past by the dozens while Link stood at the corner of Q and 19th streets, outside a bar where they poured $2 shots every time the train rolled past – the same building that used to be his statuary shop, until the landlord sold the building out from underneath him. New apartment buildings and townhomes sprang from every corner over the old *Beacon* parking lot and an array of auto body shops – all signs of the changing times.

Standing on the corner, with the train rocking and rollicking past him, Link's thoughts reverted to a few things he'd learned about himself over the past few months. During his night in captivity, he learned a Russian spy and gangster had compiled something of a psychiatric dossier on Link, which told him more than he ever knew about himself. Meditating on this profile over that profile ever since, Link believed the chief insight was that beneath his poised exterior beat the heart of obstinance. He might preach cosmic collectivity, about the need for compassion for the least among us, about living close to the earth in an urban setting, with fresh vegetables on every other street corner, but what deep down his inflexible adherence to these principles really represented ego, covered in false humility. Somehow he'd managed to glean this by FaceTiming a Russian named Anton Karuliyak, speaking from his native Novosibirsk, capital of Siberia, on the other side of the world. Link's refusal to give into their ridiculous offer of $1 million for a piece testified to his oppositional defiance – another personal characteristic revealed by the distant evil genius Karuliyak.

With the train roaring by, Link looked further inward. He had a tendency to isolate himself unnecessarily, the consequence of a superego which had unconsciously set him apart from his species. A persistent bachelorhood persisted. The Single Life served him well during a youth that tended toward delinquency until he found a chisel. He failed to establish long-lasting relationships of any kind. Everyone knew the deal with Link was that he knew everybody in town but he didn't really have any friends, except for maybe two or three drunken newspapermen he met at Benny's, the hangout for the reporters of the *Beacon*.

Maybe the afternoon bartender at the same joint. Add a couple bums from the street. Even that motley crew had dwindled. One of them – a *Beacon* reporter whose story linking a Russian organized crime operation in Sacramento to the same con artists who stole the American presidency – had blown town to take a job with the *Washington Post.*

The roar of the Union Pacific drove Link deeper into reminiscence. It soothed his nerves. It flattened out the alpha rhythms of his brain. It instructed him deeply about his place in this world.

He sought out train crossings for these moments of deeper consciousness. He appreciated being of no mind. He wallowed in the occasional flash of insight, the artistic inspiration, the revelation of a deeper truth about himself.

Oddly, however, in this moment of a perfect Sacramento spring afternoon soothed by a light breeze and warming temperatures and the bright green of the elm and sycamore and Modesto ash that turned every corridor east of 16th and north of I and south of N streets into a canopied tunnel – it occurred to him in the midst of his train trance that his mother was dead.

This was not really news. She had passed about 40 years earlier, while he was still cutting his teeth cutting logs at the Mendocino Art Center. On occasion, he contemplated her meaning to his life. He always stopped short, however, from conducting a deeper emotional investigation. The thing he always told himself was, she did her best. She loved him with everything she had, and what more can any mother do for her child than that? She provided the basics. She made sure he attended school. She made sure he graduated from high school. She cleaned his clothes. She made him sandwiches. She cooked him dinner. She saw his creative streak. She nudged him along his artistic way.

Once he got on the path, she died.

From the beginning all they had were each other. There was never a dad, never a brother or sister, never a cousin, never an aunt, an uncle, a grandma or a grandpa. They lived in a trailer on the rancheria in the foothills, and if they had family it was only the other rancherians. Their three-acre community emitted the sounds and smells of poverty. It was all that was left to Link's people after the federal government terminated their existence as a nation.

In the dread of defeat, Link ran with the pack and found his rightful place right in the middle of it. The pack brought him up as much as his mother did. The pack did the natural things boys do, sometimes with their white non-rancheria pals who lived in the encroaching suburbs. Together, white and native, they stole cheap wine from supermarkets and got wasted on hot summer nights at the age of 14. They smoked pot and did other drugs and played disorganized sports. Eventually, Link hit the six-foot marker, and the high school basketball coaches threw him the ball to see if he could shoot it, which he could. He grew bigger, to 6-4, and they also discovered he could not only put the ball in the hole, but he could also block out and grab missed shots and play good defense and dribble. Best of all, he played without self-interest. He kept the ball moving. He found the open guy. He could set a screen and roll to the hoop, and he could keep the other guys from doing the same. He made first-team varsity as a sophomore and second-team all-league as a senior power forward/center.

Link's mother supported him on a maid's salary.

It was quite a comedown from her academic training.

She had earned a Master's at Sac State and had been trained as a licensed marriage family therapist. She also got a teaching credential, and she made good money when she got a good job at the Deuel Vocational Institution right after it opened in Tracy, down in San Joaquin County, where she worked with kid prisoners – "the children," as she called the 16-to-25-year-old rapists and robbers and hardened gangsters and convicted murderers, who in turn called the facility "The Gladiator School." She thought she could turn them into college students. She experienced some success. About one out of 200 was good enough to keep her coming back. She liked it that the boys seemed to like her, even if they failed her. Of course they liked her. She was nice. She was motherly. She was kind. She was good. She was good-looking, and her Native American ethnicity, hard to pinpoint, gave her a kind of camouflage that allowed her to get over with everybody.

If Link's mother had a problem, it's that she liked the children just a little too much. Sometimes her love took her just a bit too far, like the time prison authorities caught her in a therapy session in her office with her pants down and a young man's tongue in her mouth.

Ten months later, Link was born.

She never worked a decent job again.

She took a plea early in her criminal proceedings and she didn't have to serve any jail time. She seemed to resolve to never mess around again – at least Link never knew her to have any young men around the trailer. The judge barred her from ever being able to work in a prison or school anywhere very meaningful ever again. The judge sentenced her to poverty. She didn't appeal.

She would have this child, though.

She would bear it and love it as much as any living thing had ever been loved, even if she couldn't always afford him new shoes. She would not tell the child the circumstances of his creation, even when she was lying in a bed in a nursing home in Marysville, dying of cervical cancer. She never told him who his father was, and he could never find out on his own: the name had been scratched off his birth certificate, an erasure compelled by the confidentiality requirements that governed the identities of underage prisoners.

She worked hard for her boy while she was alive. She picked peaches and plums and when Link was a teenager the two of them were hired by Juan Corona, working in the same orchards where the bodies of 25 men murdered by the farm labor contractor were eventually discovered. The unearthings prompted Link's mother to seek other employment. She cleaned houses, mainly, for cheap. She took money under the table, slave wages, from rural and suburban families of means but no morals. But she could accept the slave wages and stay on welfare, with the full range of food stamps and MediCal benefits and rental assistance to augment her monthly county check. If the county knew she was working at all, they'd strip her of every penny and throw her in jail. County welfare police suspected her of fraud and sniffed through her trash for evidence, but the house-cleaning money had been thoroughly washed. The welfare cops found nothing.

Between maid money and welfare, she did all right by Link. She suffered through his mid-teen years when he ran with the pack and his friends were more important to him than she was. She worried that he might go gangster on her.

She nurtured his artistic impulse, and no Nisenan god ever received more prayers of thanks than hers when she saw her boy breaking free. Art became more important than pack, and she jumped on the creativity, directed him to books and programs and influences that raised his soul. He was the only one in the pack who graduated. He could have gone to college, as an academic. He checked out Sac State and UC Davis. He wasn't good enough to hoop at either place, a couple inches too short and just a rat-hair's too slow to walk on at either school. Hell, he could have walked on at any D-III school in the country, maybe with help from an academic scholie – his grades were more than decent enough. So was his luck: Instead of being frozen out of educational opportunities and denied standing in American society, the country finally had begun to open up to nonwhites.

Link was smart enough and he worked hard enough and he kept his grades good enough to receive some scholarship offers, and he didn't need any affirmative action to get them. He could have played real-small college ball at schools that gave academic scholarships to players who could fill roster spots. But he was too good at his art to go all-in on his books. He settled for a Pell grant and community college and an apartment in Sacramento. His mother learned to grant-write and she found out about the Mendocino Art Center. She told him about an instructor she had heard of there, some crazy part-time teacher who babbled around town under the identity of a witch doctor. You could find him at Dick's Place, the bar a couple doors down from the Mendocino Hotel, on Main Street, every day about 5:30 p.m.

31

When she got sick, Link visited her regularly. He'd walk down from the Mendocino Art Center to U.S. 101 and hitchhike to the Transbay Terminal in San Francisco. He'd catch a bus to Sacramento and another one to Marysville. He held her hand when she died. It was just the two of them, and now it was just him and nobody else, and by the time the train had passed at 19th and Q in the spring of the second year of Trump, he flashed back to their final moment, and there were no great words of wisdom, or even many words at all. There was just her pain, and Link guessed that's probably the way it ended for just about everybody, whether they lived in a tower on Fifth Avenue or in a trailer in the dry-grass foothills east of Sacramento.

4/Butt Flick

Link showered and dressed and stepped outside to his front porch to begin the next day as he usually did – picking the newspapers off the porch and tucking them under his arm and making the four-block walk to The Shine to load up on the news of the day sparked up with an overdose of caffeine.

For the 17 years he lived on D Street, the delivery people who threw *The Beacon* and *The New York Times* displayed the consistency of DiMaggio. Five o'clock, every morning – boom! Papers bundled together and soft-tossed onto the porch of his grey-and-red high-water Victorian.

In recent weeks, and with increasing frequency, the papers didn't land until after 7 a.m., and sometimes not even then. Sometimes when Link called the *Beacon* to report this breach of the business-consumer relationship, nobody answered the phone. When they did, Link thought it probably was from a boiler room, or a prison yard, or another continent.

Nothing challenged Link's adherence to balanced detachment

more than when he stepped outside between 7 and 8 o'clock in the morning to a paperless porch. He *needed* them for his daily jumpstart. Them, and a couple cups of dark roast.

Slowly, he came to accept this consequence of journalism-by-search-engine-optimization. The papers, or at least the *Beacon*, didn't want you to read the paper anymore. They saw digital as the salvation of their industry. Link did not. He saw the disruption of his delivery service by the newspaper company as a ploy to get all their customers to switch to digital. Link vowed to resist. The pop-up ads irritated him. The flashing and dashing and sound and excitement unnerved him. He preferred the stillness and calm of the daily paper. If the paper forced him into an adjustment, Link would make it. On days when the paper failed to appear, he'd just walk downtown to the gift shop at the Hyatt Regency at 12th and L – the closest spot that carried the *Times* – and then double back to The Shine at 14th and E.

Down the stairs and into the street, he angled across to the opposite sidewalk on his journey to the Hyatt, when he passed a black SUV parked on the opposite curb. He couldn't see the driver or passenger, sitting inside, shaded as they were by the huge car's dark-tinted windows and the bright morning sun, but could not ignore it when the person behind the wheel rolled the window down and flicked a cigarette butt at him.

It landed at his feet.

Weird, he thought.

It bounced in the middle of the street and skidded along the asphalt. Link made no mistake about the message. He looked down on the cigarette butt that burned towards its filter. He crushed it with the sole of his boot, bent over, and picked it up. Then he carried it over to the SUV to present to the driver.

"You dropped this," Link told them, holding the dead butt upward with his thumb and forefinger.

His eyes still adjusting to the SUV's dark interior, all he could tell were that the two men inside the SUV looked young, and vaguely familiar.

Before his facial recognition software fully kicked in, they broke into a monkey laugh and sped away. Declining to re-litter his own street, Link put the cigarette butt in his back pocket. He followed the car with his eyes curiously, and he took special notice of their haircuts. They were trim, tight cut on the sides, grown a sticky two to three inches up top, Brylcreemed over to the side at about a 45-degree angle.

He thought to himself that it looked like both of them would have fit in very well at Charlottesville, with the tiki torchers, rallying around Robert E. Lee.

If only he knew that they had.

5/*Manuela Time*

Link once again rode the elevator to the 22nd floor of the Esquire Building in downtown Sacramento, with a woman on his mind. The same woman.

He'd found it hard, actually, to think about anything other than Manuela since the last time he had ventured into and out of the building. "Balanced detachment," bullshit. These days he couldn't separate himself from his emotional state. He fought off his interest in her, for about two weeks, before he surrendered, on a lovely afternoon in early May when he stepped off the Otis and into the lobby of the MJ Public Affairs suite.

The curved walls from the elevator to the receptionist's desk were lined with the portraits of the eight founding partners and their current associates, including the gorgeous profile of Manuela Fonseca and the list of her major clients – a major corporate television broadcaster, the most prominent art museum in town, a vintner's association from the Sierra foothills, and a couple of private foundations linked to the mayor, the founders of a half-dozen of the region's leading breweries, and an association of the most prominent chefs in the city, including one of whom – Carrick Mullaney – who had arranged for her to represent Lincoln Adams on the occasion of his totem pole being hoisted in a celebration at Cesar Chavez Plaza.

Standing in the lobby and looking over the pictures, Link looked over the profile pictures of the eight partners in the firm and saw that seven of them wore dark suits and red ties. Link saw that one of the photos stood out larger and above the seven others, a depiction of a silver-haired gentleman identified by his nameplate as Matthew Johannsen – the "MJ" of MJ Public Affairs. Link looked closer, and saw that towards the bottom of this Johannsen guy's long list of clients, one of them was identified simply as "Russia."

Interesting client, Link thought. He didn't exactly see how a lobbying firm in California stood to make any money off a country that had officially been frozen out of American business dealings. But what did he know about sanctions, or Russia? Until the previous year, he thought about Russia about as much as he did Ouagadugu, even less so, given that he once carved a dwarf red buffalo for Armand Pierre Beouindi, the future mayor of Burkina Faso's capital city. The only thing Link ever got out of Russia was a kidnapping – his own. Now, it seemed like everywhere he looked, whether he saw the Scrounger doing some kind of insane dance the night of Link's totem unveiling or laid eyes on the office wall of a woman he hoped to hustle, there it was, the R-country, or some kind of cultural reflection of it.

"Can I help you, Mr. Adams?" asked the friendly voice at the receptionist's desk that belonged to a young man who first met Link at the unveiling and had spoken to him many times over the phone.

Link replied that he only wanted to say hello to Manuela.

"Is Ms. Fonseca expecting you?" the receptionist asked.

"Only if she is prescient," Link answered.

The receptionist laughed.

"I'll call her for you," he said. "Oops. Looks like there's no need."

The receptionist looked past Link who was leaning on his elbows on the receptionist's counter in his usual get-up, a pictorial of black – jeans, t-shirt, and cowboy boots – with only a white straw cowboy hat on top breaking the monotony. His hair flowed several inches below the brim from the back.

Before he could turn around to see what the receptionist was looking at, there she was, the public relations queen, Manuela Fonseca. Increasing her spectacularity, at least for Link, was the fact that she was dressed in her workout gear.

Link had never seen her like this: the muscles rippling from her neck through her shoulders and down into her biceps, the abs flat, the waist trim, even if she wasn't skinny. This was an athletic, powerful woman, and she was big for her size, which was a little more than medium, with quite a prominent cushion on the bottom, muscular legs, bulging calves. She had to have been 5-9, maybe 5-10, and she looked like she weighed a fat-free 160, at least.

Atop her gym clothes, a pair of red Everlast boxing gloves dangled over her shoulder. She carried the headgear in her hands, and she'd just taken it off if the misshapen hair on top of her head was any indication.

It didn't take Teddy Atlas to tell you the woman had a thing for boxing, and Link, who prided himself on staying in the best shape possible for a two-IPA-a-day guy, always had a thing for athletic women. Women who were more than fit. Women who were cut. Women who could swim. Women who could hike. Women who could knock you out.

Link had gone a few rounds the year before with a muscularly lean woman, name of Angelina Puchkova, but she turned out to be a Russian spy – the introduction to his ongoing headache. Angelina oozed international intrigue. Angelina slid around between the sheets slinky as satin. It took Link a while to forget about her once his first mind told him to cut it off.

Manuela, too, looked dangerous. At the same time, she seemed safe. Stable. Set. Situated. Manuela also enjoyed one hugely favorable comparison as Link stacked her up against the ice diva from Siberia – the bronze bomber seemed like fun.

Link found it easy to snag a chuckle out of her when he commented:

"I see they don't have much of a dress code around here,"

Link said.

Manuela, of course, laughed, and as they walked through the reception room, she cuffed the back of Link's cowboy hat, to expose more of his head.

"Looks like you could use a haircut," she said. "Come on back."

"How much do you charge?"

She laughed again, before she turned flirty.

"I'll give you a buzz for free," she said.

The reciprocation settled Link down. Made him feel like less of a creeper.

It looked like this thing had a chance to go somewhere.

"Who can't use a buzz," he replied.

Link was smiling as he scanned the musculature of her bronze-colored thighs and shoulders and upper arms.

"So, what's with the gloves?" Link asked.

Manuela feigned a left-right combo. "I don't want to hurt my hands on the boys' pretty faces," she said. "Especially these boys with the camera."

"You're a fighter?"

She shrugged her muscled shoulders and nodded. "I boxed a little bit as a teenager," he offered. "I've got to say, I was pretty good at it. I could stick and move, used my height and length. There was a coach at the Auburn Y who said I had a future. But I had one huge problem."

"Let me guess."

"I didn't like to get hit."

"That is a major disqualifier," Manuela agreed. "I wasn't huge on it either, but you learn a lot about yourself from it. It's like, what do you do once you get punched in the nose? Do you back off and cry? Or do you gather yourself and punch back? Do you learn from experience?"

"I sure do. I learn a lot."

"What?"

"That I don't like to get hit in the face."

Manuela, who seemed to have a perpetual smile on her face, broke out with more laughter.

"I guess that's when you decided to become an artist."

"Come to think of it, there was an interesting coincidence in the timing of the transition."

Manuela threw the gloves and the headgear on her office couch, and Link plopped down next to them while she checked her written messages and pulled her cell phone out of her gym bag and scrolled through her texts.

"So, what brings you over, other than to rag on the way I dress when I come to work?" she said, without looking up.

"Oh, no – no ragging here. I'd say your attire is perfect for the times. Perfect for the era of Trump. Ready to fight at a minute's notice."

Manuela looked up from her phone.

"I also have a pussy hat," she said.

She nodded to the middle glass shelf behind her desk where a pink-knit head covering with the cat ears popularized during the women's marches the day after the Trump inaugural. It was fastened over a cantaloupe-sized Oakland Raiders football helmet that had been autographed by Jim Plunkett, the two-time Super Bowl-winning quarterback.

"I had a friend who tried to put one on me," Link said, thinking back to the Women's March in Sacramento. "It didn't fit over my cowboy hat."

Manuela laughed. Link's flirtatious stalling had finally enabled him to think up an excuse for his visit.

"Actually," Link lied, "I dropped by to see if I could get that Jordan kid's phone number and email. I think I lost them."

Which Manuela saw right through. She squinted her left eye and looked at Link in feigned suspicion over the mention of the young political consultant.

"You think you lost them," she said.

"I believe so," Link went on.

She laughed as she searched her cell phone for Jordan's contact information – playing her part in his subterfuge.

"So, you're going to go through with this volunteer thing?" she said.

"I think it is time, yes."

"That's commendable," Manuela said.

"I don't know about commendability," Link thought out loud. "I see it more as an obligation. If there is one thing I've got a lot of that other people do not, it is time."

Manuela looked up from her phone to listen to Link.

"Yeah," he said. "It's like, we take so much for granted. We complain and we moan and we yell at the TV, and it might make us feel good, and it accomplishes nothing. I mean, don't get me wrong. I know the imperfections of this system, just like you do – myself as a Nisenan, you as a *Latina*. We have experienced what we have experienced, yet in my readings of history, meager as they are, I am not aware of another system in the history of the world that sincerely sought to accomplish what this one has tried, on the scale that this one is trying, and has been trying for at least the last fifty or sixty years, with all of its imperfections. It seems like that might be changing."

"I tend to agree," Manuela said.

"To be totally honest, being an artist at times can be kind of scary at times, especially when you're not stimulated," Link confessed. "You can begin to freak out. So, I need some stimulation."

Manuela shook her head in the affirmative.

"I get that, too."

She looked back to the phone and found Jordan's info and texted it to Link.

He pulled out his phone and downloaded it into his contact list.

"Thank you very much, Ms. Fonseca," said Link.

"Manuela, *stupido,*" she said.

Of course he discovered that Jordan's name, number and email already had been implanted it into his device.

"Manuela," he said. "How about dinner with me at Mullaney's?

Manuela's eyebrows raised in mock surprise.

"I think I'd like that," she said.

Link pulled his body out of the couch across from Manuela's desk and made his way to the door and out of her office. Mission accomplished.

She walked him to the elevator, her scheduler in hand, to see when she could work Link in on a date, when she looked up to see him studying the photograph of the founding partner that stood above the rest.

"That's Matthew," she said. "If you're wondering about the Russia thing…"

"Now why would I be doing a thing like that," Link wisecracked, his past encounters with the nation's representatives in the Sacramento area now hanging heavy over his conversation with Manuela.

"Well, he's totally harmless," she said. "He spends most of his time at his ranch up in Sierraville where he likes to play cowboy. Nobody ever sees him around here anymore – maybe once or twice a year, and that's it. In fact, the seven other partners are in negotiations with him to buy him out of the firm. They see him as kind of resistant to the future. A few of the guys want to bring in the marijuana business, and he won't have any of that. So they've decided they don't want any of him. The only problem is, he still owns 51 percent of the company."

"Pro-Russia, anti-pot," Link said. "Not exactly my kind of guy."

"You're a pothead?"

"I puff here and there," he said, "but not so much lately. The past couple of years, all the Russia stuff has made me a little bit paranoid. Paranoia and pot do not mix."

"That's the reason I stopped smoking it, after about the first time I ever felt the effects," Manuela jumped in. "I thought I was going to get arrested."

"Where were you?"

"Kern County. Driving up the Kern River Canyon."

"This was when?"

"Mid-Eighties sometime."

"That wasn't paranoia, Ms. Fonseca," Link said.

"Manuela, *bruto*," she corrected.

"It's not paranoia," Link went on, "when you're right."

Manuela laughed, then went back to her scheduler.

"Let's see," she said. "Dinner, with crazy Indian *bruto*, the wood sculptor, at Mullaney's. Let's see if I can fit you in. What night were you thinking about, *bruto*?"

"This one," he replied instantly.

Manuela gave him a sideways smile. She liked the non-super-cool urgency of his interest.

Only, "I can't do tonight," she said. "I have a meeting with a representative of the city arts council. Looks like I'll be adding them to my client list."

"I am also free tomorrow night," Link said. "And the night after that."

Manuela laughed again.

"You make the reservation," she said, "and call me tomorrow afternoon."

6/*Frankie's Back*

Link's days usually began around 6:30 a.m. when he stirred to natural waking consciousness from dreamless sleep.

He didn't have many night-time stories erupting from deep within his dormant brain. When he got 'em, though, they were pretty good. His favorite had him right down the middle, 25 yards from the stage, just to the side of the taper's section at an unspecified Grateful Dead concert. Always, it was a great show.

Another dream story featured his mother at her best, accompanied by the emotional warmth she showered on him every single day of her shortened life.

It was a rare occurrence when something like his ringing cell phone brought him to life in the morning.

With the dawn's early light of May 11 slanting in from his east-facing bedroom window, he threw back the paper-thin green frayed cotton blanket and the thread-bare sheets that he washed without fail once a month, and he reached with his left hand to grab his cell phone that was perched on top of Ben Rhodes' *The World As It Is,* a tome on America's role in the world a thousand years ago when Obama was president.

He didn't recognize the phone number, at a minute before 6 a.m., when he clicked on the green answer button.

"You'll never guess where I am," said the voice from the other end that should have been familiar, but wasn't. It always took a minute or so for his brain waves to fire.

"Where you are," Link said, playing along as if he knew who it was, which he did not.

"The Sterling!"

"The Sterling?"

"Where else! Ain't it perfect?"

Recognition, at last.

"Frankie?" he asked.

"Thank you."

Yes, it was Frankie Cameron on the line, former reporter for *The Sacramento Beacon*, now employed by the *Washington Post*, and apparently in town for a reason that had not been previously disclosed to the journo's best friend, who happened to be Link.

"How the hell are you?"

"Good enough. What are you doing at the Sterling?"

"Well, I just finished eating a scone, and I'm still drinking a cup of coffee, and I thought I'd rattle you into the day."

"I appreciate that. But why are you in Sacramento?"

The previous year, Frankie's work for the *Beacon* on the Russian organized crime ring in Sacramento had got him noticed by the *Washington Post*, which hired him. At Frankie's request, his new bosses put him to work earlier in the year covering night cops. The editors found Frankie highly energetic for an old timer, and a good writer, too, and they asked him if he might be interested in moving up to the investigative team, or over to the political squad, or both, and when he couldn't make up his mind, they told him to pack his bags and head to California to get cracking on the seven contested congressional seats in the Golden State.

"So now I'm a hot-shot political writer," Frankie told Link.

Frankie told Link about his California assignment and how he'd be spending the next several weeks checking in and out of the congressional districts from San Diego to Orange County to the Mojave to Modesto.

Link listened casually before responding:

"I've said it many times, and I'll say it again."

"And that is?"

"There is no such thing as coincidence."

"Thanks again for the insight. Now maybe you'll want to tell me how that figures into what I'm doing here."

"All I can say is that you are now checking in with your newest source."

"Who?"

"Me."

"You?"

"Why not me?"

"How about you don't know any more about politics than the average doofus on the street."

"That may be true, but it is the doofus on the street who is supposed to be the one who holds power in this country, if the Founding Fathers are to be believed."

"Show me where they said that."

"I'm sure it's in the Federalist Papers somewhere."

"Fake news."

"I guess you haven't seen *Hamilton*."

"Neither have you."

"No, I haven't, but I kind of know what it's all about. All power in America derives from the consent of the governed."

"Man, are you serious or delirious? Aren't you aware of *Citizens United*? It couldn't be stated more clearly: all power derives from he who kisses the white asses of the Brothers Koch."

Link grinned. He'd missed Frankie.

"You sound like you're taking extremism lessons," he told Frankie.

"As should we all," Frankie responded. "These are the times

that try men's souls."

Link yawned and stood up from the bed, his phone still nailed to his ear.

"About that coincidence," Frankie asked.

"Oh, yeah," Link yawn-stifled. "You should know that I am signing up as a volunteer for the resistance."

"Oh really."

"Doing my first canvass Sunday, in Modesto."

"Modesto, huh. Well, fuck all. I guess you will be a source of mine. I'll be down there checking in on Bonham."

"Not a bad man," Link said. "He seems sincere in his efforts to prevent Trump from rounding up all of the Dreamers and placing them in concentration camps. He votes the wrong way on many critical issues, but I believe he is merely misguided."

"Sounds like they had a pretty good Poli Sci program at that art school in Mendocino."

"No," Link said, earnestly, but with a grin that suggested he got the joke. "I've just been spending more time lately trying to find out how things are supposed to work. Or not."

"I'd like to work on some things that are not working," Frankie said, "but that would violate my pledge of journalistic objectivity."

"Objectivity is subjective," Link said.

The two had watched the VCR of *Love And Death* many times in Link's living room, occasionally with a puff of the herb.

Frankie laughed, "But fairness isn't. Neither are facts. Damn, am I sounding preachy or what? As for you being sourcy, I hope you do a better job this time than you did with your gal."

"You're still calling her that?"

"Of course."

A little more than a year earlier, a good-looking woman came into Link's life. She was a Russian, a spy, a gangster's moll, and an Uber driver who picked up Link not at all by chance – the Russians had hacked his app. The spy mistress Angelina Puchkova seduced him, exposed him to the fact he still had emotions. Then she went cold. Then she went dark. Then she fled the law back to Russia with her boyfriend, the horrible

Anton Karuliyak, who had arranged for Link's kidnapping. The last time Link saw her was on FaceTime when he was a hostage.

"You'll be happy to know that I have not heard a peep out of her, or him, since our unfortunate encounter last year," Link said. But Link had a lingering doubt they weren't done with him. As much as he laughed off the whole experience, he could still feel them out there in a way he couldn't quite put his thumb on.

"All over a dumb log. Why didn't you just take the money and carve out some kind of piece of shit and get them off your back?"

"I don't need the money."

"Fine, give it to me."

"And I still have my artistic pride."

"Oh, please. Do you know how many times I wrote completely horse shit stories that I had absolutely no stake in but went ahead and did them anyway just because it was more convenient than having to fight the editors all the fucking time?"

"I'm sorry to hear that."

"Spare me. It's the way of the world."

Link steered the conversation back toward a less contentious course.

"So, what's your game plan?" he asked.

"Still coming up with one. Only thing I know is I'm going to Modesto first, like, today. You want to go with me?"

Link rubbed some more sleep out of his eyes and scratched his head.

"Possible," he said.

He rubbed his eyes some more and looked out the window into another spectacularly gorgeous middle-of-the-spring day, where blue birds floated through the liquid amber that gave him cover from new townhouses rising on the other side of his backyard fence. They chirped their greetings to the fast-rising sun.

"How are you doing for sources?" he asked Frankie.

"As usual. Making them up as I go."

"If you're looking for a real one, I might be able to help you out."

"I've heard that before."

"I'm telling you again."

Link gave Frankie the rundown about Jordan Diaz, the kid consultant hired by the national party committee to work out the defeat of John Bonham as congressional representative of the greater Modesto metropolitan agricopolis.

"I'd like to meet him," Frankie said.

"I think that can be arranged."

7/*Tako Power Lunch*

It was Frankie who insisted that they do lunch at Tako, the Korean barbecue joint on Alhambra and T. When he lived in Sacramento, he ate a bulgogi bowl at least once a week – cheap, easy walk from the *Beacon*, great. He hadn't found anything that matched it yet in D.C., where he and the wife and kids shacked up in a rental house in Silver Spring.

Link liked his Tako, too. He showered and dressed after his telephone conversation with Frankie and enjoyed his walk across midtown to the Seoul food stand where he captured an outdoor table ahead of the lunch rush.

Frankie showed up first and slid his car into the only open spot in Tako's three-space parking lot.

"My lucky day," he told Link, as he walked up and slapped his brown Reporter's notebook down on the three-seated high table.

"Buy a lottery ticket," Link responded. "When you've got it going, you've got to keep it going until it stops,"

"And, as always . . .," Frankie said.

"Be sure to pay the rent first," Link continued. They'd always gotten a kick out of that gamblers' admonition.

The two hadn't seen each other since the moving van pulled away from Frankie's East Sacramento bungalow in January, followed by a cab to the airport that drove off with Link's pal. In a matter of days, Link's balanced detachment gave way to an acknowledgment that he found life a tad emptier since Frankie left town. So long to the comfort he had known for more than 25 years that every Tuesday and Friday around 5 p.m., he could walk over to Benny's, order a Sierra Nevada or Racer 5, and spend an hour or so talking sports and politics and women and the news and Sacramento with Frankie and their other best pal, the *Beacon's* eccentric feature writer, Mike Rubiks.

Frankie took his seat at the outdoor Tako table like he'd never been away. Link stood up and stretched out his arms with a wingspan that fit his tallish frame.

"Hey," he said, prompting Frankie to get up on his feet, too.

The two men embraced for what they realized was the first time ever.

When they sat down, Jordan Diaz rolled in – last to lunch, but in way better style than the black-drabbed Link and the frayed Frankie who wore the same Jerry Garcia ties and tan khakis and long-sleeved white dress shirts rolled to the elbow and stained by several years of chin dribble. Jordan, on other hand, looked sharp. His tight-fitting electric-blue suit didn't quite reach his shoes or the end of his wrists, the coat cut off damn near to the belt line. Always the critics, and especially on things they knew nothing about, Link and Frankie opined that Jordan needed a new tailor. And a new barber: Jordan coated his shortish hair in some kind of goop and combed it from either side to a point in the middle of his forehead. To add to his dash, Jordan rode in on one of those red electric Jump bikes.

Jordan bolted his bike to the rack and looked worried as he joined Link and Frankie at their table.

"Somebody takes my bike and it's a long walk back to the office," he said. "I don't like to break a sweat during the day." He touched his hair as if to make sure it was still in place.

"Your bike?" Link said. "I thought you people shared them."

"We do, but as you can see, mine is the only one in the rack."

"Call Saudi Arabia," Frankie broke in, before his introduction to Jordan.

"Saudi Arabia?" Link inquired.

"They own the goddamn things."

"I thought Uber did," Jordan said.

"Who do you think owns Uber?"

It was Link's idea to get Jordan and Frankie together for lunch, and it occurred to him as Jordan sat down that he had not properly introduced them. Social niceties were never his strong point. Little things like introductions did not come naturally to him.

"Frankie Cameron, Jordan Diaz," he said. "Jordan, Frankie."

As the two politely shook hands, Jordan complimented Frankie for his coverage the previous year that laid out the local Russian mob and its assistance in financing the social media campaign that gave America its Trump implant. How were the poorly-educated to know that the "stories" that jammed their news feeds had been written in St. Petersburg?

"Mr. Adams and Manuela Fonseca told me it may have been the best coverage in the recent history of the paper," Jordan Diaz said.

The statement perplexed Frankie.

"Told you," he said. "You mean you didn't read it?"

"I saw the news about the kidnapping on Twitter," Jordan said.

"Saw it," Frankie repeated.

"Yes," Jordan replied. "I read the story, but I don't think, at the time, I looked at who wrote it."

"Didn't look at who wrote it."

"No, sir," Jordan said. "I am sorry."

Frankie waved it off, like it was nothing. Just another piece of evidence that the end of the world was nearer. First, a paper stops printing baseball box scores. Next, nobody reads it. Then, you work your ass off to uncover the existence of a Russian organized crime ring that stole the American presidency, and young movers and shakers don't know you from Billy Barty.

Link shook Frankie out of his reflection on the sad state of local journalistic affairs in America in the second decade of the 21st Century.

"I think you two can make some beautiful music together," Link said.

The politically-engaged artist had already briefed the consultant and the reporter on their shared interest in California CD 10 – Jordan, in wanting to flip it for the Democrats, and Frankie, to milk the best stories possible out of the Northern San Joaquin Valley race that could decide the balance of power in the U.S. House of Representatives.

The three of them walked inside Tako to place their orders. They returned to their outdoor table just in time to see somebody unbolt Jordan's bike from the rack.

"Damn," he said. "Well, I guess I don't have to worry about that anymore."

The three of them sat down and Jordan reached into his backpack.

"OK, here's the stuff," he told Frankie, as if he were about to slip him a kilo of cocaine.

Jordan pulled a manila folder out of the pack and handed it to Frankie. It was marked: "Jacob Harland Opposition Research." This was the ultra-right Manteca doctor guy who had just recently filed his papers to challenge the incumbent.

Frankie asked, "What about Bonham? Don't you have anything on him?"

"Don't worry about Bonham," Jordan replied. "We'll have plenty of opportunities to define him. For now, the person we have to worry about is Harland."

"If you say so," Frankie said.

Nobody knew much of anything yet about Harland, but Jordan Diaz knew that once the right-wing challenger came clean on his anti-immigrant stance, he figured to be a factor.

"We've been doing a little poking around," Jordan said. "I think there's some stuff in here that might interest you."

Frankie gave Link a wink that said he liked it that this kid gets right to the point. Link winked back.

The reporter opened the folder to a collection of printouts

fastened together with a small black binder clip. It looked to be pretty much a download of everything off Harland's newly-created website: pictures of the family physician candidate with his wife, dog, and children, a short bio of him being a "non-politician," and a rant about immigration and how it was changing the country in ways that some people did not like.

In his online campaign materials, Harland also harshly criticized Bonham for his semi-moderate views on immigration. The congressman's opinion, of course, had been shaped by the cheap-labor needs of the district's farmers and dairymen. Harland took the position that if the agricultural industry couldn't find Americans to work the factories in the fields, the government should go back to the older *bracero* program that benefited the farmers during World War II, and that if the workers from down below complained about their low wages, dangerous working conditions or substandard housing, they would be rounded up and bused back to the border crossing at Tijuana. Harland further castigated Bonham for the incumbent's expressed sympathy for DACA.

"All Of Them Out!" was his rallying cry.

Frankie thumbed through most of the packet and appeared unimpressed.

"Pretty standard right-wing stuff," he said, looking up at Jordan.

"Keep reading," Jordan advised.

Frankie flipped through the Harland dossier to the next bound item in the Harland packet, one that veered into a darker corner of American social and political thought.

Several pages appeared to have been printed out from an online chat room entitled "The Second Amendment People." The SAPs, as they called themselves, took their name and their cue from Donald Trump's famous campaign statement that if Hillary Clinton won the presidency, the only thing that stood between the SAPs and their guns were the SAPs themselves. Whether Trump meant to threaten harm to his opponent, the SAPs certainly took it that way. And they still took it that way, a year and a half into his presidency, at least according to Frankie's reading of their postings.

The people who wrote that they wanted to shoot, dismember and burn Hillary's body only made up the site's outliers. Mostly, the chat room was filled with support for the NRA from people who lived in the rural and mountainous Northern California outback. They were just simple country folk, religious, who still hated the Roe v. Wade decision and expressed another concern about securing America's southern border. A fourth item on their agenda, as outlined by the hosts of the cyber gathering, delved into a discussion of what they called "the preservation of the purity of the white race."

"OK – pretty standard crazy right-wing stuff," Frankie said.

"Keep reading," Jordan repeated.

Frankie scanned through the chat postings until he came to one dated the previous fall that ran under the name "Manteca Medicine Man." It read:

"Am I the only white person in this county who is aware that John Bonham is married to a Mexican?"

Frankie looked up at Jordan with a quizzical look on his face.

"What about it?" he said.

The young consultant shrugged as if he knew nothing.

"We're digging around," Jordan said.

"I'm going to need more than a Reddit post with a Manteca moniker before I can go with it, you know."

"Like I said," Jordan replied. "We're working on it."

"It's a story if you can prove he wrote it. But it's not exactly the discovery of Judge Crater's body. This Harland dude, he's basically a non-starter, right?"

Jordan cleared his throat, and he removed his coat and hung it over the back of his chair and was getting ready to lay out his take just as a Tako worker called their number.

"I'll get it," Link said. "You guys keep talking."

"Yeah, but I've got to pay you," Frankie said.

"Later," Link said. "Get back to work."

"OK," Jordan said. "As I was saying. You're right, this is just one relatively small manifestation of your run-of-the-mill northeastern California racism. But we have managed to obtain the author's internet protocol address, and it traces back to a server located in Harland's office. We've also got some fairly sophisticated IT people running some scans to see where else it goes, what other chat rooms he's contacted, what other messages he's delivered, to whom he's delivered them, and what they say."

"Fine," Frankie said. "But like I said, so what? His campaign is going nowhere, right?"

"We don't know, given this top two business. We're showing him getting around four or five percent, with his numbers rising, even though he hasn't done much more than set up his website. And this is somebody who nobody knew existed until a few weeks ago. It's fairly startling. If this keeps up, there's a good chance he'll make the runoff. And this is one of the two or three most flippable districts in the state."

Link returned with the tray full of food – a bulgogi rice bowl with the marinated steak for Frankie, the three-taco combination for him and Jordan, and a bucket load of chips with Tako's creamy, one-of-a-kind salsa.

Frankie and Jordan, who were both working, ordered iced tea. Link, who was not, made his a Sierra Nevada Pale Ale.

"I'm off the clock," he said, as he took a refreshing sip of his favorite beer.

"What else is new," Frankie snarked.

"Now," Jordan said, before biting into his Tako taco, "for the good stuff."

He took the folder away from Frankie and pulled out another, stapled packet. It was marked: "Harland Money." The first and only entry was a printout from the Federal Election Commission that detailed the operations of an independent expenditure committee established on Harland's behalf, Harland for America.

The printout showed that the committee had raised two hundred and fifty thousand to benefit Harland, and that all of it came in one lump sum from a single business located in West Sacramento, Calif.

Name of business: White Rock USA.

The only other useful information in the printout showed that the committee still hadn't spent any of the cash – all $250,000 remained available for a late dump on an election that was exactly three weeks away.

"Hmmm," Frankie hummed. "What the hell is White Rock USA?"

"To be perfectly honest," Jordan replied, "we don't really know. Our research has them identified as a private import-export company with a warehouse right next to the Port of Sacramento."

"Intriguing," Frankie said.

He repeated to himself, "White Rock USA."

He turned to Jordan and said, "Tell me more."

Jordan went on to break it down:

"Well," he said. "They've got a West Sac city business license that comes back to a warehouse on Del Monte Street. Same thing with their incorporation papers."

"OK," Frankie said. "I'm going to guess Del Monte's the address on the I.E.?"

"Nope. The committee lists an address in Rancho Cordova."

"Harland for America."

"Yes."

"Rancho Cordova," Frankie repeated, his mind going back to his previous year's coverage where the Russian mob ran its mortgage fraud and other rackets from the suburb east of town and south of the American River. "And they've got a quarter million to blow."

"That's the number."

"But no details on how they got it."

"None."

"Or how it's been spent."

"None on that, either. Actually, I don't think they *have* spent any of it, at least nothing that we know about, and at this stage of the game, they've got to report all expenditures within 48 hours," Jordan said "We've checked with all the TV and radio stations that broadcast in the district, and these guys haven't bought or reserved time with any of them. I've asked around with people I know who work for Republicans, the Never Trumpers. None of them have heard a word about who this group is or if they've hired a consultant, a buyer, anything. I mean not a peep."

"What does that tell you?" Frankie asked.

"That they're going to come in fast, late, and furious," Jordan said. "The way it works, we probably won't know who's behind the operation until the campaign is over."

"God bless *Citizens United*," Frankie said.

Frankie looked closer to the front page of the I.E. report to see who registered as the treasurer.

The name on the form said "Bob Jones," at the same Rancho Cordova address as the Harland for America committee.

"Rancho Fucking Cordova," Frankie muttered.

8/*The Warehouse*

Frankie Cameron had a lot of work to do and only three weeks to do it in, realistically. Stories that broke in the last seven days of a campaign didn't have time to percolate in voters' minds. Also, more than half of everybody already would have voted.

He gave Link and Jordan a lift to midtown and dropped them off on I Street, behind the Memorial Auditorium, before he headed over to West Sacramento, to the warehouse on Del Monte Street that had been listed as the address of White Rock USA. It was located two blocks from the Port of Sacramento, where rice farmers waved goodbye to their subsidized bounty headed off to consumers in China, Japan, and South Korea. Frankie found the warehouse and did a quick visual drive-by of an ordinary-looking complex with a half-dozen empty loading docks facing the street.

Frankie spotted an open front gate to the parking lot and slow-rolled to the end of the street. He circled back to the warehouse where he parked a few car lengths short of the parking lot entrance, on the other side of the street. He lowered his window and wondered why he gave up smoking 20 years ago.

It was time to do some surveillance.

A half-hour into his lookout, an unmarked white 18-wheel tractor trailer turned into the warehouse. Frankie watched as a skinny woman in a tan mid-thigh dress and a black buttoned cardigan and thin, brown hair with dyed-pink highlights came out of an office at the front of the warehouse and motioned the driver to a berth about halfway down the building. As the driver angled the back end of the truck into the dock, Frankie instinctively gathered his cell phone. He enjoyed an unobstructed view. The driver slid the truck into the dock and jumped down from the cab to walk around to the rear of the vehicle. He looked to be tall, beneath a black baseball cap and inside a pair of wraparound shades, a husky sort, in a tight white T-shirt and Levi's and brown workman's boots. The driver rolled up the truck's rear door and hooked a ramp from the truck to the loading dock, while the woman unlocked and opened the overhead loading dock door. Frankie zoomed in his cell phone camera as zoomy as it could get. He came into focus right when a very bright red car drove out of the truck, across the ramp, and into the warehouse. He snapped a half-dozen or so shots, until the woman pulled down the warehouse door and locked it shut from the inside.

Frankie looked down at his phone to see what he got, and what he had captured was an angled side view of what he knew to be a DeCoulomb, the all-electric luxury sedan that had become somewhat popular among elite environmentalists and other ostentatious representatives of the motoring class.

It was time to take a closer look, with his real eyes, of the real thing, so Frankie rolled up his window, stepped out of his car and walked across Del Monte Street, through the warehouse gate, through the parking lot, where he opened the office door and walked inside.

The room was empty.

He pushed a button beneath a sign that said: "Visitor Push Button."

A few seconds later he heard a jostling behind a door that led from the office into the warehouse. When it opened, he saw the thin woman with the thin, pink-tinged hair.

"Can I help you," she asked.

The accent, Frankie deduced, was Russian.

Of course.

The year before, Frankie's journalistic career had gained its biggest boost ever thanks to his stumble into Russian-influenced operations in the United States. He should have been thankful to the Putinocracy – he owed his great new gig at the Washington Post to his coverage of the Russian mob's political play in Sacramento. He wasn't so sure, however, that he wanted to spend the rest of his life on such a beat, or how it might affect his health.

"Yes, ma'am," Frankie said. "I'm a newspaper reporter for the *Sacramento Bea*...er, excuse me. That would be the *Washington Post*, and I..."

"You are a newspaper reporter? You have business card?"

"As a matter of fact, I do," Frankie said, as he pulled his wallet out of his back pocket and fumbled inside for a card. He found one and handed it to the woman.

She looked at it for a second or two and nodded.

"The famous Frankie Cameron," she said.

Unlike Jordan Diaz, some people in this town knew who the hell he was.

"I don't know about famous," he said. "Just a guy trying to make a living."

"Make living writing lies about Russian people," she responded, curt and quick, not looking up from the business card.

Frankie was well aware of the unfavorable reaction to his stories in much of the local Russian press. It painted him as a bigot who unfairly stereotyped the Sacramento Russians as white-collar crooks, political manipulators, anti-democratic, anti-American – thuggish, even. Frankie also had been subject to ugly attacks from the considerable and influential Russia clergy. Orthodox priests and Pentecostal preachers alike went after him harder than the writers, and with a more captive audience. The Russian holy-roller pulpiteers riled their believers as they railed against Frankie's stories as anti-Russian, anti-Slavic propaganda.

"Well," Frankie told the woman. "You can't please everybody."

He told her he was back in town and working again.

"And I saw that the company whose name is on this warehouse is about to spend two hundred and fifty thousand dollars on a congressional race down in Modesto," Frankie said. "Do you have anybody around here I can talk to?"

It didn't take the woman a second to say:

"No."

"What about Bob Jones? You've listed a Bob Jones as the treasurer of your political committee. Is he here?"

The woman gave Frankie his card back.

"It is time now for you to leave."

Over the years, Frankie had been thrown down stairways, nearly jailed, and shot at when he pressed his inquiries too far. He had come to know the meaning of get-the-fuck-out-of-here, in any accent. So he politely thanked the woman, and he showed himself to the door.

Walking through the parking lot toward the gate, he looked back and noticed the woman was following him and filming him with her cell phone. She stopped at the curb as he crossed the street. She continued to film Frankie as he unlocked his car and slipped into the driver's seat. He saw her zoom in on his license plate, then on him rolling down his window. He smiled for the camera, and drove away, looking in his rear-view mirror to see the woman still filming him until he turned the corner.

So that was how it was going to be.

He made it out to Harbor Boulevard and then swung a right on West Capitol Avenue, the old Lincoln Highway, where dozens of run-down motels now served as homes for the poor, the addicted, and the prostitutes. The street hadn't changed in more than a quarter-century, from when he first started working in Sacramento: shirtless men on bicycles and in a hurry, sunken-cheeked wrinkled and deeply-tanned women in miniskirts, the homeless pushing shopping carts, a store named "Cheap Cigarettes," trailer parks, massage parlors, check-cashing joints, fast-food stands, fenced-off and vacant hole-in-the-wall beer bars that missed the microbrewery revolution, huge lots that sold pre-manufactured homes, vacant lots strewn with weeds and garbage, truck yards, construction yards, storage yards, dead battery yards, lumber yards, car-dismantling yards, and heavy equipment yards where you could rent forklifts, scissor lifts, atrium boom lifts, towable boom lifts, bulldozers, and anything else you needed to build something up or tear something down. For some sick reason, the street presented Frankie with a comforting tableau. A stability of grunge – grit you could taste. In a world that spun faster with each succeeding year, he could always rely on West Cap to slow things down, bring him back to the way it always was.

Past the ballpark, he crossed the Tower Bridge into downtown Sacramento with his straight-ahead view down the Capitol Mall to the State Capitol building 10 blocks away. A right on Third Street took him past the world-class Crocker Art Museum and its collections of what California looked like before it got run over by the rest of the world. A left on U Street reconnected him with the Southside Park neighborhood that provided the backdrop to a couple murder trials he covered, its once-dangerous edge of gang elementalism reduced by regular folk who spent a half-million or more each on wooden two-bedroom bungalows with high porches that came in handy in case of a flood – always an October-to-March threat with climate change adding extra punch to winter storms that rolled into town on the Pineapple Express. Under and left, onto the Cross-Town Freeway, and east on U.S. 50 toward Rancho Cordova, where his heart beat a little faster when he got off on Zinfandel Road and made the left across the freeway to the Bob Jones address on Olson Drive.

It was a UPS mail drop.

Inside, an energetic young black woman with light skin and short, tight braided-curls was helping another customer when Frankie walked in. Wrap, stamp, print, pound, charge, and out.

"Next," she said.

That meant Frankie.

"Uh, hi," he started out – nervous, stumbling, the way he

always felt when he was about to ask somebody for information they weren't supposed to give him. "Uh, I'm a reporter with the *Sacramento B...*, er, *The Washington Post*, and I've got to tell you, I came here thinking this was an office building."

"I think you could call it that."

"Right, uh – so, I've got this address on a fellow by the name of Bob Jones that came back to here, and…"

"Bob Jones?" The woman wrote down the name.

"That's right," Frankie said.

"And you're a newspaper reporter?"

"That's right, again."

"With *The Washington Post*?"

"Yes, ma'am."

She looked straight at him, a moment of truth. Would she call the police? Would she rip him for being a member of a dying industry? Maybe she was a Trumper with a hatred of the media, or a Berniecrat with a similar disdain.

The answer was...

"That is awesome!" the woman exclaimed, to Frankie's relief. "In fact, I'm a journalism student at ARC. I'm the sports editor of *The Current*!"

Frankie never knew the name of the American River College paper. Already, he'd learned something.

"But between you and me, I'm not really that interested in covering sports," she said conspiratorially. "The investigative stuff is the real news." She winked at him.

"Sports editor, huh. What's your name?"

"Annette. Annette Smith-Bennett."

"All right, Annette. Can I maybe teach you one thing that might be helpful in your career?"

"Sure!"

"OK. It's great the way you have been immediately open to me, me coming in here like this and saying I'm a reporter and then you getting the conversation going."

"And?"

"And, the first thing you need to do, after you get the spelling of somebody's name right, is to try and verify that they are who they say they are. I know it's uncomfortable, but it'll save you a lot of embarrassment. I've had to do corrections on front-page stories after I quoted people under phony names they gave me."

"But I'm not quoting you."

"That's a good point. But you like automatically believed I'm a newspaper reporter with *The Washington Post*."

"You are, aren't you?"

"I am, but how could you know for sure?"

"Check your ID?"

With that, Frankie pulled out his wallet and showed her his *Washington Post* building pass, as well as a press pass from the National Press Club.

Annette didn't seem surprised to have been proven right, but let out a low whistle anyway. "You're Frankie Cameron? I've been reading your stories for years. I didn't know you went to the *Post*. And now here you are, and you're in my shop, and you just gave me a lesson to not trust anybody until they show you ID."

"I didn't exactly say that. All I meant was…"

"How about that babushka, the wife of one of those guys you wrote about last year in the credit card scam? Did you check her ID?"

"Uh, no," Frankie replied. "I never asked her for her ID. But I did have her ID'd about six other ways, so I felt pretty comfortable writing about her."

"Whatever happened to that story? Mainly, the crazy uncle?"

"Nikita Karlov? I've got to tell you, I don't really know."

Uncle Nikita's case had never been adjudicated. He got arrested as a co-conspirator in an identity theft case the feds filed against him and a few of his homeboys but was temporarily dismissed from trial when court-appointed psychiatrists concluded that he was not mentally competent to assist in his own defense. The last Frankie heard, he was still in a psych ward somewhere.

This was the kind of thing that had made it so hard to move to D.C., that kept California so close to him – all these open circles.

"So, are you out here to follow up on that case?" Annette

asked.

Frankie sighed. "Actually, I'm working on something else."

"I'd read it," she said unhesitatingly.

"Well, let me ask you this: would you also read a story about a mysterious company with pretty strong Russian connections getting ready to spend a quarter-million dollars to influence a critical congressional race in California?"

"What?"

"Yeah. My editors sent me out here to help out over the next couple weeks on these seven congressional races that could decide whether the Democrats flip the House."

"Okay."

"And I came across this Russian company – White Rock USA, is its name – and they opened a federal independent expenditure committee on behalf of some doctor in Manteca who is running as a right-winger in the congressional district down around Modesto. It's got two hundred and fifty thousand dollars in the bank."

"It sounds like a good one," Annette said. "Hell yeah, I'd read that story."

"Terrific. Now, would you believe that you're in a position to, shall we say, be a source on it?"

"Let me guess. By giving you information on this Bob Jones guy?"

"Right."

It didn't take Annette long to answer her own question.

"Sorry," she said. "It's confidential information. If I gave it out, I'd be fired."

And the conversation had been going so well, Frankie thought.

"Oh," is all he could say.

"But I am interested," she responded, quickly, "on getting some more reporting tips from you. Maybe you could even come talk to our newspaper class while you're out here?"

"I'd say that's possible."

She wrote her name and cell phone number down on a Post-It note. She handed it to Frankie.

She winked again.

9/*Sobriety*

After he left Frankie and Jordan, Link opted for an early afternoon stroll, to clear his head ahead of his first official date with Manuela. His feet pointed subconsciously toward 12th Street, the homeless highway of Sacramento, when he realized it had been a while since he'd had a meaningful conversation with the Scrounger. They barely spoke at the Cesar Chavez Plaza unveiling, where he saw the Scrounger dancing and picking up cigarette butts. Before that, he hadn't even seen him since Frankie Cameron's going-away party at Benny's back in late December.

Word at Benny's was that nobody had seen much of the Scrounger lately.

Link found himself searching the streets.

North, through the underpass beneath the railroad tracks, the old warehouse district where the loading docks of the brick buildings on North A, North B, and North C streets used to be the best place in town for the unhoused to go safely to sleep.

Nice weather brought out more than the usual number to 12th Street. Hundreds of homeless moved up and down the sidewalk on the west side of the busy street that acted as a freeway offramp into downtown. Men of every color from every state and a few women who clung to them and the pit bulls they held on leashes languished in the underpass, taking in the shade. Link nodded to a few that he knew and they nodded back to Mr. Generous. They asked and he answered – a dollar to each. Sacramento street people knew Link as the softest touch in town for a buck.

On the other side of the underpass, Link peered up to his left and saw several tents pitched beneath the trees at the top of the underpass's concrete embankment where several young outcasts planned their day's activities of drink and drug distribution. He took in the disconnected scene of well-dressed, white suburban kids toting stolen bikes up the embankment to exchange their contraband for that offered by the heroin, methamphetamine, and cocaine dealers. Link nodded at the addicted youth, without judgment, and continued up on the other side of the underpass, where he pushed the "walk" button at the North B Street intersection.

He waited for the light to change as streaming lines of incoming vehicles poured through the underpass, from Roseville, and Rocklin, and Citrus Heights, and all the northeast suburbs, into The Grid. He crossed on the green light to the front of the Salvation Army shelter and looked around for anybody he knew. He spotted nobody but dropped a Susan B. Anthony into a small pile of change that had accumulated next to a woman who slept so soundly on the sidewalk he felt compelled to feel for her pulse. Once Link detected one, he deposited another dollar into the pot.

He turned right on North B Street, across from Goldie's, the neighborhood sex-toy and dirty movie shop. On to Ahern Street and into an unauthorized tent city where plywood and sheet-metal lean-tos mixed in with tarps and tents and cardboard shacks that took up four blocks of sidewalk space.

Most of the people who lived in the shanties had gone about their tasks of the homeless day. Like most days, for most of them, time was mainly about survival, and sometimes that meant they had to get away from each other before they got at each other's throats.

Left on Ahern and past North C Street, Link swerved into the compound of Loaves and Fishes. This was the collection of nuns, activists, former social workers, current-day do-gooders, and former street people that fed the current street people and gave them a place to take a shower, where the down and out could sit down and flake out, for a couple hours, anyway, or go to the library and read a book or the newspaper. They provided a small shelter for women with children, a classroom for the youngsters, and psychiatric services, medical exams, day jobs, spare clothing, dog food, mail delivery, clean needles, and a social environment where people treated you like a human being. Even if you smelled as if you had bathed in urine.

The closer Link got to Friendship Park, the gathering spot at the center of the Loaves and Fishes campus, the more the people recognized him. It was no exaggeration to say that over the years of his wanderings about town, he had given away tens of thousands of dollars to tens of thousands of people. Ten bucks a day, minimum, some days 10 or 20 times that, going back a quarter-century, back to when he made his first million in casino riches due to his accident of birth. Into Friendship Park, Link said hello to the faces he recognized while he emptied himself, as usual, of what had been a full pocket of gold dollars.

As the money jingled down to nothing, Link spotted Brandon Bailey, the park manager, a big, bearded, red-haired guy whom Link first knew to be a mean, racist drunk who hated Native Americans until he got sober and decided that his true calling in life was to be a Christian Brother. In fact, Brandon lived in the friary at St. Francis on 26th and K. He walked over to Loaves every morning at 6:30 to run the homeless breakfast program that volunteers put on every day.

"Yo, Brandon," Link said, sneaking up on the big guy from behind and patting him on the shoulder.

"Link – hey, man, great to see you. Hey, congrats on the opening. Dug the totem, man. Sorry I didn't get over to say hi, but you looked pretty damn occupied."

"I guess I was. To tell you the truth, the whole evening did not feel real. But I was honored the city found the piece acceptable."

"So what's next? You got an Eiffel Tower in you?"

Link laughed, and told Brandon he didn't really know when he'd tear into another log. At the moment, he had no plans to visit the Witch Doctor. He didn't feel compelled to carve much of anything, but this was not at all like the dispiriting lack of inspiration that had plagued him the previous year.

He called this a period of determined non-production, in

search of other aspects of self.

"Right now, I'm not feeling any pressure to do anything," Link told Brandon. "I'm kind of getting into other stuff."

"Such as?"

"Politics, and other human interactions," Link said.

"Good time for it, if you know what I mean."

"I think I do."

Pressed for time with the park filling up, Brandon asked Link: "So, what brings you down?"

"I'm looking for somebody in particular," Link said.

"Maybe I can help you out. Who you want?"

"The Scrounger. Have you seen him?"

Brandon Bailey stepped back with just an ounce of hesitation. He stroked his chin with his thumb and forefinger, a nervous delay that told Link that Brandon had the info on the Scrounger's whereabouts but didn't exactly want to give it up.

"The good news," Brandon said, "is that Tomas is doing pretty good."

"Tomas?"

Link repeated the name again, just one more time. As he did, it occurred to him that he never knew the Scrounger by any other identification. At first, the guy was simply nameless, at least to Link, as he was to everybody else the guy had ever met since he began riding the rails about a decade ago. He was mainly just a "Hey, you," or "Really, Dude?" Or, "You motherfucking asshole, I'm going to kick your ass." It took Link about four or five drinking sessions with the Scrounger – on the street, in an alley downtown between J and K, outside the Pre-Flight Lounge, where Link occasionally liked to sip – before the Scrounger told him that his close friends, of which he had none, referred to him as "the Scrounger." The Scrounger's general appearance caused another person of his general class to once observe that the Scrounger looked "scroungy" which caused somebody else to give him the "Scrounger" tag, and it just stuck. It was a designation by onomatopoeia, that the Scrounger, Link, and everybody else accepted by default.

Brandon Bailey picked up on Link's confusion.

"Yeah," Brandon said. "The Scrounger has a name, and it is Tomas Marinaro, and he is twenty-six years old, and he is from Colorado."

"He did tell me once about suburban Denver," Link responded.

"Aurora, I believe. Right now, the main thing is that he's into about his fourth month of sobriety."

"Oh," Link said.

Link did not quite know what to make of this news that ran head first into his very view of human existence. He never really viewed the Scrounger – he couldn't quite associate him with the name "Tomas Marinaro" – as somebody who was powerless over alcohol. Mainly, he viewed the Scrounger as somebody who was powerless over himself. As for alcohol, it was Link's take that the Scrounger just drank too much of it, and that if you overindulge at the expense of food and an otherwise healthy lifestyle and without the discipline of work or a daily routine, there is a great chance that you will wind up vomiting in an alley.

Wasn't that the main problem with most low-bottom drunks, that they drank without rules? Without obligation?

On second thought, the more Link thought about it, the more he concluded that the Scrounger probably could go for an extended dry-out.

"So, do you know where he's staying?" Link asked. "I see he's not hanging outside the Sterling anymore."

Brandon hesitated in giving up the Scrounger's whereabouts.

But, he concluded, this was Link. If you couldn't trust him with a street person's personal information, all of humanity was finished.

"He's right around the corner," Brandon said, "up in the Quinn Cottages. But you've got to be careful if you go over there, man."

"How's that?"

"What people in the early stages of recovery need to do is change their mindset about drinking, and one of the best ways of doing that is to change your environment, including your social environment, the people they hang around with," Brandon informed. "I know you love him, man, and I know that he loves you, too, but just his seeing you could trigger an association. He'll look at you and he'll think of the way you've taken care of him over the years and the way you've treated him with dignity and respect, and that's all good. But you're a drinking buddy, man. He's going to think about you guys getting flat-assed together and the great times you've had. You don't want to get into a lead-him-not-into-temptation thing."

Link nodded as if he got it.

"You think I should stay away then?" he asked Brandon.

"No, brother. Just be aware. You're definitely going to trigger some feelings with him. Keep that in the back of your head. Maybe think about a way you can use your presence to reinforce his recovery."

"How do I do that?"

"I don't have the slightest idea."

Link knew the Quinn Cottages a little bit. They'd been around for more than 20 years, a few dozen dinky little houses around the corner from Loaves, on North A Street, named for the former bishop of the local Catholic archdiocese. They were built with the recovering drunk in mind, or any other street person with some kind of debilitating disability such as paranoid schizophrenia or AIDS or a missing limb that somehow contributed to him or her being homeless.

Chaos reigned around the cottages, with young men on bikes wheeling in and out of the tent encampments on Ahern, selling crack and crank, or making booze runs to the liquor stores several blocks away on the other side of the railroad tracks. Inside the black wrought-iron gate that surrounded the Quinns, you had the 60 two-room apartments that lined the tree-shaded compound with a picnic commons and lush green grasses, all contained within the fence that kept the neighborhood at bay. It was an oasis of peaceful sobriety where just a few feet away you'd see men who sat outside their sidewalk tents drinking Bushmills at 9 o'clock in the morning.

"It seems like the right place for him to be," Link said to Brandon. "Is he taking visitors? I mean, if he wants to see me."

"Hey, man, the place ain't no jail, or a trauma unit," Brandon said. "Give it a shot. They'll know you at the gate. Just be careful, man. Be careful for him."

In a manly fashion, Link cuffed Brandon on the shoulder.

"I will see you around," Link said. "How long have you been sober now, Brandon?"

"Three years," Brandon said. "One day at a time."

Poor bastard, Link thought.

A Ray Wylie Hubbard song came to Link's mind, the one where the story told how we – the moaning, lying, futureless mud scum – had it better in life than the raised dead. "*At least we ain't Lazarus,*" Hubbard sang, "*and had to think twice about dying.*" If such is the fixture of life, Link contemplated, then how the hell is a reasonable man – forced into this miserable existence – expected to have any respite without a daily 22-ounce dose of a local IPA?

But Link had to admit it. Brandon, for one, seemed to be a much more productive member of society since he got off the bottle. How could he forget the night Brandon came after him with a Buck knife a block away from the State Capitol, in front of the Cathedral of the Blessed Sacrament, for no apparent reason, while Link was making his way home from Marilyn's around 2 a.m. after sweating off three sets of Mick Martin and the Blues Rockers? It was one of those rare instances when Link was flat broke and when somebody on the street demanded change. Dead-drunk-in the-middle-of-the-night Brandon, sitting on the steps of the cathedral, accused Link of rebuffing him because he was white. It made no sense, but Link tried to reason with him, even offered him an IOU. But Brandon wasn't interested in the beg-now-be-paid-later plan. He reached for the knife strapped to his ankle and charged. Link was lucky in this case in that he had more on Brandon that night in terms of sobriety. A side-step put Brandon face down on 11th Street. When Brandon's blackout lifted, two cops were shoving him into the back seat of a patrol car.

Prosecutors charged him with attempted robbery and assault with a deadly weapon, with a hate-crime enhancement. Link, however, had some pals in the DA's office, and he made it clear he would not testify against Brandon. In jail, Brandon attended daily AA meetings. He kept going to them when he got out, and he hadn't had a drink since. Link could only conclude that Brandon's sobriety was for the better, though he couldn't hush the part of him that felt it was for the worse.

In Friendship Park, the two hugged goodbye, and Link made his way the few blocks over to the cottages, where security buzzed him in. He asked for the Scrounger, and they directed him to the 350-square-foot house where the young man that the guards knew as Tomas Marinaro had been living for the past few months. A knock-knock-knock-knock on the door and who should Link be seeing face to face but the former street bum formerly known as the Scrounger.

"Tomas Marinaro," Link said. "I never knew."

For the third time in a matter of hours, Link found himself hugging another man.

If Link's presence presented the danger of a Scrounger bender, the former Scrounger didn't seem to know it.

"Call me Tommy," the one-time Scrounger said – standing clean as Link had ever seen him, and healthy, with no cuts or bruises on his face and no phlegm emerging from his nose or other fluids draining from his eyes.

"You're looking, I would say, extremely well," Link said.

"Come on in," Tommy said, and Link entered the spare apartment.

The two men stood speechless while Link stood in the kitchen entryway of the tiny home, in the primary space of the residence, its walls undecorated except for the praying hands superimposed over the framed Serenity Prayer.

Tommy/Scrounger showed Link around his castle – it took about 20 seconds.

"There's the bathroom," Tommy said, pointing to one end of the house. "This is the kitchen-slash-living room. That's the bedroom."

Link poked his head into the sleeping area that was probably half the size of a millionaire's walk-in closet.

The Big Book rested on the Scrounger's night stand. Make that Tommy's night stand.

It was easy to see Tommy looked pleased to see Link.

"You're the reason I'm here," he told him, which stunned the visitor.

"Hey, don't put this on me," Link said, to the humor of the two of them. "You know what we used to say about sobriety."

"Yeah, it was the worst afternoon of Bogie's life," Tommy said, who, to be honest, didn't know anything about Humphrey Bogart's work until Link told him about it.

"Seriously," Tommy continued. "That day last year in the Federalist, before me and you went to the Kings game with Frankie? You told me something."

"Me?"

"Yeah, you," Tommy said. "You told me to call my mother."

"I did?"

"Yeah you did."

"And?"

"Well, I didn't get around to it right away," Tommy said. "But it never left my mind. 'Call your mother.' I heard it again and again. 'Call your mother. Call your mother, goddammit.' So the first of the year, I called her. It was the first time I'd spoken to her since I jumped the freight out of Denver."

Link took a seat at the kitchen/living room table, across from Tommy. The two sat silent for a few moments – awkward, unusual. They'd never been around each other when they weren't drinking, and it just didn't feel normal to either of them. Now Link started to get what Brandon was trying to tell him: things had changed, the Scrounger had changed – hell, he wasn't even the Scrounger anymore. Link damn near couldn't bring himself to say the guy's name.

"Tommy," he said.

"Yeah," Tommy said. "It's weird, but not as weird as Tomas, which is what everybody around here calls me. I mean, 'Tomas' is perfectly fine, but damn, nobody's called me that since I was an altar boy. Shit, man. I guess names can be important. It was interesting there for a while, not having one. Not even wanting to have one. The Scrounger. Shit, man, that was me. I deserved it."

Link sat, looked and listened. He tried it again:

"Tommy. Tomas. Tomasino. *Tomar* – to drink. You know, it kind of fits you."

As their soft laughter died down, the importance of the Scrounger's – Tommy's – new social environment – this one room with the praying hands – sank in deeper for Link. No way that Link was about to retreat from his own appreciation of the sacramental beer, so that kind of settled the deal – if he looked deeper into his own rituals, there was no telling what he'd find. He'd continue to let Tommy have his space.

"So what did she say?" Link asked.

"Who?"

"Your mother."

"Oh, yeah – not much. Nothing, really. Just the way she reacted when I called. Just totally emotional, a breakdown, happy to hear from me, jubilant to hear from me. Ecstatic. Hysterically ecstatic. Like I was *el prodigal* or something, which I was. Even worse. It just touched me. I felt her like I'd never felt anybody before, and I broke down, too, and I felt like a complete piece of shit, running out on her and my brother and sister because I didn't get along with my dad. Fucking me, man. What a pussy. Anyway, it was a life changing experience. I started looking at things from a point of view other than my own selfish little perspective. Maybe for the first time ever."

"I get that," Link said. "I mean, I really get it."

He thought back to his own conversation the previous year with Anton Karuliyak, the night the Russian mobster presented him with something of a psychological mirror over FaceTime, which had shown him to be something of a talented jerk.

Like the Scrounger, Link had not exactly been the same since.

He got up from the chair and dusted himself off, even though he wasn't the slightest bit dusty. It was time to go, and both he and Tommy and the Scrounger knew it.

"One thing," Link said, after the two men embraced again, after he wished Tommy luck. "The day of the unveiling of my piece in Cesar Chavez Plaza, your dance performance. I don't believe I have ever seen anything quite like it."

The Scrounger shrugged.

"I've been known to bust a move," he said. "You should see me moonwalk."

"I believe I saw a little Michael Jackson in your display," Link said. "The Russian thing, that's what I found most remarkable."

"I have to tell you, man. There was a method to that madness."

"I think I picked up on that. With the cigarette butts."

"Oh," Tommy said. "You noticed. That's not good. I'm supposed to be picking them up surreptitiously."

"I'd say you were a little less than surreptitious. What was the deal?"

"Well," the Scrounger went on, "I got me a part-time job, through that police detective friend of yours."

"Wiggins?"

Sacramento police detective Andrew Wiggins was a long-time casual acquaintance and almost a friend of Link's. Wiggins, in recent years, had worked homicide, but was assigned to a multi-agency task force investigating Russian organized crime about the time that Frankie Cameron's stories hit.

"He's the one," the Scrounger said. "We got together in Benny's, the night of Frankie's going-away. We both walked out of there about the same time, and he knew me from the hostage thing last October – did a quick interview with me, and we got to talking, and he asks me at the Frankie party if I needed a job. And I say 'What job?' And you've got to keep in mind that I haven't had any kind of job since I was a bus boy at the Blackstone Country Club, in Colorado, and that's about eight or ten years ago, and he says, 'Working for the Police Department.' Fuck me, the Police Department. Well, there's no way I'm going to be a snitch or anything like that, and that's probably the only thing I could really do for them, because I do know a lot of what goes on out there along the river banks and stuff, but he says, no, they don't need me for no snitch, but that there's this weird kind of undercover work they'd like me to try out for them."

"Inspector Scrounger," Link said.

"Exactly," Tommy said, laughing, "and I ask him to explain, and he tells me they're in the process of trying to build up some new kind of DNA databank, and he says they need somebody in my position – my position! – who could get out there and do some collection for them. And I ask them what kind of collection, and he says they could use somebody who knows how to pick through trash cans, and who can pick things up off the street, like cigarette butts, and trash and shit, and maybe I'd like to make ten bucks an hour doing that. But no more than 10 hours a week. Which is all I fucking needed. I told them straight out, 'Deal!'"

"Interesting," Link said. "I mean this has become a very big deal, you know, with this East Side Rapist guy."

A month earlier, a statewide police task force busted a former cop who lived in suburban Citrus Heights on suspicion of murdering and raping about 75 people back in the '70s and '80s, from Sacramento to Santa Ana. The investigators made their case on him based on partial DNA hits that had been donated by his relatives who were tracing their genealogical histories. A little bit of doodling around put the cop on a short list of suspects, and then they dug through his trash and came up with the perfect match that linked gunk from his garbage can to gunk collected from the scenes of the crimes.

"Yeah," Tommy said. "Interesting timing, too – I went to work a good three or four months before they announced the arrest. Basically, what Wiggins wanted was for me to collect anything on anybody who I thought was interesting, and they'd run the tests on the stuff, and if nothing else, they'd know who they had in town and maybe find some people who were wanted, or whatever, or maybe they'd get some hits that connected up with some serious shit. And if nobody was wanted whose stuff came back, they'd hang on to it, just in case something might match up against it in the future. I'm telling you, man, it's the easiest work I've ever done, although Wiggins is a little frustrated with me now because I'm not getting out as much as I used to."

"No, of course not," Link said. "You're not even the Scrounger anymore."

The two shared a smile as Link headed out and Tommy was just about to shut the door when Link stopped and turned around.

"Wait a minute." he said.

"What?"

Link slapped himself on the back side, in his left rear pants pocket, and felt the outline of the cigarette butt that the two dudes in the SUV had flicked at him the day before.

"I've got one for you," he said.

10/*View from the Berm*

In the old days, a bunch of pedestrian tunnels in the numbered streets of Midtown burrowed through a railroad berm into the warehouse district just north of the tracks. Not that anybody really needed to use them. Not that there was that much pedestrian traffic between the Alkali Flat and Mansion Flats neighborhoods and the industrial zone where the bums slept on the loading docks. They were never really a tourist attraction, either, like the paddleboats moored at the foot of K Street, in Old Town, or the McKinley Park Rose Garden, or the strip joints in Rancho Cordova where Stormy Daniels once appeared.

Even in the old days, all you'd see when you walked through them was a drunk or two, or six, doing up a jug. No harm, no foul. They were the beloved winos of lore, hobos, a who's who of town drunks and other street characters who provided atmosphere, as they say in the movies. They might whistle at you if you were female, were likely to spare-change you if you were male or female, or, if they were completely devoid of manners, they might take an unauthorized public leak when no normal citizen was around. Luckily for regular folk, the tunnel people of yesteryear policed themselves. You did something like relieve yourself in one of these hangouts and the big boys found out? You're out of the fraternity.

Everything changed with the introduction of drugs, with the crack culture, around the time when basketball star Len Bias died of a cocaine overdose. Along with crack came the crack whores, both male and female. The newbies, in Link's view, seemed to lack the basic moral standing of the hobo joes of yesteryear. They were less likely to worry about their own reputations and more likely to do anything, anywhere, in front of anybody, for about what it would cost for a pack of smokes. When the bottom fell out, the people who lived in the neighborhoods around the tunnels petitioned City Hall to do something about all this human depravity. Officialdom complied, and before long, city crews slammed shut every tunnel in town from the railyards to Sacramento State. Work crews installed iron gates thicker than what you'd find in the SHU at Pelican Bay. The closures defeated the tunnel people, who were forced to do their drinking downtown in Cesar Chavez Park, or up on the railroad berm itself, where they camped and slept and ate and defecated in the high green grass of spring, or on the sidewalks downtown. The city sure showed them.

All of this presented a sense of perhaps misguided opportunity for Link as he came out of the Quinn Cottages. He walked down North A Street, toward 12th Street, and through another compound for the down and out, this one run by the Volunteers of America, a shelter where you could stay for three months at a time if you were lucky enough to score one of the 80 beds, and when your time ran out, you could sleep in your car in the parking lot, which also served as a semi-permanent campground.

Link cut through the VOA parking lot to the alley in the rear that ran below and alongside the railroad berm, to 14th Street. Where he stood, he could almost feel his house. It was a block and a half away, just two minutes by air. Only problem was, the city shuttered the north side of the tunnel with a steel barrier that looked like it had been cut from the side of a rail car.

If Link's recollection served him accurately, he signed the petition to plug the damn things. He chuckled to himself at the inconvenience, and thought, what the hell. After all, it would have taken him a good seven or eight minutes, maybe even 10, to walk up to 16th Street and around to his house on D Street between 14th and 15th. Just for the hell of it, he scurried to the top of the berm, and he found a hole in the fence line that had been erected by the railroad. The Union Pacific put in the fence to keep people like Link from killing themselves by taking shortcuts across the railroad tracks at the top of the berm. Or so they said. The fence, along with the tunnel blockades, also segregated Sacramento's dozen square blocks of homeless real estate from civil society. What you had north of the berm now was a homeless and derelict zone unofficially reserved for homeless and derelict people. Maybe it was just a coincidence that the fenced-off tunnels and the fenced-off berm segregated the entire fenced-off mess from Link's neighborhood that had improved itself over the years. Where crack dealers once roamed, brand-new three-story homes sold for close to a million dollars on the site of the old Crystal Creamery. And here he was, climbing through a hole in a fence, to defeat a tunnel closure that he had officially sought by signing a petition the neighborhood improvement types had brought to his door.

Climbing the berm, he had barely begun to get his boots dusty before he felt the rumble beneath him. This was an entirely different feel, on an entirely different train, in an entirely different setting, from what he was used to between 19th and 20th streets. For one thing, he couldn't even see the train – he only absorbed it through the vibrations that were coming at him from a mile away, where four locomotives rolled out of the Sacramento Valley Station. The shaking of the elevated earth grew in intensity as he climbed toward the top of the berm. A couple more steps, and now he could peer over the horizon, looking west, when he saw the first engine. By the time the second passed him, and then a third, and then a fourth, he had fallen into a familiar condition.

The train trance.

First, the breathing slowed. Then, the beat of the heart. His focus: breathing and beating, heart and the lungs, air and blood. He felt the exchange of the materials of life. He felt arteries blasting life force up and down his being, up through the bottom of his jaw and into his head, down through the bottom of his belly, through his hips and thighs and the back of his knees all the way down to his toes which were confined into the pointed tips of those black cowboy boots. He felt his pulse – slow – and he stayed with that, and his breathing, and his heart, and his arteries, and his mind came to a complete and utter standstill.

In the middle of the day, a man and a woman squatting outside their car in the Volunteers of America parking lot looked up from their lunch and wondered if this tall Indian-looking dude in the black T-shirt and the black jeans and the black boots with the white cowboy hat was about to kill himself by jumping into the train. It's true that the thought had crossed his mind a time or two in the past, more out of curiosity and boredom than depression. He had determined to himself, in previous episodes of this line of thought, that the consequence of the experiment seemed rather severe.

Such a notion was not on his mind on top of the berm.

Rather, his brain froze, just *likethat*, into the state of being that those hands on the wall back in the Scrounger's crib prayed for.

His senses trip-wired a symphony of sight and sound as the fury of the speeding train thundered past him. Nothing he had ever seen or experienced came across with such brilliance. Not the top of Half Dome. Not the blue Tahoe water of late July. Not a snow pie in the face. Not the steroidal crack of Jose Canseco's bat. Not the ring of Jerry Garcia's guitar.

When the train passed, Link returned to ordinary consciousness. He scooted down the berm. He scrunched his body through the hole in the fence, back toward the alley behind the VOA. He jumped a couple of feet off the berm to the asphalt. He nodded hello to the man and the woman who had been staring at him, and he walked the long way home.

11/*Sparring Session*

Manuela had just finished a session with the 35-pound Kettlebells when Link – fresh from a midafternoon nap after his visit to the Scrounger – dropped into her workout in her open-air gymnasium on H Street, a few blocks from her office. Sweat poured off her face and head and down the middle of her back and off her muscular bronze shoulders and arms.

"All right, girl, get over here," the trainer called.

She did not expect Link's arrival, and the coach's command eliminated any chance that she'd catch him out of the corner of her eye. Once focused, that was it for Manuela – all distractions flew out the window.

The trainer, young enough to be her son, stood in the center of the ring. He held out a pair of boxing gloves and head gear for her. He looked chubby in the belly pads, his hands stuffed into boxing mitts to absorb whatever stored up anger a major league public relations woman might dish out in two-minute increments after a hard day at the office.

Manuela stepped through the ropes. She laced on the gloves. She pulled the head gear over her dyed jet-black hair. She did a couple squats and stayed low and bobbed and weaved at the waist as if she was Pernell Whitaker.

"OK, let's go!" the trainer implored, and she sprang in a flash out of the knee bend to begin the sparring session. "Jab! Jab! Jab!" he yelled, as she flicked the left at the trainer, who doubled as sparring partner and who let her get close enough to stick him in his unprotected jaw. "Body, now. Body!" She pivoted off the ball of her left foot and dug into the trainer's rib cage. The punch hadn't even landed before he quick-slapped her twice upside the head with the mitt on his right hand – nothing at all behind it, nothing at all about it that hurt, just a light tapping that came with an admonition for Manuela to pivot harder and faster and to keep her head moving forward to avoid the counterpunch. "Don't loaf!" he screamed. "Follow through!"

She stepped back and circled right, in and out. "Balance, balance," he instructed. "Relax. Dance! Rhythm. Feel the rhythm. Get a song in your head. You're dancing, you're moving. You're balanced. In and out. In and OUT!" he screamed, with emphasis. "You're not a plodder. Not so far in, back – not so far back! You're a dancer. Balance! Balance! Keep your back straight – good. Relax, good. On your toes! No heels, no heels – good! Get your feet closer together. Walk out now. Left, one step. One step only! You want to get killed? Walk – back, right, back. Good, good! OK, back on your toes! Move your hands! Arms and legs together! Pendulum. Pendulum! Looking good... looking good... looking good! Way to use your legs. The rope is showing! The rope is paying off! Great. Great! Keep your head up. Keep your eyes on your target. In and OUT!"

He popped her with the mitts, softly, left-right-left – quick! She covered up nicely, backed away with her legs beneath her, in sync with her upper body.

"Terrific," the trainer said, right when she stepped back in with a jab that popped him on the jaw with enough snap to surprise him, even stun him, and she followed up with a straight right hand that also caught him flush. "Whoa!"

Now the trainer felt pretty stupid for not wearing the headgear. Pop – another jab to the nose, and now he backed away while she danced into him. The coach backed away some more and held up the mitts.

"OK, let's see what you got!"

He backed into the ropes while Manuela crouched in with her back still straight and unleashed a solid left-right-left combination that rang against her target's pads loud enough to make a few people in the gym stop and look. Now she's back, now she's moving in again with another combination. Back, forward – jab, jab, jab, in, in, in, and when he retreated, she timed another hook into the mitt. If he hadn't been playing intentional defense with his hands, it would have caught him on the jaw. If she'd have been in there with a woman in her 150-pound weight class, it likely would have put her on the mat. She followed it with a right underneath the heart. She stepped back and unfurled a hook to the liver, another right hand to the midsection, and back, out, move to the right, stop, stick, move out, move in. Use the legs, bob, weave, up, down, keep the head moving – boom, a right-hand lead into the mitt, with oomph. Back, out, circle right, in, out, in – double jab.

Ding!

The bell ended the two-minute round, and the trainer gave her a loud whoop and a padded mitt to her rear.

Link stood just inside the garage-style door that opened the gym onto H Street and gave passersby a ringside view of the political strategists and communications consultants, opposition researchers and state public information officers, business lobbyists and labor leaders, executive assistants and computer engineers playing catch with medicine balls. Three students pounded the heavy bags with their trainers shouldering the other side. Across the gym, instructors ran about 20 men and women of all ages through a dance fitness routine.

Funny way to spend Happy Hour, Link thought to himself.

In his mind, at this time of the day, all these people should have been in their neighborhood pubs, relaxing with a cold froth. A couple hours earlier, he had woken up from a mid-afternoon nap and placed a call to Ms. Manuela Fonseca at MJ Public Affairs to finalize the details of their date that night. She told him she had a workout at the 14th Street Gym, but that it should be over by 5 o'clock. Any time after that would be fine.

As the clock approached 5, he set out on foot to watch Manuela at play.

She worked through two more two-minute rounds, same as the first. She accepted praise and encouragement from her trainer, and stepped out of the ring, and was rummaging through her gym bag for a towel and a bottle of ice water, when she looked up and spotted this tall, good-looking Native American dude in black jeans, black cowboy boots, a black long-sleeved dress shirt and a white cowboy hat, standing just inside the open garage-style door, leaning against the concrete wall, his arms folded across his chest and his right foot crossed over his left, smiling at her.

She removed her gloves and head gear and stuffed them into the bag. She glanced at Link again and saw that the same grin continued to wrap around his face. She could not suppress the smile that had begun to cover her own, and she threw back her soaking black hair. Rivers of moisture poured off her face and down her arms. She draped the towel behind her neck and drained about half the bottle of ice water. She strode across the gym towards Link.

She looked up at him and said:

"Do you often spy on girls while they're sweating like this?"

"Usually not," he laughed. "But I think I need to do it more often."

Manuela laughed back, and she retrieved the towel from around her neck and snapped it at Link.

She took dead aim at his groin.

"Low blow," he said. "Point deduction."

She stepped back and used the towel to wipe the sweat off her face.

"I'm telling you," she said. "This is totally exhausting. Exhilarating, but exhausting. Completely different than working the bags, jumping rope, or doing anything else."

"Wait until you do it with somebody who punches back."

"The veteran!"

"Veteran chicken."

"I'm working up to it," she said. "He's going to throw me in with somebody pretty soon, he says. The only problem is there aren't a whole lot of 50-year-old women who don't mind getting hit in the face."

"I would imagine there aren't *any* 50-year-old women who like to get hit in the face. Men, neither."

"I wouldn't know – nobody's hit me in the face yet."

81

Manuela feigned a jab at Link and stepped back and laughed. She took a deep breath and wiped off the new sweat that chased the drips she'd just mopped up.

Link ogled, and she caught him again, and this time she blushed.

"Lots of women do the mixed martial arts," Manuela said, "but there are damned few who get into boxing. At least damn few who get into it who actually want to fight. Lots of girls hit the bag, do the rope, do the workout, and that's all great. But there aren't five of them in this gym who are actually looking to become boxers, and there aren't any that are within 20 years of me."

"Lucky for them," Link said.

"Women are more into the UFC thing, which if you ask me is a fraud. They're all about looks, is my take. You put that Rhonda Rousey or any of them in the ring against any of 50 women boxers you've never heard of and who aren't in it to make movie deals and they'd get their asses destroyed. UFC, not my bag."

"Mine neither," Link said. "I find it unwatchable. There's no art to it. They kick you in the legs and roll you on the ground until they get you in a chokehold. There's nothing beautiful about it. Boxing, in its purest form? What has it been called from the beginning? 'The manly *art* of self-defense,' with an emphasis on art."

She gave him a look.

"An art for all the genders," he corrected himself. "As you have just demonstrated."

She sighed, "I mean I'd love to have one real fight – in a real ring where you have to walk up the steps, with a referee, with judges. Not a sparring session. I mean a real amateur fight that will be registered in the record books, and that 150 years from now somebody can go back and look up and say, 'Manuela Fonseca, huh. Undefeated at 150 pounds, amateur, from Sacramento, California.' Or, oh, she lost, and was never heard from again."

"What if you do win it?"

"Then I will retire undefeated."

"And if you lose?"

"I'll still be in the best shape I've ever been in my life."

Link struggled not to look her up and down but couldn't help nodding his head in the affirmative.

She stepped back with the towel and held it at either end and rolled it tightly with quick circular ringing motions.

"You *are* spying on me," she said, as she snapped to a sideways stance, holding one end of the towel back with her left hand that let go while she snapped forward with a backhand right – aiming, again, below his belt.

"Another point deduction," he said, loud enough to gather attention from a couple of the other gym rats. "Seriously," he said. "You are very good. I watch a lot of fights on TV. You look like you know what you're doing."

"I would hope so," she said, as she flung the towel back around her neck. "I've been doing this for a year and a half."

Manuela pulled her cell phone out of her gym back and checked the time.

"It's 5:35," she said. "We better get going if we're going to make that 6:15. Do you want to just meet me over there?"

"That sounds sensible. I am of course on foot."

"And I am of course on bike."

"Really? You don't drive?"

"Almost never, to work. Come on, I only live 15 blocks from my office. Usually, I walk. Today I rode my bike."

"In a dress? With stockings?"

"No, dummy. I keep it *cazh* at work, especially on Fridays, unless the client demands otherwise. Then, I put on the suit and the heels. It pays the bills. Then I drive. Hey, we better get going. We'll talk more about my wardrobe once I get a glass of wine in my hand."

Manuela stuffed the towel and the water bottle into the bag with her gloves and head gear and her casual work clothes. She strapped on the gym bag that also worked as a backpack. She unlocked her 10-speed and buckled the chin strap on her bike helmet.

"See you at 6:15," she said, before she pushed off with her

boxing shoes that ran above her ankles and pedaled off with the Friday afternoon rush-hour traffic.   He waved, limply, as she rode off.

12/*Mullaney's*

"Santa Lucia Highlands? Never heard of it."

"Maybe you should get out more, *bruto*."

"I think I'm doing that right now."

The venue was Mullaney's Building and Loan, one of the best restaurants in town and without question Link's favorite. He liked its sense of history, the way it gave the public access to a gem of a 125-year-old firehouse into which it had been embedded. He liked its place as a major contributor to Sacramento's food renaissance. He liked its owner who liked his wood sculpting and who frequently bought the spirits of rats and raccoons and other rodents that Link pulled out of the felled timber.

Not being a wine guy, Link of course had never heard of the Salinas Valley vineyards tucked into the other side of the mountain range that made the Big Sur coast the Big Sur coast.

Manuela filled him in on the inland winery action of Monterey County. Then she ordered a glass of the Bruliam Sobranes Vineyard Pinot Noir.

He made his an Integral, the go-to IPA from the Device Brewing Company.

"It's not as if I've never been through there," Link responded. "Back in the day, we used to hitchhike down 101 from Mendocino to Isla Vista. We'd stop on the way down near Paso Robles, and we would get quite drunk. Then, we would return in our altered state to the highway, to complete our trip south. We'd bum around I.V. for a couple days there, go to the naked beach, smoke pot, hang out. It was tremendous fun, especially in the summer when all of the students were gone."

"This is while you were in art school?"

"Calling it a school might give you the wrong impression," Link continued. "Once you got into the center, you could do whatever you liked, as long as you produced. As long as you created things they could put on display. They had their instructors who really weren't much more than babysitters, or monitors. Just people who we could talk to if we had any questions about anything, such as, where is the best place to buy a bottle of cheap French wine. That's where I met this guy we called The Witch Doctor."

"Believe it or not, I did read the stories about your sitch last year."

Manuela referred to what really was a simultaneous double kidnapping of the Witch Doctor as well as of Link. The only way the Russian henchmen were able to force Link into his involuntary subjugation was the fact that their team already was holding the Witch Doctor captive in his living quarters in a winery up in Mendocino County. Only then would Link allow his own abduction.

"Of course," Link said.

"The stories in the newspaper were pretty good."

"I'm sure you've heard that the reporter who wrote them is back in town and going over some materials with your Jordan Diaz friend."

"I have. But the *Beacon* stories didn't get into this Witch Doctor guy much at all."

"I think Frankie got distracted," Link said. "The Washington Post was recruiting him hard by the time the fires hit. To be one hundred percent honest with you, I've got to say I never even knew the guy's name was Richard Montes until I read it in the paper. He was just the Witch Doctor."

Link sipped his Integral and nodded his head in the direction of a three-foot tall statue perched on a platform inserted into the brick wall that ran along the long side of the restaurant.

"See that little guy up there?" he said.

Manuela looked up and saw the depiction of a chef, in a white chef's jacket and a white baseball cap that couldn't hold back a riot of curly hair that fell to the waist, with his arms folded across his chest and his right hand clutching a butcher knife.

"I did that one for Mullaney," Link told her. "He'd bought so much stuff from my old shop I thought I'd do one of him. I think he kind of likes it. Lots of these people from L.A. who come in here have tried to buy it off him."

"How much did they offer?"

"A hell of a lot more than it's worth, I can tell you that," Link laughed. "Crazy talk. I can tell you, of everything I've ever done, that's probably the only thing that I check up on every so often. Its spirit seems to have merged with Mullaney's. It is a good spirit."

Manuela didn't quite get it, but she smiled at him mischievously.

She was more interested in Richard Montes.

"So where did 'Witch Doctor' come from?"

"It's what he called himself," Link went on. "He said people started calling him that from the time of that *ooh-eee-oo-ah-ah* song from the 1950s. 'I told the witch doctor I was in love with you,' " Link sang playfully, banging out a little rhythm on the table.

Link had slowly gotten an idea of the Witch Doctor's story over the years, pieced together through enigmatic hints and eccentric half-stories mixed with what seemed like proverbs and mumbo-jumbo. The old man was born in San Francisco, came of age during the Beat era, hung out at Vesuvio's, did the Beatnik thing. Started messing around with wood sculpture. Got pretty good at it, made enough money to rent a room in North Beach, until the whole hippie thing happened. Moved to the Haight, got into the front edge of that scene. The kids saw him as a philosopher king, a connection from one era to the next – Beat to hippie. Smart. Funny. Well-read. Good-looking. Native American. Artist. Great story teller. What's not to like? He found a shop on Divisadero that sold his stuff, did even better for himself there. Rented a flat in the hills above the Haight, in Cole

Valley when the neighborhood wasn't so trendy and a working man could still afford those kinds of things. Life couldn't be better. Teenagers and the runaways, the young people really doing some serious searching, they wandered into his shop and he got to know them and they got to know him and they thought he had some answers, even if he was mainly about the questions. Anybody who thought he had something figured out was mainly somebody who didn't have anything figured out – that was his take.

"I'd guess he was around 30 at the time of the Summer of Love, and even then the young people looked up to him as a wise man. Which I guess he was in his eccentric sort of way. He was nice to the kids, didn't want to lead them astray, although he was not above smoking dope or drinking wine with them," Link said with a wry smile.

Manuela smiled too, and rolled her eyes as she took another sip of wine. "Sounds like a typical man who never wanted to grow up," she said. "A bit like someone else I know." She looked at him sidelong around her wine glass to see how her comment would land.

"There are similarities, I will give you that," Link said, as he delighted in the berry-citrus aromatic twist of his Integral. "He did tell me once in a while he even joined the hippies on acid trips to Baker Beach on hot summer nights. Had them over to the house for parties that would last the weekend. But he insists he never, not once, took advantage of any of the hippie chicks."

"Well, at least there's that," Manuela said.

Link had gleaned the Witch Doctor liked his women older – his age and up. He said he found them more attractive, more *womanly*. He seemed to have had terrific success with rich married women from Pacific Heights or St. Francis Woods, or the suburbs, women who were intelligent and beautiful but a little bit depressed by dead-end relationships with men who didn't appreciate their wild side.

"But he could never make it last."

Link shook himself a little as he took another sip of IPA. There were more similarities than he had ever really quite realized.

"Anyway, he started to make some serious money just as the Sixties made their weird turn, with Nixon bombing Cambodia and Charles Manson and San Francisco cops on a warpath – '*and the heat came down and busted me for smiling on a cloudy day,*' to quote the Dead. He figured it was time to get the hell out of town. He bought some land out in the middle of nowhere in Mendocino County, near Comptche, and got a good couple dozen entrepreneurial and artistic young people go with him."

"And *voila*, you've got yourself a commune," Manuela smiled.

They'd gotten about half way through their wine and brew when the chef and owner, Carrick Mullaney, stopped by their table to say hello. He knew them both: Manuela handled his P.R., and he was one of the first in town to feature Link's sculpture in his restaurant. In fact, it was Mullaney who suggested to Link that he hire Manuela to handle the press at the Cesar Chavez Plaza unveiling. He and Link had grown closer the past couple of years through their mutual support and appreciation of the city's fledgling Mardi Gras parade. It had become a wickedly fun jaunt. They hired the Element Brass Band, and it led a crowd that had grown from about 50 the first year to more than 200 by the fourth. They snaked through Midtown and stopped into a couple of bars before they rolled into the Torch Club where the band blew the roof off the joint with some do-watcha-wanna.

A smiling server sidled up next to Mullaney, who told her he'd take their orders.

"Can't you make the call?" Manuela asked the chef. "I mean, you're the expert. You never ask me how to do a public relations campaign, do you? You just say you want us to get the word out on something."

"Or not," Mullaney said.

"I don't make you order off a menu," Manuela went on, uninterrupted. This was clearly an old joke with them. "Why do you make me do that here?"

"OK, if you insist," Mullaney said. "We'll start you out with

Ray Yeung's heirloom tomatoes with Capay Valley basil and our home-made buffalo mozzarella which any Italian would tell you is better than what you can get shipped from Campania as long as the people who make it here studied under the people who made it there. And I'll have you know I spent a month in the hills above Caserta with no other purpose in mind."

"I would hope," Manuela said.

"We'll include some prosciutto and peaches along with the tomatoes, and Parma is Parma, and it can't be beat. So Parma it is."

"I would expect," Link said.

"The halibut came in from Alaska *today*," Mullaney said. "Strike that. It came in four hours ago, and you better get it now because it won't be here tomorrow. It will be grilled, with squash and a little bit of pesto *fregula*."

"Can you make that for two?" Manuela asked.

"Sounds perfect," Link threw in.

"Coming up," Mullaney said, before bowing away and off to the kitchen, interrupted along the way by other people he knew whom he stopped and greeted.

The place was nearly full, and a good number of the diners took note of Link and Manuela. Many recognized Manuela from her TV days. A smaller number read the newspapers and Link's story – his rise to artistic fame, the thing with the Russians, the totem that now stood on the 10th Street side of Cesar Chavez Plaza.

"Great guy," Link said of Mullaney.

Manuela nodded. "We were talking about communes," she said.

"Oh, yeah," Link said, a bit embarrassed to find himself saying more about the Witch Doctor than the man himself had ever said in one sitting. "He got the commune going, and over time he made his connection to the art center."

"And that's how you met him."

Link nodded. "I think he'd been there a good decade before I got there. He would come into the center two, maybe three times a week to examine our work and maybe offer up tips on technique. His advice, to tell the truth, was not all that sophisticated: make sure your tools are sharp, use them all, don't be afraid of chain saws."

"Chainsaws?"

"Yes. They're very valuable on the bigger pieces – you get to the point a lot faster."

Link had used them, and they did work, but he preferred the sweat of the hand saw. It allowed him to feel more in touch with what was inside the log, whatever seemed like it was trying to get out. The Witch Doctor was definitely into the chainsaw. He liked the noise, the authority that it brought. The sense of power. He for sure used them to harvest the logs that he brought to Link.

"Besides, you can't use them indoors," Link said. "Too much dust."

He stopped to take a sip of his beer.

Manuela smiled. "Was he a good teacher?"

Link had to think about it. "You know, when I first started, his philosophy mainly was to feel what was inside the log rather than trying to impose an idea on it. Some of us drew up these great designs of what we wanted, and he would say something like how terrific the drawing was, and that it would make for a fine piece, but that maybe you should put it on a canvas and take up the paint brush. I guess I was the only one who truly understood him. Almost all of the others left. Eventually, the art center stopped offering him space in the school. I stuck it out with him, even after he left the center, and he must have seen something in me, too."

"Now," he said, "let's talk about you."

Manuela looked at him with fake anger. "You do realize you just managed to talk for a half an hour without really giving anything away about yourself. Your time will come, *bruto*."

Link smiled. "Come on," he said. "I don't know anything about where you are from. I have a feeling I don't know half of what you have accomplished." Link leaned forward. "I have to admit, I am not much of a local TV news watcher."

"Well, you didn't miss much," Manuela laughed. "Just a lot of standups late at night on the side of I-80 when it snowed. I also got my share of late-night crime, and breaking City Hall news at night. Believe it or not, those were the toughest stories. Issues like the city passing a living wage ordinance or deciding how to react to the latest police shooting or some kind of complex land deal. You had to do lots of homework ahead of time and shoot your standup while the debate was still going on and then hang around until 1 o'clock in the morning to reshoot the story for the early-morning news. Believe me, nobody watched the morning news to see what happened at City Hall the night before. That's what newspapers are for."

Link now remembered seeing her in another TV role.

"Sometimes," he said, "I would turn on the television on Sunday nights and you would be the person sitting at the desk, in charge."

"It's called being the anchor. Man, you really are stupid." She winked. "I kind of liked that, but not as much as reporting. Frankly, about 10 years ago when the cutbacks started, I got sick of the whole thing. They chopped our news staff in half and they had me switching back and forth from reporting to anchoring to filling in on their silly mid-morning shows. I hated it, but I liked the money, and I was able to raise my son when my husband flaked out, and then MJ somehow got the word that I was dissatisfied. They reached out and I reached back. They liked me as a rainmaker, and I'm telling you: Baby, I have made *a lot* of rain for them."

"Tell me about your son."

"I take it you saw his picture in my office?"

"I did."

"He's a great kid. Worked his way through Sac State – *demanded* that he do it himself, with no money from me. Decided he wanted to be a lawyer. Waited tables through McGeorge and got out of there in three years. Now he's over in San Francisco, doing civil litigation. Not married, no kids, but he's living with his sweetheart. She's also a lawyer and they seem to be pretty happy over there, living the life. Two young, good-looking people, in love, in San Francisco. Living in a two-bedroom flat in the inner Richmond. Restaurants, fun, Yosemite,

91

more fun, Lake Tahoe, skiing, live music, fun. Walks in the park, fly off to Kansas City or Cleveland or Seattle, to see their favorite bands, more fun. Weekend beach trips to Southern California. Giants games. Warriors games. More fun."

Manuela finished her glass of wine.

"They should both be put in jail," she said.

Link laughed. A fleet of servers brought in the tomatoes and the prosciutto, the corn soup with the feta and chili oil, the two plates of bread with the olive oil-balsamic dip – Manuela, for one, was pretty damn hungry from the workout.

Manuela ordered another glass of wine. "I think it's okay with the fish, right?"

The pleasant woman in charge of the wait crew told Manuela the right wine for any food is whatever tastes best. Manuela stuck with the pinot.

Link still had about a quarter of his Integral left, and that was just fine – the buzz felt perfect.

For the first time, they let a little silence hang out at the table.

They locked eyes.

Neither felt like they had to look away.

Manuela tried to play it cool. "You're looking at me like I'm one of your logs," she laughed.

Link realized she wasn't too far off. Looking at her, he wanted to know what made her, her, from way deep down inside. The most important thing. "I'm just trying to figure you out," he chuckled.

Over their spectacular salads, she told him that she grew up in Southern California, in the San Fernando Valley, the oldest of five kids. Her father was a carpenter who became a business agent in the union and still did a little work for them on the side, on the writing-P.R. side – she thinks she got her journalistic sense from him. Her mother taught first grade. They did well enough to buy a vacation home in Big Bear where the parents now lived year-round. Her two brothers and two sisters all went to college and embarked on professional careers.

"I like to work," she said. "I love my family. I'm what you call extremely loyal."

Link told her the story of his upbringing in rural southwestern Placer County. He started at the beginning and left nothing out – the mystery of his father, his mother's wasted education, his near-solo journey through the world's obstacle course. Close as she was to her parents, Link's missing dad got her attention.

Link picked up on her discomfort. He moved to set her at ease.

"Hey, what I knew was pretty good," he said. "My mother loved me as much as any human being can love another, and that was good enough for me. I never felt like I missed anything. Would I be different if there was a man around to rein me in? I don't know. Would it have made my life better? I don't know. Wouldn't that depend on who the father was? The character and quality of the man? If it was Gandhi or Churchill, probably I'd be better. If it was Richard Nixon or Eric Trump, probably not."

"Churchill, I don't know. Wasn't he a horrible father? Didn't his son turn out to be a drunken failure?"

"I don't really know. I mean, if Ward Cleaver was my dad, I'd be who I am, plus something like The Beav, or Wally. Or what if Sonny Liston was my pop? Would I have sat on my stool after the seventh round against Cassius Clay? It is impossible to say. All I know is I like who I am, and I thank my mother for that every day."

"You don't seem to be a momma's boy."

"She wouldn't allow it. She made sure I was tough."

"And she never told you who your father was?"

"Not a hint."

He continued through his graduation from high school fuck-up to the artist who didn't know his own ability, his relative success in Mendocino County before he bumped into a million dollars that fell out of the casino sky, his move to Sac, his unexpected international acclaim, "and my accidental coincidental enjoyable meeting of you."

This unplanned verbal maneuver communicated perfectly and unmistakably his interest in Manuela.

She did not blush, but he saw a softening in her face, an ease of tension.

"I've got to say," she said, "that you are one of the more interesting men I've met in the last week or so."

Link felt compelled to reach under the table and squeeze some part of her – hand, any part really – but he knew it would probably be best if they slowed into the curve. He'd had his share of quick hitters. He wasn't desperate. He didn't exactly pine for the elusive *real thing*. They knew now that they had a connection. He knew that in time it would solidify or dissolve.

Mullaney himself swept in with the fish. The halibut melted into their mouths in a sensation of spice and sauce. The food took them so deep into the moment that they went silent a few minutes, before Link said:

"I just want to be with the fish."

Manuela laughed.

"Like Luca Brasi."

"*The Godfather*. No wonder I like you. But that's not what I was talking about."

He told her the thing about being with the fish came from a train wreck that dumped poison into a mile-stretch of the wild and scenic upper Sacramento River, one of the most popular fly-fishing spots in California, above Shasta Lake, back in 1991. He'd read a story in the *Beacon* about some mystic whose immediate reaction was to run down to the river, to, in his words, "be with the fish."

They both laughed.

Link slapped Manuela's hand away when she reached for the check and asked that they split it.

"You're embarrassing yourself," he told her.

"Manuela muttered something in Spanish but didn't make another attempt to reach for her purse.

He left a $100 tip. No wonder the servers liked him so much.

As they walked down 19th Street, she tucked herself into his side.

His natural inclination was to put his arm around her shoulder.

It felt right.

But only for a couple of seconds.

94

A dark-colored SUV steamed towards them, and screeched to a stop, the driver evened up on the one-way street with Link.

Link did not immediately recognize the vehicle, one which he had, in fact, seen before – in front of his house, peopled by a pair of asshole cig-butt flickers.

"It figures," the driver said, looking up at them. "Brown on Red. Literally."

"Better that they keep it to themselves," the passenger sitting shotgun said, ducking low to get a better view. "We don't want them to contaminate the *American* gene pool."

Link could feel Manuela bristle beside him. With her left arm around Link's waist, she leaned around the front of him towards the two men in the car, with her right arm bent at the elbow and the middle finger on her right hand extended towards the sky.

"Hey, fuck you, you motherfucking assholes," Manuela shouted at them.

Link used his body to shield her from them. He could feel the rage boiling inside Manuela as the men inside the SUV screeched away.

She broke off from him, to let her anger settle, and when it did, they eased back into each other, although neither knew quite what to say as they made it to Manuela's doorstep.

The moment of truth came when Manuela looked up at him, and Link responded with an embrace that was more than warm but was followed only by a kiss on the cheek. Manuela got the message – everything in due time. She smiled and closed her heavy wooden front door, and Link walked himself home with a sense that a lot was about to happen on multiple fronts.

The Saturday morning after his night out with Manuela, Link made his way on foot across midtown, to Benny's Q Street Bar and Grill, for a personal session with Mike Rubiks, at the writer's home away from home. The old newspaper bar still ranked as the artist's favorite in town, even though you'd be hard-pressed to find a reporter in there anymore except for going-away parties.

Rubiks was a wounded warrior from the 1990 Gulf War and the last-standing feature writer at *The Sacramento Beacon*, although that title had been abrogated, with the paper assigning him more and more to routine news coverage and even giving him a beat he hated – the local beer scene. Beer, in the Mike Rubiks world view, was meant to be drunk, not written or read about. There were more interesting topics to delve into with the pen, such as Elvis Presley, even though the King of Rock and Roll had been dead for 41 years. On a topic that would never die, Rubiks also spent a lot of his interest on the history of human warfare. He liked the off-beat, and had no problem getting a thousand words out of the pig races at the State Fair every year. He'd go down to Stockton and tell the story of 35-year-olds still playing Single-A ball. He was always good for the first drowning of the spring when the temperature hit 90 and blood-alcohol levels topped .15 while the water temperature on the Lower American stayed 55.

Politics wasn't Rubiks' beat, but it had become his obsession since Trump took office. He spent hours going over every document, every newsbreak, every assessment, every transcript, every investigative report. He knew the story better than most Washington reporters. Only thing with him, he couldn't separate himself from the information. The story drove him crazy. Trump drove him crazy, and he drove everybody around him crazy as he probed and screamed and sought to understand the country's new reality. He read the Christopher Steele report at least a dozen times, picking its details for proof of conspiracy. He spent hundreds of dollars on his own PACER account, reading every transcript and sentencing memorandum and defense and prosecutorial motion filed in the federal-court hotbeds of the Eastern District of Virginia to the District of Columbia to the Southern District of New York. He subscribed to *The Times*, *The Post* and read everything that Natasha Bertrand, Robert Palmer, and Seth Abramson wrote.

An afternoon with Mike at Benny's came with instructions, and a warning: add beer and whiskey, then stand back.

Link walked beneath the green Benny's canopy and through the front door where he bowed in greeting to Om, his favorite bartender in town, who stood behind the wood with his arms folded. Directly in front of Om sat Mike Rubiks, with two stacks of papers side-by-side on the bar in front of him. Rubiks had already pored over the so-called "Report on Russian Active Measures," released the day before by the Republican majority membership of the House Permanent Select Committee on Intelligence. He had just about finished his review of the Democratic minority's response when Link walked in.

Om shot Link a look that said, "Prepare for ignition."

The place was empty except for the three of them and the Budweiser longneck sitting in front of Rubiks.

"You're going to have to give me just a few more moments here – almost done," Rubiks said.

Rubiks took another 10 minutes to finish his read of the Democrats' 98-page evisceration of the Republican majority's 243-page rationale for doing nothing about the Russian 2016 theft of the American presidency. Link ordered a Sierra Nevada Pale Ale, a little bit early in the day for him, but what the hell – he had nothing else on the agenda. Om popped the top and set the bottle with the pretty green label in front of his tallest customer of Nisenan lineage.

Rubiks shuffled the two reports into order and took a sip from his beer..

He flipped to the first section of the Democrats' response.

He announced, to his audience of two, as if he were delivering the State of the Union:

"Three hundred and forty-one pages, my fellow Americans,

and it all comes down to this," he said.

"What's that, Mike?" Link asked.

Rubiks' read the sentence he had circled in black ink.

"I quote, from the Honorable Adam Schiff: 'You cannot find... what you do not seek.'"

The slight slur in his delivery made it sound as if this Bud was not his first of the morning.

Link and Om nodded in agreement with the statement from the gentleman from Pasadena.

"You cannot dispute that," Link said.

Mike raised his beer bottle between his cigar-thick index and middle fingers. His disheveled thin brown hair retreated from his forehead. His red-and-black plaid flannel shirt did not fit with the warming days of spring. He lifted his longneck lip-ward, as if he were about to take a puff.

Mike Rubiks pronounced, "I got shot in the fucking face, and for fucking what? For this goddamn fucking Republican Congress to abscond from their fucking constitutional duty?"

Rubiks sat up straight and looked directly into Link's eyes, which themselves observed a bloodshot quality to the analyst's world view.

"Don't these people understand?" Rubiks intoned. "They are the first branch of government. Their number one job is to keep an eye on the second. And what exactly do we have here? We've got the entire executive branch turned up missing, stolen by Russia. And what do the Republicans want? They want to investigate the guys who sent out a search party to find it."

Om whispered to Link as Rubiks blabbed on:

"He just got here from the Zebra."

Link knew what that meant. Every drinker in Sacramento knew what that meant. You walk up to the Zebra Club on 19th and P and the first thing you see is the pink neon announcement: "Open 6 A.M."

Rubiks always argued that moderate drink helped him find the deeper truth. Sometimes, he said, he needed to increase his intake to more fully behold certain lesser-seen realities.

He told his audience that the release of the "Russian Active

Measures" report required the fuller review.

"You cannot find what you do not seek," Rubiks began, again, "and these bastards – this fucking Nunes – weren't looking for fucking shit."

U.S. Rep. Devin Nunes, the Republican representative of central California corporate agriculture, was also the chairman of the House intelligence committee whose initials appeared over the "Russian Active Measures" report.

"He fucking starts out with a lie – right here," Rubiks said, flipping to the front of the majority report. "Quote: 'We were determined to follow the facts wherever they might lead.' Even an idiot could see that this is complete, unadulterated bullshit. They don't give a rat's ass about any fucking facts. They don't give a shit about what Trump and the Russians did. The only thing they cared about was protecting Trump, to keep their little game in play to turn this country into the same kind of racist oligarchy as their heroes in Russia. To that end, in this report, they only went after the leakers, as if that was the problem here, as if the people who tried to get the truth to the American people were the people who belonged in jail. I mean – fuck! But what do you expect from a dairy farmer? No disrespect to dairy farmers. But they shouldn't be in charge of the goddamn House Permanent Subcommittee on Intelligence."

"Select committee," Om corrected him.

"What?"

"It's the House Permanent Select Committee on Intelligence."

"What did I say?" Rubiks asked.

"Subcommittee."

"Of course. Select. As I was saying, we have a dairy farmer in charge of the House Permanent Select Committee on Intelligence. We can't have that."

"Depends on if they're milk drinkers," Link said.

"Very funny," Rubiks shot back.

Rubiks zipped through his notes. He laid out all the points of contacts between the Trump campaign and the Russians – Moscow-connected Professor Joseph Misfud getting in the ear of foreign policy flunky George Papadopolous who relays the information to corrupt campaign manager Paul Manafort that there was dirt to be had on Hillary Clinton. Energy-industry opportunist Carter Page, caught up as a peripheral figure working with spies dispatched out of Moscow and then arranging a deal to broker the selloff of a Russian national oil company. The National Rifle Association backchannel – Russian spy mistress Maria Butina seduces NRA activist Paul Erickson who sets up a meeting between Donald Trump Jr. and Russian banker Alexander Torshin before the NRA dumps $35 million into the Trump campaign. The Trump Tower meeting where Manafort, Trump Jr., and presidential son-in-law Jared Kushner thought they would be getting a bag full of slime on Hillary Clinton from a gaggle of Russians who weaseled their way into the building with a promise of filth. Political weirdo Roger Stone, in touch with WikiLeaks, alerting the Trump campaign and America to email dumps.

"So, you got all this," Rubiks said, "and you got Nunes going off the whole way – no collusion. No coordination. No conspiracy. Not interested in the slightest. Doesn't subpoena Misfud. Doesn't subpoena any of the Russians. Doesn't give a shit about Carter Page. Christ Almighty, he comes to Carter Page's *defense!* Paints him as a victim of the cops."

Rubiks took a long draw on his longneck.

"Totally blows off the NRA angle," he went on. "Doesn't give a flying fuck about Trump Tower, even though the biggest asshole in the universe…"

"Steve Bannon?" Link asked.

"How'd you guess? Even Steve Bannon says there was 'zero chance' Trump didn't know about the meeting. They never brought in that Russian lawyer, the woman, Natalia whatever the fuck her name is, who set the whole thing up. Never talked to Manafort. Never talked to anybody about Trump lying about the meeting a year later. Never talked to anybody about Peter Smith."

"Peter who?"

"Some Republican insider bigshot the *Wall Street Journal* wrote up for being in touch with the Russians to steal Hillary's emails. Dead now, so I guess they can't talk to him, but they didn't seem much interested in getting his story while he was still breathing."

"Oh."

"Not a single question about Manafort and his Ukrainian-Russian connections. Zilch interest in Sessions hanging out with the Russian ambassador and then lying about it. Couldn't care less about Michael Cohen trying to make Trump Tower deals with Moscow in the middle of the campaign. No collusion. No conspiracy. No coordination."

Rubiks stopped to catch his breath.

"Om?" he asked. "Could you be a good bartender and pour me up a shot?"

"Of course," the bartender said, grabbing a bottle of Early Times off the rack – the Rubiks favorite.

"So, how the fuck are you doing?" Rubiks asked Link. "I haven't seen you since they pulled the cover off your totem pole at the plaza a couple weeks ago."

"Good enough," Link answered. "No big news. My belated thanks to you for your article ahead of the event."

Rubiks had written up a short preview before the unveiling at Cesar Chavez Plaza on the life and times of Lincoln Adams – more of an info-graphic, really, than a story, something easily digestible to the non-readers whom the *Beacon* had been trying to woo.

"I can't say I know what the fuck you were trying to convey with the totem pole, but I guess it looked good," Rubiks said. "At least it looked good to me, but what the fuck do I know about art? Otter. Train. Che. Fuck, man. You are deep."

"I am thinking about adding another layer," Link laughed.

"What's that?" Om asked.

"A fourth level – 'The Nunes Report.' "

Rubiks made a supplicating gesture toward Om, standing, arms extended, bowed at the waist. The bartender slid Rubiks a fresh shot with a Bud back. In a second, the whiskey had disappeared, washed out to the sea of Rubiks' digestive system by another gulp off the longneck.

"OK, my man," Rubiks said, as he closed his eyes and took on the look of a priest at High Mass during the consecration, the feel from the whiskey shot warming him high and tight in the blood-run up his brain stem and throughout his system. "I want you to sit back and relax. I want you to close your eyes, and I want you to let it all sink in. I want you to envision Russians stealing emails from the DNC computer and from the Clinton campaign. I want you to think about the thieves stuffing them into a briefcase and walking into the WikiLeaks Pawn Shop. They open the briefcase and Julian Assange is sitting across the glass counter. He's got a monocle in his eye – just got finished looking over a diamond ring brought in by a woman who is hocking her wedding ring for a spoonful of heroin. He looks up, and he says, 'What can I do for you, boys?' And they say, 'Well, we've got these emails, and we think they could be pretty valuable, and we were wondering if you could move them for us,' and he puts the monocle down and he goes through a couple of the emails, and he goes, 'Boys, I think I know some people who might be interested, I'll see what I can do,' and he gets in touch with Donald Trump Jr., tells him what he's got, and Junior gets on his Twitter feed to tell the world to head on down to the WikiLeaks Pawn Shop to check out these emails they've got for sale."

Rubiks sipped his Bud, giving it all a chance to sink in, into his own consciousness as well as into that of Om and Link.

"Now, if that is not aiding and abetting a felony, I don't know what the fuck is – wheeling and dealing in stolen property, knowing that the pawn shop has the stolen property, telling your pals to go get some. Then, you've got Roger Stone who actually talks to the thief, the hacker, the guy who gave the shit to the pawn shop. Roger Stone gets in touch with the pawn shop – maybe directly, maybe through an intermediary, he even admits, and now he tells everybody he knows to go get yourself some free DNC emails. OK, the cops find out about it, and they start making some progress finding out who stole the shit and this conspiracy, collusion and coordination that's behind it, which just happens to include the crooks' boy who is running for president and makes 137 references to the stolen WikiLeaks emails on the campaign trail, telling his customers to check them out. The cops do their job. They investigate. So, what does Nunes do when his job requires him to make sense of all this shit? He fucking ignores the theft, ignores the receiving and the distribution of the stolen property, and he goes after the cops who did the fucking investigation."

Rubiks needed another time out. He stood up and made it to the bathroom. Link and Om could hear him mumbling to himself, before he came back to the bar to pick up the story:

"Then you've got the Nunes recommendations," Rubiks went on, authoritatively. "They are total bullshit, of course. Half of them have nothing to do with the reason those assholes did their report in the first place. The main thing Nunes is worried about is how the fuck did this shit get out to the public. That's his crime of the century, the fuck with the theft of our democracy. Nunes goes after the whistleblowers. The problem isn't Carter Page going to Russia to do business with a foreign adversary. It's the guys who asked him questions about it. This banker motherfucker, Torshin? Nunes says there is 'no evidence' he and Trump Jr. talked about the election at the NRA convention in Kentucky. How the fuck does Nunes know they didn't talk about the election? Because Junior told them they didn't? Man, I wish Nunes was the judge when I got my second DUI. He would have saved me about twenty-eight hundred bucks. Maybe Nunes might want to subpoena some of these other motherfuckers. Like the fucking Russians? Maybe this Erickson dude? Maybe the Russians at the Trump Tower meeting? And what does Nunes have to say about Roger Stone talking to the rat bastards who stole the emails? He says it was 'imprudent.' I mean that's it. Imprudence. But no collusion. No conspiracy. No coordination."

Another shot went down in a flash.

"Fucking asshole," Rubiks concluded.

Rubiks dropped his head into his arms, flat on the bar, exhausted.

Link picked up the reports, while Rubiks blubbered into abject incoherency.

"The recommendations," Link said, leafing quickly through the beginning of the document. "Twenty-six of them."

Rubiks snapped back to consciousness like a jack out of a box.

"Gimme those," he said, snatching the report away from Link. "Every single one of them – designed to do nothing. No. 1, European governments, NGOs, colleges. They need to 'practice multifactor authentication.' Now, what the fuck is that? 'Multifactor authentification?' Excuse me, but the Russians just stole the presidency of the United States. You can take your 'multifactor authenti-fucking-cation' and shove it up your fucking ass."

Rubiks took another sip of his beer, to calm himself down.

"Homeland Security should 'provide the owner or operator of any electronic election infrastructure affected by any significant foreign cyber intrusion with a briefing and include steps that may be taken to mitigate such intrusions,'" Rubiks went on, quoting from the report.

"Did you say a briefing to mitigate?" Link asked.

"That's exactly what I said. State and local governments – 'establish redundancies' to back up voting machines."

"I've always advocated redundancy."

"Number 18, repeal the Logan Act."

"Whose act?"

"Logan's."

"Who's Logan?"

"How the fuck am I supposed to know who Logan is?" Rubiks answered.

Rubiks looked at Om and asked him, "You're the bartender, man. Who is Logan?"

Om shrugged.

"Wrestler? Blond guy? Asshole?" the bartender said.

"No, man," Rubiks said. "That's Hogan."

Rubiks picked up his cell phone and punched "Logan Act" into his browser.

"I guess I've got to do everything around this goddamned place," he said.

The Google told Rubiks all he needed to know about George Logan, the Philadelphia Loyalist when America fought the British and who sympathized with the Jacobins when the United States almost went to war with France.

"Looks to me like it says that private citizens can't conduct negotiations with foreign governments," Rubiks said. "A lot of that's been going on around here, all these Trump motherfuckers working on behalf of Russia and Ukraine and Turkey. Why the fuck would Nunes want to repeal that law when you've got people all over town breaking the hell out of it? All these guys – Flynn, Carter Page, Papadopolous, Manafort. Trump himself. They're all working on behalf of foreign countries. With Trump in charge, it's almost like *we* are a foreign government. So Nunes wants to repeal the law. 'Report on Russian Active Measures.' What a bunch of bullshit. *Nunes* is a fucking Russia active measure."

"You sound contemptuous of the committee chairman," Link deduced.

"Yeah, I guess you could say I am. Recommendation 24: intelligence agencies 'should update its guidance regarding media contacts,' to make sure it applies to senior officials like the ones who blew the whistle on Trump. Recommendation 25: Congress should consider increasing penalties 'for unauthorized disclosures of classified information.' And the best of the best, Recommendation Number 26: mandatory polygraph examinations for all non-confirmed political appointees that have top secret clearances.' That's the whole ball of wax right there, baby. Lie detector tests for the whistleblowers. Find the leakers and throw them in jail, while Russia takes over the country. Jesus, Lord. If Nunes was the chairman of the Watergate committee, Nixon would still be president."

Rubiks took another slug off his beer.

"You got all this?" he asked Link.

"I do," Link said. "But I would also be interested in what you might say if you were asked to offer some recommendations of your own."

"Since you asked," Rubiks went on. "How about America

vote the Republicans out of office this. November? At least get the House. At least get the fucking House. I mean this is a dire fucking circumstance. If they win, if they keep Nunes in whatever the fuck committee he's in charge of, and all these other Trump-coddling sonsabitches who don't give a rat's ass if Russia rapes us as long as they get their tax cut..."

Another gulp of Bud, and Rubiks finished his thought:

"I'm not so sure we can survive as a country."

"You cannot find," Link began . . .

". . .what you do not seek," Om finished.

"And that," Rubiks said, "is the motherfuckingest truth."

14/*Midterm Canvass*

Lincoln Adams thought he finally understood the meaning of karma. Action determined destiny, in this world for sure, and possibly the next. A failure to act also carried consequences, especially when the times demanded it. What he'd realized recently was that this was one of those times.

It was time to get off his ass and do something.

What he'd settled on for right now was casting out the bad guys from the U.S. House of Representatives and replacing them with people with a greater appreciation of human decency.

Jordan Diaz helped him figure out his play. The young political pro sent Link a list of organizations dedicated to the proposition that the 10th Congressional District of California must be flipped.

Link settled on a labor group that had formed an independent expenditure committee whose sole purpose in this world was to defeat U.S. Rep. John Bonham, the district's incumbent representative. He signed up and hopped a Greyhound to Modesto. At campaign headquarters, he fell in with a dozen or so geezers just like him – volunteers in the army against evil.

The kids who ran the field operation taught them the front-door rap. They gave them all an iPad, and on a warm spring day beneath a blue and perfect sky, they dropped Link off on a sidewalk in a sketchy part of town.

Left to himself, on a street where working people of every race fought to maintain their economic survival on the margins, Link scratched beneath his white straw cowboy hat even though there was no itch. He poked at the iPad. The street name came up. Progress. He looked at the first address on his mobile computer. He compared it to the numbers painted on the curb of a worn but stable white-painted stucco tract house that stared back at him from the other side of the early green shoots of grass in an otherwise yellow front yard.

He gathered the courage to approach the front porch. He walked up the sidewalk to the front door – and damn if he didn't damn near fall on his ass when the silver tip of his cowboy boot caught a crack from a tree root breaking through the concrete.

Humbled by the near fall, Link regained his sense of self and purpose. He strode to the doorstep, where he observed a toddler's bicycle, a pair of soccer shin guards, three pairs of sneakers, and a man's work boots. It was a perfect morning the weekend after Cinco de Mayo.

It didn't take a genius to see that the doorbell didn't work – electrical wires protruded from the dime-sized circle where the plastic push button used to be. Somebody wrapped the grey wires neatly with a patch of duct tape and fastened them to the outer bulb of the doorbell so nobody would get hurt. A heavy black-iron screen door protected the inhabitants from intrusion in case a meth head took a wrong turn and mistook this place for a dope house. The occasional dealer and the more frequent addict served as neighborhood nuisances in a part of town mostly made up of farm workers, fast-food servers, ditch diggers, hod carriers, maids, milkers, med techs, caregivers and the care given, as well as a young mom with a smattering of preteens who came to this particular front door with all the shoes on the porch when he knocked.

"*Bueno?*" said the disembodied voice on the other side of the opaque screen.

Link could neither see the woman, nor speak her language.

"*Buenos días, señora,*" he tried. "*Uh, soy am un politico y soy un volunteer por un grupa de los trabajadaros en California, y, nosotros...,*" he mumbled and stumbled.

Then the screen door opened, and Link found himself greeted by the

heart-shaped smiling faces of three children who appeared to be somewhere between the ages of toddler to pre-adolescence. The threesome stood around and under their mother, a smallish, round-faced woman with the features of a native person much like himself.

"*Buenos días,*" Link began again, before the oldest of the kids, a girl, who looked to be about 11, maybe 12, but sounded more like 33, and who was almost as tall as her mother, told him to stop.

"It would probably be easier for everybody involved if you just spoke in English," the girl told Link.

"It's okay," the next-in-line, a boy, who looked to be about 8 or 9, said. "I could only speak Mixtec when I first went to kindergarten. They had a girl who taught me Spanish! Then English! As soon as I'm in middle school, they say they will begin to teach me French! That's the one I really want to learn!"

"French?" Link replied. "Why French?"

"I want to get Mbappe's autograph when Paris Saint-Germain comes to town!"

Link assumed this had to do with soccer.

"Mbappe. Well, that's great," Link said, sincerely. "Do you think you and your sister can help me talk to your mother?"

Link showed the children his volunteer's badge and told them how the group was trying to build a movement of the people from the ground up, beginning with this conversation at this doorstep. He'd try to keep them focused on the issues from the short list detailed on the iPad – healthcare, jobs, schools, Social Security. His next step was supposed to be getting them to sign a petition demanding that Rep. Bonham bend to the will of the people in his district.

"Here," he showed the girl, handing her the iPad. "Can you ask your mom which of these things jumps out at her the most?"

"Hmmm," the girl said, examining the iPad herself first before showing it to her mother. "They're all pretty important. I'd say for us it's education, because there are three of us, and my mom and dad worry about school a lot and want to make sure the teachers are doing their jobs right. But that's just me. She might have a different take."

The girl took the iPad and turned to her mother.

"*Mami*," she said, before sliding into one of the indigenous languages of Mexico.

The two spoke to each other for a few moments while the boy handicapped the World Cup for Link, who acted as if he understood what the kid was talking about when the only thing Link knew for sure was that the United States had been ousted from the tournament by Trinidad and Tobago.

The littlest of the three, a girl, who looked to be about 4, looked up at Link and smiled.

"Okay," the oldest said. "She says the big one is healthcare. She's really worried about it, and she's really worried that Trump's going to do what he says he's going to do and take ours away. My dad works in the vineyards, and sometimes he gets coverage and sometimes he doesn't, and sometimes he helps build houses, and when he does that he never gets any healthcare coverage there, or a pension, and we qualified for Obamacare, and it works pretty well for us."

Link concluded that the girl was a candidate for the Kennedy School of Government, if she actually was not already an analyst for the Brookings Institute.

"Maybe then," Link said, fumbling with the clipboard and the handouts while the girl handed him back the iPad, "maybe you – er, maybe your mother – or maybe both of you, would like to sign a petition that we are going to send to the congressman."

He handed her the clipboard with the petition on top.

"I don't think I can sign it," the girl said. "I'm not registered to vote."

109

"Oh," Link said, "you don't have to be a registered voter to…"

"But my mom is," the girl said. "She'd be happy to sign it."

"Great," Link said.

He nearly fumbled the iPad when the girl passed it back to him while he gave her a clipboard with the petitions. The mother needed no instructions on how to sign her name.

"Can I get your phone number and email, too?" Link asked, as he poked and prodded the iPad to put in their information.

"Tell you what," the girl said. "I'll go ahead and give you mine. My mom's not hooked up yet."

"Fine," Link said, as the girl wrote in the phone number and email on the petition. "Oh, one last thing: can we put your mother down as a contact person who might want to help us carry the word in our campaign?"

"Thank you very much," the girl said. "But we're already working for Valencia Maldonado."

Maldonado was the former mayor of a nearby town who was one of the four Democrats running for the Bonham seat.

"Oh, okay," Link said. "Anyway, thank you for your time, and hopefully we can do something about changing the way things are going in this country."

"Thank *you*," the girl said. "And by the way, you're pretty good at this – better than most."

"At what?"

"Canvassing. Believe me, we see a lot of you. You're the fourth one this week – one from the I.E., that being you – and three more from the other Democratic candidates. It's that time of year, you know."

"I think," Link said, "it's more than just a time of year.

15/*Vandals*

For three nights in a row, a warm feeling soaked Link to sleep.

He'd even been staying in bed until 7 a.m. – a relatively late hour for him. The morning of May 14, he barely made it to the Hyatt for the last New York Times, and he didn't pull up his chair at the high table at Shine until about 8:30.

He was just about to call Manuela when his own cell phone rang.

The disruption came from "No Caller ID". It could only be one person, somebody who rarely reached out to him, and when he did, it usually meant business.

"Hello, Detective Wiggins," Link greeted the caller.

He seemed to catch the policeman off guard.

"How the hell did you know it was me?" the detective asked. "My name isn't supposed to show up."

"Don't worry about it, Detective. Your identity is safe with me."

"Just a good guesser, huh. Well, guess this – they've got me working a case today that is slightly off my beat."

"That can only be good news," Link said.

"How do you figure?"

"On your beat, people only get hurt, killed, kidnapped, or held hostage."

"True, true, true and true," Wiggins responded. "But I don't know if I would call it good news that somebody either late last night or early this morning backed a truck or an SUV or something up to the Cesar Chavez statue in Cesar Chavez Park and tried to rip it the hell out of the concrete. When they couldn't do that, they spray-painted a bunch of bullshit on it."

Link digested the news as the conversation went silent for a minute.

"Swastikas," Wiggins went on. "Shit like that."

Link digested the information some more.

"It's a hate crime," the cop continued. "KKK, lightning bolts, the whole sixty-four yards. Right now, it's just vandalism. We're hoping it doesn't escalate into something more. Which is where my detail comes in. Which is where I come in. Which is where you come in."

"I'm not exactly following."

"Whoever did this sure looks like they've got you in their gunsights, too."

Link of course thought of his two interactions with the weirdos on the camera crew.

He provided the detective with the details.

"What are you doing right now?" Wiggins asked.

"Drinking coffee," Link said. "Reading the newspaper. Getting ready to make my move on the day. I'm pleased to report that it might possibly include a new woman in my life."

"I hope she's not Russian."

"No, she is safely Mexican," Link said.

"You are wising up. I know you're pressed with your usual load of pressing business of not doing anything productive, but if you could find a way to tear yourself away from it in the next five minutes, maybe you could make it over here to Cesar Chavez Plaza? The Police Department would greatly appreciate your cooperation on this matter."

"On my way."

Link clicked off his phone, folded his newspaper into his computer bag, and set off for the park. Two blocks away, he saw the flashing lights from the police cars, not an unusual occurrence on any downtown street at any time of the day since the Devante Davidson killing. Protesters seemingly had at least one major block in the grid sealed off around the clock.

On his approach to the plaza, Link saw that the entire park and its surrounding streets had been closed off by yellow police tape. TV trucks circled the block. A uniform stopped Link when he tried to walk up to Wiggins. The detective waved Link through the barrier and met him in front of the concrete landing where Cesar Chavez had been desecrated.

Link saw that a bucket of white paint had been poured over the farm labor leader's head. A vulgarity had been written across Dolores Huerta, the woman who co-founded the United Farm Workers union with Chavez, and whose likeness was included on a banner that appeared to be strapped to the back of the labor icon.

The artist and the detective had only seen each other a couple of times since the previous year's excitement. One of the occasions was the unveiling of Link's totem, where Wiggins moonlighted as undercover security.

"Let me show you something else," Wiggins said to Link.

The detective walked into the street and pointed out a heavy industrial chain that apparently had snapped in the attempted effort to pull the Chavez statue out of its concrete stand. "Check these out," Wiggins said, as he squatted next to two black skid marks next to the chain. He poked the burnt rubber with his pen.

"Looks like the tires belong to a late-model SUV," Wiggins said. "Also, it looks like they wrapped the chain around the statue to try and pull it out of the concrete. Then the chain breaks, so they get their willies instead by defacing the goddamn thing. They didn't seem too worried about being caught, either – this is right under a street light."

Link stood back a few feet, his chin in the cruck of his right hand.

"I still don't understand, Detective, why you called me."

Wiggins stood up from his crouch and straightened his brown tailored sports coat.

"Follow me," he said.

They walked over to Link's totem that had been unveiled not even a month earlier, over on the 10th Street side of the park. On the back side of the carving, a one-page note had been stuck into the sculpture at the point of a Buck knife jammed into the wood.

It read: "Your Mexican hero is gone. The Indian's piece of crap is next. You tear down ours, we tear down yours. Signed, True Sons of the Confederacy."

Link looked at the knife imbedded in the back of his totem that pinned the note that appeared to have been written on a plain 8x11 sheet of white typing paper. He could almost feel the totem's pain. Looking closer, a light bulb clicked on in his head.

"Fingerprints," he told the cop.

Wiggins gave Link a look that suggested the detective had not recently fallen off the turnip truck.

"Thanks for that advice, inspector," Wiggins said, sarcastically. "We'll get a guy right on it. As a matter of fact, we do have a forensics team in our little department, and we've got it here today. You may have noticed them."

"They're the ones with 'Crime Lab' written on the back of their jackets?"

"You are a sharp one," Wiggins said.

They walked back to the Chavez statue where one of the forensics supervisors approached Wiggins.

"Nothing," he said. "Not a single print off either statue."

"What about the knife?" Wiggins asked.

"Zippo. Clean as a whistle."

Wiggins thanked the guy for his try and paced around the Chavez statue, back into the street, around the statue again, and into the gutter, where he stooped down, into a crouch, looking for something that the vandals may have discarded before, during, or after their vandalization of the Chicano hero.

"Maybe these guys smoked, and maybe they flicked away a cigarette butt, but there are so damn many in here that it would take our people years to test them all," Wiggins said. The detective added, with disgust: "Some people wouldn't know what to do with an ash tray if it hit them upside the head."

Wiggins straightened up and put his hands on his hips. He looked slightly upward at Link, who was standing next to him in the street.

"Anyway," Wiggins continued, "the reason I called you here is because we think you might be in danger. Whoever did this, we don't know what they're up to. We just know that your piece was targeted, too, and they made an allusion to you in their note, so we are surmising that they may not stop with just messing up your totem pole. We've got to take the precaution that they also are out to harm you, and we know from what happened last year that some people will go to extraordinary lengths to fuck with you. It also looks like the bastards are personally stalking you. So the mayor, the police chief, and my lieutenant are all advising me to advise you to get out of town for a while, or let us put you in some kind of potential-victim protection program."

That made Link laugh.

The older he got, the easier it came to accept his impending demise. Fearlessness in face of mortality had always been a key component in his concept of balanced detachment. Enjoy, but do not cling, to life, Link had convinced himself, so there was no sense worrying about death, whether it came for you in a nursing home in your 90s or at the point of a knife in your prime.

"I greatly appreciate the concern, Detective," Link told Wiggins. "But I am fine, and I don't exactly want to be shipped off to Pocatello or Sioux Falls or someplace like that. I'm comfortable. I have friends. I am safe, and I know how to protect myself at all times. So, I appreciate it, but I will respectfully decline the offer."

"I told everybody you would say that," Wiggins said. "Now, tell me more about these 'incidents' you mentioned on the phone."

Link took off his cowboy hat and smoothed out his hair with his free hand, and he returned the hat to its place on his head and went over his encounters with the two guys, first in the park at the unveiling, then in front of his house, and later still on 19th Street when he walked Manuela home from Mullaney's. He also mentioned Manuela's concern when she first spotted the camera crew the night of the totem's unveiling.

The detective perked up when Link circled back to how one of the fuckheads flicked a cigarette butt at him on D Street.

"Did you say cigarette butt?" Wiggins asked.

"Yeah," he replied, "and I picked it up and put it my back pocket. I don't like people littering my block."

"What did you do with it?"

"The cigarette butt? You'll never guess."

"Try me."

"I gave it to the Scrounger."

Frankie hadn't yet heard about the vandalism when his cell phone beeped on Monday morning. It was Annette Smith-Bennett, the young woman from the UPS store, who asked him:

"What are you doing for lunch?"

"You tell me," Frankie responded.

"I get a half hour," she said. "There's a McDonald's on Zinfandel and Olson."

"I'll meet you there at noon. Can I take your order?"

"I'll bring mine. You order what you want."

Frankie had already bitten into a regular cheeseburger by the time Annette slid into the seat across from Frankie at exactly 12:08 p.m.

Annette got right to the point.

"I think I've got something for you," she said, winking at Frankie, the same way she did in the UPS shop. "I'm sorry I couldn't help you at the store, but they've got internal cameras all over the place. They're a little bit afraid that we might steal stuff – like I'd risk my job for a carton of oversized envelopes. They're also worried about private investigators coming around trying to track people down. They catch us giving any information out on postbox customers and we're fired on the spot."

"What about newspaper reporters?" Frankie asked.

"They've never even brought you up."

Frankie took that as a sad sign of the times as he munched his cheeseburger while his new friend pulled out a chicken salad sandwich.

"I guess that's one advantage of the decline in our standing in American society," Frankie said. "It used to be that people feared the *Beacon*."

Back to the matter at hand.

"So," he asked. "What have we got?"

"I just have to say," Annette answered. "I've been suspicious of this Bob Jones fellow for a long time. He gets a lot of packages and stuff that is marked 'Ukrainian Relief,' or

'Products for Belarus' or 'For Russia' or 'For Moldova,' in care of 'The Reverend Bob Jones.' And I mean he gets *a lot* of stuff. I'm not sure exactly what's in the packages, but there are a lot of them, and some of them are fairly large and heavy, like they could be TVs or portable microwaves, small refrigerators, even. And he drops in here once or twice a week, to pick up his stuff in one of these super long passenger vans, like a church bus, and on the side of the bus it says 'Russian Slavic USA Pentecostal Church.' "

Frankie nodded, almost as if he knew where this was going.

"Once a week, he comes in?" he asked.

"Sometimes two or three times," she replied.

Frankie finished his two-cheeseburger Value Meal. He slurped his medium-sized Coke and listened as Annette went on with the optimism of the 20-year-old that she was.

She didn't exactly ask him for career advice, but he told her to keep doing what she was doing – to work hard, stay in school, write stories, get them published in the school paper, and save your clips. And, in the meantime, leak him all of the information that she could.

Frankie thanked Annette for her help before she ran off back to work. Then, as he did about every 20 minutes, Frankie checked his Twitter feed for the latest news updates.

At the top, a *Sacramento Beacon* story:

"Cesar Chavez statue defaced in morning vandalism attack at Plaza. Artist's totem also attacked. Cops wonder, who did it?"

17/*Police interview*

Frankie read the story and confirmed it: once again, his friend Lincoln Adams had been certified as a crime victim. He shook his head. Go figure. From the parking lot of the McDonald's, he put in the call:

"You all right?" Frankie asked.

"Me," Link responded, "I'm fine. But the sculpture is in pain. A knife in the back hurts."

"Where are you?" Frankie asked. "You need anything?"

Link told him that at the moment, he was sitting in the back of a police car, on his way from Cesar Chavez Plaza to police headquarters on Freeport Boulevard, for a further debriefing with Wiggins.

The artist further informed his reporter friend about his recent brushes with the two goons from the camera crew and the note that had been stuck in the back of the totem from the so-called "Sons of the Confederacy".

Then he put in a request to Frankie:

"I've been getting some interview requests today, but we've decided that I should only do one. I was wondering what your availability is this afternoon."

"For what purpose?"

"To interview me."

"Interview you? Frankie asked. "Why don't you just write your own statement?"

"My press agent said it would be better if I submitted to a brief interview with a trusted reporter."

"You have a press agent?"

"Yes," Link said. He realized he hadn't yet filled Frankie in on nis new-found coziness with Manuela Fonseca. "And she thinks you should be the one who does the interview."

"I've got to check in with my desk, but I'm sure they'll go along with it," Frankie said. "You're national news."

"Can you meet us down at police headquarters?"

"I'm on my way," Frankie said, as he jumped into his rental to the Public Safety Center on Freeport Boulevard, across from the Bing Maloney Golf Course where he used to enjoy playing the back nine at the crack of dawn.

On the way to the station, Frankie realized he'd once again be dealing with Detective Andrew Wiggins.

For some reason, the two had never quite hit it off. Frankie attributed the communication problem to the natural suspicion that cops held for newspaper reporters and the suspicion that newspaper reporters held for anybody in authority. This historic distrust was further complicated by reporters' need for information and the fact that the police, in many cases, were its keepers. Sometimes in this uneasy relationship, cops needed reporters to disseminate information. Reporters most times were happy to oblige. At others, they felt used and cheapened.

So Frankie didn't quite know what to expect when he pulled into the parking lot and walked into Police HQ and was directed to the detectives' bullpen where he found Link sitting in a chair beside Wiggins'ss desk.

The detective looked up at him, contemptuously, and said:

"You again."

"Believe me," Frankie replied. "This wasn't my first choice on where to spend the afternoon."

"Well, just like I tell crooks just before I trick them into ratting themselves out, you are free to go."

"You know, Detective," Frankie said, "the last time I saw you, you were actually pretty nice to me."

"The occasion was your going away party. Wouldn't have missed it for the world," Wiggins said, deadpan.

Wiggins looked at Link and went on to Frankie, "Your best feature is your friend here."

Link shrugged. Then he lowered his head and raised his fist in a half-assed Black Power salute.

"Crazy motherfucker that he is," the detective continued, "I still like the hell out of him. I know he is true," the implication being that Frankie and his reporter ilk were not.

Frankie was left momentarily silenced.

"But your man here vouches for you," Wiggins said. "This story is going to get out, and the whole world is going to want to interview him, and we want to do it once, do it right, do it clean, and he says you're the guy."

Link was unsure of when Wiggins had become his personal security detail.

At that moment, Wiggins'ss desk phone rang.

"Okay," he said. "Send her in."

An instant later, Manuela Fonseca made her way into the detectives' room, in a sleeveless dress that did her just right.

She and Frankie said hi to each other. They knew each other a little, having bumped into each other on baby kidnappings, mistaken environmentalists' bombings of themselves, men arrested for attaching helium balloon onto their lawn chair and flying into air-traffic control radar and a few other stories over the years.

The detective led his visitors into an interview room where he dragged in a couple extra chairs.

"Don't worry," Wiggins assured the three. "The video cameras are off."

At the same time, he retrieved a small digital recording device from his shirt pocket.

"All right," the detective said, speaking directly into the recorder. "This is Detective Andrew Wiggins of the Sacramento Police Department, and I am recording this interview for my file only, and its contents are not to be shared with anybody. This interview is being conducted in response to the apparent vandalism that took place this morning, May 14, 2018, in Cesar Chavez Park, downtown Sacramento. Mr. Lincoln Adams has requested that he be allowed to be interviewed by the Washington Post reporter, Frankie Cameron. The police of course cannot prevent anybody from being interviewed, although we advised Mr. Adams that such an interview at this time would be inadvisable. We asked Mr. Adams that if it be conducted, that it take place in my presence and so that I may be allowed to interject and advise him and the interviewer on specific questions or answers that might complicate or compromise our investigation. We also informed Mr. Adams that we have no objection to the presence during the interview of his public relations consultant, Ms. Manuela Fonseca. The tape is now running, and Mr. Adams, Mr. Cameron, and Ms. Fonseca are all present. Mr. Cameron, please proceed with your interview."

It was kind of a tough one for Frankie, interviewing one of his best friends in the world, unprepared, and in the presence of cops. Still, he pulled out his own digital tape recorder from his front pants pocket, as well as the Reporter's notebook on his hip.

"So, Link, why don't you just go ahead and tell me your reaction to what happened today, how you heard the news," Frankie said.

Link took a minute, stroked his now-clean-shaven chin that used to sport his stringy goatee. Apparently Manuela did not like the Ho Chi Minh look.

"Let me see," he began, slowly. "I guess the only thing I want to say is, I'm terribly sorry about the attack on the Cesar Chavez statue. It is a depiction of one of California's most heroic and historic figures. Cesar is revered by millions. His work – wait a second there, it was more than his work – his work and the example that he set, of a simple man, with a simple idea who carried himself with honor showed that simple truth can change the world. He inspired and guided generations of people who believe in a better life for all. I hope the statue can be restored... no, strike that. I am *confident* that his statue can be restored to its previous dignity. The sculpture by Lisa Reinertson is a Sacramento treasure, and, I hereby pledge to pay for its restoration to its unblemished form, and to establish a fund to support the children of farmworkers in pursuit of the arts."

Silence punctuated the room for the next few seconds.

"Right," Frankie said, scribbling down a note. "an attack on art, how ridiculous is that. Anything you can say about these guys who had been harassing you the previous day?"

There was a somewhat tense silence as Link looked at Wiggins. The detective shook his head no.

"We'd prefer that you not get into the suspects at this point," the detective said. "We're holding off, for now, from releasing any of the contents of the note, or that one even exists. You know we're also going to get the usual lineup of nutcakes who are going to want to take responsibility. We need to be able to screen them out, and we can use the note to do that. Plus, we don't want any copycats."

Frankie shook his head in agreement, and Wiggins appreciated that.

121

"OK, we'll stay off of them for now," the reporter said. "I'll just say that detectives said that so far they have not identified any suspects."

"Good," Wiggins said, liking what he was seeing about Frankie at work. "Does that do it?"

"It does for me," Link said.

"Then it will have to for me, too," Frankie said. "I'll go ahead and type this up and call it into the desk."

"OK, everybody out," Wiggins said, as he rose to his feet. "We're done here. I've got to go get me a cigarette butt."

On the way out, Frankie filled Link and Manuela in on his intention to pay a visit to Bob Jones at the Russian Slavic USA Pentecostal Church.

The mention of the church flicked on a lightbulb in Link's brain.

"I might have a source who can help you," Link said.

"Who's that?" Frankie asked.

"Her," Link said, looking down at Manuela.

"What the hell are you talking about?" Manuela said.

"Your boss."

She still didn't seem to get it.

"Matthew Johnson." Link reminded her of the picture on the wall back in the lobby in the 22nd-floor offices of MJ Public Affairs.

"Matthew *Johannsen*?" she corrected. "What's he got to do with anything? He's barely in the office anymore. I think he lives up in the mountains, playing cowboy."

"He represents Russia," Link said.

Again, Manuela corrected:

"Not Russia. Just people who are interested in doing business over there and who might need some advice."

"Matthew Johannsen?" Frankie queried.

Frankie pulled out his notebook again and wrote down the name, and despite her skepticism, Manuela spelled it out for him.

"I must admit. It is pretty damn comfortable."

Initially, Link had resisted when Manuela offered to give him a ride in her banana-yellow Porsche 718 Spyder to wherever he wanted to go. He didn't want to impose. He would take the bus home.

"Get in the car, *bruto*," Manuela ordered.

Link complied. He'd never been in a $96,300 roadster before, or anything else that can go 187 miles per hour. The sensation of roominess seemed contrary to the two-seated stature of the sports car.

His plan for the day had been to take the 79-mph Capitol Corridor over to San Francisco to watch the Giants play an afternoon game against the Cincinnati Reds. The Giants, he could take them or leave them. He was more of an A's guy, although he liked the San Francisco ballpark better – the crown jewel of any that he'd ever been in. An added AT&T Park attraction was its location, two blocks down from the 21st Amendment brewery. He had looked forward to downing a pint of Brew Free or Die before heading over to the game, on a corner bench tucked into the windows brewery where he could watch the foot traffic up to the stadium.

He and Frankie and Manuela didn't get out of the police station, however, until well after the Reds' Adam Duvall – a former Sacramento River Cat and Lincoln Adams fan favorite – got ahold of a 92-mph fastball by San Francisco starter Andrew Suarez in the first inning and smoked it on a rope over the left-center field fence for a three-run homer.

"Do you think we could turn on the game?" he asked Manuela as she cruised north on Freeport, toward the grid.

"If you want."

Sitting shotgun in Manuela's Porsche, Link found himself stuck in his head. Never before had he worried about having these kinds of feelings for a woman – probably because they usually dissipated before they could congeal. This felt different. This one felt like it had legs. This one *felt*.

Weirdly enough, he felt nervous, a sense that something big was at stake, that everything was about to change. He had liked his total freedom, if that's what he wanted to call it, to do anything he wanted, whenever he wanted, with nobody to answer to, to wake up for, to take care of.

His reservations of feeling for other people never bothered Link, until about seven months ago, after his FaceTime showdown with the Russian gangster, Anton Karuliyak. He'd told Link he was psychologically "unclassifiable" and "oppositionally defiant." That he tended toward obsession. That he couldn't help his selfishness that nudged up against narcissism, of which he wasn't even aware. And here Link just thought he was an artist in pursuit of truth. Could it be that he used his talent as a cover, avoiding long-term relationships, avoiding responsibility to anyone or anything other than himself?

The more Link thought about the Russian's take on him, the more he came to see that the fucker was right.

He'd thought about Karuliyak's words every day since the October kidnapping. He'd absorbed them.

And now, Manuela. He wanted to absorb her.

She said nothing on the drive downtown, letting the Giants' terrific announcer, Jon Miller, describe the action into the bottom of the seventh, when Brandon Belt and Evan Longoria singled and Pablo Sandoval came up with a chance to tie the game, only to ground into an inning-ending double play.

Link clicked the radio off, and Manuela turned toward him.

"I have to tell you something," Link said.

"And that is?"

"I think you're pretty terrific."

From the comfort of his passenger seat, he leaned back, and now he felt really good, at ease, at peace, even if he once again found himself in the middle of a Sacramento police investigation. The comfort of the ride helped.

He looked at Manuela's smiling profile and thought he saw a

124

flush of blush on her right cheek.

"*Bruto*," she said, softly this time, her tone and tenor, her pitch, cutting straight to his heart and soul.

19/*Preacher Man*

Frankie typed up the Link quote and emailed it into the General Assignment desk back at the main office.

"That's it?" his editor asked.

"For now, anyway," Frankie replied.

"I thought you guys were friends. This reads like a prepared statement."

"It's all we're going to get," Frankie said. "It's all anybody's going to get, and when he wants to tell his story further, we'll be first in line."

The editor gave him a "hmmm."

"All right," he said. "Better get back at whatever the hell you're finding out about this IE."

The reference was to the White Rock USA independent expenditure committee.

"Moving as we speak," Frankie said, while making the transition from the northbound 99 to the eastbound 50 – Sacramento didn't have fancy names for its freeways like they did in L.A. or Oakland.

Destination: the greater Rancho Cordova metropolitan area.

He found the Russian Slavic USA Pentecostal Church amid the gravel pits and auto dismantling shops on the Jackson Highway, angling east and south on a path that had become more popular among Sacramento motorists the past 15 years by the placement of Jackson Rancheria Casino at its terminating end. Like all Indian casinos, the Jackson showroom featured the rock 'n roll acts of yesteryear trying to keep hope alive. Joan Jett and

Alice Cooper highlighted the summer schedule.

Somewhere south of Mather Airport, Frankie found the church that was hidden inside a parking lot that looked to be about the size of six football fields. Even if RSUSAPC – the unfortunate acronym which Frankie quickly threw at the facility – was in fact a house of worship, it didn't have a steeple. The place looked more like an indoor football stadium. Frankie estimated that it held 111,000 people, same as Ann Arbor.

When he pulled up close, he saw that the parking lot was open. He poked the nose of his rental Versa inside and began to snoop around, on wheels.

There was absolutely no action at the front of the behemoth, where several glass doors across the front looked capable of inhaling and exhaling thousands of parishioners between sermons. Only thing missing was the turnstiles. To Frankie's surprise, he found that the building was lined with red and white flags, interspersed with giant renditions of Old Glory, each of the church banners adorned in the letterings "RSUSAPC." Maybe he was a genius.

It occurred to Frankie that somebody had to raise these flags and take them down, and that whoever these somebodies were, they had to be somewhere on the premises. He drove around back, and there it was – the van, as described by Annette Smith-Bennett, white, with red lettering that said, "Russian Slavic USA Pentecostal Church," with the Jackson Highway address lettered on the side panels, right above the phone number. On the other side of the van was another just like it, and another, and another, and maybe 10 others, and all of them of identical make and with identical markings.

He parked at one side of the fleet, got out of his car, and made his way toward the glass door located in the midsection of the windowless rear hulk of a building.

"Hello," Frankie called out, as he stood just outside the doorway.

Nobody answered, so Frankie banged on the door and called out again:

"Hello?"

Still no answer, so he felt free to turn the knob and walk inside, down a dimly lit hall, and past an open door through which he looked inside and saw nobody.

A little further down, the hall opened into the backstage area of the massive auditorium.

From his right, Frankie heard a voice with a faded but discernible Russian accent.

It said:

"Ah, Mr. Cameron. We've been expecting you."

It made sense that Bob Jones would have recognized Frankie, who had already been to the White Rock USA warehouse in West Sacramento where he'd laid out his journalistic intentions to the woman with the pink hair. Word must have spread that Frankie Cameron was back in town on the hunt for a story. The woman did take his picture, and she must have forwarded it to this fellow who Frankie presumed to be her handler and probably the same guy whose name was listed as the White Rock USA independent expenditure committee treasurer, who just happened to be standing in front of the reporter right now.

"Good," Frankie said. "So you know why I'm here."

"Please assist me, Mr. Cameron."

"White Rock USA," Frankie told him. "The congressional candidate down in Modesto, Jacob Harland. The two hundred and fifty thousand dollars your committee is waiting to invest on his behalf."

"We are of course familiar with your work, Mr. Cameron, and it should not come as a surprise to you that we are unimpressed. You are universally unfair, and decidedly inaccurate. So it should not come as a further surprise to you that we will have nothing to say to you on this or any other matter."

"'We'," Frankie repeated. You said 'we.' Can I ask you, who is 'we' ?"

"'We,' in this case, would be me," the Reverend Jones said. "Me, and my church, and the thousands of Slavic peoples who attend it."

"The Federal Election Commission has identified you as the treasurer of a committee that has raised the two hundred and fifty thousand," Frankie repeated, still unperturbed.

"What committee would that be, Mr. Cameron?"

"The independent expenditure committee, Mr. Jones. White Rock. You're listed as the treasurer, and it says you've got two hundred and fifty thousand to spend on behalf of a guy who is running for Congress down in Modesto."

"Mr. Cameron, I have told you that I have nothing to say to you, and now it is time for you to leave, before I call security."

"What are you planning to do with the two hundred and fifty thousand?"

"Last chance, Mr. Cameron."

Now Frankie got the message.

"Okay, Mr. Jones. But I will give you the courtesy of a phone call before the story runs, which I believe will be in the next two or three days."

"Don't bother. Just leave."

On his way out, with the towering Bob Jones showing him to the door, Frankie, while still walking, retrieved the Reporter's notebook from his back pocket and flipped to a name he had written down back at the police station.

"Johannsen," Frankie said to Jones. "Matthew Johannsen. I guess he's the guy I should call about you?"

Frankie noticed a slight but detectable stutter in the step, if not the speech, of the Reverend Bob Jones.

"Just leave, Mr. Cameron," Bob Jones said.

Frankie put his notebook back in his pocket and retrieved his cell phone as he was walking down the hall leading to the door. Jones followed, and the church man stood in the doorway and watched Frankie as he got into his car and drove past the front of the vans that were parked in a row.

Frankie slowed on his way out of the parking lot to snap a couple pictures of their license plates.

Manuela pulled to a stop at 13th and R, right across the street from Link's corner studio. She smiled and said nothing. He got out of the car and said nothing. He wanted to lean across the console. He wanted to kiss her.

He didn't want the first one to be in a car.

"Don't forget that movie," she told him.

"Movie?"

"*Black Panther*. You said you'd take me."

"Of course. I'll call."

He got out of the car and crossed the street into his studio and he barely recognized the place.

He hadn't been there in a while.

He'd worked on the big project for Cesar Chavez Plaza around the clock from the moment he started it, late last December, just before midnight, on the night of Frankie Cameron's going-away party, to its completion in early April.

Link carved, sculpted, chiseled, painted, and lacquered the totem around the clock. When he got into the groove, nothing stopped him. He ordered out for pizza. He called in for Thai food. He sent out for hamburgers.

He cut back on his drinking.

He reduced his social life to next to nothing.

He pounded wood into the early-morning hours. He slept on the couch. He only caught a couple hours a night. His vision blurred. His thoughts fuzzed.

It's exactly where he needed to be: in a sensory netherworld conducive to finding the essence of form. Caffeine helped. Starbucks conveniently opened up a shop a few blocks up R Street. The walk cleared his mind.

By the time Manuela dropped him off, Link hadn't picked up a chisel in more than a month. He'd been to the studio only to check for mail.

Through the glass front door, he walked inside and saw the floor littered with a couple dozen more letters. He picked them up and shuffled them together and placed them on top of a couple hundred that remained unopened on his drafting table.

He sat down on the stool behind the table and went to work with the letter opener: fan letters. A request from the city of Arcata, in Humboldt County, for him to carve a totem for their town square. An invitation from a tribe outside of Vancouver, B.C., to give a talk. Requests from an Italian tenor, a Portuguese soccer star, a nationally-prominent female Democratic politician, and one from the official marketing agency for the Colombian government, to have him sculpt something for the hillside above Bogota to remember all the young men killed in the *narcoterrorista* wars.

In the middle of the new stack, he came across an envelope postmarked April 19, out of Fort Smith, Arkansas, with no return address. He cut it open to find a one-page letter with a single sentence in the middle of the page in 14-point type that in its entirety read, "We are on our way."

Interesting, he thought, and something that he would deliver to Detective Andrew Wiggins at the earliest opportunity. First, he had a phone call to make.

The Witch Doctor, in a rarity, answered the phone. Usually, his calls went straight to the screeching, hyenic laugh on his message machine, and he'd get back to you in about two weeks. He and Link would then make the arrangement to meet at the shuttered beekeeper's store in Covelo.

"Speak," the Witch Doctor answered.

The one-word greeting startled the caller.

"My uncle," Link said.

"My son," the Witch Doctor answered, in his high-pitched, purposeful deliverance. "When will you meet me at the red bench?"

"Funny you should ask that."

"I don't see the humor. But I will allow you to attempt to humor me."

"It's funny that you knew exactly why I'm calling."

"What else has been the nexus of our relationship for the past 40 years?"

"It's been the groundwork for my existence, my uncle. That is for sure."

"As it has helped shape my own. When will you be here?"

"I had been hoping to rent a van today and be up there this afternoon, but events seem to have interfered."

One of them, of course, was the Cesar Chavez desecration and the attack on his totem pole.

The news of the vandalism, of the attack on Link's creation, quieted the Witch Doctor.

"This is very troubling," he said. "The knifing of your totem could only be the beginning of what these individuals may have in store for you. Throwing paint and marking up the Chavez statue, I see that mainly as par-for-the-course racism, retaliation for the removal of the Confederate monuments in New Orleans and Memphis and other Southern cities. I would advise you to be careful. Maybe you are looking for a respite from Sacramento? If so, feel free to come up and spend some time with me. I am very much enjoying my new location."

At the time of his own kidnapping the previous fall, the Witch Doctor had been living in a winery behind a vineyard in the bucolic Redwood Valley. One of the many fires that ravaged Northern California wine country that had set the Witch Doctor free. His Russian captors fled the winery in fear of the blaze, only to die a violent death when their car flipped on a sharp turn on a country road, amid the smoke and flames. The fire went on to singe the hillsides all around the Witch Doctor's squat, and he felt compelled to leave.

He moved further up the valley from the fire area, into a cabin with running water, indoor plumbing and electricity, on the edge of a private forest, next door to some kind of monastery who owned the property and rented cheap.

"Mostly, they practice silence," the Witch Doctor said. "Now that's a religion I could get behind."

He howled at his own remark.

He quieted down some when Link told the Witch Doctor about Gathering Storm Manuela.

"Her again," the Witch Doctor said.

"Again?" said Link. "What do you mean 'again'? I just met her a few months ago."

"You know what I mean, my son."

"I can't say that I do."

"Didn't you just go through a situation such as this one? With the Russian woman?"

The reference was to Link's encounter the year before with Angelina Puchkova, the blonde Russian agent who was the main squeeze of mob boss Anton Karuliyak, the seductress who hoped to use her wiles to make Link carve a statue of her, for Karuliyak's organization.

Link couldn't believe that the Witch Doctor would liken what he felt for Manuela to his weakness for Angelina. Angelina wanted to steal his soul. Manuela wanted nothing. Or so he had convinced himself.

"They are different women," Link said.

"Yet they both share one unique quality," the Witch Doctor said.

"And that is?"

"Their gender."

In all of their years together, this was the first time Link could recall the Witch Doctor expressing a straightforward viewpoint on women. Link had never viewed the Witch Doctor as much of an expert on the topic. To the best of Link's knowledge, the Witch Doctor had never been married, never been involved in a relationship of any duration.

But there was a lot that Link didn't know about the Witch Doctor. Until a few months ago, he hadn't even known he had a name.

"My uncle," Link said. "Respectfully, I believe that you're on dangerous ground if you are suggesting that all women are alike."

"No," he said, "they are not all alike. But they all share qualities that may interfere with your own highest calling."

"I think I know where you are going with this. I've come to some realizations in recent months that make me respectfully disagree." It was a strange position for Link to find himself in—

132

the first time he could remember disagreeing with the Witch Doctor.

Link had to hold the phone away from his ear for a second to tone down the hyenic laughter screeching across the airwaves from wherever the Witch Doctor was staying these days up near the Mendocino National Forest.

"I am the first to admit," the Witch Doctor said, about 30 seconds later, after he calmed down, "that I don't know much about anything. But one thing I do know is this..."

He slowed his speech and lowered his tone.

"And that is, if you are an artist such as yourself, or myself, or ourselves, and if you fully commit – fully submit, some might say – to what we call 'a relationship,' to any committed relationship to a woman, or to a man if you are a woman, or to a woman or a man if you are gay or lesbian, then you are by definition cutting yourself off from the thing that exists that makes us do what we do."

"I don't understand."

"And this is not at all a critique on women. If anything, it is more of a commentary on those of us on this side of the sexual divide," the Witch Doctor continued. "The energy that is required to maintain this 'relationship', that enables it to survive and produce offspring and to provide for said offspring – it is all completely natural, and it is how the species survives. But there are some of us along the way – castoffs, beggars, carriers of secret truths – there are some of us who are poisoned by this impulse. We are called to shine a light, for everybody else. To give them a glimpse of beauty, of the forms as envisioned by the gods. Of creation. This spirit, this energy that comes out of us, it cannot if we are entangled in things like marriage, and relationship, and the workaday world. Relationships and families and daily labor – these are great things. I just don't think they are in the cards for the likes of you or me. At least not until we get old."

"But we *are* old, my uncle."

"I mean much older."

"You're what, 80?"

133

"Something like that. My point is, of course you can do both. But you will do neither of them well."

The speech left Link speechless. That left it up to the Witch Doctor to break the silence.

"So when are you coming up here for your next log, my son?"

"That's exactly the reason I called you, Uncle." Though now, Link wasn't so sure.

"You mean it wasn't for relationship advice?"

"You know it's not your area of expertise."

The Witch Doctor howled again.

"Dear Abby I am not, my son. Feel free to ignore everything I've ever said."

This time Link joined him in the laughter. They agreed to get together soon at the red bench on the beekeeper's porch.

21/*Chain of Custody*

Detective Andrew Wiggins left his office as soon as Link, Frankie and Manuela departed, for the drive across town to the Quinn Cottages, the collection of tiny homes for the homeless where one Tomas Marinaro – formerly known as the Scrounger – battled hard for his sobriety.

For the Scrounger, to stay clean meant to lay low. No matter where he walked in this town, he'd run into all the mistakes he'd ever known. So, he never left the cottages. Soon as he stepped out onto North B, he'd see Louie and Lyla and Lee. He'd be forced to talk to Edgar and Evangeline and Ellroy. He wouldn't be able to avoid Billie and Bobbie and Betsy – every one of them a temptation, a sharer of a story, a wild fuck, a night pushed to the edge of insanity, a companion in the back of a police cruiser. So, he stayed in the cottages. It was safe in there. Nobody could tempt him, except himself. Plus, he had 59 other people in there in the same circumstances. They knew that relapse carried a danger of death. It excited them. It made their lives in the cottages a 12-Step City, 24 hours a day.

When Wiggins rang the bell at the front gate of the cottages, he saw the Scrounger engaged in deep conversation in the main office, digging on a manager woman who had to be 20 years older than him.

They buzzed Wiggins through.

"Hey, boss," the Scrounger said to the detective.

Wiggins got a kick out of that.

"I guess I am your boss," he laughed.

"You keep paying me the way you do, I'll call you the king," the Scrounger said.

"Let's not get carried away here," Wiggins said.

"Believe me, I'm not. Life right now, I've got to say, is pretty fucking boring."

Wiggins laughed again.

"How many days you got now?" the detective asked.

"Would you believe one thirty five?"

"Why wouldn't I?"

"I drank New Year's Eve into New Year's Day, and I made it all the way through to the Rose Bowl, at Benny's, and then I had the power outage," the Scrounger recalled, to the best of his recollection. "I woke up in the hospital, if you recall."

"That wasn't a fucking hospital," Wiggins said. "It was Schmick."

Everyone referred to Sacramento Mental Health Treatment Center, the way it sounded -- Shmick.

"Did my seventy-two hours, then back to my squat at the Sterling, although they cut the bushes and made me move it around back, into the alley behind the Dumpster. Better spot, really, and the first night out, it was like, what the fuck? Then I saw you the next day."

"I remember it well."

A bad memory forced a pause in the Scrounger's rap for a second, before he pronounced:

"Roach."

135

The Scrounger was talking about a buddy of his who lived up on the levee, off of North 16th Street, behind the Ford dealership. A couple of their pals got caught up in a beef with some old guy on Basler Street who accused them of ripping him off. The old guy hired a couple of toughs to watch his place. His guys squabbled with the Scrounger's pals in front of the old guy's house. The old guy's guys chased Scrounger's pals up the levee.

That's when Roach intervened, to help his pals.

That's when Roach got stabbed in the heart.

"Of course," said Wiggins, who caught the case.

"That's when you finally put me to work."

"Sure was, and you've been doing a pretty good job. Our guys in the lab probably pulled twenty profiles off the butts you got us so far."

"Happy to do my part for a safer society," Tommy said, as if reciting the Boy Scout oath. "So what brings you down here, man? The city's up on its money. We're good for another two weeks."

"That's good to hear," Wiggins said. "Reason I came down, I was talking to your pal Link today..."

"Yeah, I see he's back in the news again. Heard it on TV. What a bunch of fucking shit that is, fucking assholes fucking up his totem pole."

"That's out already?"

"Like I said, I saw it on the radio."

"Well, yeah. And I was talking to Link about it, and he told me that he had picked a cigarette butt off the street a few days ago that some asshole flicked at him outside his house."

"Fuck, yes, and he gave it to me. I've got it right here, man. Sorry I didn't call you about it. I didn't know you needed it like special delivery."

"How would you? The main thing is, you've got it, right?"

"Sure do. C'mon."

The Scrounger and Detective Wiggins said goodbye to the manager woman and headed over to the former derelict's cottage. They stepped inside, and on the Formica kitchen table, the Scrounger pulled a Glad plastic sandwich bag out of a brown earthenware cup. Inside the baggie: the asshole's butt.

"Fantastic," Wiggins said, pulling out his digital tape recorder, which looked more like a cigarette lighter. "Now, I'm going to save you some paperwork on the chain of custody."

"I've kind of liked doing those reports."

"I'm sure, but I'm a little pressed for time. We've got a couple of scrotelicks on the loose. I'm just going to interview you, OK? Then I can get going on tracking these fuckers down."

Wiggins clicked on the record button. It took him about two minutes to take the Scrounger's statement on the cigarette butt.

He clicked it off and headed out.

"But really, man," he asked, as the Scrounger opened the door for him, "how are you?"

"Physically, I feel pretty fucking good," the Scrounger said. "Otherwise, it's not all that it's cracked up to be."

"That what's supposed to be?"

"Sobriety."

Wiggins laughed, and said, "I've never heard anybody crack it up to be anything other than a drag."

"Maybe," the Scrounger countered, "but for me, it's this or the alternative, and I was getting pretty damn sick of those fucking streets."

Wiggins stopped for a second to take that in. He looked the Scrounger in the eye, extended his hand, and the Scrounger shook it.

"Hang in there," Wiggins said, and in a minute he was back in his car and headed to the DA's crime lab behind the morgue on Broadway.

First, the forensic guys gave Wiggins the bad news. They told him it would take at least a week for them to process the new butt, given all the work thrown on them the past month by the East Side Rapist case of the serial-murderer/rapist ex-cop – the Golden State Killer, they called him now.

The good news, however, was that the lab rats had already run everything that the Scrounger picked up off the pavement the previous month at the unveiling of the totem in Cesar Chavez Plaza, and it occurred to Wiggins that Link told him how the camera crew had used the ceremony to introduce themselves to the western world.

"You got the results?" the detective asked the technicians.

"We've got them sitting around in here somewhere, gathering genetic dust," one of the techs told Wiggins.

22/Call me Rad

In the old days, Frankie Cameron made a living off the California Department of Motor Vehicles.

You needed an address on somebody, or you had a license plate you wanted to run, you called the DMV. Over the course of his career, he had tracked down hundreds of people who became sources or stories. He'd go to funerals of the dead who doubled as story subjects, write down the license plate numbers of every car in the parking lot, run their names through the paper's DMV account, and then go back and do the interviews. It was a great trick. Then some phony slimeball private investigator/stalker screwed it up for everybody when he got obsessed with an actress and used the DMV records to track her down and shoot her dead on her Hollywood doorstep. The state Legislature got a little miffed, and that was it for the DMV information superhighway.

Luckily for Frankie, the internet came along. You could find out anything on anybody, including their addresses and phone numbers. Anything, that is, except the people behind the license plates. You wanted to run a plate, you needed to know somebody, and Frankie needed to run a plate, or 12.

Frankie happened to know a few somebodies. He got on the phone with one in the safety of the parking lot of the same McDonald's where a few hours earlier he wolfed down a two-cheeseburger Value Meal in the company of Annette Smith-

Bennett.

Frankie rolled down the windows and waited while his source put him on hold. A pleasant breeze blew through his rental car.

It didn't take long.

"Konstantin Cosmenko," the voice told him.

Frankie's reaction: stunned.

"Cosmenko?" he repeated.

He thought to himself, "Wouldn't you fucking know it."

A woman named Alana Cosmenko had run a fake financial firm in Folsom and strung together a fishline of more than a dozen separate mortgage fraud rings, which employed straw buyers to purchase homes at inflated values from sellers who, for their regular fees, kicked back six figures to her, which she forwarded to her mob bosses, who used the proceeds to buy targeted Facebook ads ahead of the 2016 presidential election to depress the black and Bernie votes and to bring the nut jobs out of their isolated deplorability.

Dozens of participants in the mortgage fraud scheme were convicted on plea deals. They paid restitution. They got probation. Only one took it to trial, and that was Alana Cosmenko, and the United States showed her the consequences of that stupidity by recommending and obtaining a five-year term for her in federal prison.

"That's C-o-s-m-e-n-k-o, Cosmenko," Frankie repeated. "First name Konstantin, K-o-n-s-t-a-n-t-i-n. Middle name Ilyich, I-l-y-i-c-h.... And, yes, I would like the address if you could give it to me.... That's on River Ridge Way? In Folsom? Right, and don't worry about it. I'll find another way to trace it or I won't even show up on the doorstep. I may not have to go there anyway. But it's just good to know where he lives. So he comes back to River Ridge, but all the vans are registered in his name at the Jackson Highway address? Don't worry about it."

Frankie trembled when he got off the phone. He did not want to backtrack into the world of the previous year. These were not the nicest people. The Reverend Konstantin-Bob Cosmenko-Jones, for instance, looked like a guy who did not have good table manners. But the more he thought about it, sitting in his rental with the Skullcandy still in his ears and the afternoon breeze blowing fresh and cool, he realized he didn't have a choice.

He searched on his cell phone for the nearest Starbucks. They had the best free WiFi anywhere, and since they got publicly humiliated for running a couple of black men out of a joint in Philadelphia earlier in the year, you didn't even have to buy anything to use it. Or their bathrooms.

He found one on Bradshaw Road.

Zoom to Starbucks. Order a tall Pike. Take a seat at the rail. Punch up PACER, the online federal court file retriever system, on the computer. Run the name – Cosmenko, Konstantin. Boom – a hit. An asset seizure case to recoup unpaid taxes related to fraudulently obtained proceeds from the charitable items donated to the Russian Slavic USA Pentecostal Church by saps from all over the world – $57,000 seized from the church's bank account, uncontested. Wham, bam, thank you, ma'am – case closed. Call up the Sacramento Superior Court website. Run the name – Cosmenko, Konstantin. No hits. You're in a hurry now. Run the name of the company White Rock USA. Nothing. Damn. Let's try Russian Slavic USA Pentecostal Church for lawsuits: boom – a hit. Pull the digital file on your old account: goddamn if the motherfucker wasn't filed just two months ago – by the church, against something called the *Slavic News of Sacramento*, and its editor, a Radimir Valishnikov. Frankie downloaded the first document in the field. Take a deep breath. You don't have to run downtown to check out the file before they lock up the courthouse at 4 p.m., he reminded himself. It's all right there, in your computer. Take another deep breath. Take a nap if you want.

Click, click, click. Click to real party of interest: on behalf of the plaintiffs, The Reverend Konstantin "Bob" Cosmenko-Jones. Looks like the fucker changed his name. Click straight to the alleged facts. Click – very interesting. It looked like the *Slavic News of Sacramento – TSNS –* had been kicking the church's ass up and down Folsom Boulevard all year long. Click – *TSNS* raised questions about the church setting up an import-export

140

business, White Rock USA, to handle the charity side of the operation. Click – *TSNS* says that Russian Pentecostal shook down the flock for millions of dollars in donated goods ranging from scrap metal to late 1990s automobiles to used clothing, used furniture, books, records, baby strollers, lawn mowers, computers, TV sets, washer-dryers, vibrators, violins, chess sets, bicycles, used anything you could think of. Click – Russian Pentecostal collected all this shit under the guise of shipping it off to the underprivileged of Russia, Ukraine and other former Soviet Republics. Click – the *TSNS* said White Rock didn't ship shit to anywhere. Click – White Rock/Slavic sold all the donated crap under the cover of darkness out of its warehouse in West Sacramento. Click – nobody knew where the fuck the money went. Click – freighters came in and out of the Port of Sacramento in the dead of night and in the light of day to transport the items to the other side of the world, usually through the Mexican port of Manzanillo. Click – the stories raised the question, if there's no donated shit going out of the port, then what the fuck is White Rock USA shipping out on those goddamn boats?

Frankie thought it was a good question.

The second of the two documents in the file was the church's IRS 990-EZ report, which identified it as a 501c3 nonprofit corporation. The only officer listed was the Reverend Bob Jones. Check the contributions: $500,000 incoming contributions in the year 2017. Source: unknown. Source: does not have to be disclosed.

It was almost too much for one day.

Frankie knew he needed to slow down. He needed help. He knew of, but had never returned the telephone calls of, *TSNS* editor Radimir Valishnikov. He knew he should have been nicer to Mr. Valishnikov, despite the gentleman's propensity to bombard him with conspiracy theories on deadline. He knew he should have been nicer to the guy.

He punched the numbers of the *Slavic News* into his phone.

Radimir Valishnikov picked up on the first ring. Frankie knew right away that it was Radimir Valishnikov, because Radimir

Valishnikov answered the phone by saying:

"Radimir Valishnikov."

"Mr. Valishnikov?" Frankie asked.

"Yes, this is Radimir Valishnikov. How can I help you."

"Mr. Valishnikov, this is Frankie Cameron with *The Washington Post*."

"Mr. Frankie Cameron? Of *The Washington Post*? Formerly of the *Sacramento Beacon*?"

"That's me, Mr. Valishnikov."

"Mr. Cameron," Radimir Valishnikov said, almost sputtering, "this is quite the surprise – and a great honor."

Frankie did not know what kind of reaction to expect from Radimir Valishnikov, whom he ignored by rote, but whose weekly circulation – printed in both Russian and English – held a paid circulation north of 30,000. This gave it about 100 percent penetration in the Russian community of Sacramento. It was the largest Slavic paper in town, and the only one that did not pulverize Frankie for his coverage of the organized crime madness of the previous year.

And here the guy was praising him like he was a journalistic god or something.

"I cannot believe I am speaking to you, Mr. Cameron," Valishnikov gushed, making Frankie feel like a total asshole. "While I have got you on the line, I should tell you – earlier this year, we reprinted all of your articles from last year, with the permission of the *Beacon*, of course. And I must tell you, your articles generated more interest than anything we have ever published. I must also tell you, the overwhelming reaction to your articles has been positive. It is true that there are many, many people in our community who have avoided hard work, who despise the American system, who long for Mother Russia. But I do not believe they make up the majority of our community. Just as our readers responded well to your articles, they have expressed an appreciation for the articles I have reported on the preacher who sells snake oil."

Frankie told Valishnikov about his assignment to the California congressional races and the money trail leading him to

142

White Rock USA. He told him about his trip to the warehouse in West Sacramento, and then to the Russian Slavic USA Pentecostal Church, in Rancho Cordova, the lawsuits against the *Slavic News of Sacramento*.

"You have found the motherlode," Valishnikov told Frankie.

"It is a goddamn story, that's for sure," Frankie said. "Congratulations on stirring the guy into the lawsuit."

"Thank you, Mr. Cameron."

"Call me Frankie."

"Thank you, Frankie."

"Can you tell me something, Rad?"

"I'll try, Mr. Cam…., er, Frankie."

"What is up with this guy's name?"

"We referred to him in our stories the same way you did right now, and that is by his true last name, to which he had it officially changed, which is Cosmenko-Jones. He is known in the church only as Bob Jones, and that is a fairly recent development – I believe it has to do with his sister's legal entanglements. He had operated the church for nearly 25 years under his birth name of Konstantin Cosmenko."

"And what about this lawsuit against you?" Frankie asked Valishnikov.

"Our attorneys tell me I have absolutely nothing to worry about," Rad said. "Mainly, because everything that we published is true, and we have much of it on videotape. And there is much more that we have on videotape that we have not reported yet. Would you like to see it?"

"As a matter of fact," Frankie said, "I would like that very much."

23/Bedford…

Detective Andrew Wiggins arrived at his desk at 8 a.m. on Tuesday, May 15, with a cup of coffee in his hand and a stack of reading material piled up on his chair. He set the coffee down on his desk, hung up his brown sports coat, grabbed the printouts and newspaper from his seat, plopped himself down and dug into his reading.

First, the *Sacramento Beacon*. On the front page, the one-word, 60-point headline: *DESECRATION*, with a half-page picture of the swastikas painted across the chest of the Cesar Chavez statue. The story ran over the byline of a new reporter, Loni Cohen. It read:

"Downtown Sacramento woke up to an outrage Wednesday. The Cesar Chavez statue in the center-of-town plaza that was named for the co-founder of the United Farm Workers Union and one of the most revered Latino figures in the history of California and the United States, had been spray-painted with white swastikas and the initials KKK. The unidentified vandals apparently had tried to first pull the statue down from its concrete mooring with a truck.

"Men and women wept in the street at the site of the vandalism. City officials wiped away tears when they crossed I Street from City Hall to inspect the damage. The mayor vowed that Sacramento police would capture the villain or villains responsible for the apparent racist desecration, and he promised a $100,000 cash reward for information on whoever did it.

"This reward is a statement of Sacramento's commitment to justice, to the working people of this city and this country, and to our resolve to find and prosecute to the fullest extent of the law whoever is responsible for this abomination," the mayor told reporters at an impromptu news conference conducted on the sidewalk in front of the Chavez statue..

"Investigators believe that the same suspects who are responsible for the Chavez vandalism also apparently embedded a knife in the rear of the Adams totem pole on the east side of the park, sources said. Police Chief Samuel Kahn did not confirm the knifing or what it meant. Sources said that the knife pinned a note to the sculpture, but they did not disclose its contents."

144

Next a printout from a Washington Post article that had posted at midnight East Coast time. Wiggins recognized Frankie Cameron's byline. The headline:

Mystery money
poised to help
GOP candidate

Frankie's story stuck to the documented facts, that a company called White Rock USA had created an independent expenditure committee armed with $250,000 in cash to be spent in California's 10th congressional district, on behalf of underdog hard-right Republican Jacob Harland. The story ran down the details of California's top-two primary system and how it could freeze the Democrats out of the general election – even if their combined vote totals outpolled those of the GOP twosome. The story lifted a quote from Harland's website ripping the Republican incumbent, John Bonham, "for going too easy on the illegal aliens who are murdering our people and destroying our country." The story identified White Rock as an import-export company located in West Sacramento with unexplained ties to a Russian megachurch in Rancho Cordova. The story quoted The Slavic News of Sacramento hit pieces – protected as public information, now that they were filed as court documents – that suggested church officials had profited from a charity scam.

About five graphs down, the story picked up:

"California Democratic Party officials late last week filed a lawsuit in federal court in Sacramento to block the committee from spending any money in the 10th District race. A party spokesman said that state Democrats also intended to file a complaint today with the Federal Election Commission and the California Fair Political Practices Commission demanding an investigation into the source of the committee's funds.

"At a time when a special prosecutor in Washington, D.C., and numerous congressional committees are probing the extent of the involvement by foreign agents in our 2016 presidential election, it is incumbent upon our federal law enforcement officials and political representatives to protect us against further intrusions and attacks on our democracy," Jordan Diaz,

the party spokesman, said in a written statement.

"At the very least, we need to know where this money came from and the nature of the links between White Rock USA and the Russian Slavic USA Pentecostal Church. We need to know the source or sources of these funds before they are spent. This information needs to be publicly and immediately disclosed so that the voters of the 10th District can have this information available to them when they make their decisions on their congressional representatives. With voting by mail already underway, we think that it is imperative that a judge bar the committee from spending the money until the disclosure is made."

The story reported on Frankie's observations from the West Sac warehouse and the Rancho Cordova church. It included a no-comment from the woman at the warehouse and it quoted the Reverend Konstantin "Bob" Cosmenko-Jones as having nothing to say.

Jacob Harland, on the other hand, told Frankie in a telephone interview, *"This is nothing more than Washington Post fake news. The Post is hell-bent on pushing for Democrats taking over the House of Representatives, for the purpose of impeaching Donald Trump."* John Bonham declined to comment, and none of the four Democrats fighting it out to finish in the top two had anything to say, either.

The story went on:

"Independent polling conducted on the 10th District race shows a very close race, with Bonham attracting 21 percent of likely voters, the four Democrats each pulling between 13 to 16 percent of the vote, and Harland zooming up into double figures at 10 percent. If Harland's momentum continues, and if he outpolls the Democrats who are splitting their party's vote, a Republican would be sure to return to the House of Representatives from this Central Valley region that appeared ripe for a Democratic takeover.

Beneath *The Washington Post* story was another printout for Detective Wiggins'ss consideration – results of the forensic team's DNA testing on the cigarette butts the Scrounger picked up during his crazy dance at the Lincoln Adams totem pole unveiling. The scorecard: A guy wanted on a rape out of Detroit; a gentleman from Parsons, Kansas, arrested under six different names in four different states, all of it minor potatoes – brown-bagging a 40 ouncer in a public park in Seattle, stealing a pack of cigarettes in Portland, a bar fight in Reno, jumping the fare gate at the 12th Street BART station in downtown Oakland. Two dope dealers from L.A. who'd been clean for 10 years. A bail skip out of Tucson – residential burglary, it looked like. Three parolees – none of them absconded, all apparently meeting the terms and conditions of their releases – from right here in Sacramento.

Those were the first seven.

As for the eighth entry on Wiggins's ss worksheet, the cig-butt DNA came back to a young man by the name of Bedford MacMillian. A native of Munford, Tennessee, MacMillian was now 22 years old.

He'd been on a notable run.

Three years earlier, administrators at his high school reported him to the police for sending a racist text message to one of his teachers. A year later, Memphis police caught him spray-painting the N-word on the sleeping bag of a homeless African American man asleep on the street, down around Beale and Main. Most recently, they took him into custody when he punched a young black woman at a Memphis rally to remove a statue of a confederate Civil War general.

Wiggins signed onto his computer and ran a quick Google search. He saw that MacMillian once even made the news in a little country-town newspaper north of Memphis. It read:

MacMillian, 19, was arrested in his parents' Munford home and charged with making threatening remarks to a biology teacher who texted his students on the last day of school, "Have a great summer, and remember to read at least one book." According to Tipton County School Board officials the student responded by telling the teacher on a group text message 'Roast in hell, N-----.'"

Link rang the doorbell of the pretty little wooden yellow frame house on 22nd Street, near F Street. Amazing, he thought. He and Manuela only lived, what, eight blocks away from each other? He must have passed her house eight million times over the past 15 years, on his deep-thinking walks across every sidewalk from the river to the Capitol City Freeway, from the railroad tracks to Southside Park.

"What have you got there, *bruto*?" Manuela asked, as she took the brown paper sack out of his arms and held the door open to let him in.

She peeked inside at a collection of street tacos.

"Chando's is good," she said. "Chicken, chicken, chicken, chicken, and chicken," she said. "You couldn't find one *carnita*? I see you conserve your creativity for your totem poles."

"You did ask me to keep it light."

"Not even any rice or beans? *Bruto*, have you seen me box? I need to eat."

"I did ask for extra lime," he said.

"I see that," she said. "Very thoughtful. When they discover my malnourished body, I'll leave a note: 'I did get the extra lime.' "

Link felt so comfortable when he walked into the place that he plopped into the couch in Manuela's front room as if he owned the joint, even though it was the first time he'd ever stepped through her doorway. His smile went coast to coast as Manuela took the bag into the kitchen. He heard her scuffle around some, before the pleasure center of his brain delighted to the sound of two beer bottles popping. Manuela soon returned with two 22-ounce San Dogs crooked into the fingers of one hand and a platter filled with five chicken tacos balanced on the other. The tacos surrounded a pile of exquisitely fresh, sea-salted corn chips from the Nugget Market, inconveniently located in

West Sac. Link plucked a chip off the plate, still warm to the touch. He crunched into it.

"Send them back," he said. "It's been at least forty-five minutes since they came out of the oven."

"Forty-five minutes, huh," Manuela said, as she held her beer bottle over Link's head and gave it a tipping motion as if she were about to soak some sense into him.

Before she could pull back from the joke, about a half-ounce moistened Link's longish hair.

He didn't react to the moist sensation that absorbed into the top of his head.

"Children are starving in south Modesto," he said, "and you waste the sacrament."

She plopped down next to him, smiling. Happy. He felt a glow inside that seemed to reflect what he saw on her face.

"So," Manuela said, killing half a taco in one bite, "what do you want to see?"

"That depends," Link said.

"On what?"

"On what you got."

"You should know, then, that I have everything. If it's not in this channel, it's on that channel."

"Hmmm. It's been a while since I saw *Chinatown*."

"*Chinatown*'s out."

"Why?"

"I hate the ending."

"Everybody does. It is still the greatest."

"No, it's not. Pick another."

"*North by Northwest*."

"No. Too soon."

"What do you mean, 'too soon'?"

"This is only our second date. The make-out scene on the train is too intense for a second date. It might give us ideas."

"I have no ideas. I am just a man."

"That's what I'm afraid of. Pick again."

"*Psycho*."

"You are a terrible human being."

149

"How about... how about – let me think. How about *Damn Yankees? The Last Waltz? Sometimes A Great Notion? The Good, The Bad, and the Ugly?*"

"I'm kind of intrigued by *The Last Waltz.*"

"What do you say we save it for a Saturday night," Link said, "or when Ray Wylie Hubbard comes to town in September."

"Who's he?"

"I'll tell you in September."

"We could still go see *Black Panther*," Manuela said.

"I'd fall asleep, and my tailbone's been sore lately. Movie theaters don't sit as well with you when you can't sit as well as you used to."

"Old men really are more like big babies."

"It's really not such a bad thing," Link said.

"I've got one for you – *L.A. Confidential.*"

"That will work."

Link and Manuela finished their tacos and were halfway through their beers when she found the movie on one of the streaming services.

It didn't take Link long to go completely limp – Russell Crowe barely got it going with Kim Basinger before Link slipped into slumber. He woke up right when Sgt. Dudley Smith took a shotgun blast in the back from Ed Exley, up in the Stocker oil fields, almost the end of the movie.

He tried to discretely rouse himself, hoping that maybe Manuela thought he'd seen the whole thing. "You're maybe the best movie companion ever," she said. "I don't have to worry about interruptions from people who want to *talk.*"

"Oh, well, that scene where Dudley kills Kevin Spacey in the kitchen was the giveaway," he said. "It can be kind of tough to follow, if you haven't read the book."

"You slept through seventy-five percent of the movie."

"It has been a trying month."

"I'll give you that. Next time it'll be with coffee, not beer."

"Oh, well. I've been cutting back some lately, and I just can't handle the stuff the way I used to."

"None of us are what we used to be."

"Least of all me. But I have to tell you one thing."

"And that is?"

"This is the first time I have ever fallen asleep on a woman's couch, watching a movie or not watching a movie."

"Thanks, *bruto*. I never knew I was that boring."

"Just the opposite. It's like I feel like… I feel like I'm at home here. At home with you. I'm not worried about what's going to happen, because the moments that I'm around you are very comfortable. Like, so much other stuff just doesn't matter. You are the happening that is happening. It's comfortable."

Manuela had never received a compliment quite like that. She stroked Link's head with her hand, the first physical move of the night.

"Your hair is sticky," she said.

"I wonder why."

"It will wash out."

He smiled and closed his eyes.

She continued stroking his hair, and he nestled into her, side by side on the couch, with her soft hair floating into his chin and cheek, and him now drawing his left arm around her shoulder and pulling her into him.

Then he fell asleep again.

*****

The truth was that Link woke up on Manuela's couch in the middle of the night, alone, but with traces of woman everywhere.

First, he had been tucked in – covered in a blanket. Somebody had also placed a pillow under his head. His boots had been removed.

A heavy sleeper, Link missed it all. The evidence showed that Manuela brought out a bedsheet to slide over the couch covers, but apparently gave up on the idea once she saw that the longish fellow had gone under. Most nights of the year, Link led the league when it came to sleeping. Nothing got in the way of his unconsciousness, expect for one thing: beer. Any more than 16 ounces and he was up at least once in the middle of the night to drain the lizard.

Sure as the pouring rain in redwood winter, the San Dog

stirred him off Manuela's couch. Who knew what time it was, or where Manuela kept her bathroom. Last thing he wanted was to stumble around in the dark and have somebody wake up and break his ribs with a left hook, so Link picked himself up, showed himself to the door, and walked home.

He made it there without incident, the streets empty of sound and traffic. A light wind ruffled the trees, and streetlights illuminated the spaces between the elm branches enough to cast his shadow 20 feet ahead, down to a dozen, less, until the likeness in front of him slipped to his rear and another one appeared, each chasing the other into oblivion along the nine giddy blocks to his front porch.

Link made it to the bathroom easy enough, and he pulled back the threadbare sheets and blanket on his bed, crawling in and thinking about this real woman and the real way he felt about her.

25/*The Shipping News*

Right about the same time that Lincoln Adams snuggled on the couch with Manuela Fonseca, Frankie Cameron did a little snuggling of his own, with Radimir Valishnikov, editor of one of Sacramento's most prominent Russian-language newspapers.

Frankie and Rad did their cuddling at Café Marika, a Hungarian restaurant on J Street. All his years in Sacramento, Frankie had never been to the place. It took a mystery meeting with a Russian to finally get him to go inside.

Rad had already arrived and secured a quiet table on the side of the nearly-empty restaurant on Memorial Day night. Rad looked nothing like he sounded in his several phone conversations with Frankie. The guy had a deep, dark voice. It didn't fit with his short, squat posture, his balding top, his longish, curly gray hair on both the sides of the aisle, his bushy gray mustache already littered with bread crumbs, his four-day growth of graying, unkempt beard. Rad looked to be about 50 and a little thick on the sides, his handles protruding outward from a long-sleeved shirt about a size too tight, tucked into his light-brown, inappropriately-fashioned slim-fit dress slacks. Frankie figured that Rad probably didn't look so stuffed into his clothes back before he packed on the poundage. In fact, Frankie deduced that Rad had not been clothes shopping since the early years of the Obama administration, given his dinner companion's frayed, faded-purple collar and his shiny brown pants and his brown worn and unpolished loafers that appeared in need of a second or third trip to the cobbler.

"Good to finally meet you in person," Frankie said, taking his seat across the table from Rad, who did not stand up.

"Here," Rad said, with only a trace of his Russian accent, reaching into his briefcase after the two shook hands.

He handed Frankie five DVDs packaged in separate envelopes.

They were all marked "White Rock USA" with five recent and different dates.

Frankie deposited the DVDs into his backpack. He folded his hands on the table and looked at Rad who was looking down at his menu.

"Strongly recommend the Chicken Paprikash," Rad said. "You can't go wrong with the goulash. The stuffed cabbage is better than acceptable."

With only five entrees on the menu, Rad had just about hit them all. Frankie went with the chicken. A glass of the house cab seemed in order, he told the waitress, who doubled as the restaurant's owner. Rad chose iced tea.

"You will like these films," Rad told Frankie.

"But before we get started on them," Frankie interrupted, "have you ever heard of anybody by the name of Matthew

Johannsen?"

The name didn't seem to rattle anything loose in Rad Valishnikov's head.

"I don't believe I have," the editor said. "Should I?"

"I don't know," Frankie said. "I don't even know who he is myself."

Rad picked up his story about the DVDs.

"We shot them from the top of a rice silo, inside the port. We have some friends at the port – union men, dockworkers, upset that she would arrange for her own labor to unload the ships. We have established a very excellent relationship with them, and they have alerted us to shipping activity that they thought would interest us, all of which involved a Panamanian-flagged vessel, the *Grandeur*. They provided us an unobstructed view of the harbor operations from the silo, and we were able through public sources to obtain schedules and manifests on all vessels that come into and out of the port. It was not difficult for us to piece together which shipping companies the church and its waterfront operation employed. You tell me you have met the woman Ludmila Yolanavytch?"

"Not that I know of."

"The skinny woman who dyes her hair pink. I think you mentioned her, in association with the White Rock USA warehouse office, on Del Monte Street."

"Yes, her. We are fast friends."

"Ludmila directs White Rock's operation in the port. We became aware of her in our previous reporting on the church's charity fraud. She had organized the shipments of all the donated items out of their warehouse in West Sacramento – the shipments that according to our reporting they in time stopped making, in that they began selling off the items to sources we were never able to identify. We have long been able to film her activities, her visits to the port offices and to the waterfront itself. You will be able to see her in the disc that we have marked DVD 'A.' There is not much more to see on that one, other than the mere documentation of her frequent visits to the office and to the dock."

154

"Okay."

"The second DVD is just stock footage of the cargo ship *Grandeur*. We have pictures of its calls at ports from Hong Kong, to Incheon, Long Beach, Galveston, Novorossiysk, and beyond."

"Novorossiysk?"

"The largest Russian port on the Black Sea. The *Grandeur*, you should know, has been in operation for approximately ten years. It has moved cargo from every continent in the world, more than a hundred ports of call. It is also the vessel that the Slavic USA church has exclusively employed to ship its collections of charitable goods to Ukraine and Russia, even on the occasions – as we have alleged in our coverage – when they shipped nothing of the kind. If you check the shipping schedules at the Port of Sacramento, you will find that it sailed into harbor on New Year's Eve morning – last December 31st – at exactly three-oh-one a.m. The schedule shows that it left the Port of Sacramento approximately three hours later, and its manifest shows that it departed with only one category of cargo – two DeCoulomb Model R-x40s. There were no so-called charitable items included in the passage, as the church has represented in its solicitations for donations."

The mention of the luxury sedan sparked a visual in Frankie's brain, from earlier in the month, when he saw one of its kind being loaded off a truck and into the White Rock USA warehouse at the Port of Sacramento.

"DeCoulombs," Frankie repeated. "I'm pretty sure I told you about what I saw on my visit to the warehouse a couple weeks ago."

"You did," Rad assured him. "Which should make all of these videos even more interesting to you. You will see that DVDs 'B,' 'C,' and 'D' document additional visits of the *Grandeur* to the port here. When you examine the videos, you will see that on each of these occasions, precisely two DeCoulomb Model R-40s are loaded onto the ship from 18-wheeled trucks that had been waiting at the dock. In each of those instances, Miss Ludmila Yolanavytch oversaw the loading of the vehicles, along with the driver of the truck, whom we do not recognize. She appears in each of the videos to be supervising the shipments."

"Do we know where the cars were going?"

"The manifest says to Manzanillo, on the west coast of Mexico."

"That's interesting," Frankie said. "And the cars are brand new?"

"I believe so."

"Help me out on this, if you can, Rad: Why would anybody who has an automobile factory, in – where is it? Isn't it the old Ford plant in Hayward?"

"That is correct."

"Why would they send it to Mexico out of West Sacramento? Why not just put it on a boat in Oakland?"

"I cannot answer these questions, Mr. Frankie."

"And these cars retail for how much?"

"That would be a hundred thousand dollars each, times eight, which would equal eight hundred thousand in value, US."

"And the dates of these shipments to Mexico were?"

"You know about Dec. 31st. The others were January 31st, Feb. 28th, and March 31st."

"And this is not counting the one I saw coming into the warehouse a couple weeks ago."

"That one is an interesting anomaly," Rad said. "We are not aware of it having been shipped out yet through the port. I might add for my own purposes that the important thing to note is, none of the donated goods – the so-called charitable items – were listed on the ship's manifests. Only the automobiles, and the shipments were made in the name of some automobile broker up in Auburn."

Frankie and Rad occupied a table in the corner of the room, one of only six in all of Café Marika. Any more and the two-person crew who owned and operated the place would not have been able to keep up with traffic. Mrs. Marika brought out the paprikash with a couple of slices of French bread while Mr. Marika sat at one of the empty tables and counted the day's receipts.

"I have been watching these people for years, Mr. Cameron, and..."

"Call me Frankie, please."

"Okay, Mr. Frankie please," Rad responded. He paused and looked Frankie in the eye for almost the first time, to see if he'd gotten the joke. Frankie laughed obligingly. "I've been watching them for years, and writing about them in *The Slavic News*, and I have contacted reporters from your old paper to see if they were interested. In fact, I have sent you emails on various occasions."

"I know," Frankie said, sheepish.

"Yes. You were always polite, but always busy – harassed, it seemed. This would have been about six, seven years ago."

"When I was in the court house. I'm telling you, man, I was so slammed over there. I never had time to wipe my ass. If you weren't *in* the courthouse with a story, with a case, in front of a judge, there was just no way."

"I understand, sir. I sent you my materials because I respected your work. I did not know at the time that your work was so consuming. I must confess, I harbored some animosity toward you, and toward the other reporters at the *Beacon* who did not follow up on my theories. I just wish you were over there now, to cover the lawsuit that White Rock has filed against me. I believe that White Rock has set themselves up for a terrific lashing. You read their filing. You tell me, who came out looking worse – me, the target of their baseless allegations, or them, in the factual stories that I wrote, edited and published?"

"I've got to admit," Frankie said. "I think you win out. Unless you made all that stuff up."

"No, Frankie, that I can assure you. As you are about to find out."

Jordan Diaz monitored the 48-hour expenditure reports posted by the Federal Elections Commission. For 12 days after lunch at Tako, nothing. Then, early Tuesday, May 29 – exactly one week before the election – the $250,000 bomb landed.

Jordan scanned the internet. He saw that White Rock USA's ad buyers plastered on Brightbeat's California edition, the Daily Crawler, and Foxed News online. They pounded Facebook, Twitter and Instagram. They honed in on California, to the Central Valley, to Stanislaus and San Joaquin Counties. They red-circled the addresses of an estimated 25,000 individual voters identified as friendlies or potential friendlies from voter lists compiled by their political professionals. They carpet-bombed the internet with retweets. They masked Facebook posts to make it look like these strange entries into targeted newsfeeds had been sent by friends or family. They pinpointed their messaging so specifically that Jordan Diaz knew that he didn't know half of what they knew about their audience.

He found the ads on Reddit easily enough. He got through okay on 4chan. His problem: he could not access anybody's private emails or listen in on robocalls, nor could he check the individual Facebook news feeds that political profilers were able to target. What a combination – voters, their addresses, their social media information. If you were smart enough and worked hard enough and had enough money, and if your audience was small enough, you could damn near prepare individual advertisements for each and every individual voter you wanted to target.

Jordan Diaz concluded from his preliminary scan that White Rock made its pitch to: a right-wing, anti-immigrant, anti-Latino segment of the electorate that saw itself as the victim of an international liberal global economic order obsessed with climate change that wanted to drag people out of their cars and force them to ride on high-speed trains and take their assault rifles away and close down prisons filled with black criminals so that more money could be diverted to housing and educating the children of illegal aliens, making them more employable and harder to deport after they had graduated from the same colleges that the children of peach growers in the 10th Congressional District of California could never get into.

Jordan Diaz knew there was no counteracting the White Rock USA campaign. The hard-right play on behalf of Harland would draw a couple thousand disenchanted, normally-non-participating, out-of-the-mainstream right-wing voters into the fray. Usually, they stayed hidden beneath their rocks, but Trump had drawn them out, and now they could propel Jacob Harland into the finals.

"Bonham to non-Americans: You're Welcome Here," was the headline stamped across a caricature of a Mexican-looking man running across a dotted line with one side of it marked "Mexico" and the other labeled as "United States." That one ran on Brightbeat and the Daily Crawler. A click on the ad took the reader to a website with a picture of a smiling Bonham and his Latina wife. There were no "Home," "About," or "Contact" pages, just a series of pictures and bullet points on how Bonham supported the Deferred Action for Childhood Arrivals Act and how he favored giving American jobs to illegal aliens.

He called up the more traditional media advertising platforms – the *Modesto Beacon*, the *Tracy News*, the *Stockton Recorder*. On these sites the White Rock USA campaign took on a more practical approach. They flashed pictures of Bonham circled in red with the diagonal line through his face, underlined with the reading, "He's not a conservative." Alternatively, a picture of a smiling Jacob Harland appeared, with him wearing a red Make America Great Again baseball cap.

The sun had yet to rise before Jordan Diaz pulled out his cell phone to contact the Democratic Congressional Campaign Committee to inform them that White Rock had rolled into action.

Before he punched in all the numbers, his phone lit up with an incoming call from Frankie Cameron.

"I guess you've seen them by now," Frankie said.

"I have," Jordan replied.

"Will there be anything on TV?"

"I doubt it. It looks to me like they know exactly who to target, and they don't want to waste their money on platforms that don't work on their crowd."

"So, I just wanted to let you know I'm on it. You want to say anything yet?"

"Not me. I can get you somebody, though."

"That would be nice. Meanwhile, another name has come up. Have you ever heard of a guy who works over at MJ Public Affairs named Matthew Johannsen?"

"Sure. What's up with him?"

"Well, he's got something to do with Russia, and as you know, that is a subject near and dear to me."

"I don't know about that," Jordan said. "All I know is he's been around forever. He worked for Reagan on the sixty-six campaign, kind of a coffee boy, but it got him into the conservative movement. Mostly California-based, founded MJ Public Affairs right about the time Reagan ran for president the first time, in seventy-six. Hauled in the biggest corporate clients in the state. Got a big piece of Proposition 13 with Howard Jarvis, worked Reagan's presidential campaign in eighty, stayed west after Reagan got elected, pushed a fairly hard-right line – way more right than Ronnie. Became the California contact for the Atwater-Manafort-and-Stone group that got old man Bush elected president with the Willie Horton stuff."

"That's interesting, Stone and Manafort. And Russia."

"Became the chairman of the California Republican Party when it went into the crapper, financially. Had a little bit of a run with Schwarzenegger, during the recall campaign in oh-three. He got the thing rolling in dough, and then he just kind of got old and left town. It's been a few years since I've heard anything about him. I think he's got a ranch up north of Tahoe. Acts like he's Ben Cartwright or something. One thing I do know – he still does a little work for the Republican Congressional Campaign Committee, mostly California stuff. I mean, he's not in the everyday line of fire. I think he's just kind of doing some

160

advisory thing. Strategy things. On his own."

"Do you know if he's hooked up at all with White Rock USA?"

"Did he help out with their I.E.? I'd seriously doubt it. He's working on behalf of all the incumbents, is my understanding. If he's doing anything in that race, it would be on behalf of John Bonham. Does he have any kind of business association with them, outside politics? Not that I know. It wouldn't surprise me if he did, especially if they've got business with Russia. It would make perfect sense that if the Russians did have any such interests that it would require some advice on how to get things done. And he would be their guy. But White Rock is so, so *Russian*, to begin with, I'd say probably not."

Frankie had been scribbling furiously while Jordan spoke, and it took him a minute to wrap it up and get back to the business at hand.

"Now," he asked, "about that quote."

"I won't be saying anything," Jordan said, "but I'll get you something from Washington, D.C."

"If I needed something from Washington, D.C., I would have stayed in Washington, D.C.," Frankie said. "I need a quote from Modesto CA, is what I need. In fact, I'm down here right now. I'm going to walk precincts today with this Mary Lynne Sorenson. Feature stuff, out on the street with the candidates in a hotly-contested flip seat."

"Oh, God," Jordan said. "Not her."

"Why not her? I just met her a couple days ago. She seems great. I mean, not that I'd vote for her or anything, but she's real. From town, a nurse, gives a shit, cared about the schools, ran for the school board, won, been fairly coherent in public office. What's wrong with her?"

"Nothing," Diaz said, "except that she can't beat Bonham."

"Oh really."

"Too wooden. Too Bernie for the Central Valley. The party people are more behind this Jesse Seymour guy. Young, good looking, rich, also from the area, polls really well. Has the best chance of the four."

"Might have been nice then if the party would have endorsed him," Frankie said.

"I'm not so sure about that," Jordan said. "It actually might have hurt him. Lots of indies in this district. They don't like party labels so much. The more you stay away from them, the better. His Bay Area venture capitalist background plays okay with people around here. Half of the people who live here work in the Bay Area anyway. The Dems will go with whoever they put up, they hate Trump so much. The independents and the never-Trump Reeps might go for a Jesse Seymour type. They'd never go for Sorenson."

"Because she's a woman? Hell, man. They voted for Hillary."

"Sorenson's way more left. All those techies you see on the ACE trains going over the hill every morning? We've focus-grouped them. They like Seymour."

The Altamont Corridor Express tried to bridge the chasm between the well-paying jobs in the Silicon Valley where you needed a million dollars to buy a three-bedroom tract home built in the fifties, and the job-starved Central Valley where you could still get a McMansion for $350,000, if only you could get a job that paid more than the $15 an hour you got in the Amazon warehouse in Patterson, a growing little exurb beyond the cherry fields on the western edge of the district.

"Listen, right now Bonham is polling about twenty-five percent and Harland is looking like he's a got chance to get past all the Democrats," Jordan Diaz went on. "You can see how fucked up that is. Seymour is second at fifteen percent, with the other three Dems right on his heels. The way we see it, every vote that goes to Sorenson and not Seymour actually helps Harland, which helps Bonham, who will kill Harland in a one-on-one. Sorenson's bumping up around twelve percent, and believe me, that is her ceiling. She's going nowhere. She's tapped out. Seymour has a much higher ceiling. It'll go even higher after the primary – if he makes it through."

"I'm still going to go hang with Sorenson today. For the story."

"I can't tell you what to do."

162

"She's a good story."

"I agree."

"Whatever I do, I'm going to weave this stuff in on the ads. It plays into the other thing we talked about."

"The Russian editor's videos?"

"Yeah."

"I know nothing about that. I can't help you a bit."

"You won't need to," Frankie told him.

27/...and Beauregard

"No rush," Detective Andrew Wiggins had told Link in an early-morning phone message, concerning a break in the Chavez statue and totem vandalism case. "Just come down when you can. And just make it today."

Link took the message to heart. He took his time.

Before he called Wiggins, he dialed Manuela, who had gone into work early.

"I have to tell you, *bruto*," she said, in good humor. "You are a real live wire. You ask a girl to go to the movies and you don't even take her to the theater. Then you fall asleep on her couch."

"I, uh…"

"You don't let her tuck you in, and in the middle of the night, you leave. No goodbye."

"I did fold the blanket and placed it neatly on top of the pillow."

"I appreciate that. Next time you come over, at least let me put the sheet on the couch, before you pass out on it. What did you drink, one beer?"

"I finished at least half of that 22-ouncer."

Link explained the circumstances of his middle-of-the-night

departure; how he didn't want to wake her up, how he didn't want to pee his pants, how he didn't feel comfortable enough to take his pants off sleeping on her couch.

"A modest one," she said. "Next time, I'll leave the bathroom light on and the door cracked open, so you can find your way to do your business."

"What if you wake up and see a shadow scurry past your door?"

"I really don't think you have much to fear," Manuela said. "But I should warn you."

"What?"

"I do keep a gun at my bedside."

"You do?"

"Maybe."

"Why?"

"There have been some funny things that have happened in my neighborhood."

"Mine, too."

"There is one big difference between us, though, *bruto*."

"And that is?"

"I am a woman."

"An unmistakable fact. But there is one huge drawback to having a gun in the home, no matter your gender."

"And that is?"

"The chances greatly increase that somebody is going to get shot."

Manuela laughed again.

"Hopefully, it will not be me," she said.

"Or me," Link replied.

"That's why I'm leaving the nightlight on for you, b*ruto*."

Link's brain stalled momentarily at the idea of more overnights at her house.

Manuela broke the tension.

"You know, *bruto*, there is another way to get around the potential problem of me shooting you on your way to the bathroom in the middle of the night."

Talk about a floater she looped into him high and right down the middle of the plate, like in the slo-pitch softball games where he used to crack them out of Roosevelt Park. He let this one fall. As a younger man, he would have deposited it onto Q Street. Older and wiser, he now played coy.

"What's that?" he asked.

"Well," Manuela said. "You could always sleep upstairs."

"You have a guest room up there?"

More laughter.

"That is not what I was thinking."

He laughed some more. His nerves were gone.

"Since you put it that way," he said, "I can stop over on my way to the bus stop."

"First of all, I'm at work," Manuela said.

"I could stop over there."

"Link."

"That was a joke. I mean it was kind of a joke. I mean, the truth is I have to fight myself to keep from drooling in your presence."

Another pause.

"OK," he said. "I can wait until tonight."

"I should be home around seven," Manuela said.

"I will be there at seven-oh-one."

"You better not be asleep at seven-oh-two."

They hung up, and Link got himself together to catch the 62 bus down Freeport Boulevard to the police station.

He never did understand why they moved police headquarters the six-and-a-half miles south out of downtown, out of the gorgeous old Hall of Justice Building on 7th and H. So what if the place was so small that they had to convert the upstairs holding cells into detective work spaces.

The 62 dropped him off at Fruitridge, a couple blocks up from the inconveniently located police station. A couple minutes later, he took his seat beside the desk of Detective Andrew Wiggins.

"Feels like I've got season tickets to this place," he said.

"Yeah," Wiggins replied. "Everybody around here thinks I've turned you into a snitch."

"Well, you kind of have."

165

"Ha. My snitches either produce or they go to jail. You, you're just a victim."

"I've been a suspect, too."

"I never really thought so."

"Sure you didn't. That's why you had me arrested in the middle of the night, on my own front porch."

"You were never arrested. Just detained, for questioning."

"So, how do I become a snitch."

"First, you have to really be an asshole. You have to really do something wrong, and you have to really get arrested. Next, you have to make a deal with the DA. Then, you have to have access to big fish. You – you don't cover any of those bases."

"A regular guy can't do his part to help keep the city safe?"

"Join Neighborhood Watch," Wiggins advised before getting down to business.

"OK," he said. "I've got some news for you: we have a verified DNA hit on one of those guys on the camera crew."

Wiggins told Link about the young Bedford MacMillian, about the butt that the Scrounger had picked up the day of the totem pole unveiling, and how it matched the butt that the dudes in the SUV flicked at Link in front of his house.

There was more:

"We've got a print, or at least a partial print, off that envelope you gave us a couple weeks ago, too," Wiggins said.

This would be the threat postmarked Arkansas that Link found on his studio floor a couple of weeks earlier.

"The 'we are on our way' guys?"

"That would be the one," Wiggins said. "We think we've got the other guy ID'd. By the way, you haven't seen those knuckleheads lately, have you?"

"Nope. Not a trace."

"That's probably good. You know they're up to no fucking good wherever they are. As for the second guy, we can't say we are absolutely sure. There were fingerprints from at least four people on your Fort Smith letter. I'm thinking a couple of them worked for the Post Office. One set of them, I believe, is yours. I had no idea you were in CLETS. What the fuck did you do?"

"Juvenile indiscretions."

"Nothing since?"

"No."

"Damn."

"What do you mean, damn?"

"Well, you said you wanted to be a snitch. I was thinking I might be able to accommodate you. Back to the prints. We know about you, the postal guys are out, and we had one other partial on another son of a bitch from Covington, Tennessee. It's about fifteen miles up the road from Bedford MacMillian's stomping ground."

Link stroked his cleanly-shaven brown chin and nodded.

"You'll love homeboy's name," Wiggins said to Link.

"I give up."

"David Beauregard Barton."

Wiggins broke out laughing.

Link didn't find it so funny, that he had apparently been placed in the cross hairs by a pair of young men who had been named for Confederate generals and whose statues were being removed, in, among other places, Memphis and New Orleans.

Wiggins repeated the names, "Bedford and Beauregard," to his own alliterative delight.

"Yeah," Link deadpanned. "Rhythmic."

28/*Brazen*

Black Lives Matter activists refused to let Sacramento forget about the police shooting death of Devante Davidson. Their protests persisted into May, although the crowds dwindled from the hundreds to a few dozen. Forensic pathologists dueled over how many times officers shot Devante Davidson in the back and whether he was facing the cops or moving toward them when the first bullet struck him, in either his left thigh or left side, and spun him around in the kill zone of his grandmother's back yard.

Every afternoon, before they set off on their rush-hour marches through the downtown streets, the protesters gathered at the front doorstep of the district attorney's office, which would ultimately decide whether to file criminal charges against the police officers who shot the young man. They grilled hot dogs and swilled soft drinks on the sidewalk in front of the building. before setting off at exactly 5 p.m. into traffic to remind motorists who were off to their Happy Hours, or to their homes in the suburbs to coach their kids' Little League teams, or to enjoy an afternoon game of croquet with the neighbors, or to take target practice at their neighborhood gun range, or to tend to their marijuana plants in the age of California pot legalization, that Devante Davidson was still dead and that it didn't matter if you were in Grandma's back yard – if you were young and black and male there was a damn good chance you could get shot and killed by professional cops who were just doing their jobs.

The last Tuesday in May, about 30 or so protesters finished their hot dogs and had packed away the barbecue in the slanting rays of the late afternoon and early evening.

They had just begun to move away from the DA's building when a black SUV roared out of the Alkali Flat neighborhood to the immediate north and sped south on 9th Street, past the parade formation.

The SUV screeched to a stop about 25 yards away, in the middle of the street, directly in front of the county courthouse.

Protesters looked up, and they saw two white men jump out of the vehicle, run around to the back of the car, open the rear door, and pull out what appeared to be a six-foot tall mannequin that had been painted black. The two men stood the figure up on its feet in the middle of the street, and it appeared to the protesters that some sort of photograph had been attached to the dummy's face. They could not make out the likeness. They had no trouble, however, reading the lettering on the T-shirt that had been pulled over the torso of the dummy: the big, black, block letters very clearly spelled out "BLM."

If there was any question whether the men in the SUV were friend or foe, the two occupants of the vehicle laid it to rest when they reached into the vehicle, retrieved a pair of aluminum baseball bats, and beat the statue that they had just raised into a million tiny bits.

By the time the protesters overcame their shock, the two batsmen jumped back into the SUV and got the hell out of there.

The protesters walked across the street to examine the remains of the statue. To their horror, they saw that the photographed face belonged to Devante Davidson.

Within an hour, Sacramento police Detective Andrew Wiggins had been called to the scattered remnants of the beaten statue, in the middle of 9th Street, just a block and a half from Cesar Chavez Plaza.

Detective Andrew Wiggins was not greeted very warmly by the witnesses to the assault on the mannequin.

"This is your motherfucking fault," one man told him, in a remark directed not so much at the detective but at American society in general, for the way things had played out in this part of the world since 1492.

Wiggins ignored the comment – he was focused on identifying every one of the security cameras that were attached to the DA's building and to the courthouse and even one to the Aladdin Bail Bonds office on 9th Street, looking directly onto the crime scene. The uniforms, meanwhile, worked the crowd for witness statements.

They didn't get much cooperation.

"Talk to you?" was the average response. "When you're killing us?"

Crime scene investigators took pictures. They measured the tracks from the burned rubber that the SUV's tires left behind. With their white plastic gloves, they picked up the T-shirt with the repugnant epithet scrawled across the back and placed it into a brown evidence bag. They did the same with the photostat of Devante Davidson's face that had been attached to the statue. They did their best to gather the shards of what was left of the pummeled statue and put them in a box.

As Wiggins headed down 9th Street in his search for security cameras, the new reporter from the *Beacon* approached him from the side. He recognized Loni Cohen from her work a couple weeks earlier on the Cesar Chavez case. The detective did not hold a high opinion of her kind, but this one, he had come to think, was different.

The day the vandals hit the Plaza, Cohen found out about the note that had been stabbed into the back of the Lincoln Adams totem. She knew exactly what it said, word for word: "*Your Mexican hero is gone. The Indian's piece of crap is next. You take down ours, we take down yours. Signed, True Sons of the Confederacy.*"

When she told Wiggins she knew about the note, word for word, he asked her if she could hold off on running with it. To Wiggins'ss amazement, she complied. It cost her a huge scoop.

So many of those assholes, it seemed to Wiggins, didn't give a damn about investigations. It was all about a ridiculous competition with each other, as if that mattered in the slightest. This young woman reporter seemed different. So, the morning of the mannequin case, he didn't automatically recoil when she reintroduced herself and got down to business.

"What do you think?" Cohen asked. "Same guys?"

He looked at her through a fish eye. He always had to be suspicious of the media, even if he liked the individual reporter. It was in his DNA.

"Are we off the record?" he asked.

"Let me back up," she said. "I've already talked to enough people around here who gave me descriptions of the guys in the car."

"At least they're talking to somebody around here."

"I've also got a description of the car, and I've been told that the tire tracks match the ones from a week ago Monday."

"How'd you find that out?"

"Can't say. I guess the main thing I'm asking is, I mean, we're going to run the story – in fact, we already have posted the story on our website – about what everybody here saw and heard, and..."

"As you should."

"But what I want to know is, would it screw you guys up if I reported the fact that you have a definitive match on the tire tracks?"

It hadn't been a half hour, Wiggins thought. She was plugged in somewhere high.

"I guess I should have thanked you for holding out the stuff in the note," Wiggins said.

"No biggie – no problem," the reporter said. "No expectation. But what about here? Like I said, I don't want to screw up any investigation. It's more important that you catch these guys than for me to confirm what everybody in the world already knows."

"Which is?"

"It's the same guys."

Wiggins laughed – he really did like this one.

"Give me about fifteen minutes," he told the reporter. "Let me run it by our PIO and my bosses. Maybe we do want to put it out."

"Put out what?"

"That it's the same guys."

"Your call," Cohen said.

"You've got my number, right?" he asked.

She did not, so Wiggins gave it to her – a first between him and a reporter.

"Here's mine, too," Loni Cohen said, as she gave Wiggins her business card.

My God, Wiggins thought. Now she's developing me as a source.

"What's your deadline?" he asked.

"These days, our deadline is always. It's like, deadline is an outdated journalistic concept. Nowadays, you get it, you post it."

"All right," he told her. "I'll get back to you as soon as I can."

"Thanks, Detective."

A thought occurred to Wiggins as the reporter walked away. The boys who did this – he had begun referring to them as Bedford and Beuregard – they were getting bolder. He knew he better work fast before they turned their attention from statues and mannequins to real people.

29/*No room for imperfection*

Lincoln Adams took a nap after his bus ride back from the police station. He had another appointment to meet with law enforcement that afternoon – this one at the U.S. Attorney's Office.

Order of business: the federal trial of Ishmail Barghanyan and Dmitri Chernekoff. The two Russian muscle men had been arrested and charged with Link's kidnapping the previous October. Their trial was scheduled for summer, and Link, of course, would be the key witness.

Walking up G Street to his meeting, Link saw the big commotion in front of the county courthouse. Red lights flashed up and down the block. A police helicopter flew overhead. Up in the air, the chopper cops asked everybody below to be on the lookout for a black, late-model GMC Yukon XL. Link recognized the description. He spun left on 9th for a closer look, and who should he see in charge of the street investigation but Detective Andrew Wiggins, inside the yellow police tape, engaged in a detailed conversation with one of the crime scene investigators.

Link strode to the barrier, tall, in his black Levis, black T-shirt and black cowboy boots, his hair flowing beneath a white straw cowboy hat. He was an easy guy to spot.

Wiggins noticed him at the tape, concluded his conversation with the CSI guys and went over to have a word.

"What's the problem here, officer?" Link asked.

"Nothing to see here, sir," Wiggins said. "Move along, please."

"Seriously."

"Seriously," Wiggins replied. "It looks like your boys are at it again."

"Bedford and Beauregard?"

"Them's the ones. Looks like they dummied up a statue of Devante Davidson and then bashed it to bits in the middle of the street. Right in front of all these people."

Wiggins nodded toward the protesters who now crowded the plaza in front of the courthouse. Some of them chanted anti-police slogans. Others stood at the yellow-taped barrier with their arms folded. They watched and listened as the investigators gathered evidence. It seemed to Link like they were almost trying to listen in on his conversation with Wiggins.

The detective pulled Link further away from the crowd, towards the middle of the street.

"You might want to keep your head down," he told Link.

"I don't see why, Detective. I don't mind being seen with you."

"I'm not worried about who you're seen with. Just there's a lot of press around here and they're going to be all over you, especially after they see you talking to me."

"I'm fine with the press," Link said. "Some of my best friends are..."

"I know, I know. I'm just giving you a heads-up."

"Heads-up taken."

Link told Wiggins about his upcoming meeting with the federal prosecutors, to which the detective replied, "That's yesterday's news. These guys, I'm worried they're not going to be content with smashing inanimate objects."

"I've read a little about arsonist types," Link said. "Pryrophilia. They get off on starting fires. Maybe it's the same thing with these boys."

"I'll be sure to put a call into Masters and Johnson," Wiggins replied. "In the meantime, on behalf of your city police department, I am advising you to take some precautions."

"I'm always precautious, Detective."

"Walk with me," Wiggins said, as he resumed his work of writing down the location of every security camera on the block.

He counted four of them on top of the DA's building. They would give him 360-degree views of everything, for blocks around. The one fastened to the bail bonds office gave him a straight-on shot of where the Yukon came to a stop. On the six-story office building on the corner of 9th and H, home to some of the hardest-knocking private defense attorneys in town, he took notes on cameras that would have captured the culprits' getaway.

"There's a bunch of them shooting out of the courthouse, too," Wiggins said. "There's only one problem with all of them."

"What's that, Detective?"

"All these goddamn trees."

The greenery grew thick on both sides of the street and around the corner where the Yukon fled. It guaranteed that any view picked up by any of the cameras was going to be obstructed.

"They don't call it the 'city of trees' for nothing," Link said.

"Yeah," Wiggins replied. "That means we're going to have to rely on eyewitnesses. I can't wait to start interviewing them, they love us so much."

He took a quick glance back at the crowd. They didn't have to say anything. Their body language exuded hostility. The detective couldn't hear a thing over their silence.

If the detective was expecting any sympathy from his artist pal, he didn't get any.

"The police need to find a new way to do things," Link told him.

The detective shook his head and sighed. He liked Link, loved to argue with him, appreciated his point of view, looked forward to making fun of him. He even bought some of his wood sculptures before they got priced out of the range of ordinary working people. He just didn't understand how somebody with such good sense about him could be such a dipshit at times.

Exasperated, he told Link:

"We get a call from the neighborhood that a guy's breaking car windows with a tire iron. Then we learn somebody's smashing the sliding glass door in the back of some dude's house. Now he's squared up with another plate glass window, and we're on the scene, checking him out. How are we supposed to know he's at Grandma's? You don't think we should find out what the fuck is going on with this guy? We've got people complaining. We've got broken windows. Jesus Christ, he could be the East Area Rapist, or the Golden State Killer, or whatever the fuck they're calling him these days. What if he breaks into Grandma's and beats her head in? Then how do we look?"

"Detective, it is clear to me," Link said. "You are damned if you do and you are damned if you don't."

"That's exactly what I'm talking about," Wiggins said.

"All you have to do is achieve perfection," Link said.

"That's the pot residue in your brain talking."

"Seriously," Link said. "When it comes to taking somebody's life, you have to be perfect. You've got to be one hundred percent correct. You can't kill somebody because you can't tell a cell phone from a gun. You do it and you should be fired. You just can't be a cop anymore. Period. You've got to find another line of work. You've got to learn how to sculpt wood or write newspaper stories or teach school."

Wiggins looked at Link, stunned.

"That is so totally wrong," the detective responded. "And your law-abiding, every-day citizen knows it's wrong. They want us to catch criminals. They want us to catch killers."

"Of course," Link agreed. "The only problem is, you can't kill somebody for breaking a window."

"You expect cops to be perfect?"

"When they kill somebody, yes."

Now Wiggins laughed at Link's naivete.

"Good luck finding anybody who wants to be a cop," he said.

"Have you ever fired your gun, Detective?"

"Once. It was a domestic, and the loving husband sicced his pit bull on me. I had to put him down."

"The wife beater?"

"No. The dog." Wiggins looked around and sighed. He needed to get back to work.

"About Devante Davidson," Wiggins said. "What do you think the cops should have done? You're looking around the corner and you see what they see, and you think he's got a gun, and..."

"*Think* he's got a gun?"

"Well, we know now that it wasn't a gun," Wiggins allowed. "So let's go with pretty damn sure it's a gun and damn sure you don't want to go home dead."

"How about you try to talk to him?"

"They did."

"I mean how about trying to have a conversation with him."

"Sometimes you ask a question and the answer is, bang – you're dead."

"Have the helicopter drop a net over his head. Shoot him with a dope dart like you do a rhinoceros. Offer him a beer. Give him a kitten."

"Very funny."

"All I'm saying, Detective, is when you play God, you damn well better be right."

"Man, you are putting a lot on the poor fucking cop." He slid his hand down his face. "All right. Get the hell out of here. I've got work to do. You can take your theoreicizing elsewhere."

"As usual, we'll have to agree to disagree."

"Yeah, yeah, yeah. I'll call you later."

Link turned away from his conversation with Wiggins only to come face-to-face with Loni Cohen. She wanted to know if he had anything to say about the statue smash.

"Horrific," he said, before moving on to his appointment. "But that's off the record. I just can't say anything. It wouldn't be right, right now."

Wiggins went back to looking for security cameras when a fiftyish African American man who looked like a borderline person-experiencing-homelessness sidled up close to him.

During his conversation with Link, Wiggins noticed that the man with greying hair and a black-and-grey stubble beard dressed in clean but oversized denims had been paying close attention to their discussion. The man, up close, sounded serious and he looked grave. He told Wiggins:

"Would you be interested in a license plate number?"

Link woke with the sun on the first truly hot day of the season. A lovely breeze blew in from the window. For the first time in more than a year, he came to consciousness lying next to someone else.

Manuela Fonseca seemed to wear a smile in her sleep, Link noticed, in the grey light of the dawn that blew in through the open upstairs master bedroom window – comfortable in her muscular bronze nakedness, the white sheet pulled up over her waist, at ease, honest, full, flush, smooth, perfect, gorgeous.

Lying on her right side, facing him, Manuela lifted an eyelid as Link stirred to his feet. He pulled on his clothes and looked back at her with a soft smile.

"Out to get a paper," he said. "I'll be right back. Shall I bring you a coffee?"

"You are a dinosaur, *bruto*," Manuela told him. "It's all online. You don't need the paper anymore."

"Online hurts my eyes," he said.

"I'll print it out for you."

"No need. I'll be back in fifteen."

"Grande bold," she said.

"No room," he knew.

She was still in bed when he got back with *The New York Times*, the *Beacon*, and a couple medium dark roasts from somewhere in Ethiopia by way of The Trade, a local caffeine pusher about six blocks away, over on K Street. He dropped the papers on the circular brown oak table in Manuela's kitchen and pulled out one of the six wooden chairs with the rope-woven seats that scraped across the maple floor.

Link peeled away the first of what was now the two-section Beacon and snapped it open while he took a seat and lifted the coffee to his lips for his first rush of the day. A byline follower, he'd gained an appreciation for Loni Cohen's work almost from the day she took Frankie's slot at the paper, mostly for her coverage of routine police stories where he could tell she had an eye for detail and a willingness to get out and talk to people. She nailed it on the Cesar Chavez desecration, better than anybody, and now she was doing it again, with an authoritative report on the previous day's bizarre attack on the mannequin.

Loni Cohen had been on the job maybe four or five months and she already had some of the best sources on the paper.

Fourth and fifth graphs:

"Davis Beauregard Barton, 29, and Bedford Forrest MacMillian, 21, are both from a semi-rural Tennessee area north of Memphis, she wrote. *According to the Southern Poverty Law Center, Barton and MacMillian have been active in opposition to the movement that has challenged state and local lawmakers in the south over the past year to remove symbols and statues that celebrate their region's Confederate heritage. Both suspects were believed to have attended the tiki torch rally in Charlottesville, Va., last August that protested the removal of the statue of Confederate General Robert E. Lee from the town square, a spokesman for the SLPC told the* Beacon. *The SPLC website contains photographs of the two men that were culled from the Aug. 11 "Unite the Right" rally in Charlottesville.*

"Sacramento law enforcement sources who spoke on the condition of anonymity because they were not authorized to release information yet on Tuesday's provocation of the Black Lives Matter protesters said that investigators have determined that the pair were in the state capital of Nashville, Tenn., last month. The sources said that Barton and MacMillian attended the April 17 session of the Tennessee legislature when lawmakers voted to penalize the city of Memphis for selling parkland to an environmental group that last December removed the statue of Confederate General Nathan Bedford Forrest, whose army carried out the notorious Fort Pillow massacre of federal African American soldiers during the Civil War. Forrest later became the first "grand wizard" of the Ku Klux Klan

before renouncing his past in the years before his death."

The sound of the rustling newspaper brought Manuela down the stairs in her running shorts, flip flops and a tank top. Link put down the paper down as she made her entrance, scratching her thick dyed black hair and rubbing sleep out of her round brown eyes. Her physique, the waking smile breaking through her lips, the disheveled hair mass that dropped down to her muscled shoulders – Link allowed himself to gawk. She caught his look, and for the first time he thought he saw her blush. His smile drew her into him. He pulled her onto his lap for a deep embrace.

"Don't get me wrong," she said. "There will be entire days to spend in bed. This just can't be one of them."

He released her, but continued to gawk as she went to the cupboard to get a coffee cup before she remembered that he had already retrieved the morning supply of caffeine. She pulled up a chair next to him and snatched *The New York Times* from beneath his pile while he finished the story in the *Beacon*.

"The Police Department is considering this incident related to the vandalism of the Chavez statue and Lincoln Adams totem," Police Chief Samuel Kahn told reporters Tuesday in an impromptu press conference held in front of the district attorney's office. "The relatively close proximity in time, the relatively close proximity in location, eyewitness descriptions, the physical evidence we've been able to retrieve – it all convinces us that the two suspects we have identified are responsible for these two events."

Kahn declined to discuss or describe the physical evidence that investigators have retrieved, although one police source said detectives described the burned-rubber tire tracks at both crime scenes as being a "definitive match" to those obtained from the Cesar Chavez vandalism. The chief said that several of the protesters who saw the two men get out of the car and club the crudely-fashioned Devante Davidson statue have cooperated with the police. Leaders of the local Black Lives Matter movement pledged to assist the investigation "in any way possible."

When he finished reading the story, Link shoved the paper

across the table to Manuela.

"As my publicity agent, I believe you will find this story of interest," Link told her.

Professional that she was, Manuela had already read the *Beacon* article. First thing she did every morning, usually before she got out of bed, was to check the Google alerts on all her clients, including the one she set up for Lincoln Adams. He got a few minor mentions in the day's *Beacon* story.

"This one worked out fine for you," she said. "You weren't quoted but came out of the story looking terrific. You were seen and not heard. You projected civic responsibility, going to talk to the prosecutor. You're showing you are not a hopeless victim. You're doing something about it. This story is a grand slam. Could you do me a favor and put on a seminar for our *corporatistas* on image projection?"

"Image projection?"

"We all do it, *bruto*, even when we're not trying."

"What if I'm projecting no-image?"

"That is still a projection."

"What if I don't... project. What if I just...am?"

"You cannot 'not project,' *bruto*."

"We are going nowhere with this."

Manuela broke out in laughter, and Link bounced her a soft gaze she did not catch. He saw her spirit, and he felt this thing going into uncharted territory.

She straightened out the front section of the paper, just to see how it looked – a photo of the smashed Devante Davidson statue scattered in the street, with CSI cops on their hands and knees looking for shoe prints or cigarette butts or any other items of interest to Detective Andrew Wiggins. In the background, one Black Lives Matters protester scowled, with his arms folded across a T-shirt silkscreened with a picture of a smiling Devante Davidson.

Link, meanwhile, punched up *The Washington Post* on his laptop. He hadn't talked to Frankie in a couple of days. No problem. He was able to catch up with the reporter in his work, in a story on the bottom left of the Post's home page, the second from the bottom in its national politics section.

The headline was "Republican challenger targets GOP incumbent in ad campaign." Frankie reported only what he could document as fact – that Jacob Harland had unleashed an attack in the right-wing media on the sitting representative of California's 10th Congressional District, John Bonham, on the burning issue of immigration.

MODESTO, Calif. – A Republican challenger to a Republican congressman in a hotly-contested California district launched an advertising campaign Tuesday that paints the incumbent as soft on immigration policy, an approach that may undercut Democratic Party efforts to flip the seat.

Frankie's story detailed the figures out of the federal expenditure reports. It quoted from the advertisements placed in Brightbeat and the other conservative news sites, including some of the more inflammatory scrawlings in the conservative chat rooms. It provided the backdrop on the two hundred and fifty thousand dollar White Rock USA political fund and its ties to the Slavic USA church in Rancho Cordova. It quoted a political science professor from Cal State Stanislaus on the vagaries of California's top-two primary system and how the Republicans were primed to claim both spots even though 60 percent of the voters in the district appeared to favor the Democrats. It quoted Jordan Diaz as a spokesman for the California Democratic Party as calling the Harland campaign "a blatant tactic to manipulate the system into depriving this district of the representation that a vast majority of voters clearly wants."

At least one of the Democratic candidates in the race did not appear to be concerned about the White Rock USA expenditure, the story read. *Mary Lynne Sorenson, a Modesto nurse and a former member of the city's school board, knocked on doors just before dinner time Tuesday in the housing tracts on the city's northeast side that are encroaching into the surrounding farm fields and adding a strong suburban, super-commuting bent to the district's agricultural base. Sorenson is one of four Democrats in the race who is seeking to replace Bonham, in a congressional district that Hillary Clinton carried in 2016. Each of the candidates is polling around 15 percent.*

"To be perfectly honest, I am more focused on my own campaign," Sorenson said. "The voters in this district care about jobs and healthcare, not who is spending how much money in what fashion. They want to know what their elected officials are going to do about their long commutes. They want to know what we're going to do to protect Social Security. They want better schools, and they want to know how we're going to make that happen. That's what they want to know from me, and that's what I'm talking to them about."

The story caught readers up on the status of the lawsuit that the state Democratic Party filed against White Rock USA, demanding that the independent expenditure committee identify exactly where they dug up the $250,000. Unfortunately for the Dems, a judge killed the thing off the previous Friday.

"The judge found that 'the defendants have substantially complied with federal campaign disclosure requirements.' The source of the committee's funding, the tentative decision said, 'is clearly the committee itself.'"

Link finished reading Frankie's story and looked across the table to see Manuela staring at him, her arms folded across her chest, her face alert and happy, a coast-to-coast smile enlivening the morning. Link looked back at her in silence. He rose from his chair and walked around the table. He stood next to her. She turned toward him and stood up into him, and tugged him by the belt buckle. She led him up the stairs.

The *Times* and the *Beacon* may as well have been scattered to the winds.

31/*The DeCoulomb Trail*

Later in the week, with the clock running out on the primary campaign, Frankie Cameron knew he had no chance to pop a story on whatever the hell White Rock USA was doing with the DeCoulombs.

Newspapers generally didn't like to run kick-ass investigative pieces in the last week of a campaign – it made them look too partisan. Besides, his bosses really didn't get the story, anyway. They weren't even sure it *was* a story. A freighter ships $800,000 worth of new cars out of a warehouse in West Sacramento owned by a company established by a Russian church? You need to do some more reporting, the editors told Frankie. Right now, you've got a whole lot of nothing.

As far as nothingness goes, Frankie thought this batch carried the smell of intrigue.

From his room in the Hotel Sterling, Frankie opened the curtains to look out over 13th Street.

He put a call into Radimir Valishnikov.

"Rad man, what do you know?" he greeted him.

"Call Me Frankie Please, how are you?"

"I've been better, but I've also been worse. I don't know if you saw my story yesterday, but..."

"I did. It was very good."

"As you could see, I was not able to mention the DeCoulombs."

"I did notice that omission."

"The editors didn't see how they tied into the story."

"We still have lots to prove, my friend. It could be a totally harmless operation – a car company owned by a revanchist Rhodesian who is shipping electric vehicles worth a hundred thousand dollars apiece, through the Port of Sacramento, to Mexico, instead of directly from the factory in the Bay Area. But first, the cars are going to a warehouse controlled by a corrupt Russian preacher, who is defrauding the public in a charity scam, and who has also established a political committee to contribute money to a proto-fascist running for office. It is all perfectly ordinary, I tell you."

"I appreciate where you're coming from, Rad. My problem is I'm going to need more than sarcasm to get this story into the paper. Right now, we have parallels. What I need is intersection. Make that some intersection that we can document."

"I am sorry I cannot write your entire story for you, Mr. Frankie," Valishnikov went on, in a tone that Frankie did not care for. "I'm just a poor Russian-American publisher, of a newspaper that the mainstream media in Sacramento totally ignores. If only I had subpoena power, or an office downtown that takes up two square city blocks. Or any kind of an office, other than the one I have fashioned out of a corner of my garage."

Frankie took a deep breath.

"We're going to connect the dots," Frankie said. "We're just not going to get it done by Tuesday."

"We both know where it goes," Valishnikov responded. "You know that in some fashion, these cars are financing this political campaign."

"Through White Rock."

"And the church. They are technically distinct, as you know."

Frankie was ready to say goodbye before Rad said one final thing.

"By the way," the editor said, "I did a little checking around on your Matthew Johannsen."

"And?" Frankie asked.

"Nothing really, except for one thing," Rad said.

"What?"

"He buys my paper!"

"Subscriber?"

"No, I am sorry to say, Mr. Frankie. He only buys the occasional back issue. I checked which ones, because I knew you would ask, and it seems to me as if he had an interest in White Rock USA, and the church. They had been the lead story in every issue he purchased."

"Aren't they the lead story in *every* issue you put out?"

Rad laughed, "That is almost the case."

"You don't know if White Rock or the church were actually clients of his, do you?"

"I do not," Rad said. "But I will keep exploring on my end,

184

my friend."

Frankie signed off with Rad, and he took a long look out of his hotel window.

It was a perfect Sacramento day, in one of the town's best times of the year, late spring, when the morning sunlight splatters through the fresh leaves that fill the trees to give the city a green ceiling, especially in this neighborhood just north of downtown. The canopy of elm and sycamore and ash shaded the colorful high-water flats that used to be on the verge of collapse in a tough, drug-infested corner of the grid. In the past decade, however, the crack dealers gave way to young professionals who moved in from the suburbs and the Bay Area and fixed up their places and drove the average cost for a two-bedroom with a front porch worthy of a banjo to well over a half-million dollars. Rents zoomed upward the past three or four years at the highest percentage increases in the nation.

It had not been his choice to leave Sacramento. He just felt like he had no choice, if he wanted to remain a newspaperman. The *Beacon* used to be his perfect fit. Now it struggled to survive after top-level management decided to blow off its loyal customer base of older readers in the hope of capturing the younger generation of smart-phone consumers. The bosses half-succeeded, as tens of thousands of geezers got the message and dropped the paper. The other half of the play didn't work out so well. The young people who get their news from their telephones, they continued to browse without a paid digital subscription. Luckily for Frankie, his reporting from the previous year attracted the attention of the *Post*. He moved his family to the D.C. suburbs, which were okay, but nothing like the East Sacramento neighborhood where his kids could bike or walk to school or Little League games and meet him at his office, or at the Capitol downtown where the three of them would pick up the wife and all head over to eat fried chicken and honey-buttered biscuits and fatback-less greens at South, over on 11th Street in Southside Park. He missed the long bike rides up the American River Parkway, the 26-mile-long forest that bisected the greater metropolitan area on both sides of a blue-green tributary, with plenty of safe spots to jump in for a dip.

He missed going to minor-league baseball games and NBA and NCAA basketball games with Link. He missed the breweries and the train to San Francisco. He missed the foothill wineries and driving out to Capay Valley to hike the Blue Ridge Trail. He missed playing nine holes at Land Park and getting plastered afterwards with his pals in the tiny clubhouse grill that always had a good IPA on tap. He missed the under-the-radar blues bands that traveled the country and played the Torch. He missed the little Mardi Gras parade that started at Mullaney's. He missed walking along the docks in Old Sac and wondering what it was like around there at the height of the Gold Rush, where he stood in the very spot on Front Street where Theodore Judah kept his office and sold Collis P. Huntington on the idea of a transcontinental railroad. He missed Benny's.

He cracked open his laptop.

He Googled the name "Ian Courtney."

32/*Benny's*

By the spring of 2018, almost everybody in the world had heard of Ian Courtney. The guy was a genius – and he'd be the first to tell you so. Born in Rhodesia, into the white agricultural aristocracy. Moved to Australia when his home country went Zimbabwe on him and his family feared being eaten alive on its ranch by Robert Mugabe. Went to Cal Tech and Stanford, got a PhD in physics and an MBA on top of that. Went to law school, too, got himself a JD from the back of a matchbook cover, just for kicks.

Young Ian knew, like Eva Marie Saint told Cary Grant, that all work and no play makes for a very dull boy. So he dated the hottest chicks – poseurs, models, even some actresses. When he made his first billion and got his name in the papers, he clubbed around New York and Hollywood. He went on TV and extolled the virtues of Ecstasy, the party drug that modern-day hipsters spun as some sort of deep-thought-inducing exploratory psychedelic. In fact, it wasn't much different than street crank. Courtney, however, felt it did more for his intellectual image to be associated with Timothy Leary and Baba Ram Das.

Courtney made a big splash at the turn of the century when he blew off a rocket on a dried lake bed in the Mojave and promised that one of these days his Silicon Valley company – Courtneytronics, Inc. – would be offering round trips to the moon and maybe Mars. From space, he turned his attention to the ground and incorporated a firm he called the Bearing Company and said he could dig a tunnel from L.A. to New York and transport people across the country at 750 miles an hour underground in what he called the SuperTube. He liked electric cars and designed one for the super-rich – the DeCoulomb. It all created buzz, and Courtney rode it to the top of the celebrity pages. Wall Street liked him, too. The idea of a public offering with his car company, DeCoulomb, Ltd. garnered high enthusiasm among investors around the world. Cable business TV pundits speculated at an opening stock price of $1,000 a share.

Frankie stared into his laptop on the top floor of the Hotel Sterling. He knew the basics on Courtney. What he didn't know was why the guy's cars were taking the sea route to Mexico, from Hayward, by way of West Sacramento.

Besides his DeCoulomb factory, and his Beverly Hills lifestyle, and his space shots in the desert, Courtney had another really interesting thing going for him, Frankie found. A couple years earlier, he sold a plan to build a city in the nowheresville of the mid-southern San Joaquin Valley. Courtney City, he humbly named it, would be the birthplace and testing ground for the SuperTube. He paid off the locals, bought himself a few thousand acres of land, handed over his water rights to the surrounding cotton and almond farmers, and parlayed them into signing on to his city. The plan: hire a few hundred ditch diggers, open a country-and-western bar and a couple of strip clubs, and get the people driving up and down I-5 to stop in for some fun and watch a 750-miles-an-hour private transportation system take shape while they listened to some twang and watched city girls grind on brass poles. Get your seat on the SuperTube, L.A. to S.F. in a half an hour, direct, from Pershing to Union squares, no stops, only $1,000 ($2,000 for your own private compartment, human interaction kept to a minimum).

Courtney pitched his plan at a press conference in a fallow cotton field – a perfect depiction of the void he sought to transform into the Garden of Ian. The local politicians loved it, Democrats and Republicans alike – including one of the local congressmen, John Bonham, of Modesto – joining Courtney for his press conference in the middle of nowhere. The local papers and the Fresno TV stations jumped on the story. They embraced it as the economic salvation for their region and its historic double-digit unemployment rates.

They threw all-in with Courtney.

They came up losers.

Something happened on Courtney's journey down the SuperTube highway – something called reality. Frankie's Google search found stories on the one-year anniversary of the Courtney press conference that reported that not a single shovel-full of dirt had ever been turned. Coming up on the second anniversary, he still found no evidence of steel guitars or dancing strippers. No jobs were created, no money was made. The elders who controlled agricultural and politics in Kings County were made to look stupid over Sham City, as Frankie now called it. The whole idea, it appeared to the reporter, was a feint. His challenge now was to find out Courtney's real play.

With the election only five days away, Frankie knew that he'd have to hold off on any kind of in-depth reporting he'd like to do on the Ian Courtney conglomerate. His reporting for now would be reduced to watching polls and listening to speeches and what the candidates said about each other and any last-minute money moves and major news breaks on the seven California congressional campaigns.

You get busted for a DUI or you're caught naked on the beach with a hooker, you're in the paper. Otherwise, wait until next year.

Frankie looked at the schedule. He figured he was good for one more trip to Orange County, to write a generic feature on the three contested races down there. He called the desk. They were good with it. He'd fly down tomorrow.

This afternoon, on the final day of May, he spotted a few hours good for a break. He got hold of the internationally acclaimed wood sculptor, Lincoln Adams. He texted Mike Rubiks, the feature writer extraordinaire who was trying to save his job at the *Sacramento Beacon* from the algorithms of creative destruction.

Rubiks picked the gathering place: the elbow at Benny's.

The prime real estate at the establishment located a block down from the *Beacon* had undergone a radical change in the five months since Frankie left town. The autobody guys who used to occupy the corner of the bar had vanished. With good reason. The shops that used to employ them had all shut down, sold their space to real estate developers who had turned the neighborhood around the *Beacon* into something else. The old body shops where they worked had been transformed into construction sites where three-level town homes jammed one next to the other rose along the 20th Street side of the railroad track from R to P streets. The *Beacon* parking lot – demolished. It gave way to the soon-to-be hugest apartment complex on the grid, 250 units of mostly-luxury three-bedroom flops with a few studios thrown in to qualify the developer for a municipal subsidy.

First thing Link and Frankie noticed when they walked into Benny's was – no Om. The championship bartender still owned a fourth of the joint. It used to be a third. Only now, his 25 percent was worth more than his old 33 percent. Along with the cash he put in his pocket when he and his two incumbent owners took on a partner, the changing neighborhood boosted Benny's value, or so the smart guys in the bar business thought. In time, they'd see if hipsters spent more money than auto-body workers. Om, in any event, seemed to be doing pretty well, and that made the boys feel good. He took one day off a week, a sabbath unheard of in the previous era.

Link, Frankie and Rubiks ordered up from Om's replacement, a slinky tattooed beauty with jewelry riveted into her face and bangles the size of salad plates dangling from her ears. She seemed very well-paid and pleasant, erudite. Frankie, of course, had moved, and Link didn't get out as much, or over to his studio, either, since he finished his totem. Between the two of them, they'd made a grand total of one appearance at Benny's since Frankie's going-away party a couple nights before New Year's Eve.

Rubiks, however, maintained his regularity, and the bartender rewarded him when he bellied up to the mahogany.

She leaned across it and kissed Rubiks on the cheek.

"Elvira, I don't believe you have met my friends," Rubiks said, by way of introducing her to Link and Frankie. "Link and Frankie, I'd like you to meet The Vira, as she calls herself, and she's been running the 11 a.m. shift for, what, two weeks now?"

"Three," she said, with a smile, still holding onto Rubiks' hand. "A pleasure to meet you, gentlemen. Mike has already told me all about you. I guess it used to be a newspaper bar?" She winked as if she knew this was a topic that would get conversation going.

"When we used to be a newspaper," Rubiks said.

"You're still a newspaper," Elvira said. "You're just more than that now."

"Yeah, and a lot less, too," Rubiks said.

They ordered up their usuals – a Sierra Nevada Pale Ale for Link, a Racer 5 IPA draft for Frankie, and a Budweiser long neck and a shot of Early Times for Rubiks.

"Well, men, as you can see," Rubiks said, after a toast in which Elvira joined in with a shot of Jack Daniels, "the times they are a changin'."

"As always," Link contributed. "Some times are just more obvious than others."

"As I can see," Frankie said, nodding at Elvira, who had

moved down the bar, away from these three, to take care of a 30-ish Untuckit topped by a straw trilby. "I love Om. But I think I am in love with Elvira."

"Stay away," Rubiks said. "She and I have a beautiful thing going on."

"She's young enough to be your daughter," Frankie said.

"So what?" Rubiks said, as he tossed back the Times.

An awkward silence fell over the three. They had not been together, just the three of them, since they got together on Benny's back porch the previous summer. One guy leaves town and everything falls apart, or so it seemed to them, silently, individually, a shared understanding of the *It's-a-Wonderful-Life* syndrome.

Since Frankie and Link had been in or were reporting the news, the conversation turned to Rubiks and his status as the *Beacon*'s last-standing dinosaur.

"How're things around the shop?" Frankie asked him.

"I barely even know," Rubiks said. "I damn near don't know anybody in the newsroom anymore. They're the ones who are young enough to be my grandkids – Elvira, she's just my trophy lover. Right Elvira?"

Elvira flashed him a wink.

Rubiks went on about the *Beacon*:

"The place is half empty. I think they're going to start renting out space. In this cubicle, the education beat. Over there, a nail salon. Here, you've got the environmental reporter. Next to her, a Pilates instructor."

"That will keep you all in shape," Link contributed.

"In shape for what?" Rubiks went on. "Hell, I've got to get out of there. I mean, who am I? I'm a newspaperman. Only problem here is there's no more newspaper. Why do they keep it going if they strangle it a little more every day? Just kill the goddamn thing. Go do your online thing. Get out of the building you don't even own anymore. Move into a one-room office downtown. Save some money. Sell the presses. Fire everybody with more than five years' experience. Get to be what you want to become. Quit the pretense of transition."

"Yet they keep you around, Mike," Link said. "You know they love you. They'll never let you go."

"Don't delude yourself, man," Rubiks said. "They know, I know, we all know – I'm out on the next round of buyouts, or layoffs, whatever the fuck they do. I don't get clicks – bottom line. I'm not on board with their program. Even if I was, they could get somebody out of Sac State to do me for half the price, with a better attitude, and who's better looking. My time is done, man."

"I don't know," Frankie said. "You can still do that shit."

"I do know, man. I do know I can't stand what they've got me doing. Restaurant openings and breweries? As a beat? Fuck, man. Fuckers who care about that shit don't even read about it. It's not news. It's not a damn bit more interesting than anything else that humans do. Hey, I like beer as much as anybody. I love beer. I drink a lot of beer. I've been drinking beer for thirty-five years. Do I read about beer? Fuck, no. Who does? You drink it. You don't read about it. Fuck, man, you *can't* read about it if you drink it. No, man. I've just got to get out. Just waiting for the buyout. I'll take a layoff. Anything that pays me for nine months."

"Then what would you do, Mike?" Link asked.

"Write."

"About what?" Frankie interjected

"I don't know. Beer?"

That got a laugh out of the boys.

"A little unemployment would be nice. The pension eventually would kick in. I could find me a rich old widow."

"You're married," Frankie said.

"A patron," Rubiks announced. "Who couldn't use a patron? Frankie, make yourself useful while you're in town. Go find me a patron. I don't need much. A thousand a week? Tell you what, I'll make it five hundred. There's got to be a million rich old widows around who can handle that."

He took a long draw on the longneck.

"Actually, I have been doing some writing on the side. Mainly, to keep me from going crazy. You've got the beer beat,

192

you've got the death of newspapers, you've got Frankie moving to D.C., so what do you got left?"

"I've been a bad friend lately," Link said quietly.

"I don't think I've made many calls your way either, man," Rubiks said. "All right, enough about me. What about you assholes? Link, what the fuck is up with this statue shit? Who are these fucking crackers? You need some backup? I am still well-armed. I'll go find 'em right now and kick their ass into next week."

Link laughed, stood, and stretched at the bar, throwing his arm around Rubiks's shoulders, which took up several feet of air space.

"You are a great man, Mike. You'll also be happy to know that I happen to know a few rich widows around town."

"I'll bet you do. Now, what's the deal with the vandalism? They stabbed your guy in the back? What the hell is up with *that*?"

Link told what he knew, with an obvious lack of enthusiasm. The story had already been in the paper. He really didn't have much to add, and he really didn't want to get into it. Nobody had ever before physically attacked a piece of his artwork, so he didn't really know how to process it. Intellectually and spiritually speaking, he believed that the animistic forms he had sought to liberate had already been released once he finished carving them out. What remained – the actual piece of art – was just this physical . . . thing. An inanimate object. Some, he loved more than others. Others, he didn't love at all. He was still working on his relationship with a good number of his finished pieces, and the totem fell into that category. He never really got to know it. The two of them had never really bonded. No, he didn't like the fact that somebody shivved the damn thing, but the knifing didn't cost him nearly as much sleep as the A's blowing the 2003 American League Divison Series after they'd gone two up on the Red Sox.

He quickly moved to change the subject.

"I will tell you what really was interesting," he said, turning to Mike, "was your coverage of the story. This new reporter you have is really good."

Frankie and Mike Rubiks agreed – Loni Cohen was the real deal.

"Seems like a nice kid, too," Rubiks added. "She respects her elders."

"To Loni Cohen," Frankie said, as they raised their drinks again.

"All right, Link, back to you," Rubiks broke in. "You're not getting out of this so easy. I'm hearing some rumors about you and Manuela Fonseca."

"Manuela Fonseca?" Frankie interjected. "Man, she is too high-class for you."

Link shot them both some stone face before letting a smile crinkle his lips.

"Something is happening here, but you don't know what it is," Link sang, from the Ballad of the Thin Man, before Mike and Frankie joined in for the kicker: *"Do you, Mr. Jones."*

Frankie was about to raise his glass in a toast, before the momentousness of the news fully hit him. He knew Link had never gone more than three months with a woman in his life, and he didn't recall him ever even remotely characterizing any of his previous relationships as being close to a a lasting thing.

"My God, Link," Frankie asked. "Are you okay?"

It was a serious question. The news of Link being involved in a serious relationship could have suggested that his friend had terminal cancer and was going through the process of checking off the boxes on the bucket list.

"Never better, actually," Link said. "I think you would call it bliss."

"Don't worry," Rubiks said. "You'll snap out of it."

"I really do wonder if it is an illusion," Link said. "Actually, I *know* it's an illusion, just like everything else you see, feel, hear and touch. Like all illusions, it will probably pass. The mirage will shatter, and I will once again find myself wandering alone through the desert of life."

"Oh, fuck me – give yourself up," Frankie scolded. "Get the fuck out of your head, why don't you. You and your illusion bullshit."

"Well, there is one thing that is not an illusion," Link answered. "And that is, Manuela is way too high-class for me."

They all got a laugh out of that one.

"The trick," Frankie said, "will be to prevent her from coming to that realization."

They all laughed some more. Even Elvira, who eavesdropped from a couple spaces down the bar.

"Details," Rubiks ordered.

"Details?" Link replied.

"Yeah," Mike said. "Like, have you fucked her?"

"Jesus Fucking Christ," Frankie said. "Have you no decency? Wait a second. Did I even have to ask that?"

"As a matter of fact I do not," Rubiks said. "And I want to know."

"What the fuck," Frankie said. "Is the shot clock running down? Are we out of timeouts? Christ Almighty – why the fuck do you need to know shit?"

"Because I am a loutish, drunken, low-bottom, rat-bastard motherfucker – a two-dollar crawler. And that's exactly why you love me."

With that, Rubiks raised his whiskey shot.

"To Manuela," he said.

Frankie shook his head and clinked his pint to Rubiks's shot glass and to Link's beautifully green-labeled bottle of Sierra Nevada Pale Ale.

Rubiks threw down his shot like a jackhammer and turned his focus to Frankie.

"What about you, big shot? What you got?"

Frankie tipped a sip to his lips. Nobody talked about Racer anymore, but it was still good as any.

"Well," he slurped, "I'm going down to Huntington Beach this week to do something on the Cong races down there."

"The Viet Cong?" Rubiks asked.

"No, the U.S. Cong – the congressional races. Just a quick hitter for the weekend, catch up on whether the Republicans are going to top-two the Dems out of some of these seats. Tie it altogether with the one up here, should be readable. But the one up here is pretty fucking interesting."

"Spill," Rubiks ordered.

"Ian Courtney."

"The car guy?"

"He's more than that, but yeah, the DeCoulomb guy. Somehow his cars are getting moved to a warehouse in West Sac, on their way to Mexico. Why the fuck, nobody knows. Except the warehouse is run by the same people who set up this independent expenditure committee that's all into this congressional race in Modesto. It's all Russia, all over again."

"White Rock USA," Link said.

"Happy to see somebody around here has been doing his required reading."

"Two of us," Rubiks added.

"Thank you, too, Mike man," Frankie picked up.

"I do not believe I have seen any references to Señor Courtney in your coverage," Link inserted.

"No, you have not," Frankie continued. "You're going to have to wait for it. I've got to find out what it means. It could be nothing. Or it could be that it's part of Courtney's plan to take over the world and shoot us all off to Mars so he can have the whole planet to himself. Maybe he's laundering money, or..."

"Or maybe he's trying to throw that district to the Republicans," Rubiks said. "Or keep it in the Republicans' hands. Weird play, though, man. Like, this cat who's attacking Bonham from the right...."

"I didn't know you paid such close attention to Modesto politics, Mike," Frankie said.

"You kidding me? The whole country is watching that district. If the house is going to get flipped, that district has to turn. California Congressional District Number Ten is now a household name. Who's the guy down there again?"

"Bonham. John Bonham."

"That's right," said Rubiks. "Who's the Dem?"

"A cast of thousands."

"And the right-winger?"

"Somebody named Harland."

"Yeah, him. I read your stuff. So why does Courtney give a shit about him?"

"That," Frankie said, "is exactly what I'm trying to find out."

33/*The License Plate*

Detective Andrew Wiggins knew Robert Warrick well enough to know he didn't like him. At least way back when. Wiggins was not a racist, not even close to it, at least by the limbo-low standards white people set for themselves. He had plenty of black friends – as long as they were cops. Ex-military types, straight-up guys, exactly like himself, just brothers from a different color – he got along with them just fine. Ate dinner with them. Went to basketball games with them. Went fishing with them.

Wiggins didn't know it, but Warrick was ex-military, too – an Air Force captain. Not a pilot or anything like that. Just an organizational genius, a lifer, born in East St. Louis and raised in Springfield, who enrolled for the air to stay off the ground in Vietnam. He made a living managing ground ops for the 323rd Flying Training Wing at Mather AFB. Basically, he told the navigators of the future how to navigate themselves to the bathroom.

Warrick lasted with the Air Force until they shut down Mather and he retired on a healthy pension, bought a house in Oak Park, and somehow got himself elected president of the local chapter of the NAACP. Wiggins met him in that capacity early in his police tenure, when he was working City Hall security and had to run Warrick out of the joint one night when he refused to leave the podium after speaking for 10 minutes, eight minutes over his allotment. The topic was the creation of a police review board. Maybe if the city would have listened to the guy, it would have helped calm things down during the Devante Davidson crisis. Maybe there even wouldn't have been a Devante Davidson crisis.

Wiggins, way back when, found Warrick disrespectful. He found him obstinate. He found him odd.

He also found him helpful the day that Bedford Forrest MacMillian and Davis Beauregard Barton clubbed the fake statue of Devante Davidson into tiny little white bits outside the DA's office.

Wiggins didn't recognize Warrick at first. Hadn't seen him in at least 15 years, and in that time period Warrick's mostly-black hair had turned mostly white. Warrick also grew a beard worthy of a modern baseball player – huge, bushy, blocky, all white, enough to make you think he'd make a terrific black Santa Claus, except for the fact he was in better shape at 82 than most humans are at 22. Warrick didn't recognize Wiggins, either, even from his many appearances on television the past year, all of which had something to do with Lincoln Adams. Warrick knew Link a little bit, too, from the golden age of Benny's, when sheriffs and cops and crooks and political consultants and city council members and grifters and gamblers and entrepreneurial invaders and NAACP chapter presidents drank with the newspaper crowd, trying to get their names in the paper at a time when such things mattered.

Wiggins took Warrick inside the police tape the day of the statue bash.

"Yes," the detective told the witness. "I would like to have the license plate number. Did you write it down, sir?"

"No, officer, I did not," Warrick replied.

"Well, what are you wasting my time for?" asked Wiggens, slightly perturbed.   Warrick pulled his cell phone out of his left front pants pocket and clicked on to his photographs.

"7-H-D-F-3-1-0, and that is a California plate, sir," Warrick said.

"You took a picture?" the detective asked.

"Yes, sir, I did. Would you like me to text it to you?"

"Might as well," Wiggins said, before he realized that he'd have to give this madman-looking person his cell phone.

Wiggins thought about it for a second, but told himself, what the fuck, the guy's 80-years-old, at least, and I haven't seen his name in the paper in at least 10 years, and it was pretty damn American of him to take the picture and come out of a hostile crowd to become a civilian cooperator.

Later that night, while Wiggins was in the middle of all that security camera footage, most of which was totally obstructed by all those fucking trees, he ran the plate through the DMV computer.

The number, he found, and not at all to his surprise, did not come back to the late model black GMC Yukon XL. Rather, it traced to a Hyundai compact sedan, reported stolen, by a a woman living in a mobile home park in Foothill Farms. The next day, Wiggins put in a call to the Sacramento sheriff's car theft detail. Yeah, they had the report, and they'd be happy to email Wiggins a copy. They were sad to inform their colleague, however, that they never did follow up on the report from the complainant. They just didn't have time They had so many damn car thefts up around Foothill Farms, they told Wiggins, that they only worked things that looked organized, serialized, commercialized or politicized, mostly on multi-jurisdictional task forces.

Wiggins thanked them for their service. He waited for the email and printed out the report – the first time its contents had seen the light of day. He looked up the name and address on the victim – a young woman named Mai Vang, in her 20s, who lived in the mobile home park.

It had been a while since Wiggins'ss job took him into Foothill Farms, the classic early-Sixties blue-collar suburb that developers carved out of the grasslands, mainly to house the civilian work force that serviced aircraft at the nearby McClellan Air Force Base. Like Mather, McClellan had since gone out of business – shut down and converted to civilian use in the 1993 base closures. At its core, the unincorporated area of 33,000 clung ferociously to its white working-class status. On its edges, it gave way to an influx of immigrants from around the world and black and brown emigres from Del Paso Heights and South Sac.

While Frankie, Link, and Mike Rubiks slurped down refreshments at Benny's, Wiggins hopped into his department-issued sedan for the 20-minute drive to the victim's address. He pulled up to the trailer just as an Asian woman with long black hair flowing beneath her crash helmet, her right arm covered by a mural of tattoos, hopped on a bicycle with a stuffed backpack strapped across her shoulders.

Wiggins hailed her to a stop. He identified himself as a cop. He told her he was looking for the woman at this address who had her Hyundai stolen a couple months earlier. Mai Vang identified herself as the victim, and as late for class at American River College. But she said she'd be happy to take a couple minutes to talk to him about the crime that she thought America had forgotten about.

Mai really didn't have much to add beyond the police report.

"Detectives never talked to me, but insurance company sure did," the smiling victim told Wiggins, looking down at her bike. "They valued my loss at a thousand dollars. I used the money to buy this bike – nice ride, huh? Best thing, I park it inside, in the living room, where nobody can steal. Unlike the car. They steal them every night around here."

Mai rolled away, leaving Wiggins alone in the mobile home park.

Just for the hell of it, he took a stroll through the neighborhood. He saw the United Nations going about its day. He exchanged hellos and looked folks over, and they looked him over, and every one of them made him for a cop, including a few that mumbled to each other in Slavic accents.

For the first time, Manuela actually spent a night at Link's house on D Street. It was her idea. He was totally content just hanging at her pad, but she wanted to see how artists lived and whether they scrubbed the stains off the toilet bowl.

She found his crib a little dusty here and there, but it impressed her that the sheets were clean. She also took note that an effort had been made to sanitize the bathroom. Instead of giving Link a couple days to get his house in order for her inspection, she sprung it on him late on a Saturday night, after they went to see the Iguanas at Harlow's, on the band's every-other-year trip to Sacramento from their home arena, the Circle Bar in New Orleans.

She found the living room neat. The kitchen, wiped down within the past week. The bathroom smelled like Pine Sol.

Not too bad, she thought, for a man in his mid-60s who'd been single his whole life.

The two of them woke up early on a perfectly fine Sunday morning. They drove to the Food Co-op on R and 29th and got themselves a couple croissants and coffee. Then it was back into the Porsche and off to the capital of southern San Joaquin County.

Manteca had truly emerged as a key battleground in the campaign to flip California's 10th Congressional District, where the Republican incumbent was in a fight with a squadron of Democrats.

New homes sprouted into the outskirts south of town with driveways filled with new cars purchased from dealers in Bay Area towns like Dublin and Pleasanton. These were the super-commuters who couldn't afford to purchase a home near their Silicon Valley jobs, so they had to drive 70 miles each way to work from the $350,000 cutouts several zip codes to the east. These residents were new to the 10th District. They were very much in play in the eyes of the contestants who sought to represent them in the U.S. House of Representatives. These newbies – in Manteca, and in the other exurban towns of

Patterson and Tracy – would likely decide the future of the president's legislative agenda for the next two years, not to mention whether his malfeasance would be professionally investigated.

Manuela wheeled past Stockton and got off Highway 99 on the North Main Street cutoff that took them through Manteca's fairly substantial downtown business district.

"I never knew this town had a downtown," Link said.

"There's a lot you don't know, *bruto*," Manuela said.

In recent days, Manuela had begun introducing Link to her friends and relatives as "my new guy," which was something of a lie. The qualification left an impression of impermanence – "new" implied that Link was just the latest piece of meat she was showing around. Actually, Manuela hadn't seen anybody seriously since her divorce.

After six days of sleeping together, they'd fallen full bore into each other, and now it was on, in a way that it never had been before for him, and maybe only once or twice for her. Yes, it was physical – these kinds of things usually did start out that way. Now, their synapses synced in a way that neither could explain. Everything just kind of merged into an ineffable splat. He was her and she was him. At least that's the way it felt since Memorial Day night.

Pain and longing marked the few hours each day that they spent apart. Link's balanced detachment flew out the window. If that meant danger, so what. For her part, Manuela had thought she'd never need anybody again, period. Divorced in her 30s, she had fun in her 40s. She raised her kid on her own. Who needed anybody from that other despicable gender responsible for so much irresponsibility in this world? This thing that she had going on with Link – it wasn't a matter of need. It was just a matter of... matter. And right now, nothing else mattered.

They drove to the other side of Manteca and into fields that once grew cantaloupes and jug wine grapes. Now, the only thing cantaloupy about the area was the brownish color of the new homes that sprung from the fields all around.

"Who is this *gabacho* we are pimping for today, *bruto*?"

Manuela asked, as she bit into a croissant and sprinkled flakes all over her chest.

Link flicked the crumbs off the slinky red halter top she wore over her athletic bra.

"Some guy named Jesse Seymour," he said.

"And who is Jesse Seymour?"

"I have to confess – I'm not a hundred percent sure," Link said. "All I know is he has been endorsed by the *Modesto Beacon*."

The sister paper of Sacramento's broadsheet tabbed Seymour over Mary Lynne Sorenson and the rest of the blue crew based on what it characterized as his electability. The endorsement helped make sense for Democrats in California CD 10. The state Democratic Party failed to issue an endorsement. The national party also sat on its hands. This dereliction of duty on the part of the party left people who actually work for a living without a clue on how to make sense of this political rodeo. They didn't have time to spend every night obsessing with Rachel Maddow. They were on the freeway home. Their kids had to eat. They had to make sure the young-uns did their homework, too, and if Mom or Dad or both coached Little League or soccer or synchronized swimming teams, they damn near had to suffer a heart attack to get to practice.

Link told Manuela that the independent labor group that was running a campaign against John Bonham, the one he'd canvassed for before, did not favor any of the candidates. Now, with all this noise about the Republicans trying to freeze out the Dems in California CD 10 with a top-two showing in the primary, Link needed to make a decision. He needed to go with the Democrat who had the best chance of finishing second in the primary.

He went with Seymour.

"Personally, I liked this Mary Lynne Sorenson better," he told Manuela. "But you know what?"

"What, *bruto*?"

"We are impelled to pick a winner."

"Jordan Diaz agrees with you, too."

"I talked to him about it. He says the party liked Seymour but didn't feel comfortable endorsing him. They thought it would make all the other candidates mad enough to sit out the general election. It kind of reminded me of the old Will Rogers quote."

"And that is?"

"Something like, 'I am not a member of any organized party. I am a Democrat.' "

According to the Porsche's GPS device, they were nearing their destination. The grassy field with a kids playground and a couple of baseball diamonds on the outskirts of Manteca was so new it didn't have a name yet. But it did have what looked to be a hundred people of all ages and sexes wearing shorts and sensible walking shoes mid-morning of what would be a beautifully sunshiny 89-degree Sunday.

Manuela parked the car, and she and Link strolled across the grass just in time for a briefing provided by one of the canvassing bosses. When it was over, Link and Manuela and the other volunteers slathered on sun screen beneath hiking caps with neck shades. They flipped through their clipboards crammed with voter registration sheets and vote-by-mail documents and voter pledge cards and instructions on how to talk to voters. They checked their phone apps to find their turf. They armed themselves with Jesse Seymour literature. They snagged a handful of granola bars.

They were off to get out the vote.

Link kind of knew what to do. Manuela was basically along for the ride. They drove to a neighborhood not too far away and parked the car and pounded the pavement on their door-to-door march. By lunchtime, they had knocked on 42 doors. About half of them nobody answered. About half of the rest, they were voting for the Democrat, only they didn't know which one.

"Let me tell you a little bit about Jesse," Link would tell them, as if he and the candidate had known each other forever.

The Dem people at the doors listened and took the literature. They were very concerned about Trump. They said they wanted Trump checked out, impeached; a few even said jailed. One said he wanted Trump dead. Link didn't go down that road. He talked about healthcare and Social Security.

Surprisingly, a good chunk of the Reeps at the door were just as receptive as the Dems. They also expressed concerns about their erratic president. The ones who liked Trump made things fairly easy on Link and Manuela. They weren't nasty at all, not most of them anyway. They actually seemed kind of nice, nothing like the angry mobs they saw at the Trump campaign rallies on TV. Link and Manuela thanked them and moved on to the next door.

They finished their territory by 1 o'clock in the afternoon, headed back to the park to check out, and drove home to Sacramento.

Pulling up to Manuela's house on 22nd Street, they noticed a couple things that seemed to be out of the ordinary.

For one thing, it looked to them like somebody had driven a fucking truck up and over the curb and across Manuela's small patch of a front yard. The fucking asshole who drove the truck tore the hell out of her grass and totally wiped out two rows of California poppies and brodiaea that bloomed on either side of the walkway leading up to her front porch.

"I spent two weekends planting those goddamned things," Manuela said.

For another, they could see from the street what looked to be a pile of wood chips dumped onto the porch itself. Douglas fir, Link could tell, on closer inspection. As he picked up the chips and held them in his hand, he felt the wood. He knew this wood, intimately. He had touched it before.

He didn't even have to see the white paint that he had applied on its polished outer shell, the color of the chef's jacket he had fashioned for the little guy with the wild hair-do. He could still see fragments of his worn sneakers.

It was the piece, really, that launched Link toward celebrity. Not that he really cared for the celebrity. But of every piece he had ever done, he felt as close to this as any. He'd carved it to reflect the affection he felt for the man who had helped turn Sacramento into an eating destination, the basis of the town's ascension into its transforming identity.

Lying in ruins on the porch in front of him, Link picked up the pieces of the little statue that he had last seen suspended on a platform high on the brick wall inside Mullaney's Building and Loan.

Yet, it was only a thing. A thing that somebody obviously had stolen out of the restaurant and apparently chopped up with an axe and deposited in a pile on Manuela's front porch.

When the brief moment of emotion passed, Link actually chuckled. To think that somebody could be twisted enough to go through so much trouble.

Only, he knew this was not so funny. He knew that whoever did this was a fairly dangerous fellow, who knew exactly where Manuela lived. He knew that whoever did this also knew that Link had become deeply entangled with her.

Bedford and Beauregard were on the prowl.

As Link stood in wonderment over the demolished statue, Manuela walked around to the F Street side of the house to chronicle some additional damage: more grass churned into mud. Ground sprinklers torn out. A row of camellias beneath her kitchen window, obliterated. The side of her house, scraped by a rampaging vehicle that left behind swooshes of black paint.

Manuela, of course, became very pissed off. But before she let loose her tirade, her attention shifted from the wreckage of her yard, to the blinking police lights about two blocks up F Street from her house.

"*Bruto*," she called to Link. "I think we better go check this out."

35/*Yukon Territory*

Detective Andrew Wiggins supervised the loading of the black

GMC Yukon XL, license plate 7HDF310, onto the flat-bedded diesel tow truck. It was not how he had planned to spend his Sunday morning and afternoon – or, the way it looked now, his evening.

He had been fishing, on a friend's bass boat, down in the Delta, when he got the call. It came straight from Chief Samuel Kahn to Wiggins'ss cell phone.

"I hope you're liking the vandalism squad," the chief told him.

"Not particularly," Wiggins replied.

"Let me know what you find out about the Yukon," Kahn said. "Maybe we can get you a task force."

Wiggins couldn't believe it the morning of the Cesar Chavez desecration when he got a wake-up call from the chief who told him to drop everything else he was doing and focus on the vandalism. He was a homicide guy.

Somehow, the chief was prescient.

Cold homicides could wait, the chief said, if a warm one could be prevented.

"Take all the overtime you need, Detective," the chief told him, signing off.

Wiggins'ss fishing buddy sped him up to Freeport where a patrol car waited for him at the dock. The black-and-white ran him into Midtown to assess the F Street crash that a witness reported at 5:42 a.m. The one-man Vandalism Squad arrived at the roundabout at F and 27th streets at exactly 10:02 a.m. Standing on its head just on the east side of the traffic circle, beneath a canopy of elm and sycamore, amid the cottages and popular four-flats that used to rent for nothing but were now pushing $2,000 a month: a 2018 black GMC Yukon XL.

The traffic sergeant in charge of the scene walked Wiggins through the skid marks. They showed that the driver had attempted a feeble maneuver to make it through the circle but that he or she reacted way too late. The driver seemed to have pretty much said, fuck it, and plowed straight through the circle to an exit point at 2 o'clock. The Yukon then tried to swerve back toward the middle of the street, turned too sharply, and went into a side-over-side roll to its angled, upside-down position on the other side of the roundabout.

Some dude with a pointy haircut and a trimmy beard reported the crash. He said he got up at sunrise, as usual, to walk his dog down F Street, when the Yukon sped forward. He told the cops that after the tumble, he approached the Yukon to see if anybody needed help. No need: the two guys inside wiggled themselves free.

"And ran away," Pointy Hair told the cops.

The witness said he last saw them headed north on 27th Street. One of the two appeared to be bleeding pretty badly from his face or head.

When Wiggins reached the traffic circle, the first thing he learned was that two uniforms had followed the blood trail that began at the crash site. Up 27th it turned left on C Street. It continued west to just across 20th street, where the bike path began and paralleled the railroad tracks. More blood led the officers through a bike tunnel that bore through the berm that propped the old east-west Southern Pacific railroad line over the rival north-south Union Pacific. On the other side of the tunnel, the blood drops all of a sudden disappeared. Crime scene investigators speculated that having made it to safety, the two men stopped to treat the cut, possibly using a shirt or some other article of clothing and applying pressure to the wound. The CSI squad was still processing the area around the bike path by the time Detective Wiggins arrived at F and 27th.

The first thing Wiggins asked the traffic sergeant when he landed in Midtown:

"Did you get the VIN?"

"Of course not," the sergeant told him.

Wiggins was not surprised. What self-respecting vandal trafficking in stolen cars who was sophisticated enough to put a phony license plate on a vehicle is going to drive it around with its legitimate 17-digit vehicle identification number? If they knew what they were doing, they'd peel, file, burn, rip, or blast it off. Whatever it took to get rid of the digits taped inside the door jamb, underneath the dashboard beneath the driver's side windshield, and stamped into the vehicle's frame and engine block and other assorted parts.

So, the detective proceeded on the assumption that this car was stolen, too, same as Mai Vang's vehicle, which in all likelihood had since been ground into dust at one of the Sunrise Boulevard auto dismantlers in Rancho Cordova.

The Yukon, however, could still have tons of information to provide to investigators. Wiggins ordered it hermetically sealed and transported back to the impound shop.

"Do we know if it has been reported stolen?" Wiggins asked the traffic sergeant.

"Kind of tough to tell for sure," the sergeant answered, "without the right license plate and no VIN."

"Isn't there a database that just tells you what kind of cars somebody reported stolen?"

"We did do a crosscheck against 2018 GMC Yukon XLs. Nothing around here to verify against a plate or a VIN number."

"OK, OK, OK," Wiggins said. "Get that thing back to the yard and find me a VIN number, and get CSI to vacuum the whole damn thing from the inside out."   Wiggins watched the tow truck pull away with the Yukon. He had pivoted toward the beginning of the blood trail, when he saw a tall, lean, indigenous male person in the company of a woman the cop knew from the TV news. The pair walked up F Street and stopped at the yellow tape that sealed off the crime scene.

"You appear to be out of uniform, Detective," Lincoln Adams told the detective as he approached Wiggins.

Wiggins was wearing cargo shorts, flip flops, and a T-shirt that read "Broadway Bait, Rod & Gun."

"You again," Wiggins responded to Link. "Can't I for once work a case that involves you, without you showing up at it?"

"I'm just trying to be helpful, officer," Link said. He pointed at the Yukon. "This car," he said, "looks familiar."

"I should say it does," Wiggins responded. "I've spent the better part of the last week looking at it on film."

"I think we've got some more information for you, Detective," Manuela said.

She told him about her front yard, the sideswipe on her house, and the pile of wood chips left on her doorstep, which Link knew to be the remains of the pint-sized chef he'd carved for Carrick Mullaney.

"You might want to check with Mullaney, too, about a break-in at his restaurant," Link broke in.

After a second to process the incoming information, Wiggins said, "OK." He pulled his pocket-sized notebook out of his back pocket – he carried it with him wherever he went, even down into the Delta on a bass boat. The detective had plenty of work ahead of him. At least no asshole reporters showed up. No TV trucks, none of that shit.

At that moment Loni Cohen walked up to the tape, next to Link.

"Don't you ever take a day off?" Wiggins asked her.

"As a matter of fact, I was kind of enjoying this one," she said. "I can't help it if you've got a couple of nut cases on the loose. Oh, and nice legs."

Wiggins looked down below his cargo shorts and gave her a look. Mainly, he wondered: How the hell did she know about the wrecked Yukon? They hadn't put anything out on the news, and dispatchers, to the best of his knowledge, were not in the practice of calling reporters.

He surmised that Chief Kahn's first call, once he was alerted to the re-emergence of the Yukon, was to the detective. The second, to Loni Cohen. "Have you talked to our press people?" Wiggins asked.

"I tried," Cohen answered. "Nobody's home."

Wiggins knew that this gave him full authority to spin the story any way he wanted. Or to keep his mouth shut entirely. He could play it any way he wanted.

For now, he played it coy.

"I really can't tell you anything," he told the reporter. "Believe me, it's not because I'm being an asshole. I've just got too damn much work to do."

"So, what am I supposed to write?" Cohen asked.

"I'm sure you'll come up with something."

"And why is Mr. Adams here?"

"You're going to have to ask him."

"Well?" Cohen asked, turning to Link.

Manuela, the public relations expert, tensed instinctively before remembering she had a naturally-born perfect client.

"It's a lovely evening," he said to Cohen, "and I was out for a walk."

"You live in the neighborhood?"

"I do."

"So do I," Cohen said. "Right up the block."

"We are all very lucky," Link continued.

"Let's all count our blessings," Wiggins interjected. Turning to Cohen, he said, "If you'll excuse me, I have to talk to my victim in private."

"That would be me," Link said to Cohen, as he ducked under the crime tape.

"OK," Wiggins told him. "You've got to lose her, and then I'll meet you back at what's-her-name's house. You said 22nd and F?"

"Southeast corner. Are you going to tell her anything?"

"The reporter? I'm not sure yet," Wiggins said. "I've got to figure out what I want our boys to think they know."

36/*Raising VIN*

At the police impound yard, mechanics dropped the engine block from the Yukon to get a look at where the vehicle identification number used to be.

"Grind job," one of the grease monkeys told Wiggins.

The detective was not surprised at the news of the illegal removal. Neither was the mechanic. Expecting such an erasure, the mechanic had already put in a call to the DA's crime lab.

Not 10 minutes after Wiggins arrived, the geek stepped into the garage.

"Hello, Sammy," Wiggins said to the forensics tech. "Long time no see."

"Hi, Detective," the scientist, Sam Lillis, greeted Wiggins in return. "I think it was two years ago, wasn't it? The gangster who accidentally shot his buddy to death and got forty-to-life?"

"Down on 79th Street."

"That's the one," Lillis said. "Kind of a rough deal for the kid, don't you think."

"No, I don't think," Wiggins said. "He and the homeboys were trying to kill somebody, in case you forgot."

"Still seems unfair to me. I saw him at the defense table. He looked like a nice kid."

"Nice kid, fuck," Wiggins said. "Six guys, standing in the street, shooting up a house in broad daylight, in not even that bad of a neighborhood."

"He killed his pal, Detective."

"I'm heartbroken for the bunch of them," Wiggins shot back. "They were all fucking gang bangers. He was a fucking gang banger, and this wasn't the first time he shot somebody. Maybe you forgot your testimony about him filing the serial number off his gun."

"There was that," Lillis agreed.

" 'Nice kid,' my ass."

"OK, so what do we have here?" Lillis asked. "A VIN removal. I've done a few of these – no problem. But this takes a while, you know."

"If there's anything I've got," Wiggins said, "it's a while."

"Then let's get started," Lillis said.

With the engine block sitting on a work bench, the first thing Lillis did was set up a makeshift photography studio, with umbrellas and lights. He snapped off a few shots before setting up a magnifying lamp over the removed engine part. He brushed the area where the number had been and deposited whatever materials he picked up on a glass slide that he wrapped and retained for evidentiary purposes. Then he polished the metal and

212

gave it another once-over with a rag dipped in gasoline. For the next couple of hours, Lillis cotton-swabbed the area where the numbers had been removed with a chemical compound called Fry's Reagent. Little by little, the numbers resurfaced. Snap, snap, snap – more pictures. When the chemical dried, Lillis cleaned it again with some water and repeated the process over and over – a dozen more times over, stopping to take photographs at every round.

He ably raised 15 of the 17 numbers. He told Wiggins that's the best he could get. "Two of those fuckers are just not cooperating," the forensic man said.

Wiggins snuck in for a look before Lillis stuck in the modeling clay.

"Not bad," the detective said, examining Lillis's work with the magnifying lamp. "Not bad at all, for a liberal dickhead."

"I love you, too, Detective," Lillis responded.

Wiggins held out his hand, and Lillis slapped him five. The numbers gave the detective plenty to work with.

"Hey, man, can you give me a ride back to headquarters?" Wiggins asked Lillis.

"Liberal dickhead, at your service," Lillis said.

"I appreciate that. You're so nice that maybe one of these years I'll vote for Obama."

Ten minutes later, Wiggins was at his desk, working the DMV for VIN partials.

It came back with a hit.

It came back with a name.

It came back with a town.

It came back with an address and a phone number.

It came back to a guy who used to be a cop.

His work on the Orange County congressional races finished, Frankie Cameron returned to Sacramento on Sunday night and checked back into the Sterling. He wrote his story in the terminal at the John Wayne Airport. It cleared the desk fairly easily – noncontroversial, just an interesting, informative read on the three flippable seats, with the subtext of the right-wing losing its grip on what used to be a conservative stronghold.

East Coasters didn't know the Orange County stereotype no longer struck, probably because their newspapers kept telling the story like it was some kind of astonishing new development. The place had been liberalizing for years. It should have been renamed Purple County, it was so in play.

Frankie knew all this and tried to talk his editors out of doing what had become a journalistic cliché. When they didn't relent, he just did his job. Like a pro.

He couldn't wait to get back into White Rock and the Slavics.

From the Sacramento airport, he got a Lyft to Kupros, the bar and grill on 21st Street with about 30 handles. He downed a chicken Caesar and a pint of the new Wet Hop Willy IPA from Moonraker. Back in the hotel, he settled in with Bill Browder's book on the Russian government's murder of the tax lawyer, Sergei Magnitsky. He just got to the part where Magnitsky uncovered a scheme by corrupt Russian cops to steal $230 million from the national treasury. Then his cell phone beeped with a news alert.

He put down the book. He picked up the phone.

The *Sacramento Beacon* headline: "New attack – and possible break – in vandalism spree." The story appeared below the byline of rookie reporter Loni Cohen. It read:

"On the heels of another incident of possibly racially-motivated vandalism, Sacramento police said Sunday night that they believe they have recovered the vehicle that has been used in a series of attacks.

"Officials said they found the car after it crashed through a

traffic circle in Midtown, apparently after its occupants used the vehicle to shred the front yard of a prominent local public relations consultant. Witnesses said they saw two men running away from the 2018 GMC Yukon XL immediately after the crash, according to police. No arrests were made.

"Still, sources said investigators believe they made a significant breakthrough in the case with the recovery of the sports utility vehicle. Police impounded the car Sunday afternoon, several hours after the 5:50 a.m. crash through the traffic circle at 27th and F streets, several blocks from the vandalized front yard of MJ Affairs public relations consultant Manuela Fonseca, the former television reporter. Her lengthy client list includes local wood sculptor Lincoln Adams, whose totem pole was recently unveiled in Cesar Chavez Plaza and itself was the subject of the vandalism series that is under intense police investigation.

"The destruction of Fonseca's front yard is the third significant incident linked to the same suspects in the last three weeks. Previously, police say, two men described as Tennessee residents spray-painted racist graffiti on the Cesar Chavez statue in downtown Sacramento – during the same incident in which they are believed to have stuck a knife in the rear of Adams's totem pole. In a second incident, two men got out of the same car involved in Sunday's crash and clubbed a mannequin fashioned into a statue of Devante Davidson, the young African American man who was shot to death in the backyard of his grandmother's home in March by two Sacramento police officers.

"Police sources said the crashed SUV had been registered to a former Sacramento County sheriff's deputy who lives in an unincorporated Placer County area north of Auburn. The Beacon has learned that authorities identified the former deputy as David Allen Christiansen, 45, who had been fired from the department two years ago for what the agency described as 'racially-inflammatory conduct toward a fellow deputy.' According to a lawsuit filed against the Sheriff's Department, Christiansen had deposited several bananas on the driver's seat of a female African American deputy who had been promoted

215

over him to an open sergeant's position. The department ultimately settled the suit filed by the female deputy for $2.5 million.

"'We don't know yet how Christiansen plays into any of these incidents, or if he plays into them at all,'" said a police source who asked to remain anonymous because he was not authorized to speak on the record about the investigation. 'The only thing we know for a fact is that he was the registered owner of the vehicle that we believe was used in all of these incidents.'

"While Christiansen has not been arrested or charged in the case, the source said that he was being questioned as this story went to press. Police did not say whether or what kind of relationship the fired deputy had with the two suspects from outside Memphis, Tenn., whom authorities identified as Davis Beauregard Barton, 29, and Bedford Forrest MacMillian, 21."

The name of the fired former deputy rang bells with Frankie.

Christiansen, if Frankie recalled correctly, was having himself an exceptionally mediocre career as a patrol deputy in Sacramento's northeastern suburbs. He'd done nothing of note, but decided, what the hell – I'll take the sergeant's test. Christiansen scored in about the middle of the pack, and, as reported by Loni Cohen, was passed over for one of the open positions by an African American female deputy who scored a few points below him on the test.

There was more to the story, though, than affirmative action: Christiansen, it turned out, had the hots for the woman. He had even dated her a few times, and it was all good and funny until she got the promotion and he didn't. Then their relationship became a bit more complicated.

Frankie helped work the story when the woman went public with an internal affairs complaint she filed against the Sheriff's Department. She decided to speak out when the department responded to her complaint by rescinding her promotion and transferring her to work in the Rio Cosumnes Correctional Facility, the sheriff's lockup for sentenced, longer-term felons. The Branch Jail, as they called it, also served as a graveyard for the careers of veteran deputies who had fallen into administrative

216

disfavor.

She sued, and a year later when her case was about to go to trial, the county settled the case with the $2.5 million payment. The term of the settlement included her reinstatement as a sergeant – and the termination of David Allen Christiansen. Then she quit the department and became chief of security for the Sacramento Kings professional basketball team. Christiansen filed a lawsuit to get his job back. It went nowhere.

After reviewing the Christiansen stories in the *Beacon*'s electronic library, Frankie Googled the former deputy. In the two years since his firing, Christiansen had become a licensed car broker up near Auburn.

What a weird business, Frankie thought. Who'd want to pay a guy to go shopping for cars? Whatever he saved you would have to be more than his fee, right? Which meant that his fee had to be pretty low, or his customers had to have lots of money, or they didn't give a shit about whatever the hell they drove, or that they were a couple of white boys from Tennessee looking to do some white nationalist damage in Sacramento.

All of a sudden Frankie kind of wanted to be working for the *Beacon* again. This statute-shattering thing, it looked like it was developing into a hell of a story.

First, he needed to check up on his pal.

Link picked up on the first ring.

"Hey, man," Frankie asked. "You all right?"

"Hold on a second, Frankie," Link answered. "Altuve's up."

For no sane reason, Link did not turn off the Sunday night baseball game, even though the Boston Red Sox were leading the defending world champion Houston Astros, 9-3, with two outs in the bottom of the ninth. A blowout, in early June, and still he watched.

Frankie heard the babbling of the non-stop yakkers in the background. Under no circumstances would they ever shut up, he thought to himself. Like Mick Jagger said: a bunch of useless information just to drive his imagination.

Frankie could hear Link click them off.

"Fly ball to right," Link reported. "Game over. How are you,

Frankie?"

"I asked you first. What's up with this shit?"

"To what might you be referring?"

Frankie laughed. Nobody could turn down the volume on a crisis better than Link.

"Well, there is this story about these knuckleheads from Tennessee tearing up your girlfriend's front yard and then rolling their ride through a traffic circle somewhere near her crib."

"Yes," Link said.

"And it's usually customary for friends of the person or persons involved, to ask them afterwards if they lost any limbs, or had their eye put out, or were somehow inconvenienced by the unusual event."

"Are you referring to anybody I know?" Link said.

"Yes," Frankie replied. "I believe that one of the persons involved, if the *Beacon* story is accurate, would be you."

"Oh, yes. Me," Link said. "What would you like to know?"

"Everything," Frankie said, on his way to exasperation.

Link stopped playing it obtuse.

"It appears Manuela was targeted by the same fellows who have been causing so much consternation around this city the last couple of weeks," Link said. "The two of us are sitting in her living room right now, on the couch, looking out the front window. She has armed herself with some kind of weapon, and she says if she sees these guys again, that it will be the last time the two of them participate as members of this life."

"She's got a gun?"

"A nine-millimeter pistol."

"A Glock 17," Frankie heard Manuela say in the background.

"One thing we know about guns," Link said.

"I know – you keep them around, and the likelihood goes way up that somebody gets shot," Frankie responded. "You've said that many times."

"An irrefutable fact. Yet Manuela seems insistent on exercising her inalienable Second Amendment right. She purchased the weapon several years ago and took lessons as a matter of home protection, I guess. I have tried to dissuade her –

218

I have informed her of my statistical assessment. Have I informed you of her response?"

"As a matter of fact, you haven't."

"Manuela?" Link said.

He held the phone within range of her voice that did not need much amplifying. She exclaimed, in its general direction: "Damn right somebody's going to get shot, and it's not going to be me."

"Yes, sir," Link continued. "If these boys are smart, they will not show up around here again."

Manuela was not smiling.

Frankie and Link went over the events of the day, and Frankie was assured that his friend was not in imminent peril. It was very similar to the way Link had responded the previous year, when he was held hostage for a few hours by a couple of Russian meatheads. The clearer and more present the danger, it seemed to Frankie, the more detached and unemotional his friend became.

The conversation swung around to the topic of David Allen Christiansen, car broker.

"I can't say that I remember him," Link said, when Frankie relayed his reporting on him of a few years ago, followed by Loni Cohen's story of just a few minutes ago. "Detective Wiggins called a while ago to update me. He mentioned the name. Nobody I know."

It had been a few minutes since he read the story, but only now was Frankie beginning to feel the sensation, this very real physical thing that he felt overtaking him. Who knows where in his body it began. The only thing Frankie knew was that he was exploding out of his sides, just like he'd always felt, from when he was a kid and ran out on ghetto murders in the middle of the night in L.A., to now, in his mid-50s and aging rapidly, yet still an addict to the adrenaline rush.

The inflammation of nerves and tension came on like the first stage of an acid trip. He heated up from the inside out. He felt an inflammation of his nerve endings. His heart rate escalated. His brain waves stepped up the pace. He surrendered to a psycho-electric surge. It made him think smarter and faster. It made him lose sleep. It made him want to smoke cigarettes. It made him need to get off the phone with Link and drive up to Auburn, right now.

"Wiggins," Frankie said to himself, though Link was still on the line. "I need his number."

"I'll give you his cell," Link said.

38/DeCoulomb Connection

Detective Andrew Wiggins did not expect the call from Frankie, certainly not at 9 o'clock on a Sunday night, after he'd spent all day in the field, investigating a traffic wreck.

Maybe the 18-year-old Glenlivet on the rocks softened him up. Maybe he was just relaxed and feeling good. Maybe he just knew it was time to drop the pretense of his dislike for reporters. Maybe he liked the way Loni Cohen turned her stories, telling the public what it needed to know and at the same time allowing him to shape events to the benefit of his own work. Maybe he liked working with her.

Maybe he listened when she told him that Frankie Cameron was her hero.

"I hear you're not really such a horseshit guy," Wiggins told Frankie, as the Scotch smoothed out the detective's evening. "If I was horseshit to you, it wasn't personal. We just had a lot of stuff going on last year with your pal."

"You could have fooled me, it wasn't personal," Frankie responded – relieved that he was finally getting over with Wiggins, but chuckling a bit about the detective's assessment of their relationship. "Like the time in Benny's when you told Link you wouldn't talk to him as long as I was sitting there."

"Now hold on there, cowboy," Wiggins shot back. "I did not say I wouldn't talk to him as long as you were sitting there. I just said that if you didn't shut up, I was leaving."

Frankie knew better than to argue with a cop's memory. They

never forgot anything, down to the smallest detail. There was no such thing as a distinction without a difference. Still, he couldn't resist replying:

"I don't really get the distinction."

Now Wiggins had Frankie where he wanted him, with enough Scotch swirling through his system to soften him up.

"That's why you're a reporter and I'm a cop," he said. "We mess up just a little detail like that and the next thing we know some douchebag is walking out of jail. We know that everything is distinct. Everything has to be precise in our world. Yours, not so much."

Frankie stayed quiet.

"You still there?" Wiggins asked.

"Yep. I don't want to argue with you, Detective. I mean I get it that you don't really respect what we do. But I'll tell you who does: the... "

"Hold it, hold it, hold it," Wiggins said. "Don't be such a whiny bitch. Nothing I'm saying here..."

"...the Founding Fathers. They knew that without us, we'd have a much, much different country," Frankie broke in.

"...is meant to be disrespectful of the news media," Wiggins continued. "Hey, I still subscribe to your paper, even without the box scores or the fact that it never has shit about last night's games, and you've got to wait two days to find out what happened at the City Council meeting, and the damn thing isn't even half the size it used to be. I support the fucking press. Like I was about to say, nothing I said that night at Benny's, or any other time, was personal. I was on a federal task force, and there was no fucking way they could have been perceived as cooperating with 'the enemy of the people.' They were very sensitive times. They still are." "Understood," Frankie said. He needed to steer the conversation back to the Yukon. "About this Christiansen guy."

Wiggins sipped his Scotch and wondered:

"Why does *The Washington Post* give a shit?"

Frankie told him, "It's a good story."

Wiggins couldn't disagree.

"I think so, too, although I'm no expert," he said. "So what do you want to know that I haven't already told that girl who took your place at the *Beacon*?"

"Can you confirm that everything she's got is accurate?"

"Off the record, yeah."

"Anything else you told her that she didn't use?"

"Not really. I think she got it all in there."

"She didn't get at all into what Christiansen told you guys. I think your people were still talking to him when she posted the story."

"Yeah," Wiggins said. "I guess the bottom line is that we're going through his interview pretty closely. It looks like he lied to us about a couple of things, but if you print that you'll never be talking to me again. Said he didn't know these crackers until they came to him to lease a truck, back in April. Denied knowing anything about the missing VIN numbers."

"Do you believe him?"

"Not on everything, no. We need to do a little more work on him."

Frankie didn't want to push his luck too far with Wiggins, but he felt compelled to remark: "I mean, this had 'federal case' written all over it from the beginning," Frankie said. "How come the FBI isn't on this case?"

"We're in touch," Wiggins replied. "They're really hinky though."

"Why?"

"All the shit in Washington. Prosecuting white nationalists is not exactly this administration's top priority. Now, if the guy who stabbed your statue in the back had been a Honduran immigrant, they'd have sent us a squadron. But these were just a couple of crackers from Tennessee, so they're slow-walking it – no-walking it would actually be more accurate. But they're coming around, I think."

"Kind of interesting, isn't it," Frankie said, "that a couple Tennessee racists come out here and get hooked up with an ex-cop who got kicked off the force for being a racist."

"Birds of a feather, man."

"But Christiansen denies he's got anything to do with what they did?"

"Yep. Our people spent a couple hours with him today, with the feds listening in – one guy. They found him to be very cooperative. Also, it looks like he's doing fairly well for himself."

"What do you mean?"

"Money-wise. Lives in a little tract north of Auburn. Nice enough neighborhood – I'd live there."

"Sounds pretty normal, for an ex-cop."

"But one thing about it wasn't normal at all."

"What's that?"

"What he drove."

"What's he drive?"

"A DeCoulomb."

39/Down Goes Frankie

A blood orange glow highlighted the Sierra skyline when Frankie pulled his rental to the front of the apartment building in suburban Citrus Heights. Awaiting his arrival at the curb: the editor of the the *Slavic News of Sacramento*.

"I did a little research on your David Allen Christiansen," Radimir Valishnikov told Frankie, as he shut the car door behind him. "I couldn't find anything other than what you already know."

"Good," Frankie said. "For once, I'm even with you."

They hit a drive-thru coffee stop and got back onto I-80, headed for North Auburn to see what they could see.

Morning sunlight gained momentum as Frankie and Rad turned north off the freeway, onto Highway 49, a stretch of California gold country that was damn downright ugly. Traffic backed up in the other direction, toward the interstate, filled with white people one to a car. They wanted country living. They settled for a sprawl of fast food joints and auto body shops and sand and gravel depositories, car dealerships and the Les Schwab Tire Center, NAPA Auto Parts, the Walgreens-Anytime Fitness-Carl's Jr.-Golden 1 Credit Union onslaught that just happened to be located on the edge of the forest. Somebody forgot to put in sidewalks, but who needed them, anyway, when nobody got out of their car? Who in world history has ever *walked* to a Best Buy, or a Mel's Diner, or a Taco Bell? The Dollar Tree or the Chevy's? No car, no truck, no service. Only a nut got out of their car in Highway 49 through North Auburn. You walked at risk of death. You could get run over walking to Big Five to buy the components easily assembled into an assault rifle or to Little Caesar's for some fine Italian dining.

"This is worse than Orange County," said the reporter, who had just spent three days there.

"I've never been there," Rad replied. "For the last number of years, I haven't been anywhere. I guess that's the way it is when you're obsessed."

"And you are obsessed with?"

"Konstantin Cosmenko, of course."

Over the past couple of weeks, Frankie had developed his own unusually deep interest in the Russian Slavic USA Pentecostal Church minister, who wanted to be known as Bob Jones. The night before, it had taken him a couple of minutes to stir from the catatonia that overtook him when Detective Wiggins told him about the DeCoulomb observed in David Allen Christiansen's driveway.

It meant something. But what?

What was really weird was that when Frankie asked Wiggins for Christiansen's address, the detective actually gave it to him. On the hush-hush, of course. He really was getting over with the cop.

Frankie, meanwhile, thought it wise to bring in the Russian-language press on the story, and Rad Valishnikov was more than happy to take the trip to Christiansenville.

They stopped at the Panera Bread in the middle of the Highway 49 mess to come up with a game plan.

"First of all, it is not illegal to own a DeCoulomb," Frankie said. "It could mean absolutely nothing. The fact he's a car broker makes this even less likely to lead anywhere."

Rad, thick in the middle, did not let heavy conversation get in the way of a meal, especially when someone else was buying. He bit into his scrambled bacon and egg on ciabatta. He spoke with his mouth full.

"I agree with you, Mr. Frankie," Rad told his partner. "But let's be clear on our instincts. We both believe that this car is a piece of the puzzle. We would not be here otherwise."

Frankie picked at his oatmeal. He was more nervous than hungry. He wired himself up on coffee, and thought about buying a pack of smokes, just like the old days whenever he was out on a big story.

"Really, what do we have here?" Frankie asked. "We've got a guy who rented a car to a couple of white supremacists who come out from Tennessee to destroy a statue of an iconic labor leader, at the same time that the statues of their own heroes are being removed by their local governments. Now we find out that the guy who gave the racists their SUV drives a DeCoulomb, and we know that these cars are being moved out of here in the dead of night through a warehouse owned and operated by a company loosely linked to a Russian church that it just so happens appears to be financing another racist upstart's renegade campaign in Modesto, apparently to keep the Democrats from flipping the house."

"Yet it all could mean absolutely nothing, like you say," Rad said, gleefully raising an eyebrow.

Frankie was too involved to play along. "And what the hell does Ian Courtney have to do with this?"

"I have my suspicions, Mr. Frankie," Rad said.

Frankie pulled out his cell phone to check the time. It was about 10 minutes to 8.

"Hold on to them for now, Rad," Frankie said. "Let's get up the hill."

They returned to Frankie's rental for the drive up the Gold Rush Highway, a quarter-mile short of where the forest reclaimed the scenic upper hand.

Rad mapped the trip out on his cell phone. He directed Frankie to Christiansen's address: Right on Dry Creek Road and a couple more lefts and rights onto a cul-de-sac cut into the surrounding, oak-studded foothills, still slightly green from the winter rains. At the end of the block was a tired-looking, three-bedroom rancher that looked like it had been converted into a parking lot. No fewer than 10 vehicles were parked in the driveway, on the front lawn, and angled into the curb in front of the house: a couple late-model pickups, an SUV, one Mini Cooper, a few sedans from Japan, Western Europe and Detroit, and right in the middle of them all – a brand new candy-apple red DeCoulomb Modern Deluxe VXP.

"Goddamn," Frankie said, looking back at the DeCoulomb as he wheeled around at the end of the cul-de-sac. "That thing looks just like the one I saw in West Sacramento."

"You know what they say about candy-apple red DeCoulombs," Rad said.

"What's that?"

"They all look alike."

Frankie chuckled.

"Well, let's see what the driver looks like," he said.

Frankie circled the cul-de-sac and parked about five houses down, almost at the end of the block, and he and Rad got out and walked in silence toward the Christiansen address. Frankie checked to make sure his *Washington Post* press pass dangled from around his neck. Rad didn't believe in press passes. His press pass was the search for the truth. He wore a camera for a necklace.

Up Christiansen's driveway, another camera – the surveillance kind – recorded their approach to the house.

They made it about halfway up the driveway before a mid-40-ish-looking man stepped out the front door to greet them. He was muscular through the arms and chest, with a bit of a paunch in the midsection. He wore a white T-shirt and blue jeans and brown work boots. His short brown hair had been tapered above the ears and down the neck.

For some reason, Frankie weirdly thought that the guy looked more familiar to him that he should have. He had seen Christiansen a couple of times in the courthouse, but only briefly, at very brief court hearings, a couple years back. He knew he'd seen the guy more recently than that, but he couldn't quite remember where from. Couldn't quite place the face.

With Christiansen approaching in a huff, Frankie held up his press pass and identified himself as a reporter. Radimir Valishnikov didn't say shit. Frankie introduced his partner as a member of the local Russian-language media.

Christiansen sounded as if he expected visitors. "I know who you are," Christiansen told Frankie. "I thought you quit that local rag that's dying on the vine."

"Well, I did go to Washington, to the *Post*," Frankie responded. "But they sent me out here to cover the California congressional races. Then your name came up."

"Don't tell me," Christiansen said. "One of your Sac PD buddies gave you my address to come up here and harass me some more."

"I did see in the *Beacon* that you came to their attention."

"Yeah, and it's a bunch of bullshit."

"You mean you don't own that car that crashed in Sacramento yesterday?"

"I leased a car to a couple guys who called me up looking for one. I find leases for people all the time. So what?"

"Do all your leases have their VIN numbers removed?"

Christiansen chuckled to himself.

"The fucking cops," he said. "What are they doing telling you shit like that for?"

Frankie said nothing.

Christiansen picked up his end of the impromptu interrogation:

"Hey, I just leased them the truck. I don't know what the hell they did to it. That's on them."

"So, you're saying they removed it?"

227

"I'm saying I don't know anything about it, and that's what I told the cops last night, and they believed me."

"Can I quote you on that?"

"I don't give a fuck what you write. Nobody believes a word of it, anyway."

"I'll take that as a yes."

Christiansen had barely noticed Frankie's partner until he piped up. "Mr. Christiansen," Rad said. "I was admiring your vehicles, and I see that you have one of those very hard-to-find DeCoulombs."

"And a Modern Deluxe VXP," Christiansen answered. "I don't think you'll find fifty of them in the world."

"Can I ask you, where did you buy it?"

"Where the hell do you think I bought it? From the showroom."

"But Mr. Christiansen," Rad countered. "I've done a little research on this car, and I can tell you – there are no dealerships in the world that handle that particular model."

"No wonder you're hanging around with this *Beacon* reject," Christiansen said to Rad. "You get everything wrong. There are at least five of them in Northern California."

"Not this model, Mr. Christiansen. The VXP is not for sale yet to the general public."

The VXP, of course, was a cut up from the standard Model R-x40.

"Well, maybe I'm not the general public," Christiansen said. "Maybe I know somebody. Maybe I bought this one right off the assembly line."

"Or maybe off White Rock USA," Rad said.

The mention of the business arm of the Russian Slavic Pentecostal Church seemed to stop Christiansen cold. His attitude changed from surly to potentially violent. He raised an eyebrow and looked at the editor.

"What are you talking about?" he said.

"You've heard of them?" Frankie asked.

"I read the news," Christiansen said. "I see that somehow you've made them controversial for legally participating in the democratic process."

"It's all public record, Mr. Christiansen," Frankie said, "and people have the right to know."

"And you have the right to know that it's time for you to leave."

"I understand, Mr. Christiansen. Just one last thing, before we go. What can you tell us about Bedford Forrest MacMillian and Davis Beauregard Barton?" Frankie asked. "That's the reason we came up here."

"The two guys from Tennessee?"

"Yes."

"Nothing. Now, why don't you get the fuck out of here before I call the cops? These guys up here ain't like the pussies you've got down there in Sacraghetto."

Frankie nodded his head. He'd already gotten more than what he expected out of the morning, which was nothing.

He turned to walk away, when a picture flashed through his head – where had he seen this guy before?

Before he could compare the guy in front of him with the mental image that had popped up in his head, Rad Valishnikov raised his camera to eye level to take a picture of the car broker.

It was David Allen Christiansen who snapped.

"You son of a bitch!" he yelled at the editor. "Give me that fucking camera! I'll break your fucking neck! You think you've got a problem with these white trash boys from Tennessee..."

Rad and Frankie backed out of Christiansen's yard, toward the street.

"Come onto my property and take my fucking picture?" Christiansen said, at the end of his driveway, standing face to face with Radimir Valishnikov and grabbing for the camera, while the editor held it away from him.

Frankie tried to step between them when Christiansen hauled off with a right hand aimed at Valishnikov. Like a misdirected North Korean nuclear missile, the punch instead caught Frankie Cameron on the side of the head, knocking him sideways and to the ground. Frankie got up at the count of two and jumped back in to try and corral Christiansen in a bear hug as the ex-cop

229

moved in on Rad.

This time, Christiansen flung Frankie away, and he grabbed Valishnikov by the shirt with his left hand and clutched for the camera with his right. Rad spun to his right and did a 180 in that direction toward the street, nimble for a fat guy, with the camera still in his possession – when he looked up to see the arrival of reinforcements.

Coming up the street: a parade of Sacramento police vehicles, including a crime lab on wheels.

At the head of the pack, on foot, and dressed in his regulation brown sports coat, tan slacks and brown loafers, this time with a purple tie:

Detective Andrew Wiggins.

40/*Warranted*

Frankie picked himself off the deck when Christiansen backed off amid the show of force.

"You all right?" Wiggins asked him.

"Sure," Frankie said. "Good enough."

"It would have been nice if we could have just come out here and served our search warrant and gone about our business," Wiggins said. "But I saw this man here hit you for no particular reason, so now I've got to ask you if you want to press charges, like a pussy."

"Since you put it that way," Frankie responded, "I will defer."

"Good decision," Wiggins said, before he turned to the car broker who had since caught up with Valishnikov and held him by the shirt with his right hand while reaching with his left for the editor's camera. "Let him go," Wiggins said, "or you're going straight to jail."

Christiansen released Rad.

"David Allen Christiansen," Wiggins informed the ex-cop. "I

have a warrant to search your house and the surrounding premises."

Frankie and Rad spent the better part of the rest of the day in the greater North Auburn area, Frankie with a bit of a headache but nothing too serious from the haymaker Christiansen landed just above his left ear, and Rad wandering up and down the street, talking to himself. Rad, under pressure, had a tendency to act a little strange, Frankie thought.

They watched for a couple hours while the Wiggins-led search team did its thing. One by one, a parade of tow trucks swung around the cul-de-sac and backed up to Christiansen's property to haul his cars away. Early in the afternoon, Frankie and Rad retreated to the In-N-Out Burger near the freeway for a couple Double-Doubles. By the time they returned, they saw that they had lost their hold on the story. Loni Cohen was standing with Wiggins and watching the last of Christiansen's vehicles saddled up for the trip to the Sacramento police garage.

"Fuck me," Frankie said. "I thought this was my fucking story."

"It's okay, Mr. Frankie," Rad said. "The more the merrier."

If Frankie was pissed off at the site of the rival reporter, he damn near popped a cork when he saw Wiggins hand Cohen some kind of document.

"What the fuck," he said to no one in particular as he broke off from Rad and quick-stepped it down to Christiansen's curb.

Soon as Frankie broke in on the cop's conversation with the chick reporter, Wiggins pulled out another copy of the same document and handed it to Frankie.

"Calm down," Wiggins told him, noticing the frantic look on Frankie's face. "There are plenty to go around."

It wasn't every day that the cops handed out copies of search warrant affidavits as if they were handbills on the street. Once in a while they'd leave them accidentally lying around the courthouse for reporters to somehow find and write salacious stories to dirty up a criminal defendant. Frankie wasn't about to question Wiggins's act of generosity. He happily accepted the offering.

"I take it this is for immediate release?" he asked.

Wiggins laughed.

"My new job – PIO, on my own cases."

The department's actual public information officer arrived the same time as the TV trucks.

"I've got to run, before they ask me to be on TV," Wiggins said. "Not comfortable with the camera."

Frankie retreated, his nose in Wiggin's sworn affidavit, which laid out the probable cause for the search. Back in his car, Frankie flipped through the parts where Wiggins laid out his experience and credentials, zipped through the details of the previous day's Midtown rollover that featured the GMC Yukon with a license plate removed from a stolen vehicle, and finally dipped into the juicy stuff.

"Your affiant," Wiggins wrote, "obtained a partial VIN number on the GMC Yukon retrieved from the impressions generated from the chemical analysis conducted by forensic technician S. Lillis. Your affiant ran the partial VIN number through a Department of Motor Vehicles computer. The computer search turned up four close matches. One of the close matches came back to a 2018 GMC Yukon XL. The registered owner of the GMC Yukon XL with the partially-identified VIN number was identified as Subject David Allen Christiansen of North Auburn, CA. Your affiant dispatched two detectives to contact Subject Christiansen at his home. Subject Christiansen admitted to leasing a Yukon to Subjects Davis Beauregard Barton and Bedford Forrest MacMillian. Subjects Barton and MacMillian are the prime suspects in at least three (3) recent acts of racially-motivated vandalism in the City of Sacramento. Subject Christiansen said he knew nothing about the VIN alteration on the GMC Yukon. Investigators' plain sight observation, however, revealed the presence of a 900 Watt Electronic Flat-Head Angle Grinder on the front porch of Subject Christiansen's residence. Your affiant has previously conducted approximately twenty-five (25) auto theft investigations. In his experience, your affiant knows that professional car thieves and 'chop shop' operators who deal in stolen auto parts commonly use items such as hand grinders to attempt to obliterate VIN numbers stamped into engine blocks. Investigators also observed on Subject Christiansen's property the presence of an additional ten (10) vehicles of various makes and sizes.

"In the course of his investigation, your affiant examined a variety of Internet 'chat rooms' and websites operated by so-called 'white nationalist' political groups. One of these websites your affiant examined was run by an organization that calls itself 'The White Right.' In examining 'readers comments' under news articles posted on 'The White Right' website, your affiant observed extensive written exchanges between one author identified as 'White Cop' and another author identified as 'Nathan Bedford Forever.' In an interview with Sacramento police officers on Sunday night, June 3, 2018, Subject Christiansen admitted that he corresponded on 'The White Right' website under the name 'White Cop.' Subject Christiansen also informed officers that the author who corresponded on 'The White Right' website under the name 'Nathan Bedford Forever' was in fact subject Bedford Forrest MacMillian.

"Based on his 15 years of experience as a criminal investigator, it is your affiant's belief that Subject Christiansen is involved in an operation that provided a motor vehicle to Subjects MacMillian and Barton for the purpose of their vandalism schemes in the Sacramento area, and that he either participated in the removal of the vehicle's identification number or had reason to believe that it had been so removed, and that when he was interviewed the night of the June 3, 2018, rollover of the subject utility vehicle he concealed and attempted to conceal that information from Sacramento police investigators. It is also your affiant's belief that Subject Christiansen may be in the business of providing vehicles to other so-called 'white nationalists' for their endeavors in other jurisdictions in the United States and that he maintains some of those vehicles at his residential property in North Auburn, Calif.

"Based on information obtained in his current investigation, your affiant requests the search of Subject David Allen Christiansen's residence for the following items: one (1) 2018

MINI Cooper, three (3) 2018 Chevy Volts, one (1) 2017 Toyota Tundra pickup truck, two (2) 2017 Ford F-150 pickup trucks, one (1) Ford EcoSport Compact SUV and one (1) 2018 DeCoulomb Modern Deluxe VXP. For the purpose of examining the vehicles, your affiant requests that a seizure order be obtained to take possession of the above-cited vehicles for the purpose of transporting them to a Sacramento Police Department facility to conduct forensic examinations on them to determine if their Vehicle Identification Numbers (VIN) had been altered or otherwise damaged. Your affiant also requests to conduct a search of the residence at Subject Christiansen's above address for any and all records pertaining to Subject Christiansen's vehicle leasing and brokering business, to determine whether he has had any other contact with known 'white nationalist' political organizations. Along with the vehicles, your affiant requests the authority to seize a 900 Watt Electronic Flat-Head Angle Grinder from the property as well as any other tools or devices commonly used by automobile theft rings to alter vehicle registration numbers."

As a side dish, Wiggins clipped a second search warrant affidavit to the copy of the warrant he provided to the reporters. This one was addressed to Christiansen's cell phone service provider. It laid out the same probable cause as the first affidavit. Instead of cars and business records, this search warrant sought and obtained permission for the cops to retrieve records on all of Christiansen's phone calls and text messages beginning from the date one month before the Tennessee legislature took its vote to slam the city of Memphis for its role in the removal of the Nathan Bedford Forrest statue. Wiggins wrote that he wanted the phone and text information "to determine the extent of contacts between subject Christiansen and subjects MacMillian and Barton leading up to the May 14, 2018, vandalism of the statue of Cesar Chavez in Sacramento, CA."

A third attachment also came with Wiggins's package: a search of Christiansen's bank records.

Frankie pushed the driver's seat in the rental car as far back as it could go. He opened the driver's side door and pulled the lever to pop the trunk. He got out of the car and walked around to the trunk to retrieve his backpack. He pulled out his laptop computer and got back into his car. Before he started writing, he called his editor back in Washington, D.C.

To the voice on the other end of the phone, Frankie said:

"I think I might have a daily for you."

41/*Arson Squad Callout*

On Tuesday, June 5, Lincoln Adams journeyed to the outskirts of Modesto to get out the vote. He drove his Zip car into an office complex of flat, single-story concrete bunkers and into the field headquarters of Jesse Seymour for Congress.

It was getting to be around 2:30 p.m. on the afternoon of Election Day when Link parked in front of an office suite that had been converted into a ping-pong parlor. He never knew they had such things.

Himself an emissary from Sacramento, Link observed that license plate holders on other cars in the parking lot showed legions of volunteers rolling in from liberal outposts such as Berkeley and Davis, San Jose and San Francisco, Oakland, Mill Valley, and one from as far away as Carmel-by-the-Sea.

Their drivers had two goals in mind: Flip the House, screw the president.

He found the campaign headquarters of Democratic congressional candidate Jesse Seymour in the rear corner of the office park. The line of volunteers stretched out the glass door of the Seymour office, all of them ready to roll for their guy in California's 10th Congressional District.

A man about Link's age stood in front of him while they all waited for their turf assignments, to lead Seymour's supporters by the hand, if need be, to the voting booths.

"You ever done this before?" the man asked Link, pleasantly.

"Can't say that I have," Link responded.

"Me neither, at least not in the past forty-two years," the guy said. "I mean, I did a little volunteer work for Tom Hayden back in college, when he ran for the Senate. Same thing for the farmworkers thing."

The 1976 farm workers initiative, Proposition 14, would have locked in funding for California's newly-created Agricultural Labor Relations Board and allowed Cesar Chavez's organizers to go into the fields to get workers to sign union cards. Growers didn't much care for the idea. They spent millions to ensure its defeat.

"Late night, door-hanger stuff," the man said. "Then you get busy. You get married. You have kids, your job... you vote, but that's about it."

"Sometimes, you don't even do that much," Link said. "At least I haven't."

"I've sat out a few elections," Link's chatty new acquaintance said. "Sometimes I hold my nose and vote, usually more when I'm against than for somebody. 2004 with Bush – I had my problems with Kerry and his 'I was against the war before I was for it' crap. That was weird, man. But Bush, Cheney and those swift boaters – that was a total 'anti' vote on my part."

"I feel you."

"Then Trump got elected."

The man stood almost as tall as Link. His grey hair strung shoulder length beneath a round straw shade hat to protect against another sunny San Joaquin Valley day. He was long and lean and he wore a plaid, short-sleeve shirt, over blue jeans and sandals – colorful next to Link's black jeans, T-shirt and cowboy boots, and the white straw cowboy hat.

Maybe a hundred people stood with them in the line. Most were fellow geezers, but there were a good number of college kids, and Link noticed a smattering of families.

Link knew the drill from his previous canvassing. Their apps contained the identities of all likely Seymour voters in the district, obtained through their previous efforts. Now it was time to make sure they voted.

"Can you believe this?" the man said to Link. "All these people, coming all this way, for a congressional race in Modesto? So where are you from?"

"Sacramento," Link answered.

"All right. And have you ever in your life given up a day to go knock on doors for a *congressional race* in *Sacramento*, let alone Modesto?"

"I can't say that I have."

"Me neither. Yet here we are."

"That is an undeniable fact."

"Because of your revulsion, I would presume, with the things that our so-called president has done over the past seventeen months."

"I have been properly revulsed."

"The lying. The dividing of people by race and ethnicity. The collusion, the obstruction of justice, his general asshattery. His attempt to kill healthcare, the tax bill for the rich."

"Don't forget climate change."

"The weird dance with North Korea. The infrastructure lie. The attack on black football players. I could go on."

"And on."

Link eventually made his way into the office where a young blonde-haired woman with ruby-red lipstick looked into her computer and gave him his turf for the day: the countrified far northeast corner of the district. His app showed him that he would be contacting exactly 27 people whom previous canvassers had identified as self-confirmed Seymour voters.

"Every vote is going to count," she told him. "Knock on every door. Make sure they know their polling place. If they don't have a ride, give them one. If nobody's home, go back. Don't come back until you've contacted everybody."

"Or the polls close."

She nodded and allowed a brief smile. This was serious.

Link headed out on Highway 120, about halfway to Sonora, beyond Oakdale, a good 45 minutes away. He opened his windows and enjoyed the fresh air as it blew through his car on a perfect, 88-degree day. One by one, he hit the doors on the little ranch houses with friendly people who seemed happy to tell him that they'd already voted for Seymour, mostly because they couldn't stand Trump.

By the time 8 o'clock rolled around, Link had reached 25 of the 27 people laid out for him in his app. He checked back in at Jesse Seymour HQ in Modesto where the woman with the ruby-red lips synced the information from his phone into her computer.

"This is excellent," she said. "25 out of 27. Believe me, we are going to need every one of them."

"The two I didn't get, I think they were meth labbers," Link told her.

"Fantastic. We'll see you again in the fall?"

"If we make it," Link said, before getting into his Zip to do a little ballot-box monitoring in uptown Manteca, prior to hitting the road for the 70-mile drive back to Sacramento.

As soon as he got off the 99, he called Manuela to inform her that he would be arriving at her house in the next couple of minutes.

"Please don't shoot me when I come through the door," he asked.

"Don't worry," Manuela said. "I put the gun away. I think those white boys aren't dumb enough to come around here again."

When Link walked through the door, he saw that Manuela had made a visit to the Food Co-op and picked up a bucketful of what looked to be parmesan-covered chicken wings. She put them on a plate which she shoved into the microwave. Forty-five seconds later he had one in his mouth, with sides of roasted red potatoes and multi-colored grilled vegetables.

Manuela popped him a 22-ouncer of Bike Dog Mosaic Pale Ale and set it on a coaster on the coffee table while they settled in front of the TV to watch the night's election returns. They chomped wings and switched back and forth between MSNBC and CNN, with an occasional peek on FOX. They also worked a local channel into the rotation to get a read on the congressional race down in Modesto.

First click: Bonham, easily in first with 30 percent. No surprise there. Then, the scary part: Bonham's Republican rival, Jacob Harland, holding down second with 25 percent. In third, less than 100 votes behind Harland, the leading Democrat: Jesse Seymour.

It stayed tight all night long, with Harland and Seymour swinging back and forth in and out of the second playoff spot.

Manuela slipped off to bed around 2 a.m., and Link fell asleep on the couch not too long after that. He woke at 6 a.m., not to the morning news hosts jabbering away on the television, but to his ringing cell phone The voice on the other end, to Link's surprise, belonged to Samuel Kahn, Chief of Police at the Sacramento Police Department, who did not call to update Link on the results of the congressional race.

"Mr. Adams," the chief said, "I regret to inform you …"

Link waited at the pause and wondered who was dead.

"Your totem pole," the chief said, of the celebrated Lincoln Adams work of art in Cesar Chavez Plaza, "has been torched."

42/*Moving On*

Link woke up Manuela to tell her the news, and she got dressed. Link still had his clothes on. All he had to do was pull on his shoes and brush his teeth.

They walked in silence to Cesar Chavez Plaza where the flashing lights of fire engines and cops and TV news trucks blinked and blared.

Link saw a police detective in a brown sports jacket whom he knew to be Andrew Wiggins.

"I'm getting tired of my own victimhood," Link told Manuela.

They got closer to the park and picked up the strong smell of

239

gasoline.

The totem had been burned beyond recognition. It tilted at a 15-degree angle, weakened by the heavy destruction to its bottom. You could no longer make out the finned feet of the otter. The rest of the piece had sustained the equivalent of third-degree burns. You needed a healthy imagination to determine that the torso of the structure had once featured the headlight on a northbound train, pointed in perfect accordance with the compass embedded in the concrete beneath the granite base. Even an expert in Cuban revolutionary history could not tell you that the head and shoulders belonged to Che Guevara.

"The fire guys tell me the whole thing is going to have to come down," Wiggins told Link, when the detective approached them at the edge of the grass behind the damage. "Only a matter of time until it all falls down."

Link nodded.

He thought about the people he met on Fisher Lake Drive in Mendocino County the previous year, who lost their homes in the wildfires the night he was kidnapped and held under arms in his own studio. They'd lost everything except their lives, which was more than nine of their neighbors in the woods could say. The more he thought about it, the more he realized he had lost nothing, really. Same as it would be for Michelango in the event somebody broke into the Galleria dell'Accademia and took a sledgehammer to the David. Everything alive was living on borrowed time. Why should inanimate objects deserve a break? Maybe he could restore the totem, but what good would that do? He thought about Lazarus having to think twice about dying.

Even if there was no chance of salvaging the totem, his sense of accomplishment hadn't been singed in the slightest. Isn't that the main thing that mattered?

Link stopped for a moment and turned off his brain. He stepped outside himself. He looked at the way he felt, without emotion, with balanced detachment.

Objectively speaking, how did he really feel about the torching of this totem?

Bottom line was, he didn't really feel anything.

240

No emptiness. No nothing. No sense that it mattered, at least compared to the Fisher Lake people.

If he was ever under it, he was now over it.

"It would be nice," he told Wiggins, "if somehow I could get ahold of the remains. I could rent a truck and take them to my studio."

"You conducting an autopsy?"

"More like a funeral," Link responded.

"It's going to be awhile, probably late in the afternoon at the earliest," Wiggins said. "The arson squad still has some work to do."

"Of course," Link said.

"Come here," Wiggins said. "I've got to show you something."

The detective led Link to the totem and pointed to the remnants of the dowel, about four feet off the ground, where the totem had been inserted into the granite.

"Check this out," Wiggins said, taking a ball-point pen and sticking it into a hole that appeared to have been drilled into the dowel. "We've got three more of them," the detective said, directing Link's attention to additional holes. "It looks like whoever did this stuffed the holes with some kind of explosive – gunpowder maybe. Then they soaked the goddamn thing – er, sorry, your statue – with gasoline and set it on fire. The fire and the powder exploded on ignition, it looks like. The Fire Department got here pretty quick. Otherwise, we'd be looking at a pile of charcoal."

"Allow me to make a wild guess, Detective," Manuela broke in. "The same assholes who have been pulling this shit the last few weeks, they did this one, too."

"That would be a pretty good guess, Ms. Fonseca."

"Well, allow me to ask another question," she continued, "and that is, why the hell haven't you caught them yet? You know their names. You've got their car, or at least one of their cars. You're questioning the people who sold them the cars. These guys don't strike me as criminal geniuses. They've got to have paper trails, right? Do they use credit cards? You can't put a task force together to find them? Another thing – it's just you and a bunch of geeks in plastic suits. What about the FBI? Didn't these guys cross state lines to get here from Tennessee? There should be a hundred of you here."

"Believe me, ma'am..."

"You see where they're going, don't you?" Manuela went on. "What if I would have been home when they tore up my front yard? Do you think they would have stopped at my lawn?"

"We still haven't recorded any injuries, Ms. Fonseca."

"Don't get smart with me, Detective. I am asking you good faith questions about a serious situation that is getting worse. Somebody's going to get hurt, and soon, and I'd feel a whole lot better if I saw some guys out here in dark jackets with the big block letters 'F. B. I.' across the back."

"Like I was about to say, Ms. Fonseca, I've begun to get some help."

Link broke off from the conversation and circled the blackened hulk. Standing there in the park, he opened himself up to whatever might emerge from whatever was left from the offering from the Witch Doctor's forest in Mendocino County. He couldn't pick up a thing.

He walked around the detritus, back to Wiggins. "On second thought," Link said, "I don't think I have any use for this thing anymore."

He pulled his cell phone out of his left pants pocket.

He texted the Witch Doctor:

"Ready," he wrote, "for another one."

43/*Hold All Tickets*

It had been a few days since the primary, but it was probably going to be another week before anybody knew the results on the

10th Congressional District scramble.

John Bonham for sure would be in the runoff, but he only had 29 percent of the vote. The big question: would he face a Republican or a Democrat? With 100 percent of the precincts reporting, it looked like GOP challenger Jacob Harland would sneak through. Harland closed out on Election Night with 15.1 percent. Jesse Seymour led the Democrats with 14.9 percent. About 200 votes separated the two. While it was true that all precincts had reported, it was also true that not all the ballots had been counted. As was their right, and as Link had witnessed on election night in his capacity as a vote monitor, a smattering of moms in shorts and flip flops with babies on their hips and farmworkers just back from the cherry orchards walked in their by-mail ballots to the voting booths at exactly 7:59 and 59 seconds. No need to rush these things. Meanwhile, thousands of democracy practitioners didn't mail in their mail-in ballots until Election Day, and post offices all over the state put people outside to collect and post mark them right up until the 8 p.m. cutoff. This meant that the procrastination vote couldn't even begin to be counted until Thursday or Friday of election week at the earliest. Then it could take another two weeks to finalize the tally.

The smart guys knew to hold all tickets until the results were official. For Harland and Seymour, it was going to be a long fortnight.

Andrew Wiggins didn't have to wait so long. By Thursday afternoon, he got the phone and the bank records back on David Allen Christiansen.

They were interesting.

The same day, he also had the examinations completed on all the vehicle identification numbers in Christiansen's front-yard parking lot.

Those were not.

None of the numbers on any of the cars had been altered – all the vehicles had been accounted for properly, their VINs intact, their paperwork in order.

Unfortunately for Christiansen, there still was the matter of that hand grinder he left on his front porch.

Forensic investigators lifted a number of prints off it, and dammit if a few didn't come back to Davis Beauregard Barton, and fuck-all-further if they also didn't line up with the partials retrieved from the envelope mailed to Link's studio from Fort Smith, Ark.

Now we're getting somewhere, Wiggins thought.

At the very least, the prints gave Wiggins cause to go back up to North Auburn and fuck with Christiansen some more. He had him cold on lying to the cops, and now there was a good chance he could ring him up on a conspiracy rap.

Friday afternoon, June 8, Wiggins put a call into his friends on what was left of the Sacramento Local Russian Organized Crime Task Force, the unit the feds put together to investigate the previous year's mortgage fraud, computer hacking, and identity theft trifecta that investigators believed helped finance the Russian purloining of the 2016 presidential election, not to mention their later work in the Lincoln Adams-to-the Witch Doctor kidnapping parlay. Manuela was right. It was time for him to get some help.

Before the detective could dial his task force pals, his own phone lit up with an incoming call.

Frankie Cameron's name occupied the screen.

Wiggins rolled his eyes and clicked the green "accept" button.

"Wiggins," the detective answered.

"Yes, Detective Wiggins," Frankie Cameron said. "Frankie Cameron here. You told me to give you a call today about the search warrant return?"

"I thought I told you to call me Monday," Wiggins said. "This is Friday."

"Oh," Frankie lied. "I must have written it down wrong."

Being a cop, Wiggins remembered what he told people, and he made a point of watching Frankie write it down in his notebook.

Another vile reporter trick: faking incompetence to get a foot in the door. Another reason he didn't trust them.

"Yeah, yeah," Wiggins said. He knew the guy was hungry for

244

the story. He had to respect that. Maybe he'd do the guy a solid.

"Well, I haven't had time to think about the return yet, and I just got a load of crap back yesterday, and I haven't gone through all of it and I probably won't be done until late next week, so I won't be filing the return until next Friday. Maybe I can give you some hints, but you fucking cannot use it until I file the fucking thing."

Frankie promised to hold off on submitting anything to his editors. Wiggins told him:

"So here's what you need to know… and I swear to God, if you write this before I file it, I'm going to come after you with a chokehold."

"Nothing," Frankie said.

"Okay. The cars – we got nothing. Everything's legal on everything we towed. No obliterated VINs, all the paperwork in order."

"Even on the DeCoulomb?"

"Yeah, even on the DeCoulomb. What's the big deal about that?"

"Well," Frankie said. "The model Christiansen was driving isn't available to the general public yet."

"So fucking what? The fucker who makes them can go hand them out on street corners like candy for all I care. The only thing I care about is that the documentation is in order, which it is, with the transfer made out direct from the factory to the fuckhead."

"The fuckhead being Christiansen?"

"Yes. Now, for the most interesting thing on my part – the hand grinder. We printed it and it showed that one of the Tennessee dickheads handled it. I can't think of any reason for their prints to be on a hand grinder on Christiansen's front porch, other than to use it to rub out the VIN number. This means that Christiansen is a lying son of a bitch, at the very least, and that he may be an aider and abettor to a string of federal hate crimes that now includes arson, and he and they can go to jail for a long time."

"Which dickhead?"

245

"Barton, if it matters. Now, all this other shit with the bank and phone records doesn't mean a goddamn thing to me, but being that you're into politics these days, I'll go ahead and fill you in on what we've got. You can do with it whatever the hell you want, but not until after I file the return. Got it?"

"Absolutely."

"OK, here we go," Wiggins said.

He paused a beat for effect.

"The phone records," Wiggins continued, "show multiple contacts between Christiansen and Barton going back to last year when they first started posting on that fucked-up website."

"The White Right?"

"That's the one. Now, Christiansen can explain away all these contacts as legit, right? Like, the Tennessee fucker had a constitutional right to rent a car, right? Nothing illegal about that, right? Christiansen's in the phone book, easily reachable by anybody who Googles his name. Right? The Tennessee fucker calls him – no crime there, right? Next thing you know the Tennessee fucker's got a GMC Yukon. Everything's still legal."

"If you say so."

"Now, for the interesting stuff, as far as the phone calls are concerned: Christiansen had multiple calls, first coming in, and then going out, and then going in and out, from a phone number that comes back from that warehouse in West Sacramento you've been writing about. We've also got his cell phone on multiple occasions pinging from the closest tower to the warehouse, which pretty much puts him in it, as far as I'm concerned."

Now, the light bulb went on in Frankie's head.

"Holy shit," he told Wiggins. "I've seen him there!"

"Where?"

"At the warehouse. Christiansen. First time I went over there, on the White Rock story. He was the truck driver! Loading the DeCoulombs into the warehouse, from his eighteen-wheeler."

"I don't recall reading about him in your stories."

"I didn't recognize him at the time, although I should have. I got a little bit of the story when that woman sued the Sheriff's

Department over his leaving the bananas on the seat of her patrol car. I'd seen him around the courthouse a couple times before they settled it. Totally forgot about him, until you guys ID'd him for the SUV. Thought I recognized him when we braced him the other day, me and the Russian reporter, but I couldn't place the face, from either the courthouse or the warehouse."

"You'd a made a lousy cop," Wiggins consoled him. "We have built in facial-recognition software."

"Same as good politicians," Frankie added.

Wiggins ignored that. "Not that I read your stories when you wrote them, but I Googled 'White Rock USA' for the search warrants, and they popped up. I think: well, here we go again with this Russian shit. I call the chief, and he gives me a deep-throated 'holy shitfuck,' and we talk about your stories on this weird-ass political committee that's doing some kind of crazy bullshit down in Fresno or wherever."

"Modesto."

"Yeah, Modesto. He texted me all your stories on that congressional race, and the *Modesto Beacon*'s stories, and the mentions about the warehouse, and the Russian church in Rancho Cordova, so now I get the picture. I've got to admit – it is a real interesting fucking story, the money, the politics, the Republicans trying to fuck the Democrats out of the primary. Then we get the return back on Christiansen's bank records, and boom – he's got a couple hundred thousand, at least, coming into his bank account here from a bank account *in his name* in the Cayman Islands."

Frankie's mind very quickly rolled through what he heard and what he knew: expensive cars rolling from the East Bay to the Port of Sacramento, on their way to Mexico. Phone calls between Christiansen and the Tennessee terrorists. Phone calls between Christiansen and White Rock USA. Major money transfers to Christiansen, from himself.

He asked Wiggins, "Do we know why Christiansen has a Caymans account, and where that money came from?"

"We do not," Wiggins said, "The only thing we know is we still have a hell of a lot of work to do."

Link knew.

This thing with Manuela was real.

He knew it so well that he thought it was time to introduce her to the most important human being in his life.

He knew it was time to introduce her to the Witch Doctor.

On their way up to Covelo, to the beekeeper's bench where Link met his mystically-inclined, marijuana-influenced mentor, they first had to stop in at the Robertson Rancheria to say hello to a couple of Link's old Pomo pals. He'd known them since he was a kid, when their moms enrolled them all in cultural identity school. Link's mother was concerned that even though he lived on his own rancheria, he was growing up too white. She did some research and found a couple of Native American faculty guys at UC Davis who ran weekend programs a few times a year for parents of kids like Link, who feared the destructive influence of Ozzie and Harriet and Gilligan's Island on the mindsets of Native American youth.

These days, Link's cultural-identity buddies from back in the day ran a casino in the general Clear Lake area. Link always made sure to drop a couple hundred bucks at their blackjack tables. They appreciated it so much that they'd comp him a club sandwich – two, on this occasion, since he brought his girlfriend along. Link and Manuela lost their money, ate their sandwiches, said their goodbyes, and then continued onward, on a warm, lazy Saturday afternoon, to Mendocino County on Highway 20.

A few miles past the casino, Link instructed Manuela to pull the Porsche over, at the site of a state-sanctioned historical road marker.

Wind brushed the high grasses of the late spring, quiet in the surrounding reclaimed meadow, on the lightly-traveled road where breezes ruffled hillside copses of oak and juniper 500 yards distant that had witnessed historic atrocity.

The marker designated the hill in the distance as "Bloody Island," which really wasn't an island anymore, since the white people in the last century leveed up the north end of Clear Lake to make way for 1,650 more acres of farm land. They could never have enough, Link thought to himself.

Manuela got out of the car and walked over to read the marker that Link had long ago committed to his memory:

"One-fourth mile west is the island called Bo-No-Po-Ti (Old Island), now Bloody Island," the bronzed engraving said. "It was a place for native gatherings until May 15, 1850. On that date, a regiment of the 1st Dragoons of the U.S. Cavalry, commanded by Capt. Nathaniel Lyon and Lt. J.W. Davidson, massacred nearly the entire native population of the island. Most were women and children."

The highest estimates on the loss of life numbered 800, a figure compiled two months after the killings by an officer in the same U.S. Army that perpetrated the massacre. If Major Edwin Allen Sherman's math was correct, it would put Bloody Island right there at the top when it came to the all-time single-incident mass murders of native peoples on United States soil, since the undocumented European immigrants overran the continent beginning in 1492.

"Nearly-two-and-a-half times the number killed at Wounded Knee," Link told Manuela. "George Stoneman was one of the co-conspirators."

Manuela's looked at him with a wrinkled brow.

"...'til Stoneman's cavalry came and tore up the tracks again..." Link was singing a line from "The Night They Drove Old Dixie Down."

Still nothing from Manuela. Maybe they should have watched *The Last Waltz* that night at her house. He gave her an abbreviated rundown on The Band, old backups for Bob Dylan who helped define the sounds of modern Americana, even though most of them were Canadian. The reference in the song described General Stoneman's efforts to help drive a stake through the heart of the Confederate resistance at the end of the Civil War.

"My whole life, or at least since I first heard that song, George Stoneman was a hero of mine," Link said. "I'm an American. I love my country. But I have since grown dubious of Stoneman."

Link gave Manuela a little off-the-top-of-his-head background: Fifteen years before Stoneman laid the wood to the Confederates – and 119 years before Robbie Robertson memorialized him in song – Second Lieutenant Stoneman laid in wait to murder Indians.

"The Pomo roamed from what is now the Napa Valley wine country to the coast, from Bodega Bay nearly to Mendocino, inland a hundred miles from there," Link intoned. "The genocide started with the Gold Rush, and then with the settlers. The whites pretty much enslaved the Pomo. The people starved, and the settlers raped and murdered them. Five Pomo killed two farmers, and the white Army retaliated. They came here, to Bloody Island, to Bo-No-Po-Ti, where the Pomo lived. The Army attacked and killed many Pomo there, women and children included. They drove the Pomo into the water. When the Pomo swam to shore, Second Lieutenant Stoneman and the Dragoons under his command systematically shot them. Later, he was promoted to General, where he supervised the rear-guard attacks on Lee's forces that fled Petersburg. Later still, Stoneman was elected as the second governor of California."

Manuela let Link's words waft over the surrounding silence, as he led her down a road to the island, where they poked about in silence and Link listened for the screams of the long-dead Pomo. What had been the far-north end of a lake that fed a people had now been reclaimed into scrub brush, for the benefit of more settlers, more farmers. Walking the road back to the car, Link imagined the shoreline, where the people swam and were gunned down under the direction of the cavalry lieutenant who tore up the tracks again.

The Witch Doctor looked relaxed. As usual, he left his car – a 1960s era Volkswagen Bug – parked half a block up the main road in downtown Covelo, along a row of corrugated-metal bookstores and subcontinental fashion boutiques and hydroponics outlets that catered to off-the-grid tastes. He didn't want his view obstructed, from where he sat on the beekeeper's red bench. Manuela, on instructions from Link, swung the Porsche around and parked it a half block in the other direction.

Link and Manuela, who had spent the night at a bed and breakfast in Ukiah, made the drive fairly early on a cool Sunday morning along the winding Eel River past Holmen Ridge and into the Round Valley flats that encompassed Covelo. At 8 a.m., they stepped out of the Porsche and up to the porch, where the Witch Doctor was reading a book.

Before they could say a word, the Witch Doctor told them:

"It's about the heroes of the sixty-eight Olympics, the black brothers who raised their fists on the medal stand in Mexico City," he said. "I forgot that they had trained beforehand at elevation, near Lake Tahoe, in the land of your people, my son. The Nisenan."

"Manuela, I would like to introduce you to my uncle," Link said.

"I am not really his uncle," the Witch Doctor said before Manuela could say anything or extend her hand in greeting. "He just calls me that."

"And I am not really his son," Link responded.

"And I am very pleased to meet you," Manuela said. "Link has told me about you."

The Witch Doctor mock recoiled.

"He has, has he," the Witch Doctor said. "I can assure you,

whatever he said, it was not complete."

"That's true," Link nodded in agreement. "Much of this man is unknowable. For instance, I didn't even know his name until last year."

The Witch Doctor nodded. They were both thinking of the night he'd been abducted, which had led to the publishing of his name in the news. Link had been held hostage too. The memory was so potent that Link was able to say, without preamble:

"Interestingly enough, that night turned out to be one of the best things that ever happened to me."

"So you've told me," the Witch Doctor said, with what Manuela detected to be a sneer. "Somebody you've never met gives you a rundown on yourself and all of a sudden you know yourself."

There was an edge of harshness to the Witch Doctor's voice, something Link had never heard before – and something that Manuela picked up on immediately. The Witch Doctor had his moments. Back in his teaching days, Link had seen the WD so riled by obtuse art students, himself included, that he would beat them unmercifully with an oaken staff. But this was different. A howl of laughter usually accompanied the artistic beatings. This sarcastic interpretation of Link's cross-continent chat the previous year with Russian organized crime boss Anton Karuliyak came without even a twinkle in the Witch Doctor's eye.

Maybe it was the presence of the woman that altered the rhythm of the interaction, this being the first time that Link had ever sought out the Witch Doctor to introduce him to a female companion.

A silent discomfort erupted between the two men who took their seats on the red bench, Manuela observing from where she stood on the sidelines, respecting this space that Link had told her had been the site of so many exchanges between the two.

"You have great ability," the Witch Doctor told Link, the old man's tone taking on an even harder edge. "Then some crook pulls a theory out of his ass and you think you have discovered a truth. The next thing you know, your work turns to shit."

This criticism stung, and for just a second, Link's feelings were hurt. His first reaction was to defend the piece. Instead, he sat in silence, with a cool morning breeze massaging his cheeks. He took some relief in his foresight, to bring along his Levi's jacket, and Manuela, towards whom he looked in response to the Witch Doctor's critique. She stood mute, interested to see how her man would respond.

Ready to go on the defensive about the totem, Link instead found himself saying:

"Come to think of it, the thing never did speak to me."

A look of smug self-satisfaction covered the Witch Doctor's face. Another expressive first.

"How could it?" the Witch Doctor responded. "You might as well try to have a conversation with the three faces of Eve."

Link accepted the perspective on his totem that reflected both man and beast as well as machine. He nodded, in silent agreement.

Once again, he knew, the man who beat art into Link was right.

"These fellows who burned it down," the Witch Doctor continued, "they may have done you a favor."

Link thought about it. Maybe so.

The Witch Doctor gathered his bones beneath him. He aligned them in a manner that allowed him to stand up with the least amount of strain on the sinewy connections in his body, especially the ones in his back. He made it to his feet, and stretched. He twisted left to right and released a crack loud enough to start a 100-meter dash.

"I thought you were coming up for a log," he said to Link.

"So did I," Link responded.

"I think you're going to have a hard time getting it back to Sacramento in that," the Witch Doctor said, with a nod toward Manuela's roadster.

"It is not an efficient vehicle for transporting much of anything other than two human beings," Link said.

The Witch Doctor turned to Manuela. Link braced himself for whatever might come out of the mouth of the wild card from

Mendocino.

"Miss Manuela," he said. "Link has told me that you hold a special place in his heart."

Manuela was about to smile and say something polite, but the Witch Doctor went on.

"I fear that you could destroy him. As an artist."

Manuela looked over the Witch Doctor respectfully, the same way he had looked over her.

"Destroy him as an artist," she repeated.

"That is my concern," the Witch Doctor said.

Manuela had encountered this masculine, go-it-alone routine before – this idea that somehow love and family can sap a man's potential. It was the line her ex laid on her when he walked out – the super lawyer whose name was in the paper every day for his high-profile criminal defense of anybody, regardless of offense and their ability to pay, as long as their case made the news. He told Manuela he couldn't be the best lawyer in the world and a husband and father at the same time.

She knew the ex's line was a bunch of bullshit, and a cover for his cheating on her in the hyper-sexualized world of the legal warrior. She didn't know the motivation here, but she did hold to the same position she reserved for her husband's line – it was a crock.

And this seemed to be as good a time as any to take it head on.

"Well," Manuela went on. "my concern is this: you have mentored this man, and you have helped him attain a level of greatness, and that is a fantastic thing. Now I think it's time for you to back the fuck off."

"Hold on, Manuela," Link broke in.

"Seriously," she continued, unabated, to the Witch Doctor. "You have been a great inspiration and teacher. But you know what? I think there's something else going on here, with you, and him, and you over him, and you exercising an element of control over him."

"Control?" the Witch Doctor let loose in a high-pitched crack, before he launched into a hyenic scream. "I control nothing. Not even myself!"

Manuela's analysis caught Link cold. In their blossoming relationship, he had filled her in with great detail on his relationship with the old man, in hours of conversation, at Mullaney's, on her couch, on their drives to do their politicking, in their walks along the river from between Old Sac and the Crocker Museum.

Each time, all she did was nod, and listen, and absorb.

Now, she spoke.

"I don't think it's intentional," Manuela went on. "It's just that he can't help it. It's the way of the male elder, and once one of *you*" – she looked the Witch Doctor in the eye – "gets your hooks into one of him" – hello, Link – "the trajectory will roll forth into history unimpeded, until and unless, a leavening force presents itself."

Manuela, still standing next to the red bench, raised her arms to the sky.

Link and the Witch Doctor looked at each other. Simultaneously, they shrugged.

"There she is," the Witch Doctor said. "The leavening presence."

"Her theory," Link added, "makes sense."

For maybe the first time in his life, the Witch Doctor looked chastened.

Manuela continued, "For you to suggest that I, in any way, in loving him and taking care of him and entering into a life with him, might 'destroy' his artistic impulse – well, I think you're full of shit."

The Witch Doctor took a few moments to let Manuela's remarks sink in. A few minutes, really, as the three of them sat in silence on the beekeeper's bench.

In time, the customary smile returned to his face, to replace the odd and ill-fitting surly countenance that had marked his previous demeanor. The Witch Doctor knew he had wandered into the territories of women and relationships that was far removed from his wheelhouse of knowledge.

But a control freak? He'd have to take a deeper look.

In the meantime, he broke into more polite laughter.

"Miss Manuela, sometimes men need to be told what they do not know. I am a man who knows but one thing for sure, and that is that I don't know very much about most things," he said, apologetic – thoroughly leavened. "However, I have long felt an obligation to hold forth on topics of every sort of which I have absolutely no knowledge. We call this *bullshitting*, and nobody is better at it than men. Usually, it takes ourselves to correct it in ourselves. Yet there are those occasions when it takes a woman to step in, a 'leavening presence,' as you said, to set the record straight. I do hereby declare this as such an instance, and I would apologize to you, Miss Manuela, if I only knew how."

"I accept," Manuela said.

Laughter filled the deserted street in the empty town.

46/*The Christiansen File*

The morning of June 14, before Detective Andrew Wiggins was supposed to file his search warrant return in Sacramento Superior Court, Frankie Cameron received a telephone call from a *Washington Post* editorial assistant.

Back in Frankie's early days, when he was one of them, they called themselves copy boys or copy girls. Somehow, those terms became objectionable. Besides the whole gender thing, and beside the fact that some copy boys and girls were in their late 20s, there was no longer any such thing as "copy." At least there was no more paper. And you for damn sure didn't have young people anymore running it all over the newsroom. But you still had to have somebody to answer phone calls from crackpots and tipsters.

From people like David Allen Christiansen.

"He wants you to call him back as soon as possible," the copy boy told Frankie.

"Was he armed?" Frankie asked.

The copy boy laughed.

"It sounded to me like he was carrying a samurai sword," the copy boy said.

"I'll approach from a safe distance," Frankie responded, as he took the number and thanked the editorial assistant.

It was nine days after the election, but Frankie had convinced his editors to let him stay in California. For one thing, the cliffhanger in Modesto between Jacob Harland and Jesse Seymour for the right to challenge John Bonham for the 10th Congressional District seat in California had not been resolved. Frankie also wanted to keep digging on this weird connection between the Jacob Harland campaign, a Russian church in Rancho Cordova, and a couple of statue wreckers from Tennessee.

It all came together, Frankie believed, through the person of David Allen Christiansen, and boy oh boy, would he like to talk to him.

Last time Frankie saw Christiansen, it was from the mat, decked by a right hand that caught him upside the head and put him down for a mandatory eight, on the dude's driveway, in North Auburn. Now, David Allen Christiansen wanted to talk to him. Frankie, from his room at the Sterling with a commanding view of the elm canopy around H and 13th streets, returned the call, and Christiansen answered on the first ring.

Christiansen sounded apologetic for the previously-delivered right hand to the head.

"I was going for that weasel with the camera," Christiansen said. "You just got in the way."

"I didn't take it personally," Frankie said.

"Thank you for that," Christiansen went on. "Now, I've got a whole lot of stuff to tell you. But not over the phone."

Christiansen, it turned out, was in Midtown, and Frankie directed him to the Weatherstone, a coffee joint on 21st Street, between H and I.

"I'll meet you there in 15 minutes," Frankie said.

Fourteen minutes later, Frankie spotted Christiansen in the far back corner of the Weatherstone's patio, next to the water fountain. Christiansen sipped coffee from a large white porcelain coffee cup. Two minutes later, Frankie cradled one just like it with both hands while he backed through the glass doorway leading to the patio.

Christiansen did not get up. All he said by way of greeting was, "I am not taking the fall for this."

Frankie slid into one of the metal chairs at Christiansen's table. He was already nodding. It looked to him like Christiansen hadn't shaved since they had last seen each other, 10 days earlier. It also looked to him that Christiansen may not have even slept.

"You shouldn't be taking the fall for anything," Frankie agreed. He left it right there – an encouragement for Christiansen to continue with his story. The good cop.

"I'm just minding my own business, leasing my cars, brokering a couple sales, getting over my anger, moving on with my life, making decent enough money – honest money," Christiansen said. "Out of nowhere, I get a call last year from this woman with a Russian accent. She says she is calling me in my capacity as an automobile broker. She says she might have some good business for me. She says her name is Ludmila."

"I think I've met her," Frankie said. "At the warehouse, in West Sac. And it has since occurred to me, since our meeting in your front yard, that you were the guy driving the truck that unloaded a DeCoulomb at the warehouse."

"Yes, I was."

"And Ludmila was the woman with the pink hair."

"Sometimes it's pink. Sometimes it's purple. Sometimes it's orange. I remember the day you walked into the office to try and talk to her. She told me all about it. I couldn't believe it was you. You've got a pretty shitty reputation with people like her, and me, you know, and I offered to go out there and kick your ass. She told me not to."

Now that Frankie had pinned Christiansen as having an association with White Rock USA, he pressed the fired former deputy on how it began.

258

"She calls, I think it was last June," Christiansen said, picking up his story, "and she asks if I'd be interested in making some big money, and I tell her, 'Who isn't?' She starts in about how she'd read these stories about me – in your newspaper – and how she thought I was typical of 'strong white men' who had been oppressed by 'the American system.' By this time, I'm pretty much over my shit with the sheriff and the lawsuit and my getting fired. I've got the car business going, and it's going pretty good. But, yeah. I'm still a little raw – I did get a raw fucking deal, you know. So, yeah, I agree with her that I got screwed, and she goes on with this business proposition for me. She invites me out to the warehouse in West Sac, and she tells me she needs my help in what looked to me to be a legitimate business transaction. And it was legitimate, except for this one little problem."

"And that was?"

"Economic sanctions against Russia."

Christiansen paused to let that one sink in, and Frankie took a sip of coffee so as not to give away any emotion.

"The sanctions had been in place for three years," Christiansen said, "and she's telling me how unfair they are, how Russia was only taking care of its own people, how the Russians were being oppressed in Ukraine by having to live under a new government that wouldn't deal fairly with Russia and the Russians, all that crap."

"I get it," Frankie said.

"Then she tells me that she knows a few 'gentlemen,' as she called them, who happened to live in Russia and who happened to have some money and who happened to have developed an interest in buying these ridiculously priced electric cars. She said she's got about a dozen of these guys, maybe more, and that they're very rich, and that it would be nothing for them to spend a hundred thousand each on a nice car. They saw their cars as status symbols. It had become a competition with them, to see who could out-do the other, and the big deal became who could get a DeCoulomb into the country, even with the sanctions in place. Ludmila

259

wanted to know if I could help her out. Help them out."

"Help them out how?"

"By shipping the cars to automobile dealerships in Mexico that would then transfer the ownership of the vehicles to the oligarchs or whoever the hell she wanted them shipped to. I'd truck them over from the factory, she'd store 'em in the warehouse, and late at night we'd ship 'em out."

"Why the secrecy?"

"I'll get to that in a second, but the main thing that drew me in was the money. It was huge, like twenty-five thousand a car."

"That's your end?"

"For me, right. Now, I had a sense the whole thing wasn't on the up and up, but I checked it out with my lawyer and he said he couldn't find anything illegal about me obtaining a car in the United States and shipping it to a dealer in Mexico, as long as I followed the rules and paid the fees. How was I supposed to know what they'd do with it in Mexico? It wasn't any of my business. Besides, Mexico hadn't imposed any sanctions on Russia. And even if I did know that they were trying to get around the sanctions, so what? Everything I would be doing was legal."

"And she was willing to pay you twenty-five thousand a car?"

"'No problem,' she tells me. I got the sense she'd budgeted me for even more."

Before Christiansen went on, Frankie removed the brown Reporter's notebook from his back pocket. He flipped it open. He pulled out his pen.

The presence of the notebook seemed to elicit a measure of introspection on the part of the interviewee.

"Man, I've got to be careful here," Christiansen said. "I mean, you see what they do to people over there, don't you?"

"Over where?"

"Russia. You know who Magnitsky is, I'm sure."

Frankie told Christiansen he was reading the Bill Browder book. "I'm aware of the Magnitsky Act, yes."

"I guess what I'm saying here," Christiansen said, "is I need to know how you plan to use the information I'm about to give

260

you and whether it's going to be attributed to me. Your cop friend, by the way, has offered me witness protection, and if and when I accept it, which could be as soon as tomorrow, you'll probably never see me again."

"You're talking to Wiggins?"

"He came out to my house again last week, after the search warrant. Now he wants to get me together with the feds – like, tonight. To talk about witness protection, if I tell them everything I know, which I think I'm going to do. I'll have to plead out to something. Wiggins also told me I probably shouldn't be talking to you. But I felt I owed you one, for slugging you."

"I appreciate that," Frankie said.

"So," Christiansen continued, "how would this work, if I tell you my story? When would you publish it? Would I get to look at it first? Would you mention my name – all this shit."

Frankie had to think the whole thing through. This was a little more complicated than your average interview. He had never before interviewed somebody who the next day was likely to disappear.

"I guess all I can say is that the search warrant return is supposed to be filed tomorrow," Frankie said. "Depending on what it says, I may not have to mention that any of this information is coming from you. Obviously, you're a big part of this story, your name has already been published, and it's going to be published again if and when you make your plea deal in open court. Otherwise, I can say that ethically speaking, journalistically speaking, that everything you've told me so far is totally fair game for me to use. You called me. You know I'm a newspaper reporter. We had met. You knew I was covering this story, and you knew I'd be writing a story on what you told me."

"So that's how it works," Christiansen said.

"All that being said, you seem to be having some second thoughts now about going public. Believe me, no matter what you think of me, or of newspaper reporters, or of the mainstream media in general, the last thing I want to do is get anybody killed. If you pull the plug on the interview, or if you don't want your name used, I'm going to respect that, and I won't use the

261

stuff you just told me until we flush out our ground rules."

"Okay," Christiansen said.

Frankie continued:

"The main thing I guess that I want to know," he said, "is everything. The whole story. Once I know that, it can help shape everything that I write, even if I can't use all the details. Let's do it that way – everything right now is for background only, not to be used unless I can get it verified by other sources, and under no circumstances would any of the information be attributed to you. Even then, I probably couldn't use it, even if you wanted me to, unless I can get some kind of corroboration, through documents or official sources."

"That sounds reasonable."

"It sounds to me like you want this information out."

"I think I do," Christiansen said. "Right now, based on everything you and everybody else has written or said, and based on this case that got me fired, I look like the worst person in the world. Usually, I wouldn't give a shit about what anybody says or thinks about me, as long as it's based on correct information. Right now, it's not. At least it's not based on complete information."

Frankie stayed silent while Christiansen sat back in his chair, and looked over the crowd in the Weatherstone – mostly young and studious, men and women hunched over their laptops, enjoying the afternoon. They were just a little bit younger than himself, a little more entrepreneurial. Local. Artistic.

It seemed to Frankie that Christiansen liked the atmosphere.

"I think I'd like all these people here to form whatever judgments they form based on true and complete facts," Christiansen said.

"Then let's keep going – background."

Christiansen didn't need to be prodded.

"Okay," he picked up. "I began moving the cars for Ludmila about a year ago, in July. Four of them to Manzanillo on a shipping line that Ludmila told me to use. One ship in particular – the *Grandeur*. All I have to do is bring the cars over from the DeCoulomb factory in Hayward, store 'em in the warehouse in

West Sac, load 'em onto the boat, and they take it from there. No money changes hands. No sanctions, no worries. The cars go to Mexico, to the dealerships. I pay for the shipping, and then I don't know what happens to them. They ship them to Russia, I don't know. Meanwhile, Ludmila tells me to open a bank account in the Cayman Islands to work these transactions through. I talk to my lawyer. He says no problem. The Mexican dealerships wire me four hundred thousand. Ludmila gives me an account number in the Caymans for White Rock USA. I wire them three hundred thousand. I keep one hundred thousand for myself, which just about doubles my annual gross. Everything's on the up and up."

"I take it you wired the hundred thou to yourself, to your bank account here?"

"I did. Declared it, too, to the IRS, even. Remember, my lawyer told me this was a legal transaction."

"Maybe," Frankie said, "but didn't you have any suspicions? Like, why didn't the money go to the DeCoulomb guy? Why did it go to White Rock?"

"I did ask Ludmila that very question."

"And?"

"She said it was a, quote-unquote, 'charitable donation,' from the car guy to the church," Christiansen answered.

"From Ian Courtney?"

"Yep. Him. I think they used the money they got from selling the cars to buy a fleet of vans for the church, at least that's what they told me in July. It seemed legit to me."

"So they said it was going to the church?" Frankie asked. "Not to White Rock?"

"What's the difference?"

"Well, one's a church, a non-profit, charitable organization. The other is an import-export company."

"Oh. Well, they do everything hand in hand. They're one and the same, really. Bob's the preacher, and he's also the main guy at the warehouse, although you'd never see him there. That was Ludmila's thing. She ran it. But he was the brains."

"How'd you know Bob was the guy behind the warehouse if

he was never around?"

"Ludmila told me," Christiansen said, with just a hint of sly in his eye.

Pillow talk, Frankie deduced.

Frankie remembered seeing the vans behind the church in Rancho Cordova on the day of his face-to-face conversation with the so-called Reverend Bob Jones.

"But you've got to be suspicious now, right?" he asked Christiansen. "Like, why should they go through all this trouble to donate money to a Russian church?"

"Tell you what. You pocket a hundred grand, you don't ask questions. I know everything I did was one hundred percent legal, and what White Rock or Russia or Ian Courtney or the Mexican car dealerships or the oligarchs – anything they did was totally about them. I was about me, and I obeyed the law."

"All right. I get all that. But there's still one thing I don't understand," Frankie said. "Like, why couldn't they just have the shipment made out of Oakland? Why did they make you bring the cars here first?"

"I can only surmise," Christiansen answered.

"Surmise what?"

"Well, remember – the church is receiving hundreds of thousands of dollars in donated crap. You've seen their ads on TV, how they're using it to take care of widows and orphans overseas. They're getting these donated items from all over the country. They collect the stuff and they store it in the West Sacramento warehouse, and they make this big production on how they were shipping it out on freighters to the Ukraine, Russia, Belarus, and everywhere. Now I swear to God, I didn't see a thing, and Ludmila didn't tell me a thing, but they've got all this stuff in the warehouse, and the pile goes up and down, and if you wanted my opinion, I'd say that they were selling the stuff out of the warehouse in the dead of night to second-hand stores, junk dealers and a zillion other operators. It wouldn't surprise me if Bob and Ludmila pocketed hundreds of thousands – millions – in proceeds. Meanwhile, what's going out in the ships that they're using in their television ads? Maybe they've got a couple used toys on board, for the kids in Batumi. But I know they've got some luxury automobiles on 'em, too, going to Mexico."

Frankie nodded his head. Radimir Valishnikov, it seemed, had really been onto something.

While he had Christiansen in his presence, Frankie hazarded a guess.

"What about Matthew Johannsen?" Frankie asked.

"Matthew who? Never heard of him."

"Big time California political P.R. guy, has a side business trying to help people who need advice about Russia. His name ever come up?"

"Like I said – never heard of him," Christiansen repeated. "Can I go on?"

"Sure."

"About December, Ludmila calls me again. She says she wants to ship out a couple more cars on New Year's Eve morning, and she says there will be more orders to come. I tell them: no problem. Everything's the same as before – I go pick up a couple of DeCoulombs in Hayward and I drive them to West Sac a week ahead of time. The morning of the thirty-first, I take them to the port, and they're off to Manzanillo aboard the *Grandeur*. The Mexican car dealers wire me two hundred thousand in the Caymans, I send a hundred and fifty thousand to White Rock, and I keep fifty for myself. We do it three more times, in January, February and March, and it's like I don't have to work anymore for the next couple of years. I got my sheriff's pension, you know, as part of that wraparound settlement with the county. Then Ludmila gives me a bonus – the VXP."

"That's the one that just came in a couple of weeks ago, that I saw in your driveway?"

"That's the one."

Now Frankie had to slow things down. He thought he saw the whole picture: a crooked preacher ripping off the public on a charity scam while at the same time laundering secret in-kind campaign contributions from a billionaire industrialist transportation visionary from San Francisco by way of Rhodesia who was illegally financing a renegade campaign to screw the Democrats out of a congressional seat in Modesto.

"I guess you saw that two hundred and fifty thousand that went into that congressional race down in Modesto," Frankie said.

"I did read that somewhere," Christiansen said.

"It had to come from the proceeds from the automobile sales."

"I did ask Ludmila about it, after your story ran."

"What did she say?"

"Fake news," Christiansen said.

47/A Cop Comes Clean

David Allen Christiansen found it a little tougher to talk about the Tennessee boys, when Frankie steered the conversation to the ex-deputy's postings under the name "White Cop" on the website called "The White Right."

"Yeah," he told Frankie. "It was not one of my finer moments."

Frankie tried to be sympathetic. "I guess we've all got a lot to learn when it comes to racism," he said.

Christiansen got defensive. "What the fuck are you talking about?"

Frankie stayed calm. "You just said your hanging around on 'The White Right' website wasn't one of your finer moments. Made me think you were talking about racism."

Christiansen went silent and he stayed that way for about 30 seconds. It looked to Frankie like something was sinking in.

"I was still very pissed off about what the Sheriff's Department did to me, what the press did to me," Christiansen said. "I lashed out."

"Bananas in the patrol car?"

266

"I mean *really* fucking stupid."

"But not racist?"

"Shit, man, of course it was racist. But I swear to God, I have no animosity toward black people. Dammit, I might even have been in love with a black person. I know I was in lust with her. I liked having sex with her, and when she shut me off after the sergeant's thing..."

"You left bananas in her patrol car."

"Like I said, really fucking stupid, and I was really fucking mad, and I was really fucking hurt, and when you're mad and hurt, you lash out at the people you're closest to, and that's the way I chose to do it."

"Which pretty much everybody would agree was racist."

"From an appearance standpoint, it sure looks that way. All I can tell you now is that I'm pretty damn sorry all that shit happened."

Frankie found Christiansen's story of redemption to be commendable. But he was too much of a reporter to buy it just yet. No matter. He didn't have time to decide whether Christiansen was still a bigot or ready to volunteer for the NAACP. He was a reporter, working on a story, and he made a living by not being too judgmental. He'd let the readers make their own conclusions on Christiansen. For now, he only had a few hours to pull out whatever Christiansen had to say before he slid into his new life as a protected witness. As for Christiansen's emotional state, he'd let him duke it out with a psychiatrist.

"What made you check out that website?" Frankie asked.

Christiansen searched inside himself some more.

"I don't know," he said. "Once I got fired, I actually did feel as if I'd been racially aggrieved. You know the whole concept about people getting pulled over by the cops for driving while black? The way I looked at it, I got fired for complaining while being white."

"You left a bunch of bananas in the woman's patrol car."

"Hey, I'm not saying I was right. Then I made the mistake of spending too much time on the Internet. All sorts of shit out there, right? Racist shit, and I mean real racist shit, and that's where my head was at then, and I checked it out. Then Charlottesville happens, right? I sympathized with the idea of preserving the statues. It's American history, you know – bad as it was."

"I don't know if I'd call it American," Frankie said.

"Whatever you want to call it, I was checking it out, and then I found out about that 'White Right' website, and I checked it out, and I made the connection last summer with those two assholes."

Frankie Cameron did not disagree with Christiansen's characterization of Davis Beauregard Barton and Bedford Forrest MacMillian.

"One thing that was odd," Christiansen said, "is that I never told them I was an automobile broker. Or that I lived in California. Somehow, they knew I was out here, and somehow they found my name and number and email."

"But you had talked to them first, right, or at least communicated with them, on the racist website?" Frankie asked.

"Yeah."

"How'd you come across that?"

"How do you think?"

"I don't have a clue."

"I'll give you one – her hair is pink, unless it's purple. Or orange."

"Ludmila?"

"I mean, I already had been checking around on Reddit and some of the other chat rooms for... like-minded people. And Ludmila and I do our first deals with the four cars, and... she and I found each other attractive. We jumped each other's bones."

"I see," Frankie said, his suspicions now confirmed.

"And one day she sends me an email and says, hey, check this out, and I do, and it's got a link on it, and goddamn if it's not this 'White Right' thing," Christiansen said. "I check it out. I start clicking on stories, and I get into one about all the Charlottesville shit, and the removal of the Confederate statues, and that's where I come across the older one."

"Barton?"

"I guess, I don't know."

"This is when?"

"Some time after Charlottesville. I'm not exactly sure. Maybe September, October. And we keep it up, into the next year, and then this Barton guy really gets steamed when the city of Memphis votes to get rid of the statue of the dude who founded the KKK,"

"Nathan Bedford Forrest."

"That's the one, and he and I get talking in the comments sections of the stories that get posted on this 'White Right' website. For me, it was just a venting exercise – like, I thought I'd gotten over all the shit from when I got fired, but Ludmila had stoked me up again pretty good. I mean, I kind of agreed with Barton on all this heritage crap, but really, I could give a shit about their fucking statues. Then the story dies down, and I drift away from the website, but back around April of this year, he calls me up."

"Who?"

"Beauregard Barton."

"That's what he called himself?"

"Yep."

"And you gave him your telephone number?"

"I'm in the book. Kind of hard to run a business without a phone number, you know. I'd told him my name, told him about my firing. And I'm not hard to find. Anyway, he calls, and he tells me he's in California and wants to lease an SUV."

"I thought you were a broker."

"I am, but I do a little leasing, too, and I tell him I've got a line on Yukons, and he said that would be perfect, and I ask him when he wants it, and he says 'Right now.' I tell him I can do that, but I'm going to have to hustle a little bit, and that it's going to cost him a premium, and we agree on six hundred a month, no problem. He shows up at my place about an hour later, with some other little cocksucker. I guess the two of them drove all the way out here, straight from Nashville, in a couple of days."

"MacMillian?"

"MacMillian who?"

"The second guy."

"I don't know what his name was. All I know is they get here, and I ask them why they need to lease a car from me when they're already driving one, and they tell me, 'you don't need to know, you don't want to know.' What the fuck, I get them the truck, and they thank me, and then they start in with how they're out here to do some damage and that I might be reading about them in the newspapers fairly damn soon. I really don't want to know what the fuck they're going to do, and I say goodbye, and Barton goes back to their car and pulls a hand grinder out of his trunk. He shows it to me, and I know exactly where they're going with that. I've got to confess, this is not the first time I've brokered a lease on a car for somebody who didn't want the vehicle to come back on him. I tell them I'm going to have to increase their rate, to a thousand a month, and they say it's no problem, and I say you can't do any of your shit here, but I do direct them to a body shop guy I know on Highway 49, and they go do their business and they come back to my place, and Barton says thank you very much, and says to me, 'Hey, man, you need a hand grinder? We got no use for it anymore, and I think to myself, what the fuck, just leave it on the porch."

In plain sight.

Christiansen paused for a sip of coffee.

"My mistake," he said. "I should have at least put the goddamn thing in the garage."

Frankie digested the information.

"I'd say you're in some fairly deep shit," was all the he could muster up in response. "Knowingly leasing a car to a somebody you know is up to no good. Somebody who you knew or should have known was going to alter the VIN number."

"Hey, I didn't know exactly what they were going to do."

"What did you *think* they were going to do?"

"I didn't *think* it through," Christiansen countered, a little anger flaring. "I made it a point not to know. I just kind of liked the money."

"Shit, man, you'd already made hundreds of thousands of dollars off the DeCoulomb transactions."

"Once you get a taste," Christiansen said, "you never want to go hungry."

Never having been much for money, Frankie was forced to suspend his judgment. It had always helped him in situations like this.

"I take it," he said, "that you told all of this to Detective Wiggins."

"Well, I lied to his boys about it at first. But, yeah, I did eventually come clean with all of them. Tomorrow, I'm supposed to tell it all again to the feds, officially, and it might be the last time anybody sees me under my real name for a long, long time. So, so long, David Allen Christiansen. Except from on the witness stand."

"Testifying against?"

"Who do you think?"

"The preacher?"

"And Ludmila."

"What about Courtney?"

"I told them everything I know," Christiansen said. "I don't know what they're going to do about him. I'm a little bit removed."

"You trucked the cars over here from the factory."

"There was nothing illegal about that. For all I knew, and for all I still know, they were charitable donations to the church, and I was shipping them to car dealerships in Mexico."

"Out of the warehouse of a Russian import-export company."

"Excuse me, but that company is incorporated through the California Secretary of State's office. They're as American as General Motors."

*****

Walking back to his hotel from the Weatherstone, where the elm trees burst in early-summer green, Frankie thought to himself that Christiansen's story rang true.

It also rang incomplete.

While Frankie sorted out the additional layers in his mind, something else rang: his cell phone.

On the line: Jordan Diaz, with a big piece of news.

271

"I just got the word from the Stanislaus and San Joaquin county election people," Jordan said. "The results are official. Jesse Seymour sneaked through."

It was on to November.

48/*In the Tunnel*

Manuela's trainer removed her boxing gloves. She unwrapped her hands on her own and wiggled her fingers and flexed her shoulders to loosen them up.

Just inside the pull-down steel door, a young man stepped inside to watch the action from behind a pair of wraparound shades. Just as unobtrusively, he stepped out. She didn't notice him. The sun had already set on a fairly productive day.

Earlier in the week, she landed nine top chefs of Sacramento as new clients for MJ Public Affairs. More accurately speaking, they had landed her.

Carrick Mullaney introduced them to her, as key cogs in his plan to do something about human suffering in Sacramento. Mullaney's idea was to open something on the order of a double-duty soup kitchen north of downtown. To feed the homeless, for sure, but there was more: along with the mere shoving of food down their throats, the chefs would teach the wandering destitute how to prepare it. How to season and slice and make it look pretty. How to cook.

To paraphrase the proverbial wisdom, the cooks knew that if you gave a man a meal, he'd wolf it down on the spot. On the other hand, if you could teach him how to flip a pancake, he'd be able to stuff himself today and tomorrow – and also find a job in a town where a new restaurant opened about every 15 minutes.

The chefs found an abandoned furniture millwork on 14th Street with blue-metal corrugated siding to serve as test kitchen and laboratory for their social experiment. They envisioned a dozen street people rolling sushi over here and another 12 or so twisting gnocchi over there. Or maybe they didn't want to cook. Maybe they'd like to manage. Maybe they *did* manage, before the wife left them for the meter maid and their lives went to shit and they wound up at the bottom of a whiskey bottle or in the drudge of the crack pipe. Or maybe all they wanted was to wash dishes or bus tables or learn how to be nice to somebody when you served them a pork chop.

Done with her workout, Manuela said goodbye to her gym people and headed over to the millwork, to check in with Mullaney and help flush out his vision. She'd spent the greater part of her day on a conference call with him and a few of the other cooks while they free-associated on their homeless human assistance employment program.

Manuela set out on foot on a gorgeous late-spring evening beneath the freshly-green elm and sycamore giants. Her pace quickened the closer she got to the millwork – past The Aura, a Korean-Japanese restaurant with candied fried chicken, and past the coffee place where her boyfriend liked to hang out in the morning and read the newspapers.

Fourteenth Street, of course, dead-ended into the railroad berm, and the chefs identified this as a problem. Not so much the berm. What irritated the chefs was the fact that the city gated off the tunnel that connected one side of the railroad tracks to the other. For no good reason, they thought. According to the chefs' thinking, heroin and whoring constituted minor nuisances compared to the public good they proposed of improving access to their program.

Mullaney and the chefs made it clear to the city: get rid of the gate, or we might have to take this project across the river, to West Sac. Plenty of homeless over there, too.

Approaching the millwork, and the tunnel, Manuela saw the power an excellent saucier could wield in a town where restaurants were valued almost as much as the Kings. The gate, she observed, had been cut away, the steel railcar door on the other side had been removed, and light once again was allowed to flow through the tunnel from one end to the other, and back.

The vision pleasantly surprised her. Before she took her P.R. gig, Manuela worked in the same neighborhood, a few blocks west, at the TV studio that housed one of the network affiliates, and she did the story when the city destroyed the tunnels. The closures, of course, had zero impact on the dopers and hookers. They just shot and smoked and screwed up on the berm, or at the dead-ends the closures created, or in the parking lot of the furniture millwork, or in Cesar Chavez Plaza, or under the awning at City Hall, or any other place that was convenient, now that they'd been forced out of the tunnels.

Darkness, meanwhile, rolled over Midtown, and Manuela thought about Link. He told her earlier he was going to spend an hour or so at the Torch Club to see Mind X. He also told her that on occasion he was known to take a puff in the parking lot around the corner with some of the regulars, to help catch the groove.

Manuela, who did not puff, did not understand the impulses that led to such mind-altering behavior. She thought that this would be an interesting issue to resolve between her and Link, and she thought about it so deeply that she never saw the guy coming at her from behind.

The young man with the wraparound glasses was no longer alone. He'd been joined by another man, maybe a few years older, and this one had a baseball bat. Manuela never him swing, but she sure felt it, the tip of the weapon striking her across her back and sending her stunned and sprawling to the sidewalk.

Before she could piece together what happened, one of the attackers grabbed her arms and the other grabbed her legs, and they dragged her into the tunnel at the end of 14th Street.

"I get her first," she heard one of them say, as the two of them ripped at her clothes. They tore off the T-shirt that a friend had recently bought for her, which memorialized the night Tony Lopez took the lightweight championship from Dingaan Thobela

274

in Arco Arena. For some reason the words on the T-shirt sat perfectly in her mind while they stripped her down to her athletic bra and she felt them ripping at her shorts.

A jolt of adrenaline brought her to a state of abject clarity. Manuela came to a complete understanding of what was about to happen. Talk about a pain-killer – her internal neural transmitters flooded her with chemicals that numbed her from the impact of the baseball bat. She summoned her strength, and it responded. She struggled to her knees and was able to get her right leg underneath her, which enabled her to swing her hips – with leverage. Now she had energy and power from the middle of the earth that came up through the ground, into her legs, through her core. Here it came – channeled directly into her right elbow while she swung it with the force of each and every one of her own 150 pounds, her legs acting as the fulcrum between her upper torso and the weight of the earth.

The blow caught the younger attacker in the sweet spot of his jaw, and it knocked him out, cold. In almost the same motion, Manuela whirled into a boxer's stance to face the bigger guy, who still had the bat. He took another swing at her, which she ducked, bending at the knees, before she fired out of her crouch into his midsection. She used the momentum of the energy he'd wasted on the swing- and-miss against him, and she hit him like a blitzing linebacker, separating him from the bat and driving him into the ground with her right shoulder. That's where she'd been hit, but she couldn't feel it anymore. He was a big one, way bigger than the twerp she'd just KO'd. He must have outweighed her by at least 50 pounds. She wrestled him with everything she had, but as strong as she was, the son of a bitch used his weight to regain the advantage and pin her on her back. She rolled and they grappled and it was on between the two of them in the middle of the tunnel. He thought he had her subdued, on her back with him sitting on top of her, before she rolled and bridged herself up to her knees and again summoned an extra measure of strength to whirl on him with a reverse elbow to the midsection. The blow knocked him back a step. He absorbed the shot and retrieved the baseball bat that had been deposited to the side of the tunnel. He swung and she ducked, but this time he made sure to keep his momentum in control. They circled each other, moving to their right, Manuela using her footwork to duck in and out while the bastard looked for an opening to cut loose with a swing.

She had worked him around so his back was to the north side of the tunnel, when, out of the corner of her eye, she noticed a silhouetted figure appear almost out of nowhere, his medium frame outlined against the illumination of a street light a half block away. She didn't know who he was or what he was doing there or if he had any kind of intent, but she did know she wanted to keep both the attacker and the silhouette in front of her, in her field of vision, together. Now she danced side to side, back and forth, left to right, no more circling. It was then that she saw the silhouette pull something out of his pants, and she saw whoever it was swing it with force and fury – a one-timer, as they say in hockey. Things started to blur, and she did not see the tire iron connect with the back of the head of the man with the baseball bat, with a launch angle of a perfect 25 to 35 degrees.

But she sure heard it, a thud-ish whomp, with the added crack you might hear when steel meets bone. Blood spurted from the back of her attacker's head, as he fell forward and landed face first at Manuela's feet. She saw the oozing of the brain matter, and she knew right away he was dead.

Manuela looked up at the silhouetted figure. He looked to be maybe in his mid-to-late 20s, and battered, from years of alcohol abuse.

She thought she recognized him.

She did recognize him.

The silhouetted figure extended his hand toward her, to help her straighten up.

"Are you all right?" he asked.

"I think I am, and thank you," she said, to the man she, like most everybody else on the streets of the old warehouse district north of town, and along the riverbanks and in the alleys, knew only by his nickname:

The Scrounger.

A half a year later, in the second week of December, the editors once again dispatched Frankie Cameron to the capital of California.

It would be his third tour of duty.

Sent west on his first assignment to cover the primary elections with a focus on the Golden State's congressional races, Frankie wrapped that one up in late June when Jesse Seymour moved past Jacob Harland and beat him by more than 500 votes to win the runoff spot in the 10th District congressional race. His first trip morphed into a return to the police beat when a couple youngsters came out of their caves in the rural suburbs north of Memphis to take up the Lost Cause, and he had just hit the send button on Seymour's advance when he got word of the Tennessee boys' attack on Manuela Fonseca.

He ran over to 14th Street in time to see the Sac PD crime labbers comb through the tunnel. It was decorated, on the north end, by the body of the dead Mr. Davis Beauregard Barton, covered by a police tarp. Off to the side of the street, over by the millwork, the local artist Lincoln Adams lingered outside the police tape with Sacramento celebrity chef Carrick Mullaney and other foodies. On the other side of the street, in front of the parking lot filled with Amador Stage Lines long-distance buses, Loni Cohen of the *Sacramento Beacon* sat on a curb and pounded away on her laptop.

Frankie checked in with Link, who seemed OK; Manuela, the artist told the reporter, had emerged from the ordeal in okay shape.

"They took her to the hospital as a precaution," Link told Frankie. "Lucky for her, the dead guy was off with his swing. Had he caught her in the back of the skull, she would be in very serious condition right now. As it is, it appears she only suffered a bruise across her back and shoulder. They're going to keep her in the hospital overnight for observation."

That's where Link was headed right now. Frankie offered a ride, but Mullaney already had car keys in his hand.

Even before he headed to the tunnel, Frankie had put in a phone call to the night desk in Washington. They told him there was no way he could work that story. It was okay to snag a quote the time somebody knifed Link's statue, but they didn't want him working as the lead guy on the attack on his buddy's girlfriend. They'd find a freelancer.

The day after the incident in the tunnel, Frankie had to eat some bad news on the matter of the David Allen Christiansen story. Despite the assurances from Detective Andrew Wiggins that the bones of the investigation would be laid out in a new slew of affidavits, federal and prosecutors insisted that the returns on all the search warrants be sealed. The sad fact for Frankie was that there would be no public disclosure on what Wiggins had already told him about the phone and bank records on White Rock USA, the **Russian Slavic USA Pentecostal Church**, the residences of the Reverend Konstantin "Bob" Cosmenko-Jones (his legal name, as far as the cops could tell) and Ludmila Yolanavytch, not to mention David Allen Christiansen's house. The prosecutors didn't want defense attorneys to know what they had until they had time to process the evidence haul themselves. Wiggins told Frankie he'd have to wait until the indictment. Bottom line: he couldn't write any of it, nor could he go into any meaningful detail in print on what Christiansen told him during their afternoon conversation at the Weatherstone.

Frankie stuck around in Sacramento for a couple of days after the assault in the tunnel and visited Manuela and Link when she returned home from the hospital.

Then he went home to Maryland.

Five months later, Trip Number 2: the editors dispatched him once again to California to chronicle the November congressional elections in the war to flip the house. Again, his focus would fall on the crucial 10th District. Same as the primary, the results weren't made official for more than a week after election day. Same as election night, thousands of votes poured in by mail ahead of the postmarked deadline of November the 6th. Same as the primary, it took a while for the vote counters to do their thing. Same as the primary, Jesse Seymour cruised to a substantial victory once all the ballots were counted.

Hanging around town for the results, the fire broke out in Paradise. For more than a week, the smoke from Paradise poisoned the sky over the 2.4 million people who lived in metropolitan Sacramento.

They were the lucky ones. Their only problem was that they couldn't breathe.

Not a single one of them burned into nothingness when the wildfire caught them, in their homes, in their cars, running from their cars, down the mountainside, into town, out of town, out of this world. Not a single one of them were among the 14,000 families whose homes were destroyed. None of them saw their town extinguished. None of them had to live their lives surrounded by their nightmare. They didn't have to arrange funerals for loved ones amid blackened trees and the piles of ash that used to be their homes.

Frankie excused himself from politics for a couple of days to drive the hundred miles north to trudge through another fire zone, just like he had done the previous year in Sonoma County when he still worked for the *Beacon*. He didn't go home to Silver Spring until the week before Thanksgiving.

By early December, a series of seasonal storms had cleansed the Sacramento sky, and the diminishing days of the second year of Trump broke free of the clouds. Morning sunlight shafted earthward at different angles. It collided with the moisture that clung to the reds and yellows of the foliage that hung from the Eastern oaks and liquid ambers, a final burst of color before autumn gave way to the mild but distinct north-valley winter that seemingly contained less fog than it did when Frankie moved to town more than a quarter-century ago. A phone call had brought him back out west, an apology of sorts from Detective Andrew

Wiggins, who wanted to make things right from the promises the cop could not keep when his case went federal. Indictments, the detective told the reporter from long distance, had just been filed under seal. They're going to be unsealed on Friday, Dec. 14, once we get everybody in custody. You might want to make sure you're in town on Thursday the 13th.

It was perfect.

He couldn't remember the last time he'd seen Mind X at the Torch Club, which you could only do on Thursday nights.

He flew in that day and arranged with everybody to meet him there that night at 5:30 – on his tab.

50/*A Theory*

Mike Rubiks had already parked himself at one of the high tables in the back of the room when Frankie walked into the Torch about a half hour before showtime. The two hadn't seen each other since the fire in Paradise, which they double-teamed for purposes of economy. They shared notes and a coveted motel room in Yuba City, and disdain for a president who couldn't get the name right on the town that had just been destroyed.

"Of everything Trump's ever said or done, that was the cupcake," Rubiks said, about how the president fucked up the name of Paradise and called it "Pleasure" before a worldwide audience. "Eighty-five people, dead, and the motherfucker can't remember the name of their town. And these were his people! This alone should have been enough to impeach him."

Right above their table, a window opened out over the sidewalk to 15th Street. Usually, on a cool December late afternoon such as this one, the metal shutter would be closed. Rubiks, however, burned hot, and he kept it open. His rumination on Trump inspired him to hang his upper torso out of the window and scream as loud as he could:

"What's it going to take, people?"

His Howard Beale-inspired rant caught the attention of two 35ish looking dudes who were smoking a joint outside the bar before the Mind X jam.

"He can't even get the name right on the disaster area, America!" Rubiks yelled.

One of the pot smokers held in his hit and nodded to his buddy in silent agreement, as Rubiks returned to his stool.

"I guess you told them," Frankie said.

"Damn right," Rubiks shot back, a smile plastered across his face as he grabbed his Budweiser by its long neck. He poured about half of it down his gullet.

It was the first time Frankie had seen Rubiks smile in more than two years. Now, in the final month of Trump's second year, Americans who held Rubiks's views, if not as vociferously, had reason to smile again. They flummoxed Trump in the suburbs of Philadelphia. They kicked his ass in Key West. A Native American lesbian knocked him on his keister in Kansas. They slaughtered him south of Salt Lake City. They were dancing in Chicago, down in New Orleans, up in New York City, and beyond the west Texas town of El Paso, out in the badlands of New Mexico. Most of Minneapolis, outer Richmond, inner New Jersey, and the island nation of Staten Island – all of them also registered their disgust.

In California, the seven congressional districts that the Dems targeted all turned blue.

Frankie was just getting up for another round when the front door of the bar opened and in walked the young political consultant, Jordan Diaz, who saw their table and came over to take a seat.

"Ladies and gentleman, Mr. Jordan Diaz!" Frankie shouted, as he stood from his stool to give the young consultant a standing ovation.

Nobody else could say with certainty that they knew who Jordan Diaz was, but a few of them knew Frankie, and they knew that if he was giving anybody a standing ovation, it was good enough for them, so they stood up and applauded, too, while Jordan broke out in unguarded laughter. First time Frankie had seen it.

"Jordan Diaz, Mike Rubiks. Mike Rubiks, Jordan Diaz," Frankie said, as he sat back down and yanked a stool away from an adjacent table and slid it into theirs. "You two, you have nothing in common."

Jordan sat down and said he was looking forward to seeing the band.

"This will be a first for me," the young consultant said. "The Torch Club."

Frankie went for the drinks and returned in the nick of time with two Hazzah New England-style IPAs from the Blue Note brewery in Woodland, for him and Jordan Diaz, and a Bud longneck and a shot of Early Times for Mike.

It looked by then that Rubiks and Jordan had known each other for years.

"Your boy was just telling me about the Jacob Harland case," Rubiks said.

Which reminded Frankie of some unfinished business. He asked Jordan:

"Did we ever find out what Ian Courtney's deal was?"

Jordan kind of shrugged while he took a sip of his hazy Hazzah, which he found curious but tasteful.

"I asked around," he said, "to some friends on the other side."

"The other side?" interjected Rubiks. "You mean the Russians?"

"No," Jordan said. "The Republicans."

"Same thing these days," Rubiks growled.

"There are still a few people in the other party who are honest and legitimate, and they are just as concerned about what's going on as you are," Jordan said. He took another sip and nodded, deciding he approved of the Hazzah. "Like everything else these days," he said, "it looks as if the most audacious behavior we see is taking place in plain sight and on the record."

"Tell me," Frankie said.

"I don't really have the whole story," Jordan said, "but I feel like I have a workable theory."

"Let's hear it," Frankie said.

"Well, when you sort everything out, you have to first look for the thing of value, and in the end, that was the cars that Courtney delivered to the warehouse that Christiansen sold to the oligarchs."

"Wait a second. How do you know Christiansen sold the DeCoulombs to the oligarchs?"

"You told me, Mr. Cameron."

"I did?"

"The night of the midterms. The Young Democrats party. At the Shady Lady."

"I believe whiskey was involved," Frankie said

"It most definitely was," Jordan laughed.

"It's coming back to me now."

Jordan gave Frankie a moment to piece together the night he held court at the R Street bar with Diaz and a number of other sharpies, when he blabbed on about the David Allen Christiansen story that he was never able to write.

"I mean, if there were no cars, then there was no cash, and there would have been no last-minute Harland play on the immigration stuff," Diaz continued. "Or at least nothing that would have had a two hundred and fifty thousand-dollar below-the-radar advertising campaign behind it."

Frankie nodded, readjusting to the present.

"What we don't know," Frankie said, "is why the hell Ian Courtney gave a flying fuck about Jacob Harland and the Tenth Congressional District."

Diaz took another sip of his Hazzah. The elders could see that the kid was getting loose.

"It should be pretty obvious," Diaz said.

"Enlighten us," Mike Rubiks implored.

"Well," Diaz said. "Mr. Courtney, as you may remember, the biggest thing he had going in his world – bigger than the cars, bigger than the space shots, all that stuff – was the SuperTube. Right?"

Frankie and Rubiks looked at each other, quizzical.

"The fuck is he talking about?" Rubiks said.

"This was his big idea," Jordan said, getting excited about his theory now. "He had the cars, he had the space technology, he had his businesses – all of that. But this was the thing that would make him the Jonas Salk, the Thomas Edison of his time. If he could come up with this transportation alternative that would replace the car and save the world from climate change, he'd go down as the next Jesus. And here he is, in the most experimental place in the world – California. An eight-hundred mile long laboratory, where right in the middle of it you had an outback, the Central Valley, where you can do just about anything you want if you've got the money to buy off the politicians."

Another sip of the Hazzah and Jordan went on, "And Courtney really thought he had one on the hook."

"Jacob Harland?" Frankie asked.

"Quite the contrary."

"Who?" Rubiks inquired.

"Representative Bonham, Mr. Rubiks."

That brought a silence to the table as everybody took a sip. Rubiks told Diaz to hold that thought while he went over to get himself a little shot of Early Times.   "You're   familiar   with Courtney City, right?" Diaz asked when Rubiks returned.

Frankie had a vague recollection of the failed development in the heart of the San Joaquin Valley.

"If you go back through all of Bonham's election cycles," Diaz continued, "you'll observe that Ian Courtney had reached the maximum contribution level on behalf of Representative Bonham every two years. Early in Mr. Bonham's first term, Mr. Courtney approached him about the SuperTube idea and the attendant plan for Courtney City. Bonham latched onto it, saw it as a great economic boost for his poverty-stricken district."

Frankie and Mike Rubiks nodded.

"Like I said," Jordan went on, "everything was in plain sight. The Tube, the city – it all received extensive publicity, both in California and in Washington. And meanwhile, Bonham does his work as a solid Republican backbencher in Congress, and he gets on the House Transportation Committee. If he would have won this race against Seymour, and if the Republicans would have held on to their majority, he would have been the chairman. Of course, Courtney would want to assist in any way possible, and Courtney, being the highly intelligent business and political person that he is, he could see from as long ago as Donald Trump's election..."

"You mean his theft of the presidency," Rubiks broke in.

"Courtney could see that once Trump took office, that there would be very strong opposition to the president, especially in California, and that Trump in office would set off one of the biggest political backlashes in American history. Mr. Courtney, actually, is very Democratically inclined – he's your standard liberal on social and environmental issues, and an extremist, even, when it comes to climate change. He was not a supporter of President Trump. But he did like Representative Bonham very much, given the congressman's enthusiastic backing of Courtney City. Yet there was only so much Courtney could do, given the limitations on campaign contributions. He always could have formed his own I.E. on behalf of Bonham, but he knew that if his name was attached to it, it would likely work against Bonham – Courtney is not the most popular figure in the state, you should know. His favorables poll in the low teens. Again, being politically astute and attuned, when he saw an opening in California's top-two primary system with this crazy right-winger to keep the Democrats out of the runoff, he jumped through it. He figured that was the way to go, to get the outcome he wanted, and to keep his name out of the papers. He knew Bonham would have crushed Harland in the runoff, while he would have had a very difficult time with any of the Democrats. So the big challenge for Courtney was to make sure Harland made the runoff."

"That's all very interesting," Frankie Cameron said. "And you know this, how?"

"I don't really know it at all," Jordan said. "Like I told you, it is just a theory."

"A theory," Mike Rubiks said.

"Well, maybe more than a theory," Jordan said.

Frankie and Mike Rubiks stared at Jordan, waiting for the punch line.

"I just got together with some of my Republican pals the other day, and they tell me they're hearing somebody actually did put this plan together."

"Let me guess," Frankie said. "Matthew Johannsen."

51/*Detective Does The Torch*

Frankie and Mike Rubiks were so engrossed in Jordan Diaz's theory about Ian Courtney that they hadn't even noticed when Sacramento police Detective Andrew Wiggins walked in the door, with Samantha Fish blaring on the juke box while the Mind Xers rolled in with their instruments.

The lawman contrasted sharply with a crowd that was mostly bathed in tie dye and reeked of reefer. Frankie told him that he'd stick out like a sore cop if he wore his usual slacks and sports coat.

Wiggins, of course, came in looking like Jack Lord. It was the only look he knew, except when fishing.

"Funny smell around here," Wiggins told the three. "A year ago, I'd have you all in cuffs."

"That was a year ago," Frankie said. California, of course, had since legalized pot.

"I test positive from all the second-hand smoke around here and I will personally come find you and lock you the fuck up," Wiggins said, pointing his right index finger at Frankie. "Of all people to cost me days, you ain't the one."

Now, Frankie knew. Detective Andrew Wiggins was beginning to like him.

"You didn't have to come."

"And I won't be long. But I told you'd I'd fill you in on Bob and Ludmila and tomorrow's indictment to the best of my abilities, and one thing I do not do is not do what I say I'm going to do."

"I appreciate that."

Before Wiggins began, he insisted on introductions.

"Detective Wiggins," Frankie said, "this is Mike Rubiks, the star feature writer of the *Sacramento Beacon*."

"I've heard of it."

"Make that, the only feature writer left on *The Sacramento Beacon*," Frankie added.

"I've read your stuff," Wiggins told Rubiks, obviously in a high mood, if not second-hand high gathered through no fault of his own. "Can't understand a word."

"Fuck you, too," Rubiks shot back with a laugh, and not missing a beat.

"Now that's what I'm talking about!" Wiggins responded. "This guy I like!"

Being totally unfamiliar with the world of police, Jordan Diaz was somewhat intimidated by Wiggins's commanding presence. He actually shook a little bit when they shook hands.

"Don't worry, dear," Wiggins said. "I won't bite."

It wasn't clear how Diaz was going to respond. He hesitated just a second, biting his lip, before he shot back:

"That's not what they tell me – at the bathhouse."

Everybody roared – including Wiggins. Diaz looked pleased with himself.

"Now that I've been outed," Wiggins said, "what the fuck do you have to do to get a drink around here?"

"Let me," Frankie said, making a move to the bar.

"Scotch and soda," Wiggins requested.

It was easy for Wiggins to enjoy himself now at the Torch, now that the vandalism series had ceased, and that its tentacles to other interesting developments had begun to come into focus.

He told the group that the feds had indicted Konstantin "Bob" Cosmenko-Jones and Ludmila Yolanavytch for conspiracy to violate federal campaign finance laws.

"They'll be turning themselves in tomorrow," Wiggins said.

"Always a chance they might catch the first thing smoking to Moscow, but I doubt it. At least with the reverend. He is too invested here. Ludmila, if she flees, so what. There'll be another one right behind her, no matter what she does. The Feebies found an eighth of an ounce of methamphetamine when they tossed her apartment. They turned that one over to the Yolo DA. There's a good chance they can turn her, somewhere down the line."

The young Bedford Forrest MacMillian, meanwhile, had spent the last six months on the 8th Floor of the downtown jail, in the solitary confinement wing. He still awaited a preliminary hearing in Sacramento Superior Court, for the attempted rape of Manuela Fonseca and the felony murder of Davis Beauregard Barton. Prosecutors regularly used the felony murder approach on gang bangers – your buddy gets offed in a shootout, you're just as culpable as the guy on the other side who pulled the trigger. The Sacramento DA also charged him with six counts of vandalism, all of them carrying hate-crime enhancements. Just for fun, the feds aimed a conspiracy charge at him for the vandalism series. Crossing state lines to be a dirtbag could get you life.

Wiggins stood up from the table and motioned Frankie to follow him to the other side of the room for a word in private: David Allan Christiansen, he told Frankie, would be charged with single counts of aiding and abetting the alteration of a vehicle identification number and then lying to the police about it. He would plead guilty in federal court and be sentenced to a year's probation. No charges had been filed for his role in the cars-to-cash money laundering scheme.

Christiansen also accepted enrollment in witness protection. He would be arraigned the next day in absentia and his proceedings suspended until after he testified at the Cosmenko-Jones and Yolanavytch trial about his role in their political money laundering scheme.

"He said to say hello," Wiggins told Frankie. "He appreciated your never running anything about your interview with him."

"Yeah, yeah, yeah," Frankie said. "That's an afternoon I'll never get back. What about Courtney? Anything happening on him?"

"He didn't do anything illegal," Wiggins said, keeping his tone even. "All he did was donate a bunch of cars to a church."

"What about the cars being sold to raise money for a political campaign?" Frankie inquired. "You boil everything down and you have Russian oligarch money financing the attempted manipulation of the American political system. Courtney had to have known where the money from those cars was coming and going."

"Only thing is, proving intent is a bitch," Wiggins said.

52/*Scrounger Gonna Scrounge*

Annette Smith-Bennett was next through the door. Right behind her, making their entrances separately: *Slavic News of Sacramento* editor Radimir Valishnikov, and *Sacramento Beacon* reporter Loni Cohen.

Annette ran right up to Frankie at the overstuffed table and nearly shouted, "I got an internship at the *Beacon*! I start in January!"

"Congratulations," Frankie said.

"I can't thank you enough," she said.

"I had nothing to do with it," Frankie said modestly. "I just told them you know a story when you see it. What're you going to cover?"

"The Russian church beat," she laughed. "No, seriously – features. Sports and news."

"I don't think they've ever brought in a junior college intern

before,"
Frankie said.

"About that," she said. "I've been accepted at Sac State. I start there Spring semester. I'll be writing for *The State Hornet*, too."

"You are making all the right moves."

Annette did a little dance next to the table, complete with a toe-behind-heel 360-degree twirl, that brought her face-to-face again with Frankie, who smiled an approval.

"I'd introduce you to everybody here," he said, "but they are all boring as hell."

"Hello, boring people," the ebullient Annette waved.

Frankie backed up his stool and pulled in a table to make more room for her and the rest of the growing crowd. Loni Cohen took the seat right next to his. They'd always seemed to meet around police tape, so he'd never had a good chance to look at her. She looked to be about 25 or 26, maybe 27, tall, fairly dark skin for a white girl, frizzy long black hair pulled into a lengthy ponytail, dressed down in jeans, a Down vest, hiking boots and a Levi's jacket. She looked like a street reporter, on duty – which she was.

Frankie had heard about her coming to the *Beacon* just before he left. She had a great reputation – San Jose State journalism grad, worked for an alternative weekly in the Bay Area before she swung the gig in her hometown.

"Hey, I've always meant to tell you," Frankie said. "Fantastic job on all these stories."

She thanked him for the compliment, but turned him down when he offered to buy her a beer.

"Make it a soda water," she said. "I'm working."

"Okay," Frankie replied. "Well, I guess I don't need to introduce you to anybody around here. You know Mike from the office."

"I do."

"And I believe you met Rad up in Auburn."

"I did."

"And I don't know this for an absolute fact, but I have reason to believe that you are acquainted with Detective Wiggins."

"I am."

She and the detective acknowledged their acquaintance in predictably demure fashion – smiles and head nods, not wanting to betray the kind of overfamiliarity that might get a source burned or a reporter frozen out.

The front door at the Torch swung open again. In walked the Scrounger, to a loud ovation from the table.

The Scrounger had always been a hero of sorts – more of a belligerent antihero when he was on the street advocating for himself and others like him, even if it was just for beer money, and just plain hero when he enlisted a homeless army to free the kidnapped Link, and once again, for helping Manuela take out a white nationalist terrorist only eight months later.

A few other folks in the bar recognized him, too, from the news accounts of his heroics. They joined in the applause.

By the time he got to the table, everybody who knew the Scrounger and who had seen him since his turn to sobriety could see that there was something new about him that reminded them of something old. That is, that the Scrounger had been drinking. It sounded to Frankie and Wiggins and Rubiks that The Scrounger might be in need of a 12-step call.

"Who's going to buy me a fucking drink around here?" the Scrounger ordered, once the applause died down.

It looked like he'd already had a few. It looked like he'd already had several.

Mike Rubiks, who had only recently begun to understand the Scrounger, said he'd take care of him. Frankie dirty-looked his friend but did not resist Rubiks's offer to buy the Scrounger a drink.

"I'll have what you're having, Elvis," the Scrounger told Rubiks.

Rubiks made a move on the bar, but stopped first to tell the Scrounger, "That was a hell of a performance a couple months ago," Rubiks said.

"I only did what any self-respecting dry drunk would do when he sees a woman getting beat up," the Scrounger responded.

"That too, but it's not what I was talking about. That dance, man, the day of Link's opening. What the hell was that about?"

"Some people carve totem poles," the Scrounger said. "Some people write stories that nobody reads for a newspaper. Some people drink, and some people dance. Me, I drink *and* dance."

"It looks like you're definitely drinking," Frankie broke in.

"It looks like you're very observant," the Scrounger semi-slurred.

"Everything okay?" Frankie asked. "I mean, I'd heard you were living at the Quinns, and doing pretty well."

"Well, maybe I decided that being sober wasn't such a great plan," the Scrounger said. "And maybe I decided I couldn't stand that fucking place and all those fucking dry drunks living on edge twenty-four hours a day. Since when is sobriety so fucking much of a thing?"

Rubiks returned with the round and the Scrounger threw down his shot.

"I decided that me and the Quinns didn't see eye to eye, and that it was time for the Scrounger to be the motherfucking Scrounger again!" the motherfucking Scrounger said.

"Makes sense to me," Rubiks contributed.

Detective Andrew Wiggins finished his scotch and soda and got up to get another. "Just keep picking up those butts," he told the Scrounger, putting a hand on his shoulder.

"Will do, Chief," the Scrounger told the cop while reaching for his longneck.

Turning toward Mike Rubiks, the Scrounger announced, authoritatively, "I've always said this about Rubiks – he is the greatest American I have ever met."

Rubiks grunted. "You never fucking used to say that when I told you to shove it up your ass whenever you asked me for a dollar," he countered.

"That's only because you never gave me the dollar," the Scrounger said. "Seriously. You get shot in the face for your country, and you survive – it's just as good as giving your life. Mike Rubiks deserves that recognition and respect, and I don't want to hear any fucking argument from any motherfucker in this room, or we are going to have a problem."

292

Nobody argued, and the Scrounger spewed on.

"The Quinns, I'll have you know, kicked me out about three weeks ago."

This was news to everybody at the table.

"For what?" Frankie asked.

"Drunk. I killed a man, and I got drunk. I smashed him on the head with a tire iron, and I saw his brains spilling out at my feet. You see some motherfuckers attacking a woman, in a dark tunnel, at night, and I'd a killed the other guy too if I'd a known he was there. And I get my recognition in the paper and everything and the city councilman puts me up for a heroic honor-type-of-shit thing and they argue about it because why the fuck is some former inebriate carrying a fucking tire iron down his pants? Shit, man. Just because you're sober doesn't mean you no longer have to protect yourself. So that's what I carry, and it all turned out all right, and it was all right for a couple of days, a week, a couple weeks, and then I decided I needed a drink, and goddamn if I didn't go out and get one, or two, on one or two nights, and the Quinn people rolled with me, said they understood, that I'd been traumatized like I was in a war or something, even though I wasn't. And after about my fifth or sixth drunk, they said they couldn't put up with my shit anymore, and they said maybe I needed to go to a psych ward, and there was no fucking way I was going to commit myself so they kicked me the fuck out."

Silence gripped the table.

"I mean, I'm not going to go into any fucking 72-hour program," the Scrounger said. "I know I need some mental health. I know I've got issues. With my dad. With authority. With myself. I know I drink too much. But I don't need to go to no hospital. I don't need to live around a bunch of motherfuckers who white-knuckle their way through the goddamn day and night, and goddamn fucking right – I like to fucking drink."

"Where you staying?" Frankie asked.

"Here and there," is said. "I'm thinking of moving back to the Sterling. In the alley, out back. Next to the dumpster."

53/ *"Hazzah!"*

Rad was about to interrupt the Scrounger by saying something very important about his very important work when a white straw cowboy hat popped through the open window. It sat on top of the salt-and-peppered head of a tall Native American fellow dressed in a nice black Levi's jacket and a black vest and a turquoise and silver necklace and black jeans and black cowboy boots.

"Hazzah!" the voice belonging to Lincoln Adams shouted.

Mike Rubiks had a stool waiting for him when Link slunk down the back wall to their crowded table, while Frankie jumped into the bar line to nab four more Hazzahs, two additional shots of Early Times, a Bud longneck, and a vodka on the rocks for the editor of *The Slavic News of Sacramento.*

"You seem to be in a good mood," Mike Rubiks told him.

"Hey, man – it's Christmas," Link said. "The season always makes me feel good."

"Makes a lot of people feel pretty shitty," Rubiks countered.

"I can understand that," Link agreed. "The traffic is terrible. There's not enough time to get everything done. It can turn you into a nervous wreck. I've been there. But I'm here now."

Link scanned the gathering and smiled. He gave soul-shake hugs to Frankie, Mike, Wiggins, and the Scrounger. He acknowledged Jordan's smile, and he shook hands for the first time with Rad, Annette, and Loni.

For a moment, the table went silent. It was Frankie who made the invites, and this was his gathering, but it was Link who brought in the crowd, who everybody knew would be there, who

294

everybody wanted to see.

"Where's Manuela? How's Manuela?" Frankie asked, breaking the silence.

Frankie hadn't seen her since the day after the tunnel, when Link brought her home from the hospital in a Lyft.

"She is fairly well, and thank you for asking," Link said. "Unfortunately, she couldn't make it here tonight. She's actually back in her office writing meaningful messages on her Christmas cards to everybody who expressed concern about the unfortunate incident in the tunnel. She's not too far away from being sociable again."

Link took a sip of his Hazzah and looked at Loni Cohen, who looked right back at him. She had attempted to interview him from the day of the first knifing of his statue to the day of the Devante Davidson demonstration and then over on F Street. She got a couple of reactive one-word answers out of him, but never an in-depth interview.

Everybody broke into sidebar conferences now that Link had officially been welcomed to the table. Left alone among the many, he noticed Loni Cohen looking at him funny.

"When am I going to get to get to interview you?" she asked, without preamble.

"With me? Why would you want to interview me? I'm really not newsworthy."

Loni laughed.

"No less interesting than anybody else," she said. "You do things. People care about you, about what happens to you."

Link smiled at Loni.

"Since you put it that way," he said, before turning the conversation toward her.

"Your work has been phenomenal," he said. "Your reporting – it is sensational. Your writing is that of a seasoned professional, yet you don't appear to be that old."

"I'm twenty-seven," she said.

"I know what it takes to get any information out of him," Link said, nodding in Wiggins's direction, who was engrossed in a conversation with Rad. "I've got to tell you, as somebody who devours newspapers as my daily bread, I have never seen anybody grasp the profession in the manner you have. At least not anybody of your generation."

She looked at him with the same quizzical look on her face. She handed him her card.

"Whenever you think the time is right, please give me a call," Loni said.

Link accepted the card, a bit mystified. He could tell that this woman was not flappable. He sensed that she practiced something along the lines of balanced detachment.

Before Link could say another word, Loni Cohen's cell phone rang – at almost the same exact time as Wiggins's device also went off.

"I've got to take this," Loni told Link, while Wiggins stepped out the front door with his cell pinned to his ear.

The two of them returned to the table in sync.

"Gotta run," Loni said. "A shooting in Oak Park. Frankie, thanks for the invite. Mr. Adams, interesting meeting. Rad, Annette, everybody – nice meeting you all."

Detective Andrew Wiggins ducked his head into the barroom door right when Loni ran out.

He waved goodbye.

"It'll look really bad if she gets there first," he said of the now-sprinting Loni Cohen.

And he was gone.

54/*Matthew Johannsen's Ride*

Mind X finished its gig, and Link and the Scrounger and Mike Rubiks and everybody else emptied out and headed to wherever people go in the middle of the week when Happy Hour ends on the edge of downtown. Link, who had downed a pair of Hazzahs,

296

same as Frankie, observed as Mike Rubiks and the Scrounger made it out under their own power – wobbled, but were still standing, arm in arm, the best friends you'd ever seen, under the neon torch that marks the Torch. Frankie offered to give Mike Rubiks a ride home and the Scrounger a lift to wherever he wanted to go. They declined, and Link deduced that the pair's night was just beginning.

For Link, it was off to the Esquire Tower, to liberate Manuela from Christmas card duty. He'd take her back to her home, where he'd moved in almost six months ago after putting his house up for sale. The two of them passed the 90-day test, through the initial explosion of attraction and emotion that gave way to the long haul of long-lasting relationship, to something called commitment.

They discovered that they worked pretty well together. They found that they could maintain their individuality while at the same time forging a partnership. For the first time in his life, Link felt something that he had never felt for anybody other than his mother – a sense of devotion. Of unquestionable love.

Talk about resilient. That was Manuela Fonseca. Somebody clubs her across the back with a baseball bat to bruise the hell out of her, and they damn near had to put her in restraints to keep her in the hospital overnight. They let her go first thing in the morning, and Link and her had not been apart a single night since. She was back to work the next day.

Everybody in the office knew to act as if nothing had happened. Manuela went about her routine taking care of clients. None of them knew at first that she had even been victimized. By policy, most major news outlets did not identify sexual assault victims, or even attempted sexual assault victims, unless the victims offered to go public. Manuela did not – at first. As a good public relations woman, the last thing she wanted was to *be* the story. She changed her mind, however, when discussions with some close friends – one of whom happened to be the host of the morning "Insight" program on Capitol Public Radio – suggested that her story might be inspirational to women. After all, she did knock one of the attackers cold, and she fought a much bigger guy to a standstill and was about to lay waste to him (she said), before the Scrounger stepped in with his tire iron. So, she did "Insight," and it was a huge deal for a week, then it died down, and everybody went back to normal, and for Manuela that meant a return to the gym to put a daily beat down on the heavy bag.

Out the door from the Torch, Link pulled his flannel-lined black Levi's jacket tight against the evening chill for the four-block walk to the Esquire building with the streaking blue light that flashed 22 stories into the sky and was visible all the way to the Cal Expo fairgrounds.

The security guard at the desk recognized Link immediately and buzzed him in with a smile. He'd become a regular.

Up to the 22nd floor, he got off the elevator and walked through the empty receptionist office at MJ Public Affairs, and into Manuela's corner office that overlooked the sparkling white dome of the Capitol, where he found her writing personal little notes on each Christmas card.

"*Bruto*," she greeted him. "How was your night?"

"I always enjoy hanging with my peoples," he said. "It was nice of Frankie to pull that together."

"Did you smoke any pot?"

"You're going to have to guess."

"Hmm," she said, with a feigned frown of disapproval.

He laughed, and put his arms around her. The big news, of course, was the Scrounger blowing out of the Quinns and returning to drink.

You could argue that Manuela owed her life to the guy, although she would debate it. Still, Manuela appreciated the help.

Link took her over to the cottages to visit the Scrounger about three weeks after his intervention on her behalf and two weeks after the city hammered the tunnels closed again. This made it tough on the chefs' project at the millwork, but not that tough – people found their way easily enough down to 12th Street or up to 16th to make it around to the other side of the berm.

The Scrounger never did enroll.

When Link and Manuela visited him, he still seemed a little

unsettled after having taken a man's life, even if Barton's had been a fairly despicable one.

"Who knows," the Scrounger told them. "Maybe he could have seen the light. Maybe he could have turned his life around. Maybe he could have found the cure for cancer."

"He was trying to rape and murder me, Tomas," Manuela said.

"Well, there was that," the Scrounger agreed. "Maybe if I would have just knocked him out."

"Please don't worry about it too much," Link chimed in. "He can work on improving himself in his next incarnation."

"Unless he comes back as a rat," Manuela said.

"Even rats have to work out their karma," Link responded.

Neither Manuela nor Link had seen the Scrounger since they thanked and hugged him on their way out of his cottage, until this night, when the Scrounger showed up drunk at the Torch.

"Recovery," Manuela said, "isn't for everybody."

Link concurred, and the two of them strolled out of Manuela's office to the elevator. It was getting close to 9 p.m., and everybody from MJ Public Affairs had blown out of the building, except for Manuela and her Christmas cards, and some tall guy about Link's height who was standing next to the elevator. He had just pushed the button when the couple walked up on him.

The lingerer wore fashionably pre-washed designer blue jeans, Link noticed, and a sheepskin jacket that fell almost to his knees, and a pair of alligator boots that should have gotten him arrested for some kind of environmental crime.

The man greeted Manuela and Link as they walked up to the elevator.

"Miss Fonseca," he said. "Working late I see. Always such an asset to the company."

"Hello, Matthew," Manuela smiled. "How have you been? It's been, what, a year since we've seen each other?"

"That sounds right," he responded. "Last New Year's Eve, maybe." He looked at his watch. "I was very concerned to hear of the attack a few months ago," he said. Manuela lowered her eyes. "But I am so glad to see that you are back and bringing in more business than ever."

He seemed sincere in his concern about Manuela's earning power. Just by looking at what stood in front of him, Link knew he and this man were like the yin and the yang. He hadn't redeemed himself in his first few lines of conversation.

Manuela could only laugh. Up until recent events, she mostly found Matthew Johannsen amusing. Old, a bit out of touch, massive ego. She'd always viewed him as a classic of yesteryear, in a three-martini dark-red-leather-booth-in-a-steakhouse sort of way, combined with the high-fashion California country twist that exuded a faux rugged individualism that was common in the West. It was an image that Johannsen worked on at his spread up in Sierraville, mending fences and branding cattle.

Johannsen's original client list formed the basis of MJ Public Affairs' wealth. Oil, ag, timber, industry, tobacco. Old school. Knew everybody in town over the age of 65. Matthew Johannsen looked at money the same way Red Sanders and later Vince Lombardi looked at winning – it was the only thing. It's how you kept score, as George H.W. Bush once said. Even if the world was moving on from the Johannsens of the world – to cyber, to political correctness, to the do-gooders and the chef-ocracy who Manuela represented and who actually made the firm bags of money – she knew he was the reason she worked where she did and enjoyed the success that she had and made the money that paid for nights out at Mullaney's. She knew she had to show him respect.

"I've been back at work for six months, Matthew," she said. "But thank you for your concern." She changed the subject. "What brings you down from the ranch?"

"Oh, nothing much. Took the wife to dinner – at the Esquire of course." He pushed the elevator button again. "She's going to be picking me up in about one minute."

"They don't have any restaurants up there in Sierraville?" Manuela inquired, trying to stay amiable.

"Not really," Johannsen said, deadpan. "I've also got some business down here tomorrow. We'll be spending the night at the Sawyer. I like that Kimpton chain."

Finally, Johannsen recognized that Manuela was not alone.

"And this must be the famous Lincoln Adams," he said. "I've seen your work, but that does not make me unique in this town. You'd be happy to know that many of my friends up in Sierraville have given your pieces places of honor in their homes."

Matthew Johannsen introduced himself, with an extended hand that Link accepted with a manly grip in which each tried to squeeze the other's into dust. The two men smiled at each other, both on their best behavior, as they stood for a moment, in front of the elevator – toe-to-toe, eye-to-eye, soul-to-soul, recognizing each other as yin to the other's yang, representatives of opposite world views that, for the moment, would go unreconciled.

"A pleasure to meet you, sir," Link said.

The elevator opened. The three of them stepped in, and they rode in silence to the bottom floor, from one lobby to another. On their way out of the building, Johannsen held the door open with his hand and motioned to Manuela to please go first. She thanked him. Link was next out the door, and he thanked Johannsen, too.

They performed the same dance at the glass door leading out to 13th Street, with Link holding the door this time, and Johannsen, very politely, thanking him for the courtesy. Like clockwork, the titan's wife turned their car out of the parking garage.

"Right on time, as always," Johannsen said. "She is a good wife."

A valet raced to open the passenger-side door for him, and Manuela took note of the Johannsen family ride. She was something of a car buff herself, with her Porsche 718 Spyder, but this was a vehicle that she did not recognize.

"Wow," Manuela said, as Johannsen handed the valet a $10 tip. "What the hell kind of car is that?"

"Oh, this old thing?" Johannsen replied, with a lilt in his voice. "It's a 2019 DeCoulomb Modern Deluxe VXP."

Johannsen plopped into the passenger seat. He shut the door and buzzed the window down.

301

"And," he yelled back to Manuela and Link, as his wife shoved off, "you've got to know somebody to get one."

Acknowledgments

Thanks again to:

Megan Anderluh – a great editor in the line of Anderluh women that includes her aunt and my wife,

302

Deborah.

Cindy Love, a Downey and Hardly Strictly Bluegrass girl – she knows how to cover.

Dara Slivka – the terrific eye behind the shutter.

Doug "The Assassin" Kelly – typo killer.

And always, Deb and Andy – the best.

Made in the USA
San Bernardino, CA
11 November 2019